EAST GOES WEST

THE MAKING OF AN ORIENTAL YANKEE

EAST goes WEST

BY

YOUNGHILL
KANG

KAYA

First edition published by Charles Scribner's Sons in 1937
Second edition published by Follett Publishing in 1965

Published by Kaya Production
133 West 25th Street, Suite 3E
New York, New York 10001
www.kaya.com

Jacket design and photography by Darryl Turner
Book design by Juliana Koo
Manufactured in the United States of America

Distributed by D.A.P./Distributed Art Publishers
155 Avenue of the Americas, 2nd Floor
New York, New York 10013
(800) 338–BOOK
www.artbook.com

Library of Congress Catalogue Card Number 94–75597
ISBN 1–885030–11–8

CONTENTS

BOOK ONE

1

AN UNDYING BIRD...forever lives, forever breathes, forever, with its two wings fluttering, flies. That is the universe. It was there when there was the empty space of our non-existence. It is here moving still. Where it is, silence is never there.... And speaking with an Asian's natural bias, it seems to me it is wrong to say, time passes. Time never passes. We say that it does, as long as we have a clock to calculate it for us. The two hands go, the iron tongue tells hours, we sense the experience of our own duration...we are illusioned. It is not time that passes, but ourselves. Time is always there...as long as there is life to use it. Only if no life existed, there would be no time. Time was because life was...as it is the mortal life to travel over the immortal time. The bird flies with the two wings, on and on. But the same time that occupied the Roman lovers is the same that Hamlet was insane in, and in the same I write and think of time....

In the perpetual merry-go-round of the universe, suns, moons, planets, stars, the whole body of all ten thousand things shift with the shifting space and the eternal time that Orpheus asserted was in the beginning, but had itself no beginning. I, too, with my own life have skated upon the great time arena. I seem to have traversed much time, more than most men, although I am still in the early thirties. To the old-fashioned Oriental, life goes back, step by step, to many forefathers, in unbroken chain, and onward into descendants which are somehow he, not in any abstract coldly philo-sophical sense, but as the solemn vehicle of his Ghost and his God, his most material ghost which eats with them. My own life in actual books still extant in my Korean village was traced far back in this way to ancestors with the bodies of men and heads of cows. This lifetime, threaded to theirs over the mellow-gold distances of time, can it be the same which now sees New York City?—And I ask myself, did I fall from a different star?

Up to a short while ago, the other side of this earth was like the turned face of the moon to people of the West. But there once the men, the women and children, the plants, fruits, gardens and animals, all traveled together in a forgotten leisure. They sang songs, made love and ate heartily, because there was always time. There life grew in manifold harmony, careless, free, simple and primitive. It had its curved lines, its brilliant colors, its haunting music, its own magic of being.

> Life, like a dome of many-colored glass,
> Stains the white radiance of eternity
> Until Death tramples to fragments...

Shelley has said. It was my destiny to see the disjointing of a world. Upon my planet in lost time, the heyday of life passed by. Gently at first. Its attraction of gravity, the grip on its creatures maintained through its fervid bowels, its harmonious motion, weakened. Then the air grew thin, cooler and cooler. At last, what had been good breathing to the old was only strangling pandemonium to the newer generations....

I know that as I grew up, I saw myself placed on a shivering pinnacle overlooking a wasteland that had no warmth, that was under an infernal twilight. I cried for the food for my growth, and there seemed no food. And I felt I was looking on death, the death of an ancient planet, a spiritual planet that had been my fathers' home. Until I thought to stay would be to try to live, a plant on the top of the Alps where the air is too cold, too stunting, and the wind too brutally cruel. In loathing of death, I hurtled forward, out into space, out toward a foreign body...and a younger culture drew me by natural gravity. I entered a new life like one born again. Here I wandered on soil as strange as Mars, seeking roots, roots for an exile's soul. This world, which had sucked me in by its onward, forward magnetism, must have that in it, too, to feed and anchor man in the old durability...for in me has always burned this Taoistic belief in the continuity of living and of time....

It was here...here in America for me to find...but where? This book is the record of my early search, and the arch of my projectile toward that goal.

2

From an old walled Korean city some thousand years old—Seoul—famous for poets and scholars, to New York. I did not come directly. But almost. A large steamer from the Orient landed me in Vancouver, Canada, and I traveled over three thousand miles across the American continent, a journey more than half as far as from Yokohama to Vancouver. At Halifax, straightway I took another liner. And this time for New York. It was in New York I felt I was destined really "to come out from the boat." The beginning of my new existence must be founded here. In Korea *to come out from the boat* is an idiom meaning *to be born,* as the word "pai" for "womb" is the same as "pai" for "boat"; and there is the story of a Korean humorist who had no money, but who needed to get across a river. On landing him on the other side, the ferryman asked for his money. But the Korean humorist said to the ferryman who too had just stepped out, "You wouldn't charge your brother, would you? We both came from the same boat." And so he traveled free. My only plea for a planet-ride among the white-skinned majority of this New World is the same facetious argument. I brought little money, and no prestige, as I entered a practical country with small respect for the dark side of the moon. I got in just in time, before the law against Oriental immigration was passed.

But New York, that magic city on rock yet ungrounded, nervous, flowing, million-hued as a dream, became, throughout the years I am recording, the vast mechanical incubator of me.

It was always of New York I dreamed—not Paris nor London nor Berlin nor Munich nor Vienna nor age-buried Rome. I was eighteen, green with youth, and there was some of the mystery of nature in my simple immediate response to what was for me just a name…like the dogged moth that directs its flight by some unfathomable law. But I said to myself, "I want neither dreams nor poetry, least of all tradition, never the full moon." Korea even in her shattered state had these. And beyond them stood waiting—death. I craved swiftness, unimpeded action, fluidity, the amorphous New. Out of action rises the dream, rises the poetry. Dream without motion is the only wasteland that can sustain nothing. So I came adoring the crescent, not the full harvest moon, with winter over the horizon and its waning to a husk.

"New York at last!" I heard from the passengers around me. And the information was not needed. In unearthly white and mauve, shadow of white, the city rose, like a dream dreamed overnight, new, remorselessly new, impossibly new…and yet there in all the arrogant pride of rejoiced materialism. These young, slim, stately things a thousand houses high (or so it seemed to me, coming from an architecture that had never defied the earth), a tower of Babel each one, not one tower of Babel but many, a city of Babel towers, casually, easily strewn end up against the skies—they stood at the brink, close crowded, the brink of America, these Giantesses, these Fates, which were not built for a king nor a ghost nor any man's religion, but were materialized by those hard, cold, magic words—opportunity, enterprise, prosperity, success—just business words out of world-wide commerce from a land rich in natural resources. Buildings that sprang white from the rock. No earth clung to their skirts. They leaped like Athene from the mind synthetically; they spurned the earth. And there was no monument to the Machine Age like America.

I could not have come farther from home than this New York. Our dwellings, low, weathered, mossed, abhorring the lifeless line—the definite, the finite, the aloof—loving rondures and an upward stroke, the tilt of a roof like a boat always aware of the elements in which it is swinging—most fittingly my home was set a hemisphere apart, so far over the globe that to have gone on would have meant to go nearer not farther. How far my little grass-roofed, hill-wrapped village from this gigantic rebellion which was New York! And New York's rebellion called to me excitedly, this savagery which piled great concrete block on concrete block, topping at the last moment as in an afterthought, with crowns as delicate as pinnacled ice; this lavishness which, without prayer, pillaged coal mines and waterfalls for light, festooning the great nature severed city with diamonds of frozen electrical phenomena—it fascinated me, the Asian man, and in it I saw not Milton's Satan, but the one of Blake.

3

I saw that Battery Park, if not a thing of earth, was yet a thing of dirt, as I walked about it trying to get my breath and decide what was the next step after coming from the sea. It was oddly dark and forlorn, like a little untidy room off-stage where actors might sit waiting for their cues. The shops about looked mean and low and dim. A solitary sailor stumbled past, showing neither the freedom and romance of the seas, nor the robust assurance of a native on his own shore. And the other human shadows flitting there had a stealthy and verminlike quality, a mysterious haunting corruption, suggesting the water's edge, and the meeting of foreign plague with foreign plague. I walked about the shabby little square briskly, drawing hungry lungfuls of the prowling keen March air—a Titan, he, in a titanic city—until in sudden excess of elation and aggression growing suddenly too hot with life, as if to come to grips with an opponent, I took off my long coat; and sinking down on a bench, I clapped my knee and swore the oath of battle and of triumph. The first part of a wide journey was accomplished. At least that part in space. I swore to keep on. Yes, if it took a lifetime, I must get to know the West.

Well, mine was not oath of battle in the militaristic sense. I was congenitally unmilitaristic. Inwoven in my fabric were the agricultural peace of Asia, the long centuries of peaceful living in united households, of seeking not the soul's good, but the blood's good, the blood's good of a happy, decorously branching family tree. In the old days the most excitement permitted to the individual man, if he got free from the struggle with beloved but ruthless and exacting elements, was poetry, the journey to Seoul, wine, and the moons that came with every season. His wife, usually older than himself and chosen by his mother and father, would be sure to know no poetry, but she would not begrudge him a feminine companion in Seoul, or even in some market place near-by—one of those childlike ladies who having bought—or more often inherited—the right to please by the loss of other social prestige, must live on gaiety, dancing, and fair calligraphy. But any wholehearted passion would have shivered too brutally the family tree. And I had done far worse. I had refused to marry my appointed bride. I had repeated that I would not marry, at the ripe age of eighteen. I had said, with more pride than Adam ever got out of sinning in Eden, that I must choose the girl, unhelped by my forefathers or the astrologers or the mountain spirits. And this rebellion against nature and fatality I had learned from the West. Small wonder I had struggled with my father over every ounce of Western learning. I had gone against his will to mission schools, those devilish cults which preach divorce in the blood, and spiritual kinships, which foster the very distortions found, says the golden-hearted Mencius, in the cleverish man. I had studied in Japanese schools and it must be confessed, my studies had brought ever increased rebellion and dismay—to me as well as my father.

The military position of Japan—intrenched in Korea in my own lifetime—forced me into dilemma: Scylla and Charybdis. I was caught between—on the one hand, the heart-broken death of the old traditions irrevocably smashed not by me but by Japan (and yet I seemed to the elders to be conspiring with Japanese)—and on the other hand the zealous summary glibness of Japan, fast-Westernizing, using the Western incantations to realize her ancient fury of spirit, which Korea had always felt encroaching, but had snubbed in a blind disdain. Korea, a small, provincial, old-fashioned Confucian nation, hopelessly trapped by a larger, expanding one, was called to get off the earth. Death summoned. I could have renounced the scholar's dream forever (plainly scholarship had dreamed us away into ruin) and written my vengeance against Japan in martyr's blood, a blood which like that of the Tasmanians is strangely silent though to a man they wrote. Or I could take away my slip cut from the roots, and try to engraft my scholar inherited kingdom upon the world's thought. But what I could not bear was the thought of futility, the futility of the martyr, or the death-stifled scholar back home. It was so that the individualist was born, the individualist, demanding life and more life, fulfilment, some answer to his thronging questions, some recognition of his death-wasted life, some anchor in thin air to bring him to earth though he seems cut off from the very roots of being.

And this it was—this naked individual slip—I had brought to New York.

"Dream, tall dreams," I thought. "Such are proper to man. But they must be solid, well-planned, engineered and founded on rock."

Had I not reached the arena of man's fight with death? I sat there on a park bench, savouring rebellion, dreaming the Faustian dream, without knowing of Faust, seeing myself with the Eastern scholarship in one hand, the Western in the other. And as I sat it grew colder. I had thought a little of spending the night on that bench. It appealed to me to wake up here with the dawn and find myself in New York. It would not be the first night I had slept roofless in a large city. But in the inner lining of my cap, I had four dollars, all I had left, in fact, after my long gestation by boat and by train. I decided to get myself the birthday present of a room.

"Begin tomorrow, trouble. See if I can't have some good dream. An unpleasant dream in this dark lonely park would be bad luck."

Clouds over the denser uptown regions trembled with the city's man-made whiteness, a false and livid dawn light, stolen from nature. I turned my face toward the dawn light as to a pillar of fire. And as I walked, steadily progressing toward the harsh curt lights and the Herculean noise, I wondered if the sight of a rainbow would be lost, the sound of thunder drowned here.

4

At last I found a hotel to my liking, neither as tall as a skyscraper—to choose such a one would not be modest the first night—and yet not a dingy one either, which would be inauspicious. The hotel had many lights inside, but not too many, not the naked glare which clashed from canyon to canyon along the outer runways of the great hive; these had a luminance more proper to honey cells and inner coffers. The fat six-foot doorman with red face seemed an imposing sentinel. Past him, I saw inside the people walking to and fro…talking mysteriously, perhaps of Michelangelo, but more likely of stocks and bonds. I tried to catch his eye. Always he looked past me, or without looking exactly at me, he would shake his head mournfully, directing his thumb toward a side door. But while he was engaged with one of the fortunate insiders who came outside, I went in. To me the gilded lamps, the marble floorway with its carpet of red, were luxurious and full of splendor. How gentlemanly, engaging, yet frankly businesslike, the sandy-colored hotel clerk, as I asked for a room, in my best high-school English which I had prepared to say before coming in!

And as I wrote my name down—Chungpa Han—in my unmistakably Oriental handwriting, which unconsciously dwelt on a stroke, or finished in a quirk that was not Western—I was elated that I had voted not to spend the night with the waifs and strays, but was enrolled there tangibly as a New Yorker.

I had engaged a small room for two dollars. This was half of all I had. I was satisfied. I thought I had a bargain. I had heard that all the hotels in New York cost ten and twenty dollars a night.

"They are worth that!" I thought, as the elevator boy danced up, a rich tobacco brown, well-formed and neatly mannered like his dress. He seized my big suitcase of brown cloth purchased in Seoul, Korea, a roomy bag which yet carried little besides a few books, some letters of introduction and a toothbrush.

The elevator went zk! and up we shot. A funny cool ziffy feeling ran into my heart. It was my first elevator. Fast climb…I thought…like going to heaven.…

My room was small, white, nakedly clean, as characterless and capable as the cellophane-wrapped boxes in which American products come. The elevator boy smoothed the bed and pinched the curtains and examined the towels and looked in the wastepaper basket and picked up imaginary papers.

I sat down in the chair, and crossed my legs. He stared at me dubiously. He waited. He didn't seem interested in my conversation. I asked him if he liked Shakespeare. He giggled and said coldly, "Who, suh? Me, suh? No, suh!" I know now that he was waiting for a dime. I was not sure. Besides I had nothing but bills, those four dollar bills which rested in the inner lining of my cap. I committed my first New York sin. I gave him nothing, neither then nor when I left next morning. I am sorry. I would like to go back and make it right. I have been a waiter myself. I know the importance of tips. But I would not be able to find that bell boy now. There must be fifty thousand bell boys in New York and they never stay in the same hotel long. Even the hotel may not have stayed. New York—its people, its buildings, its streets, are like a rushing river, the flood of which is changing all the time, so to be a New Yorker, one must feel like Heraclitus, that nothing is changeless but the law of change....

The bathroom was almost directly across from my room, beautiful, shining, glazed, so ordinary here, and yet a marvel of plumbing and utility. Even a prince in the old days could not have had such a tub. In Korea, the tubs were not of marble, nor machine-turned porcelain, but of humble intimate wood, and they were never used except for a grand occasion. Then all the water must come out from the well. In summer man bathed in streams, in winter from a great hollow gourd, a shell of the summer.

"But here," I thought, "a man has only to press a button. All the streams leap when he calls."

I let the water run—shee!—shee! as hot as I could stand it, as cold as I could stand it. I washed with soap—in my childhood, people still used an old-fashioned paste of ashes for that purpose—once more with soap, and then thoroughly with clear water. Even my hair I washed...everything.... I was washing off the dirts of the Old World that was dead, as in my country people did before they set out on a Buddhist pilgrimage. Now I had washed everything. Everything but the inside. If I could, I would have washed that as thoroughly, I suppose, and left a shell. But the inner felt the echo of the outer.

In my room again, I listened at the window. That incessant hum of wheels and screech of brakes...how different from the brawling mountain streams, the remote grass-roofed villages of Korea.... Korea, kingdom that was no more, taken by the little blue-clad soldiers to be a barrier against Russia, to be a continental point in Asia from which to punish Manchuria and China for their deep and stubborn resistance to the Machine Age.... In sheer amazement at life, I suddenly stopped at the mirror to see if I had changed, as well as my environment. For me an unusual act. In my Korean village there were mirrors, but mostly small ones, about the size of a watch, and generally with covers. Besides, the people who had mirrors usually hid them. It was thought some kind of vice to look at one's face. Some people like my uncle, the crazy poet, never properly saw themselves.

I have read that the Koreans are a mysterious race, from the anthropologist's viewpoint. Mixtures of several blood streams must have taken place prehistorically. Many Koreans have dark brown hair, not black—mine was black, so black as to have a blackberry's shine. Many have naturally wavy hair. Mine was quite straight, as straight as pine-needles. Koreans, especially women and young men, are often ivory and rose. My face, after the sun of the long Pacific voyage, suggested copper and brass. My undertones of the skin, too, mouth and cheek, were not at all rosy, but more plum. I was a brunette Korean. Koreans are more animated and hot-tempered than the Chinese, more robust and more solid than the Japanese, and I showed these racial traits as well. At eighteen I impressed most as being not boy but man. I needed to shave every morning for the thick growth of hair that came overnight. My limbs retained a look of extreme plasticity, as in a growing boy, or in a Gauguin painting, but with many Koreans, even grown up, they still do. In more ways than one, I looked an alien to the Machine Age and New York. One could not tell from my outside that I had lost touch with dew and stars and ghosts.

I tried to go to sleep, to rest baptized in the roars of Manhattan traffic, as Virgil had been in the Hellenic stream. But all my old life was passing through my brain as if I had not been able to wash out the inside at all. My eyes seemed to turn back, not forward. I saw the village where I had spent my boyhood, and where my father's father's forefather had spent his. I saw my father, responsible for the whole family, uncles and aunts and cousins every one, and I, his only son, his vehicle through time, who had made a wide parabola from him. I saw my *paksa* uncle and my poet uncle and many more…. Yes, a synod of ancestors seemed coming to visit me, watching me disapprovingly in that high Western bed, which had renounced plain earth so literally beneath. What can you hope to find here? they said. Life, I cried. We see no life, they said. And yet they did not scold me now. Just waited, arms in sleeves, with the grave and patient wonder of the Asian in their eyes. And with a pang, I saw before me my uncle's studio, through which blew in summer the pine-laden breeze. I saw his books and the thousands of old poems in Chinese characters I knew and loved so well. Must I leave all this behind at the portals of America?… Couldn't they at least pass through into the world of the machines?… And against my will, a poem came into my head, one I had heard long ago. All in one throbbing moil it revolved, mingling in a hopeless incoherence with the foreign noises outside, of that most spectacular city so far over the rim of the world to me and yet a greater cycle in time than in space onward. It annoyed me that I could not quite rearrange the lines of this poem, nor remember the rhymes perfectly.

It was written in Chinese characters, but it was a Korean poem. One, I think, written by my crazy-poet uncle—although I am not quite sure. (Poetry writing then was so often anonymous. Men cared for the poem, not for the fame.) It dealt with a tragedy that had happened in our province, perhaps a hundred or more years ago, yet still remembered and sung. A young lady of the house of Huang, or Autumn Foliage, had been suspected of unchastity. In Korea, this was such a terrible thing that the family in which it occurred would be disgraced forever, even by rumor. The young lady did the only thing possible in her environment. She gave orders for the building of a wooden coffin and said good-bye. In the wooden coffin she embarked on the sea as to the land of death. Miles away, beyond the sphere of her trouble, as if in token of true innocence, she was picked up by men of the family of Li, or Plum Blossom. She became a daughter of the Li household and married one of the sons.

In this poem, she speaks of herself symbolically. A leaf of the family of the Autumn Foliage floats loosely upon the sea. It is blown to rest against the branch of the white spring plum blossoms. That leaf of the yellow foliage is carried so far away that if one wishes to see her, he must ride on the back of the white crane.

This poem was very short, but contained in four short lines an Asian drama of fate which might have been entitled Hail and Farewell, or Autumn Saved by Spring, or Distance Bridged and Unbridgeable, or many more names besides. And the images were such that it was a poetic experience to write them in dynamic calligraphy, surrendering to the natural motion of leaves and scattering blossoms, of autumn and spring and the waves. In the end I had to rise from bed and write down this poem on paper, to get it all straightened out, before I could fall asleep in my high Western bed.

5

My second night was not spent in a New York hotel.... But of that trouble, later.

I was up early and checked out, while the streets were still: quietly rumbling. Half-past eight—it is perhaps the emptiest time. I did not know then that the people were in the subways.

The man in the "Quick Lunch" I entered had plenty of time on his hands. He had nothing better to do than to stand on one foot and the toe of the other, and look at me quizzically while I was eating my two doughnuts and milk. I had been inspired to order these by a previous customer, a taximan who finished so quickly that when I looked a second time he had only half a doughnut left; by the size of the last bite, I saw how he did it—half a doughnut for a bite.

"Third breakfast this morning," he had mumbled. "First one at four, second at six.... Been up all night."

"Tough," said the quick-lunch counterman laconically. He was blonde-looking, Uneeda-cracker colored, with deep wrinkles cutting his face, so that he seemed forty-five. But I think he was about thirty-five, or he may have been ten years less. His eyes were dry, semi-humorous-looking, and in his dirty apron, he had a dry, casual ease as if, behind his counter, he would not have changed his pavement view of humanity even for the Prince of Wales.

"Don't eat the hole!" he said to me finally, with a faint, dry grin.

I couldn't think of anything to reply to this in English, so I just nodded and went on with my doughnut.

"Guess he don't speak English," said the man, still regarding me like a sceptical parent, and addressing a waitress only by a rakish cock of his sandy curls. "Look at his suitcase there. The guy just came. Guess he don't speak any English yet."

"Sure he does," she said good-humoredly. She was tall and skinny and young—about seventeen but big. Her face, long as a colt's, had a confectionery pink-and-whiteness. There was something friendly and good-natured about her.

I took it for encouragement and began. I asked the man his name.

"MacNeil," he said jauntily, his arms still folded; "Scotch."

I asked him, did he know "MacFlecknoe," an English poem which I had learned in Korea.

"Who?"

And I quoted:

> All human things are subject to decay:
> And when Fate summons, monarchs must obey....

"Unhuh—that's fine," he said sceptically, with a wink at the girl. "And who's that other Mac, the son-of-a-bitch?"

"Yes, that's what all Mac means: son-of—"

"Well, I'll be darned if Mac means 'son-of-a-bitch'!"

By this time I felt for a piece of paper to write things down to memorize. The conversation was getting beyond me. I said if he didn't mind, I would take a few notes on what he said, to help my English.

"Yeah? Go ahead."

Without change of countenance, he moistened his thin, gray lips as he gravely took a swipe at the counter with the soiled towel over his shoulder. Nothing was too fabulous for him to accept dryly in this quick-lunch world of downtown Manhattan.

"What was that you said? Not son of Mac but son of—"

"Son-of-bitch...it's what you say here in America when you get mad."

"And mad?"

He made a fierce expression to show it.

I wrote that down.

I regarded my tutor hopefully.

"What's that?" I said, pointing to the vinegar.

"A skirt," he said. "Do you want to know that?"—indicating the salt. "'Kiss.' Ask the girl for it. Let's hear you say it. Good word to learn."

The girl broke into a young loud guffaw, not prudish nor coquettish, but evidently full of delighted appreciation for his pavement wit.

"Say, Paul, you're getting fresher every day," said she, admiringly.

I left them with reluctance, for they were touched for me with the magic of the city and its first encounter. But soon I became convinced that everyone in New York felt the same way as this dry-voiced, kidding man I had first met...the need of sustaining a role, a sort of gaminlike sophistication, harder and more polished than a diamond in the more prosperous classes, but equally present in the low, a hard shell over the soul of New-World children, essential for the pebbles rattling through subway tunnels and their sun-hid city streets.

But I was not a New Yorker yet, though fast becoming one. I set out to present a letter of introduction. It was to the head of all the Y.M.C.A.'s in New York, urging him to interest himself in my behalf, and I got directions by showing the address to people as I went along. By the time I reached him New York was very busy again, and his office, high up in a skyscraper, seemed one of the busiest places to judge by the typewriters all about him clickety-clacking at enormous speed.

"Ah," I thought. "Not like the missionaries, with whom it is difficult to get anything done."

When he said, after reading the letter, "Yes, and what can I do for you?" I told him I needed a job.

He said with businesslike finality, "Mr. Allen in our Harlem branch at 125th Street is the very man for you."

I waited while he did some telephoning, arranging for an interview around seven that evening. I started at once. I went on foot. That seemed to me simpler and besides I should see some more of the city.

Whom did I find to talk to on that day? I don't remember, but I know I talked. The New Yorkers were not hard at all to talk to, though they could understand me better than I could understand them. But I sat down in all the parks I came to and standing my bag beside me, rested, deliriously stretched my feet, and watched. I practised my English until I could hardly turn my tongue any more. Oh, how hard to say "r" and "th" and "w"! They had to be torn from the throat and reared high like the skyscrapers. The sounds were dry and ponderous and without juice. My own language rolls from the gullet and is inextricably mixed with moisture and nature's fire. But now with all its energy, my tongue moved between teeth and lips rigidly, to pronounce "Roman Catholic" or "Methodist Rise," as a Greek methodist-preacher gave me some lessons in a New York park. Even "Fifth Avenue" was hard for me to say, and many times I practised that because I liked to say it.

I lunched with the crowd. I ordered frankfurters and sauerkraut, not because I liked them, but because the man next to me was eating them. Already I was beginning to feel at home in New York. But my hair was too long. Somebody told me so—asking me if I wanted to look like an "Indian." I judged from his tone that an American should not. It must be cut. I wanted to make a good impression on Mr. Allen and grab that job.

I went into one of those glassed-in barber shops. The customers were wrapped up in white like Buddhist monks, only rather cleaner. I also was put to bed with a sheet. I told the barber what I wanted, saying it as well as I could by my hands, because my tongue was very tired. Here was a chance to rest, I thought. And I could not be robbed, in sight of so many people of New York. In the Orient, one goes to a barber shop as to a picture show. There is one entrance fee for everything inside.

Whenever the thin, dark barber with the sharp eyes close together said, "Do you want?" I nodded. Four or five times it was repeated, like courses of a table-d'hote, and each time I said, "Yes, that too." He cut my hair, shampooed it, oiled it, perfumed it, combed it and brushed it with an Italian flourish.... I was so tired after walking, that I almost went to sleep. "My, you get a lot for your money here!" I was thinking in dozing admiration. "They certainly find things to do." A Negro boy shined my shoes on my feet too.

Drowsily, I asked, "How much?" $1.60. I woke up. For a haircut, it couldn't be true! I jumped out of the chair just as I was, in my sheet. They had to show me the itemized account. Everything was there with a corresponding price. And I had thought it was according to the Oriental custom, where every luxury in the barber shop is included at the cost of one barbering, and that a very low one well within the means of everybody! There was no getting away, I had to pay the price. I had only $1.70 in the world. In less than a minute, I had only ten cents left.

"It's a good thing I went to work about a job right away," I thought. "But I must ask for an advance."

It was in sobered mood, not to say humbly downcast, that I entered Harlem...in blinking astonishment looking around.... The pale people with steely eyes and ridged noses and superior shrewdness had faded away. Negroes peopled the world, big and small, rich and poor, fat and thin, light and dark, old and young, men and women and children...barbers, hair dressers, undertakers, cabaret-singers, employment agencies, theatres, restaurants, poolrooms, dance-halls, all belong to this other kingdom, this Negro kingdom, more secret, more mysterious, more luxuriant, more soft, more exuberant. Here was no standardization. Every individual bubbled out on the streets absolutely different from everybody else in clothes, in gestures, in color. Their effort to adapt themselves to a natureless environment resulted in odd freaks at every turn. And nature glinted here, not to be routed. Everywhere laughter was more hearty, the air was richer in suggestion, more emotion-filled; the colors had more depth, so had the smells; the lights, though not so numerous, seemed mellower, gaudier, more picturesque, the spice of Africa was in the atmosphere. Their native jazz came through the windows, from brassy phonographs, a raucous, inarticulate rhythmical cacophony which I remembered having heard elsewhere as I walked...indeed it penetrated through and through New York...the soul of man dancing amidst machinery...for it expressed not Africa alone, it had caught up the rhythm of America—this Negro jazz—it had taken possession of the Western planet, working upon all hitherto known cultures and civilizations, flamboyant lazy magic of disintegration.

I walked along and the street lights came on in Harlem, and the smell of pork chops cooking with onions—a poor but a savoury dish—made well-nigh visible figures against the blue night air. And the atmosphere was very rich and husky, suggesting, in amazing juxtaposition, the warmth and humbleness of home, and the plaintive, alluring sadness of life's farthest exile…a dimmer, vaster captivity than the Babylonian one.…

6

My interview with Mr. Allen ended without satisfaction. The vacancy which he had and which I had hoped to fill must not be given to a Negro or an Oriental, he told me frankly, precisely because his branch was up in Harlem. And I left, reflecting bitterly.

Under a street lamp, I consulted my next best letter, the address of Mr. Jum, a Korean who had left Korea some time ago, and who lived now in New York—he gave out—permanently. He was not allied with the missionaries; he was one of the few Koreans in America who were not. I had not yet met Jum, though we had corresponded through a mutual friend. The understanding was that I should look him up as soon as I came to New York.

I had hoped to appear before George Jum as one already possessed of a job. I saw it was not to be. The hour was late. I must look him up without delay. I found his place after more walking…a respectable-looking dark house on 72nd Street with only a surface-car track between it and Central Park. I rang the bell. Nobody came. I rang and rang. A very fat, short lady with broad, pale face almost the color of her faded fuzzy hair, answered the door. Fifty perhaps, she was built like a barrel and was wearing a one-piece pink-and-tan pajama with big flowers. She spoke a broken English. (I later found she was Hungarian.) All I could make out was that Mr. Jum was away. Whether temporarily or forever I did not know. He had left no word for me and no address. The lady closed the door abruptly, though otherwise not unkindly, and again I was alone.

And since there was nothing else to do, I went on walking. I had in my suitcase introductions to two other Koreans, but from none had I expected so much as from George Jum. It was too late anyhow to look them up. I entered Central Park. I walked and walked. What a wide, dark park! As big, it seemed, as all the city of Seoul. Here were trees and grass and winding asphalt. The trees rattled stiffly in the March wind, and the shaking sound of traffic was almost left behind. I stiffened too, tightening myself.... Here you could pick no roses in December.... To combat the cold, I had to keep on walking. I searched my brain. There seemed no way to get a room and something to eat with only ten cents. Anyway water is free.... I took a large drink from the concrete fountain bubbling there for any passerby. But it takes a long time to starve anyone, I knew from experience.

Out of the darkness of the grave, tense park, into the lighted jungle of concrete and steel again.... By chance I issued on Fifth Avenue. I read the signs. I saw the tall green buses, still more suggestive of joys than gondolas in Venice, and realized where I was. Fifth Avenue. My spirit echoed. My head lifted, my tired feet worked more firmly. A man should be aristocratic here. Magnanimous. And wound up again to my dreamlike tune of New York, I walked, still without running down. Koreans are walkers, always.

Fifth Avenue eventually brought me out at Washington Square Park, small, dark, urbane and rather still. The motor cars rolled curtly, deftly by, making no more noise than possible. My feet ached dully. I did not blame my body but my shoes. To the east of the park was a large building, one of those in which many years later I was to become a teacher in New York University. Close to this building, several people were lying on newspapers, with newspapers to cover them. I went up to them, and picked out an unoccupied place against the wall. I had escaped the homelessness of Battery Park, only to become one of the waifs in Washington Square. The wind seemed to take a real satisfaction in blowing. Merciless and businesslike, it attacked newspapers, trees and men.

We were all miserable and benumbed. I could not make out the figures or the features of my companions, and they could not make out mine. Every man was silent, hunched down. Every once in a while, as wearily as a dead leaf, a man left the cluster and drifted down the dim street, seeking some more sheltered spot, or some mean refuge known only to himself. Most went in silence. One man proved an exception. He muttered something.

"Too cold," he said. "I'm going!"

"Where?" I asked.

"To a room I know. It's too cold here."

"May I come?"

"It'll cost you a nickel."

A nickel I had, two in fact.

"I have," I told him eagerly.

I watched him gather all the newspapers he could, in spite of the curses of the other men, whom he treated like dead bodies.

"Why?" I asked, indicating the newspapers.

"It's cold there, too."

After some time my guide led down into a large basement of a tall, dark house in a desolate slum district. Down in this cellar was a vestibule with a desk. On the desk was a shoebox with a slit. As you went in, you had to deposit a nickel there. Two or three men were just going in as we arrived. Behind the desk was seated a weary, tired-looking man slightly better fed and better dressed than the rest. Not much, though. If he had been in among them, he would have been able to pass as one of the insiders. The place was unheated and while on duty he wore his shapeless old-fashioned hat and wrinkled overcoat. His hands trembled as he received the nickels and put them in the box, as if he were a man past the time of active work. He was a little bit deaf, so you had to shout to make him hear; but he had good eyesight—so good that nobody could pass without his "O.K." I knew, because my guide got into loud argument—louder, because the other man was deaf. My friend was trying to get by on three cents. He said he had no more. He turned his pockets inside out. At last he was allowed to enter on credit.

We passed into "the room." And room was all it was, nothing but floor. Men lay thickly on the floor. From a bracket on the clammy wall an open gas jet flared. Nothing bad must go on during the night. My guide warned me in a frank, loud tone about thieves. "They steal the hat off your head here," he said bitterly, "so hold on to it. They'll change it while you're asleep, if your hat's better than theirs." Oh, the smell of the place! Sour alcohol, sickness, stench from decayed clothes! Misanthropes withdrew to corners and tried to get away by facing the walls. Others huddled up together. One or two had brought shoe-shining boxes, emblems of an unsuccessful trade. Nobody took any notice of me, except a very tipsy man, who was carefully mixing the contents of two bottles. He offered me a drink. I grinned, spread my hands, pretending I knew no English.

The only experience I have had to compare with this was in a prison of the Japanese. But the people—Korean revolutionists—had been put there for a single integrated feeling, a hard bright core of fire against oppression. These men were like pithless stalks, and the force that swept them here, the city's leavings, was for the most part the opposite one, a personal disintegration. And yet I clutched to a new world of time, where individual disintegration was possible, as well as individual integration, where all need not perish with the social organism, or, as in Japan, all rise in savage blood, a single fighting man.

...During the night one tried to sing and others cursed him. There was no spirit of brotherhood in endurance as in my Japanese prison, though each man looked like another under that dim light, unshaven, frail and gray. I distinguished individuals only by their voices. This voice was drunk, that bitter and jeering, that other suffering, and that voice so much like a woman's that I jumped, while the rest laughed, addressing it as "Violet." Some wretched sleep must have gone on, for there was snoring. I put my head down on my suitcase, as the bootblacks theirs on their boxes, and rested my tired legs. Without trying to form plans, I waited stolidly for the night to pass. And in the end I slept quite soundly, for I was very strong and young, carrying still the heritage of another age....

7

I awoke very early, while the lost men around me were still sleeping, a crypt of roughly piled bodies. I crept out. The man who had taken my nickel was asleep at the desk. His mouth was open, his neck bent crookedly. He looked like a corpse. Outside I drew a deep breath of keen new air, brought to this mart of the world by its servants, the morning winds.

"Well, you find that better than the Salvation Army, eh?"

I glanced around and there was my friend of the night before hurrying after me. He chuckled and ended up coughing. I saw he was tall, thin and pale in the close look—black in the far look because he was unwashed and unshaven. Only his pinched nose had the faint pink of real blood. He wore a shirt without a collar, which once perhaps was white. The lapels of his threadbare coat were turned up, for he had no overcoat. One fairly good shoe he had, but the other was completely worn out, and both very likely he had picked up from the garbage can. As for socks he wore none, but a bloody rag was tied around one of his ankles to serve the purpose.

"What is the Salvation Army?" I questioned.

"You don't want ever to go to the place!" he emphasized with disgust. "It costs 35 cents. That there's a flophouse," with his thumb he indicated the building from which we had just issued. "It costs only a nickel, and you don't have to pray inside. Want some free coffee now?"

I saw he was a bum of long standing. Gesturing for me to follow him, he shuffled along cheerfully, though he was bending his back to the wind and shivering. (I didn't see how he could last long; he trembled like paper.) On the way we passed by a massive stone water trough for horses. He paused to drink from the trough by means of an empty bottle; offered it to me, and I drank too. He sopped a small dirty rag around there with trembling hand and washed himself feebly. I did the same with my handkerchief. After that we both felt better. He led the way, spreading his dirty rag out on his hands to dry in the sun. I did the same with my handkerchief. We talked as we went along. He couldn't see how I had never heard of Chinatown (which was where we were going).

"Where all the Chinee people live? Ain't you Chinee?"

I couldn't make him understand about Korea.

Pretty soon we came to a tangle of tracks. El's, subways, at the juncture of the great Manhattan Bridge. Turning off to the right, in the shadow of a three-story el, lay the winding alleys and lanes of Chinatown, with their intricate signs in Chinese characters.

Our destination was not so much Chinatown as a certain rescue league which maintained a bread line there. The bread line advertised itself.

Down a narrow, crooking street, in gloomy shadow even now by day, stretched a herd of coughing men looking like hungry goats. Chinese signs overtopped them high on either side, and above, the el was so near it seemed to rumble over our heads, fenced by the scrolling network of unlit tin calligraphy.

We had to go to the end of the line. Here two men were fighting over a cigarette stub, unusually long, smoked evidently by a luxurious smoker, perhaps one of the prosperous young men who had been through on a slumming party the night before. Both claimed to have seen it on the street first. I pointed out this scene to my guide. He shrugged and fished out of his own pocket a handful of butts, all very short, none much larger than a good-sized fingernail. He politely offered me to choose. But I did not know how to smoke yet.

We came to the soup window at last, and my friend received a plate of thin soup, a slice of bread and some coffee, but I was refused. Like every New York executive, the soup-kitchen preacher was evidently a business-man, grim, with the eyes of a lynx and an alert and legal manner. He said he couldn't give me soup unless I had a soup ticket, with my name down on a charity organization in some other part of New York. But the junior attendant sympathized with me. All I had to do, he said in an excited and emotionally thrilled voice, was to go get a soup ticket. He emphasized with paper and pencil. When I came back, there would still be coffee and bread left. And he wrote down full directions to somewhere many blocks away, requiring nothing else but carfare money. He struck me as one who would have been at the front in five world wars, although I believe he was too young to have been in the last one.

I dropped out of line and stood on the pavement with his slip of paper in my hand—another letter of introduction, this time to a charity organization. Up and down the streets were rows of Chinese restaurants. Every house in fact was a Chinese restaurant! They served something more than coffee and bread, neither of which yet seemed like food to me. I thought a bit. Contrary to what one might suppose, being a New York bum required training, recognition. It was hard work to be one; and to be a good one, still harder. It might take as much time as a bank president's work.

I gripped my suitcase again and entered a Chinese restaurant. A Chinese waiter brought me the Chinese menu at once, not the American one. It was good to be able to read that bill and to know what I was getting. I ordered something thick, honest and humble. It was soup, filled up with Chinese vegetables slightly cooked, and big pieces of cow's stomach. I ate two huge bowls of steaming rice with it. To appreciate this sort of thing, one should fast for two meals. I took time in eating, after the first bowl, and began to think how I could "save face" without any way to pay for what I had eaten.

The proprietor lounged on a stool behind the cash register; as tranquil as a mossy stone. He looked like a fat magnanimous man. I asked him for a sheet of paper. Taking, as theme, lines from a famous Fu on vegetable soup, "Alas! why is it that my life is poor and narrow as of a hare in flight? How can the Muse of Poesy descend upon me with my bowels a core of vibrant thunder?" I wrote a poem in Chinese characters. The characters and the rhymes were in classical Chinese, but the poem was my own and had a modern signification. I spoke of the tired wanderer in a foreign wilderness who finds the remote kinsman home, and when he is given the same food eaten in China Land, through the vapor, out of a sea of soup, rises Li Tai Po's old playfellow, the moon. The ideas were not much, but the form and calligraphy fairly good. I gave it to the waiter, and he, as I expected, showed it to the boss.

I had written my own letter of introduction. So strongly is the Chinese classical culture ingrained in the East that the educated man is at once noted by the assurance and deftness of his strokes in writing. And the classical gentleman, says Confucius, is to be the "measuring rod of Heaven and Earth."

Well, the proprietor came over and talked with me. I knew only a Northern dialect, he only the Cantonese, in spoken language, so we conversed in writing to help out the English. He sympathized with me that I was Korean. The Chinese always regard Korea as a part of China, although the Koreans do not, for Korea has had a long, independent history before it was taken by Japan. He knew the Koreans had a hard time with the Japanese. He, too, wrote a poem in Chinese, one of Li Tai Po's. He apologized for his lack of skill in calligraphy. But his writing was not without feeling, for one of so little training as he had had. I asked him then if I might eat in his restaurant by the month and run up a bill. That was all right, he said. I asked him, too, if he could recommend me a room. He promptly gave me a number not far away. I left my suitcase in his restaurant while I looked it up.

The address that had been given me was not exactly in Chinatown. It was in the Italian quarter which enjoys the Chinese elbow to elbow. The landlady was a broad-bosomed, fiery-eyed Italian. She knew very little English, but it was wonderful how we could communicate without any language. She held up fingers, and I could understand the price of the room. I nodded my head to say yes, and pointed to the name of the Chinese restaurant man on the card he had given me, indicating that I was a friend of his. I arranged that I would not need to pay for a while there either.

8

It was a ghostly world to be lost in, this town that was neither in America nor in China. Certainly Chinatown is less American and more segregate than any other foreign colony in New York. The Chinese elect their own mayor, administer their own justice, and their houses and their homes are to the outsider impenetrable. The Japanese, in spite of their fanatic patriotism, do not live like this in one great organism. Koreans abroad of course are too small in number to admit of much generalization; later I found that on the whole (though with exceptions) they do stick together rather closely, but with none of the formidable breastworks of the Chinese. They do not have the money or the American footholds, as have these Chinese merchantmen, who practise Westernization with such inviolability that sons are still sent back for education, marriage, death. I found myself still in the shadow of the Confucian world. The unreality of it in New York, and my own helpless immobility filled me with a curious trance-like despair, as I waited, penniless, for George Jum.

But I talked with many Chinese businessmen, touching little on the vulgar topic of money, mostly on the glories of Li Tai Po. I walked and observed a good deal, not only around Chinatown, but throughout lower New York. I could not improve my English—the Chinese, tenacious of old ways, spoke little English. I am reminded of the story of a Chinized Korean, who, living in Canton, doing business there, wished to visit New York also on business. He knew no English, but on his return three months later, reported in the most glowing terms that he had not needed it. Americans spoke Chinese. It seems, on landing, he hailed a taxicab and said "Chinton," which really means, in Chinese, town of the Chinese, and being driven promptly to Chinatown, he had no difficulty there in conversing fluently in the Canton dialect.

Yet if I had not been so worried about the future, I must have vastly enjoyed Chinatown. However gloomy and impassive, Chinatown is one of the most picturesque quarters of New York. Before you approach Chinatown, you can smell it—the incense, the rice cakes, the Oriental perfumes, the cold, earthy smells of giant turnips and strange green vegetables, the teas, the musty smell of sawdust out of China, and through all a peculiar kind of dirt, more discrete than Western dirt, fainter, less frank, yet there. And much of the smell is due to salted shrimps. You are struck by colors everywhere, colors which are not exactly Chinese and not exactly Western, but are a mixture, an exotic hybrid of the East and West. The shades of these colors give you a sense of uncomfortableness, yet once in a while they are strikingly effective in their combination. As you enter Chatham Square, you begin to hear the sounds of the Chinese language. Newsmen pass by with a peculiar shamble, shouting in the American style, but their words are in Chinese. Later, as the day progresses, there will be the tinkling of distant musical instruments behind the shuttered upper balconies, the clash of cymbals thin and high, the shrilling dissonance of strings.

It's an odd triangular quarter, centering at Doyer Street and issuing off Chatham Square…lying in Mott, Bayard and Pell streets. The section itself is so small that you can borrow a spoon in one end of the town to eat porridge with in the other, without your porridge growing cold. Yet it never increases nor decreases. A few years before my arrival, such a flood of strangers moved in that you would have expected to see Chinatown swamped, overwhelmed, obliterated, but there was no change to the outward eye.

Later on, after the immigration laws, no more Chinese could enter, and many returned to the old country. But this section did not change. If there are more Chinese to live there, then people become more thick. If there are less, it is just the same, and people have more room. Yes, the whole quarter could be made into one big modern apartment house. But houses are mostly old, as American houses go, and in that harmonize best with the Chinese; an old race in old buildings does not look bad. Most of the buildings are three or four stories, with dormered attics. The stairs one enters from the street are black and warped, with uncarpeted, crooked, narrow treads.

As I walked along, I would gaze in the little shops. In the windows was the oddest mingling, beautiful flowery garments for women and men, together with American felt hats. Here were corsets, suspenders and a woman's Chinese fan. All sizes of gorgeous embroidered shoes were ranged side by side with old-fashioned long-sleeved American underwear. And the Chinese characters everywhere inside these windows were written not upright, but across the goods in Western style.

In the midst of a junk-heap of things for sale, I saw a few real Himalayan jades, as green as greenest sea. They might even be the most expensive kind, as rare as the Egyptian pearl. I looked at them and fell into a revery lasting many minutes. Time could not wrinkle nor stain such pieces and on them was always to be seen the dead jade carver's pains, intense as lovers' pains. Only an old, old culture could have produced such gems. After seeing them, I spun around as if my thoughts were being pronounced on air. What strange spell, what haunting little tune was that coming out of the window on a New York top floor? It seemed the flute had a touch of magic sound, recalling memories of long ago, some ancient Cheung Chow night, some distant idyll, in a landscape weirdly different from that I saw before me now, a world of nature, green and gray harmonies, houses irregular and ever curved—not straight—a world where human feelings were patterned otherwise, the human heart more shy, Pan-toned, and clear. Was it another existence that I lived? In retrospect, my past and future blended (at least within one book, within ten years), it seems to me at that moment I sought in the past for a brother, a future friend, who was to go with me through these pages, who was always to shadow for me old realms of thought even as he guided me into the new…that here for the first time I sensed one as exiled as that tune, carved by the Asian centuries as intricately as that gem, my friend, my dear friend, Kim.… I even walked up that clifflike stairway, three flights in pursuit. But the ghost was gone. I found only a room in the Hip-Sing society, some silent images about, a smell of incense, and Chinese ink permeating all, a Chinese record going on the Western victrola—and two young Chinese men discussing football.

9

The house I slept in was as dingy and as dark as those in Chinatown, but unlike the half-familiar feel of Chinatown, it was wholly strange to me. It had a back stairway where no light ever came, and where there was no lamplight either. I sometimes passed people who looked rather frightful going in and coming out. For instance, the big flushed swarthy man on the second floor, who ran a pool room just outside of Chinatown, had a very rough look. He never wore a collar or a tie but only a shirt with handkerchief around the neck; yet he was kind to me, going out of the way to be friendly—particularly when drunk. At such times he often came into my room of his own accord to talk. His Italian name was Machelozzi, he said. He first shortened this name to Michael and then to Mike—these were its evolutions over thirteen years of living in New York. I could not gather much from his conversation except that Dante was the greatest poet, Italy the most beautiful land. He still hoped to go back to Italy and resume the Machelozzi again when he had made enough money to afford it.

The Italian section was also colorful. Unlike the Chinese, all the Italians seemed to be on the streets day and night, quarrelling or laughing or singing at all hours. Even their business was conducted mostly on the street. There were bright-colored markets everywhere and tropical fruit wagons. Yes, the Italians were as voluble and perpetually excited as the Chinese were noiseless and impassive. My landlady often opened the window on the second floor where she lived and talked to the woman on the fourth of the house across the street, using both the tongue and the language of gesticulation. And then she would grow enraged like winds and storms and slam the window down hard enough to break the glass.

The days I spent in this unpaid-for room seemed endless, though I think in reality they were not more than ten. But ten days is a long time to go on five cents in New York. Early I had found a place where my five cents would buy two loaves of stale, hard bread. On this I lived, soaking first in water the bits I hacked off with my knife, going into the Chinese restaurant only every other day, so as not to run my bill too high. My bread was almost gone. I had known the famines of poor rice years in Korea. Now, in utter solitude with a chilling heart, I feared pavement famine, with plenty all around but in the end not even grass to chew. While in the shadow of New York's skyline, sunny hours were few, evenings seemed to be cold, dreary, long. In my unheated room during the cold night hours, I spent some monstrous intervals in studying Shakespeare. But it was hard to concentrate. Even in the midst of Hamlet's subtlest soliloquies, I could think of nothing but food. I often passed that charitable soup kitchen, but it, too, wore a closed and alien look and I shrank from passing myself off in there. My only hope was George Jum. Almost every day I walked up to his house. There was no news.

BOOK TWO

1

THE NEXT PERIOD of my life must properly be dedicated to George Jum. He attempted to be my teacher in things American, and certainly he had left all Asian culture behind as a thing of nought. If I am not a very shining example of his precepts, the faults must be laid to me and not to him.

Yes, even that first endless and helpless period of mine had a help and came to an end...for Jum appeared at last. The evening before my rescue, in a restless misery I could not bring myself to re-enter my dreary little room. I had eaten well in the Chinese restaurant and this food had revitalized me with a nervous energy. All night I prowled on tireless padded feet, like a creature caged. Central Park I reached at 59th Street, just as the sun was stealing up and the dews slipped down. The patient trees of winter spread their arms more hopefully, as the sun washed off the night dirt, showing the dust crystals in the blue and violet light. The homeless bum sat up on the bench. Another day had begun. Milk wagons, street-cleaners, policemen....
And now the sun, well-risen, was splashing the façade of George Jum's house

with a strong, cheerful light. It was half-past eight, no longer too early to call and inquire once more.

What a change in the Hungarian fat lady! She was all warm personal interest and smiles now.

"He expects you. Go right up—Mr. Jum came home."

Through the warm, steam-heated house hovered a morning incense of American breakfast bacon and a Korean or Hungarian odor of garlic, too. (Probably Hungarian, for George disliked garlic now, he was so sophisticated.)

"He's on the third floor. You'll see his name on the door. Go right up, Mr. Han."

And she encouraged me with many nods and waves of her pudgy hands, before disappearing through a long curtain in the hall below.

Before I had finished the first knock, George Jum jumped out. "Han? Chungpa? Son-of-a-gun! Why didn't you write you were coming? Then I would be here," he exclaimed jovially in English. "How long have you been in New York? How are you? Come straight in. What is the news from the homeland?"

George Jum looked very Americanized in his red leather slippers and a bathrobe of heavy striped black-and-gray necktie silk. Even now when he had just risen from bed, with hair not combed or parted, but all streaked down, he had a fresh, debonair appearance. His forehead was smooth and marble-white without a scratch, his eyes were a light black and always dancing with a smile, his nose was round, well-shaped: only being too round it looked better in profile. He had a demure, impudent grin. His figure was neat, his movements rapid as those of a cat after a mouse. And as he pushed me into the room before him, he was very cordial, and seemed to have known me always, not just by mail.

"This is my room. You're welcome here. Not bad? Large enough to have a small dancing party in. It is all yours. This house is practically private, except for the black kitten which is very seldom seen. But the lady—Mrs. Flo—is seen once in a while. She has very good whisky when I have a cold. There is the couch and this is the bed. Choose which you will have. This door leads to the closet," and he opened it to show me. It was neatly filled up with shoes, hats, suits, overcoats.

"They all belong to you?" I asked incredulously.

"Oh, yes, but nothing unusual. When I start work again, I will buy more.... This door leads to the bathroom. Perhaps you will want to wash up. Where have you been staying these last few days when I wasn't in New York to show you how to do things?"

"Oh, you have a bathtub, too! Luxurious!" I exclaimed, too busy looking to reply. (My landlady in Little Italy had no bathtub.)

"Sure!" said George. "That is nothing. In New York it is necessity, not luxury—where dirt is common property."

He came in after me and said he would instruct me how to do things—how to use things.

I looked at George's bathroom shelf. I had never in my life before seen so many things to put on the human body—the hair, the teeth, the face. "What's this—and this—" I marveled.

George shaved and I watched him do it—so I would know how, he said. He washed hands and face first. Then he rubbed his shaving paste with the shaving brush, making a lather. Then he put his brush to his face, was for a minute lost in foam. After that he shaved in rapid strokes up and down.

"It's a good razor, the kind that never cuts. Unless you have a pimple or some kind of extra pointed-out flesh."

"Yes, sharp!"

"But it does not matter if it cuts, because I have a pencil."

He showed it to me.

"It's a white pencil that can't write."

"Then what's it for?"

"To use in place of sea-glue, of course."

"You mean it stops bleeding?"

"Yes," said George, and he purposely cut down a small pimple to make it bleed and held up the pencil. "You see? This is the way...."

Later he put some perfumed water, smelling like spring flowers, on his face, and last, some cream-colored powder out of a round box with a black-haired gentleman's head on it.

"Powder on face!"

George grinned.

"Ladies have to grease it first. Which I don't."

He took out a clean white shirt and freshly-pressed pants. A fast worker he was, I noted. In a minute he was fully dressed, while, fascinated, I still prepared to take a bath at George's instruction. George came in just then to comb his hair. I turned the bathtub on and the shower ran down over everything.

"For God's sake, turn that off!"

I meant to turn it off, but it came on more vigorously.

"I don't know how!"

George turned off the shower, and unloosened a rosy-colored bath curtain looking beautifully fresh and new; he told me to get in there. When I got in, he closed the curtains.

"Now you can turn the water."

It was marvellous, like being inside a flower. Water came down as if it were harnessed rain, a tropical rain. But I could make it as cold as I wished. George said…either polar or tropical. Down it ran, over my hair, face, body.

"That was wonderful!" I exclaimed, coming out. "Never a bath again! Only a shower."

But poor George! I had made him all wet. He had taken off his pants, and was examining them. "These will have to be pressed. Hell to it!" He saw my worried look and reassured me. "That's easy. I have an electric iron. Anyhow, it is better to cook without the pants."

He gave me the American dressing gown and he himself tied the girdle around my waist. He pointed out to me the red leather slippers. "Wear these." Then he said, "Now we shall have breakfast. Wait. It flows too much. It moves." He was referring to the long wide shirt in which he was still clothed, although without the pants, "The reason I put this on." And he put on his vest, leaving his neat compact legs bare, down to his garters and socks. "Now I will show you the American breakfast."

The kitchen was a big cabinet in George's bedroom. When open, it was a little alcove, very complete, with small electric ice-box, gas stove, dish cupboard, etc. When you got through, as George explained, everything folded back and you closed the doors. He took down a loaf of bread.

"Grandmother's," said George with a wink, in reference to the wrapper around the bread. George winked slowly. It was the only thing he did slowly. But winking is difficult for a Korean unless he practises it very much in youth.

George cut the slices very thick, trimmed off all the crust, and prepared to make toast. He balanced himself, this way and that, watching everything without appearing to do so. When he took cups and saucers down, he made the cups turn a somersault, catching them in mid-air. The knife he juggled, whirling it three times round, before cutting the grapefruit with one stroke; then taking out all seeds at once with one motion of the grapefruit jack, he poured in powdered sugar quickly. He buttered the toast, smoking hot, until each piece was soft clear through.... Coffee, too, was ready by this time.

"Be seated," said George with a bow.

Over the breakfast, I told George my troubles since arriving in New York. How he pitied me! Especially because I had walked up to his house so many times.

"Good Lord, I wouldn't do that for anything. Unless a beautiful girl accompanied me or I got paid for it!"

I said it was good training. I would have to know New York if I mean to live here and find a job. All my optimism and assurance had come back, with George.

'Well, don't worry about not having any money," advised George. "Not in New York, which is wealthier than all Asia. Tonight we will go to Chinatown and pull out some lottery. Later I will teach you to cook. As a cook, I can boast myself an artist. The wages of a good cook are $50 a week with board, room and laundry. Better than a bank clerk or college instructor, you will find. And it's *much* better money than when I was an ambassador for the Korean government in Washington, D.C."

"But I don't know the spoken language very well yet. You must speak only English with me so I can learn."

"Sure," said George genially. "I like to speak English. I myself know how to employ the idiom."

Now I lay back on George's bed, comfortably stretching in the sun-filled room. The luxury of being here was almost too much. I loved the effect of space, after narrow, tortuous, dark Chinatown. Two double windows opened toward Central Park and there was besides a smaller window in a side wall. White net muted the light. There was some kind of artificial Persian rug on the floor. Two cheap Western pictures were hung—one with three Shepherd dogs' heads with tongues hanging out, another, a Maxfield Parrish print of a girl with bare legs sitting against a romantic blue.

My eyes traveled from the big desk with three drawers at the bottom and a row of books at the top, all brand-new bindings, to a dressing table very neatly kept. On it were George's father's and mother's and brother's pictures, and another in an ornate silver frame, of a blonde Western girl. George had shut up the kitchen and was busy with his pants and a big steel cake. He pressed a button, as he explained, and electricity made it hot enough to press the pants which were laid across a cloth wrapped board held up by two chairs. George put a wet cloth over the pants and pressed hard.

"Better than the stick our mothers used, huh? This line has got to be exactly straight. You see? That is it. Girls don't like it, if it is not."

I asked George if he was thinking of getting married, that he took such pains.

"I am thinking of love, not of marriage," said George. "Marriage from love is vinegar from wine, as the poet says. I have done a lot of thinking on this subject. Marriage as an institution here is a failure because it is a law-abiding. Anything that law commands in the form of thou shalt not, that thing man wants more. That is the symbol of this Western civilization. Man makes laws. And laws make his wants more complicated. If the law says you should have one wife, then you want more than one. If the law says live with the same woman, then you want to try different ones. Isn't that funny? That's human nature. Just like the wild ducks. They are monogamous in their wild nature and become polygamous as soon as domesticated. The guinea fowl does the same. That is, civilization depraves the birds and the animals as well as man. But then civilization is a good thing. We enjoy motor cars and bathtubs. And who would not enjoy having more than one wife? I would rather choose civilization and more than one woman than go back to wild life and marry one woman for life. Let us never forget, we owe all this pleasure to the progress of civilization. It is because nude women are prohibited on the streets that the beautiful half-naked women dancing on the gymnasium floor under deep-colored lights of soft evening are beautiful, or the three-fourths naked women by the seashore under a glowing summer sky. Man makes laws and sometimes law does help psychologically."

I let George see that I was interested. Willingly he spoke more on the same subject.

"I don't believe anybody in New York has gone around with more girls than I have. Still I have more to find out about them. I make a study of them. It's the greatest line of research in the West. You know women are funny and different. And you have to treat them accordingly. They do not have the same psychology that we do. Sooner or later they will get mad. Watch out for that. That man who said he couldn't get on without them or with them seems to have understood them, so that the best thing is to make the best out of them. Now pants are done."

He asked me what I thought of the picture on his dressing table.

"All right. But the girl is very fat."

George got into his pants. They fitted him to perfection. He was evidently very careful about his clothes. Yet he never looked stiff.

"That picture is the most deceiving thing in the world," he said warmly, taking it up to examine. "She is much much better looking than that. I met her five years ago. In Washington, D.C."

"When you were ambassador?"

"Washington!" George sighed.... "What a place for beautiful girls! The job alone counts. My! I was in love with her for two years. Now we write to each other, that is all. It's sad.... If you don't like her, I'll change the picture."

And he brought out the photo of a girl in cossack boots and Russian dancing dress.

2

I fell into a gentle slumber, exhausted by my efforts in reaching the real America at last. When I awoke, George was sitting at his desk. Beautiful note papers of various kinds were spread out before him. There was mono-grammed paper with the initial of his last name very large and the initial of his first name very small inside, there was paper with his name written in gold in beautiful Chinese characters, and there was a third kind with the Korean national flower at the top in color.

"What are you doing?" I said.

"Writing letters."

"Very boring," I said. "Letter writing has always seemed to me a waste of time. My! how I hate it!"

"That is because you have never been in love. Letter writing is very important in the art of love. Sometimes a letter can do more than actual meeting. Especially if the letter is a suggestive one. That's where art comes in."

"Confucius does not list love among the different branches of the arts and knowledge."

"Does he list cooking? But isn't cooking an art? And so is love. They are much the same. Each requires the highly skilled master, and each gives pleasure in its own way. Confucius, I admit, has nothing to teach on the subject of love. That's where I leave him behind. For love is the beginning of a real, new and true life leading you into the Garden of Paradise, maybe Eden. It's a pity that they in English say falling in love. It is not a falling, but it is a rising. If it is a falling action, you will have no more life. But because it is a rising action, you get more done. But maybe in English they have a more ironic attitude toward love than I have...."

"Are you writing to that girl?" I asked idly, indicating the new photograph.

George thought a bit, then shook his head.

"What I have written is too good for her. Besides, it is in Korean."

"What will you do with it, then?"

"I will save it. Very often I write what is too good to send right away." He opened a drawer in his desk. "See. These are all kinds of love letters for various occasions. Some are finished, some roughly sketched, some only once revised. They are in English, Korean and Chinese. I write them as they come into my head. Then when I am in a hurry or need to act with sudden inspiration, I select from these."

I saw he got this idea from the Orient where the village scribe used to keep on hand certain especially good letters for birthday greetings, or for partings or congratulations on the birth of a son. Then he rented them out as they were called for, always being careful to keep the copy.

"But what a pity that I have written this letter in Korean," said George, shaking his head. "Not many beautiful Korean girls can get away from Korea to come over here. I don't know any. They all get married too young when they are beautiful, now that the men are becoming civilized over there. But I will put it away for my Ideal!" And he told me he also had an ideal imaginary girl to whom he wrote regularly, posting her letters in a certain drawer.

"Why not translate?" I suggested, after reading George's letter.

"All right."

"And I will help you."

When we got through, it ran in English something like this:

My dearest heart,

You left an everlasting image upon my soul. Every sinew of me bleeds and my lips shout your name, scattering it with the winds of the Hudson River. Ten thousands of tears and sighs have been accumulated upon my heart like New York dust, and engraved on it "I love you." My heart's restless sea, perpetually beating upon the shores, can never become a serene and calm lake sleeping in the eternal quietness until I have you in my arms.... Darling. I can't say it except with a bunch of red roses—every dewdrop is my tear, every thorn is my anguish, every red petal utters love.

Yours, until I may have life and love,

GEORGE JUM.

"My Lord, you are a genius!" exclaimed George.

"Yours until" particularly pleased him. That had double meaning, he said. And he wrote it all out on monogrammed paper, using the greenest green of shallow sea ink. He had a neat and beautiful handwriting even in

English, which can't show much of the calligraphic art. "Chungpa, you know the written language better than I."

"That is because I have read Shakespeare."

George said he regretted at times that he had not had more education in the Western style. He had never been to a Western university and knew only what he had picked up.

"I can interpret Shakespeare to you," I offered.

"Fine. And you can be my secretary from now on. I will pay you well for that."

George went to look at the rice that was cooking, for it was approaching four o'clock. He now served a late lunch with the promise to read to me from one of his Korean plays immediately afterwards.

George had tossed off a number of Korean plays, but his English was not adequate to translate them. The dialogue was witty, but obscene. It had early been his ambition, George explained, to become thoroughly Westernized, not just Christianized (which is often the direct opposite). He was the son of one of the earliest Christian converts in Korea.

"My first years were spent in a church school associated with my father's Methodist church," George said. "But I could never prove an acceptable Christian. Later my father sent me to the Christian academy in Seoul. But I hated it like the devil. And they said I was a devil. Everybody knew from the start I was a bad egg. It was hopeless to beat it. Such eggs never make decent omelet. Still, my school days in Korea were not unfruitful. I learned enough Chinese literature to make me classic (if not a classical scholar), and I made friends with my equals to lead them in games, and my superiors took me to winehouses. My first experience in love was with a young girl at a famous winehouse, where she was the daughter of the landlord. Confucius, Christ, Buddha, I found all were wrong. There is more meaning of life in woman's arms than in all the written words about the soul's paradise. I was forced to separate from her because of Christian parents. And later, she died, young. But I have been true to first love and what it taught me. Life lies with women, not with the classics or the ancestors."

As George read me one of the scenes from his play, I pointed out to him that though it might have two actors, it could not have an audience.

"Oh, well," said George. "You're right as usual. We hasten on then to the soliloquy."

The last scene showed the hero speaking ecstatically:

"Wonderful woman! wonderful life! wonderful love!"

"I consider that," said George, "almost Shakespearean."

3

It grew dark outside, and the blue-black wind curled about the sparkling street lamps, lifting the tinselled papers; it was time to go downtown and try our luck at the Chinese lottery. George put away his love letters and his plays with affectionate hands. Now, he said, he would show me how to dress.

"First, your underwear. It will have to be cut down." It was Korean underwear, long-legged and long-sleeved.

"But the wind is cold."

"That can't be helped." And he got scissors at once and cut it down while it was still on me. "Now. Get dressed. I'll keep these pieces to dust out my desk with."

When I was dressed, George looked me over again, shaking his head. He said he liked me all right, except for my hatless head, my shirtless condition, my dirty shoes, my schoolboy suit, and my minister's overcoat. From his own supplies he gave me a long white shirt of very good quality, a necktie of black and gray and mild red combined, gray socks, garters, a hat, a short coat to match my trousers as nearly as possible. He said he would have my shoes shined on the sidewalk.

"No," interposed George. "That isn't the way to tie a tie. It must be tight." And he tied it for me. "And your socks. Remember. Tight. If you want to give a good impression with girls, always be tight. Even in a kiss, it should be tight. Many Western marriages are broken up because the man is not tight."

"In dress I fear I can never be tight, any more than my poet uncle—"

"Then you will lose your opportunity. Don't you know that whenever you are with girls, they look first at your necktie, then at your socks, then at your shirt, then at your shoes, then at your cuff buttons? When they like all these things, then they will like you. I remember the impression I made once with my cuff buttons. She noticed them at once. 'Oh, these are not ten cent ones!' 'They aren't!' and she was just delighted. Don't take a chance. Girls may be very beautiful. You don't want to lose them. One of the easiest things is to be well dressed. Maybe two girls in a million won't care. But even with these two, it cannot hinder if it docs not help."

We went downtown on the subway and that was my first experience underground. "My wild ride with God." Everybody in New York seemed to be right there with us. It looked like a fight going on. George instructed me how to get into the car.

"The best way to get in there is to walk back and then come forward."

I did this and it worked very well.

"You have to push and force in, to get anything in New York," said George. "Nobody has any pity. Nobody cares what you are doing. Nobody sees. It makes people unconscious. They wouldn't care if you had two heads and three eyes. In this they are different from the people of Boston, who look at you though you have only one head, if that head is Oriental."

We went down into a large basement. There were about fifty Chinese and a singing noise of the Chinese language, Cantonese dialect. Here was a big lottery headquarters. George paid one dollar for me and another for himself. For that we received slips of paper with certain characters. The characters read: "Autumn harvest in the vast universe," and "Winter heaping under mystery moon."

"I like the looks of these," said George.

But the mystic picture words did not work as much as George wished. We got nothing at all. Again we picked and punched and waited around.

"Do you play this game often?" I asked.

"Yes," said George. "And never win. If I ever get that highest reward, I will spend one half on a scholarship for my brother."

Then he got much excited. "Good Lord, we almost got $2000, the highest reward."

Quickly he spent another dollar in my name. On that I got ten dollars. It seemed like a fortune, and I was as delighted as if it had been $2000, almost. George said it was all mine; it had been won on my luck, not his. I paid back the two dollars George had spent for me on the lottery. We went to that restaurant where I had a bill. I ordered a feast, big lobster with meat sauce, and beancakes with pieces of red steak and Chinese greens, and a soup of chicken giblets cut in the form of flowers. My bill for the entire ten days of soup was under two dollars, and after paying it completely and for our dinner that night too, I had enough left to pay my room rent, which was not high.

George was well satisfied with this restaurant, as the cooking was good, yet he warned me never to bring a girl here. Wasted advice, as I was not much Westernized.

"It is a favorite place with me though," he said. "I often come here, but always alone. It has no atmosphere. You see, here the Chinese wear those black Chinese coats like pajamas and their Chinese slippers like bedroom ones have no heels. Girls may think this place is not clean—especially if they come from Washington, D.C."

Next we went to my room, to liquidate things there. George examined the few effects I had brought with me from the homeland. He himself packed for me, while I read to him from Shakespeare. I read him the love scenes between Romeo and Juliet and Hamlet's soliloquies. "That's the stuff!" And right off George liked Shakespeare. But we differed on which characters we liked. I said I preferred Hamlet's part to Romeo's.

"Well, I like Romeo," said George. "Anyhow, Juliet is great. 'Give me my sin again.' If I could only find a woman as artistic as that, I could do better than Romeo."

And as we passed through a bit of the park to get to George's house, he pointed out two young lovers seated on a park bench in each other's arms. George said, "O, that this too too solid flesh would melt." Combining Romeo and Hamlet, so to speak.

4

There was a Korean Institute in New York, where students and the other exiles met. George took me here.

"It is easiest to find the first job through a Korean. Besides, if you are going to college, you will surely want to meet the Reverend Ok." (There was a demure look in Jum's eye.) "He is the most famous student that I know. At least in length of time. He has been going to college now for sixteen years!"

The Korean Institute was in the Chelsea district, a grimy old-fashioned brick building that had seen better days. The section was very dirty, noisy, and plebeian, but the house inside was quiet and dignified. The most attractive feature was the community dining room in the basement, where real Korean food was prepared and served. Up on the ground floor were some rather bare clubrooms for playing games, and a hall for the Christian Koreans to sing hymns in. The rest of the house was given over to bedrooms, occupied by certain well-known students at small cost.

It was a center for all kinds, bad atheists like George, good Methodists like Ok, communists, capitalists, and all other categories, rich and poor. Of the rich, of course, not many. Koreans were generally ruined by this time, by the Japanese occupation: besides, those counted as rich men in Korea were poor men in New York, where incomes dwindled to one third by the exchange. But not a few belonged to old and distinguished families in the homeland. There were several princes. Now they could only get along by doing housework; royalty had been ruined more than the barons or the rich men.

As the men were standing around waiting for dinner, and George was playing pool, an old and gray-haired gentleman, looking very refined and distinguished, came up and shook hands with me. He had known both my uncles through their reputation, the uncle who was a lunatic poet, and the eldest, most aristocratic uncle who was the *paksa,* the most famous scholar of our family. We began to talk on classical poetry. We even got rhymes and practised. Both of us seemed to get intoxicated. The Koreans here were not so modern as George, but here proved to be a man of two generations behind the others, not only in age, but also in spirit. His calligraphy was very beautiful. It reminded me of the poem written by Han Yu:

> The years deepen, but how these pictures avoid cracks!
> One sticks a scaly monster like a writhing knife;
> The phoenix pair wings; numberless genii hover;
> Coral and jade trees interlace their branches;
> Golden thread and iron cable knot in powerful clasp;
> An ancient tripod is plunged in water;
> Back and forth the soaring dragons weave.

The old gentleman proved to be a real scholar, and in fact had several literary degrees from the old Korean government.

"I am greatly surprised to find that you have studied so much in the classics," he said at last. Saying it, he sighed. I knew what that sigh meant. Alas, what good would it do me? More harm than good.

"I study no more of that now, but only the Western literature. Shakespeare," I murmured in a subdued voice.

He looked with caution all around, then said, low and whisperingly: "I have read many English writers, but I have never found anything in them that could be compared to the classical poetry." But he dared not say it aloud before these young fellows who had studied in the West and now saw nothing except the new writers.

With the easy perspicacity of youth, I suddenly saw into Doctor Ko. His presence here seemed to me almost irony, an irony to which he was oblivious. Ko spoke an excellent English, and would give any American meeting him the impression of a man, if not Westernized at least thoroughly Christianized. Scratch him—and underneath was still that Old-World Confucian. Doctor Ko was a valued adviser on church administration, a leader in the service always, and he supported church and institute with his money, giving lavishly. He was not wealthy, but having been for many years a merchant for Korean ginseng roots in Cuba, he had enough to live a quiet life of retirement with frugality. And what is more, Ko really believed himself an earnest Christian. Odd illusion! Every inch of the man I saw—his mind, his spirit, all his values, were those of a Confucian scholar. He had simply changed the letter of his faith.

I found out soon, he wrote Korean articles in support of Christianity, English articles, too, for Korean papers published in America. Ko was not a bad journalist in English or Korean. But what a lifeless, stilted one! How different from his work in classical poetry, which showed his fire and elegance and real distinction!

Presently George came up and drew me aside, saying in a whisper:

"Over there you see the Reverend J. P. Ok, A.B., B.D., A.M., S.T.M., sometime to be, if God helps, Ph.D. The people here in the institute call him Doctor, because he is hoping to get that title soon. And he is pleased to be so. Mr. Ok, or Jimmy Ok, to him, does not sound so good or so exciting as Reverend Doctor Ok, Ph.D."

George beckoned and Mr. Ok came toward us, bowing and smiling and holding out his hand.

"Probably I can tell you something you are wishing to know about American universities," said Ok, mincingly. "Come up to my room. I will have no time afterwards, as I am going to speak before a ladies' missionary society at nine o'clock."

He handed us a card all printed out, announcing he was to speak. Reverend Doctor Ok, and just as George said, A.B., B.D., A.M., S.T.M. after his name.

Mr. Ok had a very large, clean room upstairs in the Institute, where he had been living for over a month. We went there now. In one corner I noticed about one hundred Bibles, leather-bound, gilt-edged on India paper. I examined one. It was in English. He was glad to have me look at them, and explained that he was selling these to help out his scholarship. He made me a very good speech on the Bible, "The Book of Books," "The Inspirational Book," "The Greatest Literature ever written," etc.

"He has no money to buy Bibles. He wants to go to college like yourself," George interrupted. After that Ok wanted to show me cheaper pocket editions.

"Where would you advise me to go?" I asked hastily.

"Oh, South," said Mr. Ok. "South."

"Why South?" I said. "They told me in Korea I must go North."

"Oh, South by all means. The professors are really interested in the Orient down there. They will be kind to you...."

"Kinder than in the North?"

"Oh, yes, I mean they would not flunk you. They always remember that English is not your own."

"I guess you got good grades," George said.

Mr. Ok smiled modestly.

"My grades in the South were very good. I remember, I got an A in New Testament Greek.... Unfortunately I had to leave Georgia, because they don't give the Ph.D. down there. Besides, my idea was to get the doctor's degree in a bigger place for a change, and maybe I can be more service with that...."

"Whew! you discourage me! It takes too long," said George bluntly.

"Well, I don't mind telling you, if I get my Ph.D. I am not going to study any more. No, not anywhere. It is not good for you to study all the time," explained Ok ingenuously. "Hard on the nerves. But this Ph.D. is a very hard one. I have a language requirement in it, French or German. I am taking French. But I always fail. Still, I am going to try French in the fall again."

"If you take time, maybe to pass that French will not be necessary," said George. "They may give Ph.D.'s in the Southern university in a few years."

"You think so?" Mr. Ok asked with interest.

"Or maybe they will give you an LL.D. on your success in giving service."

"Hee hee!" laughed Mr. Ok.

"But what are those?" I asked.

"Those are my golf sticks."

"And that?"

"His tennis racket," said George, examining it. "Son of Gun, it's a good one!"

"You know how to play tennis, Mr. Ok?" I questioned.

"Yes, tennis, too. A bit. What I like the best is football. Not to play. I am not heavy enough. But fun to watch, hee hee! That's what you learn in college."

Our interview was almost ended. Mr. Ok was busy brushing up his suit and hat. He sprinkled perfume out of a small bottle on his handkerchief too. You saw he had shaved the second time that day, and there was powder on his cheek, just the kind you smell in a five-and-ten-cent store. He took out of a well-filled closet a light handsome overcoat, and he felt in his pocket and drew out the headlines of a speech, which he examined hastily with moving lips.

"Perhaps you can come and hear my speech this evening," he invited.

"No," said George. "Sorry. We have another engagement."

We left him conning the headlines of his speech, and George sniffed on the stairs:

"You heard it anyhow."

"When?"

"His only speech. It is about the Bible. He has a fine introduction from a missionary friend in Korea and another from the head Y.M.C.A. office in America. Every time he comes to New York on vacation, he hunts up a different church. There he speaks through these letters of introduction—in the church at least once, and maybe also in Sunday school. Meanwhile he will get a list of those same church members to visit during the next week for his sales. He has memorized that speech on 'Book of Books' and all the kind you heard. This speech is good—and really kills two birds by throwing one stone. The same speech he uses for selling Bibles as well as speaking in church." Our glances met.

"So that is Doctor Ok," I said thoughtfully. "Certainly he is the best-dressed Korean of the Institute except you, George. And he's very nice and good. And there's nothing at all wrong with him that I can see. Of course, he has awful calligraphy, I see on those notes he made. And he doesn't know the classics at all. But as Doctor Ko says, who reads the classics nowadays? He can't speak English very correctly either."

"And yet he has been studying logic, systematic theology, homiletics, homogeny and ecstasy, not to mention hygiene and sanitation, for the past sixteen years," said George.

5

While waiting for dinner, I met a number of people besides the Reverend Ok. Especially I took notice of Pyun and Hsun, as I hoped from one of them to get some job. Hsun had a tea business which employed many boys. Pyun was head of an Oriental employment agency for house servants.

"Come around to the office tomorrow morning, both of you," said Pyun.

Hsun said he would give me a job in his tea business if I could find nothing to do at Pyun's.

"But with Hsun you will learn no American efficiency," said George.

Pyun seemed to think this very funny. He laughed and laughed.

"That's all right," said Hsun good-naturedly. "We get along all right."

"I also have a hard time," said Pyun bashfully, "to learn these business ways."

And now George and Hsun laughed at Pyun.

These two men were very different. Pyun, so emaciated, tall and ever bending in, Hsun so short and stout and ever curving out. Pyun's long, pale, hollow face was like a narrow cupped hand with the forehead more prominent than the nose, so that if he grew a pointed beard his face would be a crescent moon: his chin was bald, however. But Hsun's face was like the full moon except that it had whiskers though every day he shaved. Pyun wore a well-fitting suit of navy-blue serge and a tight necktie. Hsun on the other hand was loose; he was dressed in the ill-fitting clothes of Third Avenue, had a shabby twisted necktie and dusty shoes, and long blowing hair without a part. But Hsun had a heartier look than Pyun and seemed a better friend to George; in swearing he was not so good as George, but he was pretty good.

Nobody else swore here except these two. But then George always became a center of disapproving interest in the Korean Institute, it was so dignified and self-respecting. The Korean conservative—whether at home or abroad—is no more tolerant than the Puritan New Englander, and this made George the more mischievous. He never could stand respectability that covers up.

So now he began, to Pyun and Hsun, but loud enough for all around to hear:

"You know it is almost impossible to get close to a Korean girl. She is not like an American. You may sit right across, plenty of opportunity to kick beneath the table. You may even grab her while you are playing games. But she won't respond. She will not talk or flirt with unmarried boys as is the custom in America." George paused and looked around. "Isn't that so, Pyun?... Only the married women...."

This displeased the married men there very much. But it fascinated them, too. All were afraid of George with their wives, knowing that he was an Americanized pagan.

"Are there many Korean girls in New York?" I asked.

"No, very few. Are they good-looking, I see you want to ask. Even an optimist could not expect it. Only the intelligentsia is here. None are good-looking of course except those married."

"But how about the girl you were telling me about the other night?"

"American-born in Hawaii," said George. "I will point her out to you at dinner. She is putting herself through the New York music school by waiting on tables in a Broadway restaurant. She has no other education of any kind, except she is a good piano player. She can play jazz too, but she prefers, 'Onward.' Isn't that just like a Korean girl? Plays in a Korean church every Sunday."

"But, George, you said she was good-looking, too."

"Well, much better by back than by front," said George. "If all the women in the world could be lined up and covered with a big pillow, all but hands and legs, she'd have a good chance. Even when you saw her face, it would not be so bad, as you would still have the legs. My! legs! Those are grand, stunning, swell!"

"Man might get an old woman that way, George," teased Hsun. "An old woman sometimes has the best legs."

"Not I, never!" said George. "I can tell by the expression in legs, whether old or young."

"So you don't like Korean girls' faces, you say, eh, Jum?" grinned Pyun. "Only legs?"

"I don't say that. Beautiful girls have faces as well as legs. Am I right,

Mr. Pang?" and George turned to a tall ill-favored Korean with gray hair, tortoise-shell glasses and bad teeth who had been listening attentively. Long and lank like Pyun, he was dressed like Hsun in badly fitting clothes, yet not so cheap. Hung-Kwan Pang had a reputation for being rich. "But perhaps you're no authority on ladies' charms? Well, I am, I tell you. I have no degree from American universities like Reverend Ok. I have no intellect to write that dissertation on American business like Mr. Pang. But love—I study it. Confucius doesn't teach it. Nor does St. Paul. Nor all those professors North or South, in literature, commerce, or theology. But in my field I may be said to have the Ph.D. Naturally I have formed my idea of a beautiful woman. Her beauty has to do somewhat with features—complexion—shape. Not necessarily blonde, as I used to think on first coming over. Brunettes, they may be stunning wonders! And I can tell you, too, I like a Korean girl. If she is beautiful. A flirting Korean woman can be the most beautiful in all the world—when she makes up her mind to study American methods outside as well as inside college. Unmarried ones, as well as married ladies."

I could not understand why Hung-Kwan turned violently red and moved away, with every sign of irritation. Of course, none approved what George was saying, for Koreans didn't like those American methods George had been mentioning. But Hung-Kwan withdrew to the hall, to the head of the basement stairs, where with back turned he remained, thrusting his head downward, as if he would tell by smelling how nearly dinner was done.

"But first of all she must have pretty legs that can be judged," went on George. "And it is a good thing now that girls wear short skirts so you can see their legs. You know, legs ought to look like this." George drew a perfect picture and passed it. Even the Reverend Ok tittered. He had joined us too, by this time, light overcoat hung up in the hall, and all ready to address that missionary meeting, immediately after dinner. "Not the kind that looks like a bundle of hay. Neither those too thin, like T.B. in them. But they should be just right. I can show you a good sample any time on Fifth Avenue. It's a pity that the Koreans cover up ladies' legs with a heap of clothes; the Japanese are superior in showing the female legs. Even they have much to learn from America. Look at the silk wrapped Western leg on Fifth

Avenue—this is progress...still better, the bare legs on the Coney Island bathing beach."

But the waiting Hung-Kwan now gave the sign and everybody moved downstairs where the food and the ladies were. The Korean pastor and his missionary friend had just taken their seats side by side, and Mr. Ok there, too, when Pyun called softly from the top of the stairs, "Oh, Jum, come here. You forgot something."

George went to the foot of the stairs and peeped up. I took a step after him and peered up, too. Pyun was gesticulating with a flat sort of flask as concave as he.

"Sh!" said Pyun, and pointed toward the washroom.

"For the Lord's sake!" ejaculated George. "Bring it down! What's the secret here?"

But Pyun came down awkwardly, with flask concealed. Nobody there was willing like George to flaunt proprieties. They called it being obscenely Westernized.

BOOK THREE

1

GEORGE AND I were to leave New York about the same time. Pyun had found places for both, as he said he would. Since I could not cook, though George was charitable enough to recommend me, they said I must go as a houseboy, in company with another Korean, Mr. Pak.

"I know Mr. Pak," said George. "And you will have no trouble there."

I became optimistic then:

"My first American step, George, in economic life. I will make money now like Hung-Kwan Pang. On that I will be come educated like J. P. Ok, A.B., B.D., M.S.T., M.A., Ph.D."

"I'm sure of Pak," George added, "but I am not sure of Pyun. Pyun has himself learned the American efficiency, though he would be ashamed to say that he is a good businessman...this shows he still has some Orientality about him. But all the same he may be sending us both out just to get a commission."

"But he is a good friend of yours!"

"I do not like him much. In some ways he is an interesting type of Oriental successful in America.... Pyun's Utopia is not unlike that good old Epicurus...he believes in eating good meals. He also believes in hard work. So he spends his days in hard work and his nights in good times—a typical New Yorker. He really knows gin. Those who come for the party enjoy themselves and have no headache the next morning. He has an apartment uptown where I often go to play poker (mostly losing). He keeps the entire floor for himself, so he can bring his friends privately. (His friends are mostly girls.) But he will never get anywhere. He has no poetry, no romance! Just skating!"

"Remember," said George to me, "it is not always the money man who is the best dancer, the best drinker, or the best dressed human being at all. He often leads the dullest existence. That is because he does not know how to create an enjoyable life. It may be that money does not come to the man who knows how to spend it for a good time. But then you can't afford to have a dull life. At any rate—make money; but don't sacrifice mystery to make money. When you say, 'Never mind—that will come when I accumulate wealth,' then it may be too late. To scorn delights and live laborious days, that will not do."

I was packed long before George, and presently Pak came in a taxicab with his two suitcases. They were old and worn, not so good-looking as George's. The handle of one was wrapped with strings. Pak was very big and tall, with a phlegmatic face. He had a stubborn hesitating accent; three times his tongue would flutter, sometimes even more, before he could utter a sentence.

He was a most typical Korean, an exile only in body, not in soul. Western civilization had rolled over him as water over a rock. He was a very strong nationalist; so he always sat in at the Korean Christian services, because they had sometimes to do with nationalism. With his hard-earned money, he supported all societies for Korean revolution against Japan. Most of his relations had moved out of Korea since the Japanese occupation—into Manchuria and Russia—but Pak still lived believing that the time must come to go back, and even now, with a little money sent in care of a brother-in-law, he had bought a minute piece of land to the north of Seoul. For fifteen years his single ambition had been to get back there and settle down. On Korean land, he wanted to raise 100 per cent Korean children, who would be just as patriotic as himself, and maybe better educated in the classics. But still he did not have enough money to travel back, get married, settle comfortably down. This made him rather suffering and gloomy, always looking on the dark side of things.

George went out and got some beer to cheer him up. Real beer it was, in a paper carton. Pak drank beer and light wines—never gin—and smoked Luckies, but very temperately.

Pak, too, was worried, not about George's job, but about his and mine.

"Eighty dollars a month for two. That is not much!" he sighed. And George agreed.

"What is the matter with Pyun? Is he trying all the worst places first?"

"That trick was played on me many times before," said Pak.

"I guess your place is all right. The woman has two kids. She must be normal."

Pak shook his head gloomily.

"Normal you say—or as I say, not—American woman is hard to understand," insisted Pak, shaking his head. "I have had only one good job in America. For seven years I had a good job. A very nice man. Very nice wife. Nobody ever was mad at me. But he was mad at her, she was mad at him. Finally both become so mad with each other, they divorce. Nobody can see a reason why. The man goes to live in New York hotel. The lady goes to live with a friend in California. I was so happy with both!" Pak was almost crying. "Neither could take me. The lady cried, saying good–bye. Then the man came, separately crying. But—all up! Our home was broken. One month's pay, $100 from the man. From the lady, a wonderful letter recommending me. I use this letter ever since. But never find another job like that. No more jobs like that in America!"

"Well," said George philosophically, "Their jobs are like their marriages. In the American civilization, especially in New York civilization, a married woman is no more than a kept woman, and no kept woman could be kept long. Thus divorce comes. It costs money. But they have it. So social life is a burden to them...."

"Western marriage is no good in New York!" agreed Pak mournfully.

"But being a bachelor in New York is not bad!" Pak didn't see it that way.

"Not good for a man to be unmarried. Indecent Western way."

"Look here, Pak, you are not Westernized," exclaimed George, rising up to preach. "You are not civilized. What is the matter with you? You can't enjoy the bachelor life when you have it. It is something we don't have in the Orient. This is one of the advantages of Western civilization. Listen, I read you advice."

George took down a big fat notebook. He put on glasses.

"These are the wisest of Western men—the greatest of thinkers," he opened to his self-made index, hunting advice whether or not to get married." (Not because they are wise and great, but because I agree in what they say.) First. Take Socrates. When asked whether to get married or stay single, Socrates said, 'Whichever, you will repent.' (You see, Socrates encourages marriage 50 per cent. He lived in Western classical times.) Another writer says, 'One was never married and this is his hell; another is, and that is his plague.' Hell may be bad, still it would not be as bad as plague. The wisest advice I know is that given by the great philosopher and thinker, Bacon, 'Young man—not yet! Elder man—never!'" And George shut the book with a whack, pleased with himself.

Pak still stood by his own conviction. He seemed not to have heard Jum's words at all.

"Forty-five years old I am. Not yet married. Already I lose at least five children by not marrying. And no children—no more me! This is fault! This is sin! This is crime...of the race suicide!"

2

In the station Pak bought a newspaper, which he could not read. He only bought it to look at the advertisements. He had not had much education at home and none at all in America. I offered to read some to him. But he was only interested to know what had happened in the Korean revolution, which had already quieted down. At least in American papers.

We were met at our destination by a lady in a big shiny car, all enclosed, and she was driving it herself. I examined her somewhat curiously, remembering the stories of George and Pak. She looked very artificial to me and not very friendly.

"He talk not much English," said Pak, and, uneasy how I would behave, he nudged me. As we assembled our suitcases, he said in Korean:

"Leave everything to me. You just keep in the background. Be shy like a Korean bride."

I tried to be shy. But the lady would not allow me to do this. As we rolled through suburban green lawns and semi-countrified streets, she directed all her words at me.

"You are the houseboy, aren't you? What? No experience! I hope we won't have too hard a time to train you"...and on and on.... My role seemed more a star than Pak's.

"And you must say 'Yes, *Madame*.'"

The car stopped. All around was free land, laid out for houses regularly with streets, but on it now were only small trees. There was one house. I did not care for the house. It ought out here to be a farmhouse but nobody attempted to make it a farm. It was a three-story concrete, very abrupt to look at in that flat space. There was a tiny hedge a little dog could jump and an artificial lawn with gravel paths. On the wind also you could smell the sea, but there was no sea smell about the house. It negated Nature, but the city was not transported yet. In a few years there would be many houses. I saw on the horizon another going up. I would not be able to recognize this place in 1975. Now, with neither society nor privacy, it was desolate.

"Get out," said the lady, who seemed a society-pioneer here. "And open the door for me. No, I mean you." And she pointed at me.

I had difficulty though to open the door for myself. Pak tried to open it too, but it stuck. There was a trick in the button. The lady opened the door, turning around from her seat in front. Then my suitcase, which was on top of Pak's two suitcases, fell out and opened and all my books fell out, and

I fell out of the taxi after them. There I stood and didn't know whether to pick up my books or open the door for the lady. For she would have to step out on the books.

"Go round to the other door," said Pak to me in Korean. And he jumped out after me.

"Yes, Madame."

I tried to get there so fast that I stubbed my toe on Shakespeare and fell down. I jumped up and got the door open at last, and the lady had to step out in a kind of flower bed, while Pak crammed all my books back into the suitcase, and shut it, but only by one lock on one side: the other side wouldn't close.

"That was very badly done," said the lady. "Leave the suitcases there—no, on the gravel, not on the lawn. Get into the car and try that over again."

This time I did very well. Pak breathed a sigh of relief.

"Now whenever I come in, you stand out here and open the car door...."

She was moving toward the house in illustration. I grabbed up my suitcase again and followed after. Pak, too.

She opened the side door with her key.

"Here, you must help to take my coat and overshoes."

"Yes, Madame."

I dropped my suitcase again. Again it broke.

"Never mind now," she said in vexation, "just remember another time."

I picked up my books.

"I hope they have no germs," she said, shuddering as she saw the dingy Oriental covers of some second-hand books I bought in Yokohama.

We went inside. Pak took off his coat the first thing. But I kept mine—a missionary had told me that a gentleman never takes off his short coat in the house; forever he must wear it, just like shoes. The lady handed us two white aprons, badges of servitude, ordering us to try these on. Pak tied his around his armpits. But mine was too long. I tied it around my neck and stood attentively.

"No, no, not that way."

"Yes, Madame."

Dejectedly I tied it around my waist under the jacket. The upper part looked man now, the lower, woman. Certainly it was a very long skirt. It almost trailed on the floor. The lady was looking at me analytically.

"H'm! What is wrong with you? Well, these are the best I can do until I take your sizes. My former cook was a very tall Negro. He was able to do the work of two. But I hired you to be presentable. Tomorrow I will go into the city to get some white coats—if everything else is satisfactory," she added with emphasis.

A cultured Korean lady takes small and calm steps full of leisure. This American lady moved out vice versa.

We were late. We must rush to get the first dinner. I only peeled carrots and beans. Then I cut my finger. But I had to wait on table. Pak couldn't do it for me. O Lord! George had forgotten to tell me how. I had a short lesson from Pak.

"Fork on left, spoon on right...pour water over right shoulder...offer meat on left...don't take away plate under soup bowl till end of soup...."

How was I to remember all this? It was like learning the Chinese book of rites in five minutes.

Then I forgot all when I brought in the soup. A girl of eighteen stood there in trousers and shirt like an American man, with long leather boots reaching to the knees. She sat down.

"Oh, I'm so hungry," said the girl. "I rode clear around the riding school.... My horse was in fine spirits and..."

She caught sight of me and giggled. Her brother, a boy of twelve, laughed too.

I returned to the kitchen and described the girl to Pak.

"It's the way women dress on Long Island," I said.

Pak, however, took it as sinister.

"This job won't last," he gloomily shook his head. "Girl dressed like man, hair cut short, Westerners all like ten hells."

"But she has to, to ride on a horse."

"Yes! Rides on horse! Son-of-ingenuine-woman!"

The lady's bell rang peremptorily.

"Quick! Tell me what next."

But Pak couldn't. His tongue wouldn't move that fast.

"Get back," was all he said.

I went back in and the lady said, "Take the soup off."

"Through?" I said as softly as I could.

"You must say 'Yes, Madame.'"

What had Pak said? Don't take the plates under soup bowls? I left the plates. It was wrong.

"Take these plates off!" said the lady angrily.

"Yes, Madame."

"Hey, give me some more water, Charley, before you go," said the boy.

"Yes, Madame."

The girl and the boy seemed to be giggling and laughing the whole time. They never took their eyes from me. I went into the kitchen again, where Pak was still mumbling to himself about the unnatural evils of Western civilization.

"What would my grandmother say? Running round over country on horseback dressed like men."

"How can I be there like Korean bride?" I asked indignantly. "The girl and boy are laughing at me all the time."

"Get back!" was all Pak said. "Before she rings. Here. Put napkin over arm."

I went in as noiselessly as I could. That was very noiseless. I was facing the boy and girl but the lady's back was to me. She didn't know I came in. I stood by the sideboard like a statue, napkin over the arm. The boy and girl were delighted.

"Ain't we got style?" said the boy. "We got a butler."

The lady laughed, "Peu! peu!" But she didn't see me.

Pretty soon I had to sneeze. I struggled for control. I must be Korean bride. No help. It was an awful sneeze. The lady jumped and said "Oh!" She turned in a hurry—the boy and girl buried their faces in napkins and weakly howled. I, too, must laugh to look at them. "Hee!" I, too, put the napkin to my face. But the lady didn't laugh. "You may go!"

"Yes, Madame."

3

Pak worked slowly, but he did well, and he was a good cook. To me he was always kind. I complained to Pak about the lady, who interviewed me much more than Pak.

"It is not good that all the time she should get angry—not good for her, not good for me."

"No man can understand American ladies," he said patiently.

I had to work from morning to night. I had never worked so hard in all my life with no time to myself. First, beds to make. Pak helped me in this, for it was hard. Pak preached like George, be tight, but for a different reason.

"All Westerners roast the feet to freeze the nose. Western feet are cold, while Western nose is tough, tough as the elephant's trunk."

But next day the whole thing was to do over again. I was discouraged.

"All Westerners kick, these more than most," said Pak. "It is bad conscience maybe. I will buy big safety pins to pin the end sheets and blankets so they won't come off, after once being done, when the lady kicks at night."

Then there was so much dusting to do, all seemingly an unnecessary labor to me. Surely such quantities of furniture were only in the way! In Korea, the beauty of a room is in its free space. "The utility of a vase is in its emptiness." I did not believe Americans got much out of Shakespeare—American domesticity gave no time. And yet there were all sorts of labor saving devices in the kitchen, even an electric egg-beater. I could not understand why I did not get through safely and quickly like George, with plenty of leisure time.

Whenever the lady saw me, she got nervous and irritated. Before she spoke, she would give one big artificial smile, and the bigger that smile was, the angrier she was going to be. She would preach:

"Always rearrange pillows after I—or others—sit on the sofa...."

"Always put on a clean apron before coming out of the kitchen...not one spotted with jam...."

"Never leave off your apron as if you were a guest in the house...."

"Dust under each chair with an oil rag, not with a feather...."

"Dry the saucepan before putting it away...."

"Dishwipers must be washed at once after being used; then hang them up carefully...."

"Never use the front door except to open it for others...."

"Don't stay here...go...after being called and serving..."

This last was vice versa to the orders of Pak. Always when I came out of the dining-room while the family sat at the table, he ordered, "Back!" He didn't want me in his way either.

It was interesting in a sense, being treated just like a dog or cat. One could see everything, and go unnoticed, except while being scolded. But how tired my feet got! How discouraged I was! How hungry to get away somewhere, even if I starved! "To keep on is harder than being a prisoner," I thought. And I remembered George's advice not to scorn delight and live laborious days.

Still another day of chore work in domesticity began. It was a beautiful morning. I looked out through the window at the green fields of the first April, juicy and wet. Outside the spring odor was penetrating and lyrical. The perfume of the bursting sods and quickened rootlets, all swaying in the west wind, intermingled with the salty tang of the sea. But inside it was tough and bitter, for I had slept too late, having gone to bed too late the night before. Shakespeare was to blame for it. He was too beautiful to be left unread, too poignant to be left uncried. I wished to write letters to my ideal as George did. "From you I have been absent in the Spring...."

The clock indicated that I was an hour and a half late when I got up that morning. Pak did not wake me, because he thought I needed a little more sleep after the night before. He was too kind to me always. Alas, kindness was to spoil the whole business!

I went into the great white mechanized kitchen. Pak said:

"Fired!"

"Something is burning?" I cried, running to the electric stove.

"No. Fired! Job doesn't last!"

But hoping still to make good, I dragged the vacuum cleaner in to do the living room, my usual morning task. The girl, who was always the latest breakfast-getter, was already up, and so was her mother. They were standing, looking at the living room which was just as it had been left the night before, when the girl, who was already a candidate for somebody, entertained company.

The girl as usual giggled when she saw me. But the lady did not. She looked at me with a hard and spiteful smile:

"I have telephoned for a house servant, not a comedian."

4

Well, we were fired, and given one week's pay, fifteen dollars for Pak and four for me. A good share of this must go to Pyun. Pak was not angry with me for our failure. He said he did not believe that I would ever make a good cook, or even could keep a houseboy's job, but he wished me luck—he thought I ought to make a great scholar. And he asked me to make him a copy of his letter of recommendation—the original was too old and worn out to show now. He was not even very bitter against Pyun. Pak was so patient. He went back to Pyun's employment agency immediately.

"Here all is alike. Nothing lasts in America," said Pak stoically. "Such trick is known as business efficiency."

I however had learned my lesson. I would not try Pyun any more. I went to Hsun. Hsun was extremely sympathetic. He hired me at once, saying he would not be able to pay me much, but by staying with him, I could be assured of living expenses and a little over, and besides have plenty of time for studying. Hsun always saw the importance of studying. In most things, he remained an Oriental, in his habits, his imperfect ways of American dress, his method of housekeeping and of eating and even of doing business.

Hsun occupied an entire floor on an upper story of a tall building at 74th Street and this was his home and his tea business at the same time. The front room was once very large, but Hsun had put up a tall carton partition, making a separate storeroom for tea, incense, and the other things he was selling. At top, the storeroom was open, but there was a door and a key to lock it by. On the other side of the partition, at a folding card table, I worked as Hsun's secretary. The work was easy. Hsun's business correspondence was almost entirely confined to the Korean student directory, which stood permanently on my table. The letters he told me to write were not like business at all...they had more to do with how boys were getting on and how they need not send money right away unless they had something beyond their school expenses, etc. To those who had not enough funds to carry them through the summer, he wrote, saying he would be glad to send them some tea on credit to sell. To penniless students, west, south, or north, who wanted to come to New York, he wrote encouraging them and enclosing part of the fare, saying that when they came, they could make it up to him by selling tea.

This work was all done by the end of the morning. Always my afternoons were free. Hsun himself fixed our lunch and dinner. He usually made something that was his own invention: it was a sort of Chinese chop-suey, Korean kimchi, Japanese skiyaki, Italian ravioli, and Hungarian goulash, all combined. To pour over this, he always kept some red-hot pepper sauce.

After lunch, I took a walk, or remained at my desk, reading, until the students who were Hsun's salesmen thronged in from summer classes. In New York City alone, more than twenty boys were trying, off and on, to sell his tea. They peddled it from house to house. Harlem was a favorite selling ground. They did not get kicked out there. But it was found that incense was more profitable than tea in Harlem. Some Negroes have the superstition that burning incense in a house prevents disease and brings prosperity in business ventures, especially incense sold by Asiatics. Because of this and because the boys liked Harlem, Hsun had added incense to his stock, labelling it "Good-Luck Incense" and wrapping it about in golden paper.

5

One of the outside men who visited Hsun's once or twice was Chinwan. The interesting, or rather, notorious gossip about Chinwan was that he was a Japanese consul, on leave of absence. This was not noised about at once, as Chinwan was very quiet and didn't talk much.

It is a very rare thing for one of Korean birth to be in Japanese diplomatic work. But it would not be much of a surprise for any one who knew Chinwan's past life. Chinwan was born in Fusan, the Korean seaport nearest to Japan. Now Fusan is the gateway to Korea, and the Japanese came over there first. For decades, nay centuries, there was a large Japanese colony in Fusan. The migration of the peoples moved both ways. Long before Japan took Korea, Chinwan had emigrated to Japan and he remained there. As a child, he had passed through the Japanese schools, and he had taken degrees from the Imperial University of Kyoto, and in all things he was pretty well Japanized. Many of his Japanese friends did not even know he was a Korean. But he spoke Korean and knew Korea well. And at present he wanted to associate with Koreans, perhaps because he had just married one.

Nanchun, his wife, was a modernistic artist of some reputation. She had lived for a long time in Paris and was one of the few Korean women in the emancipated realm. It was well known of Nanchun that before Chinwan married her, she had loved, married, and divorced, all in the Western passion. Indeed, it was said of her former husband that on the honeymoon she took him to the grave of her first lover and cried there all the day, while the newly married husband was left sitting by.

Chinwan had met Nanchun in Tokyo while he was studying law. A more paradoxical match than theirs would be hard to imagine. Chinwan had a radical wife, but he was not at all modernized. He had traveled for more than a year in Europe and now he was spending the rest of his time in New York, but he had no conception of the Western world. And he seems to have had little idea of the condition of Asiatic politics.

The Koreans thought that Chinwan was infamous, because he had a Japanese government position. But he was not in any sense a spy for the Japanese. He had shown himself too good a friend to Koreans for that.

During diplomatic service in Manchuria, he had helped many revolutionary Koreans who were arrested carrying news and bombs from Siberia to Shanghai and from Moscow to Seoul; today many Koreans in Germany and France tell me that their heads would have been chopped off long ago if Chinwan had not befriended them. But neither was Chinwan a Korean spy. He was a good friend to the Japanese, too. He was just a lenient kindly man, not fitted to be a harsh official. On the other hand, he was the farthest possible from a revolutionist type.

A harmless man was Chinwan, thoroughly human, enjoying the good things of life, wearing good clothes, liking good times, always sociable. Whenever friends around him talked about things seriously, Chinwan kept quiet, as if he never thought about anything serious in his life. So there was never any argument. He just left all betwixt Tweedledum and Tweedledee. He was shapely in body and feature, healthy, vigorous, a good-looking average type, and through and through a peaceable Oriental. I saw him one Sunday in Central Park and we walked together, for I had missed him on his first visit to Hsun's. He invited me to come and see him and Nanchun in their uptown apartment. He said the dean of my Korean college had told him to look for me when he came to America. He bought peanuts for the squirrels and the tamed pigeons, and showed a youthful, childlike gaiety in speech and actions.

Chinwan came to Hsun's because of a few students who studied in Japan when Chinwan was studying at the Imperial University of Kyoto. That was before word got around that he was a diplomatic-service man. But after that, a Mr. Lin brandished his long cigarette-holder and said he had ordered a sword for Chinwan and soon he would get rid of *him*. I did not think he was serious. But one of Chinwan's friends advised him not to come round there any more, saying Lin was a dangerous man.

One night about this time, there was a nationalist meeting in the Korean Institute. Naturally, all the Koreans who were interested presented themselves there. My, how they could gather in from all over the city, as well as from near-by places such as Massachusetts, Connecticut, and Pennsylvania! Most were passionate national patriots—and a few still more passionate communists, the latter being there to raise objections. As usual they all sang the Korean national hymn to the Auld Lang Syne tune and there was a speech or two delivered, but to any outsider, it would have seemed an innocent gathering. The little institute was well peopled and a great social activity was in the air. Amidst all was Chinwan the diplomat, sitting quietly as ever somewhere in the rear. His wife was in another section among the ladies, very original and serious, a strong personality (I knew from hearsay), except in looks, in which she resembled many a beautiful woman with a perennial smile and soft words. I admired her. I was thinking I would like very much to call on them. Meanwhile a certain Korean was making a long speech. Others beside myself moved restlessly; complaint could be seen about the speech being longwinded, too much repetition with afterthoughts. Nor did the speaker flame up the fire of enthusiasm. People wished for something more worthy of the occasion.

Suddenly Mr. Lin ran in from the side door with a sword in hand. It was the sword he had ordered and sharpened—a large butcher knife. He approached Chinwan and cried out in a loud voice:

"You son of devil, this is no place for you. Tonight I will send you to hell."

There, before everybody, he stuck the dagger in the traitor's neck. Blood spurted, blood was over all, women screamed, but it was not the accurate hit that Lin intended. Seeing life in Chinwan, he tried a second blow. Somebody grabbed his hand from behind. Friends of Chinwan hurried the wounded man to a hospital.

Promptly the Korean papers in America held up to praise Lin's action, which was as heroic, they said, as you would want to see. Telegrams poured in from Europe, from all over Asia, even from South America, congratulating Lin. Lin became a hero and his name a household word. A few days after the affair, in an underground Chinatown barbershop, a group of Koreans were discussing it. I took part, and narrowly escaped death. I found it was dangerous to deny Lin's act as heroic. You simply could not comment on it as being "narrow nationalism." All discussion had to be centered on the side of Lin versus the Japanese.

My comments in Chinatown spread out and went to Lin. Lin came to me himself and asked me with gravity to go to dinner with him. It was not to a Chinese restaurant that he took me this time but to an expensive place in the Fifties. Conversation, I soon found out, was to be on Chinwan.

"Oh, why did I not better use that opportunity!" Mr. Lin bemoaned. "My best chance to serve the fatherland! I failed. I want to know the address of the hospital where he stays. Do you know that?"

(I knew from other sources that Lin had already tried very hard to find it out. But nobody knew where the hospital was, and New York is so big that one can easily keep oneself hidden in it anywhere, anywhen and anyhow.)

I was alone with Lin, but thought I might as well try escaping death again. I preached in my turn.

"Nothing in the world could be done that way, Doctor Lin. You have to know what is barbaric and what is heroic."

Lin stared at me a moment. He waved his long cigarette holder vigorously for silence. Then solemnly, he wanted to know if I understood why he did it.

"But why did you do it? Chinwan was a harmless man, nice to everybody, kind and friendly. One never could dislike him."

"I like him very much," insisted Lin. "There was nothing personal in my attack."

"Then why? There was absolutely no spying on his part. He was just interested in what Koreans are doing. What gain could there be in taking this man's life?

Mr. Lin continued to speak to me in a sad, beautifully sonorous Korean, and his motive was now clear in inviting me to dinner. He was preaching to me a long and solemn sermon, the gist of which was:

"I would not be a true Korean if I did not feel that what I did was right. You are going to hell and ruin. You forget your country, your country's cause. But I—I am only sorry that it was unfinished and I could not give my life to get Chinwan."

But it was as if I saw Korea receding farther and farther from me. Lin failed to arouse my patriotism; he merely italicized my loneliness and lack of nationalist passion, my sense of uncomfortable exile even among my fellow countrymen, where the homeland was constantly before my eyes. The rebellious individualist in me could not accept his Asian arguments for that bloody attack. It seemed to me not only savage, but futile. And yet I could thrill to the suicide of my countryman, the great Baron Lisangsul, before the Hague Tribunal, who scattered his blood throughout that conference chamber over all the diplomats seated there, that Korea's lost cause might be remembered. That was heroism in the classical tradition. But not this attack on poor harmless Chinwan. Here in this cosmopolitan city I saw Lin as living in a narrow world, a small world in a large. No message came back and forth from the large world to the little nor from the little world to the large. The big world did not know the small world, nor the small world the big. That act of Lin's went down on no police record, nor was Lin ever arrested. In his own group, he received no condemnation for that, only praise.

Later I heard the report that Chinwan was magnanimous, on coming out of the hospital. Of course he refused to prosecute, and he said:

"I am glad he did it, if it was for Korea. Because it was done for love of country, I am willing to accept it as punishment, and not as a crime on Mr. Lin's part."

He and Nanchun disappeared after that; they had to keep their stopping place secret from the Koreans. I lost my chance to make my call on Chinwan.

6

We floated insecurely, in the rootless groping fashion of men hung between two worlds. With Korean culture at a dying gasp, being throttled wherever possible by the Japanese, with conditions at home ever tragic and uncertain, life for us was tied by a slenderer thread to the homeland than for the Chinese. Still it was tied. Koreans thought of themselves as exiles, not as immigrants.

When we reached the West science was the thing: science, economics, social problems, and all the troublesome themes of the twentieth century. Literature was "out." Korean students felt even less interested in literature than the modern Chinese, specializing in science, philosophy, economics, at Columbia (unlike the quieter conservatives of commercial Chinatown, who were thoroughly old-fashioned and not at all "up" on recent trends in thought). As I sat day after day in the sunny tea-fragrant office, teaching myself English by means of the *Golden Treasury,* a paper-backed edition I had bought in Yokohama, I was considered a funny fellow for my interest in either Eastern or Western poetry.

Summer was coming on, with one day like another for us all, at Hsun's, marking time, never inching out of desperate poverty. Hsun's business, while not good, kept on, so that we could win our daily bread and struggle to fight with Nanking bugs at night. His place remained the meeting place of the flock of homesick birds flying back from their classrooms, or from the scorned and unwelcomed labor from house to house. They felt they were coming home. Yet there was no home. There was no comfortable chair to sit on, yet still they came as if they had to be somewhere. Perhaps all they got was only the sound of a tongue that had been heard since the days of the cradle until they left their native land. Day after day, late afternoons and evenings, prisoners of the eternal time, waiting, waiting...for what...the Judgment Day?

BOOK FOUR

1

"MY, I'M GLAD to see you back!" I said to George when he appeared suddenly in Hsun's office during the middle of July. "But the job? You're not leaving Long Island, bathing beach and millionaires' playground, just when summer is here!"

"Man, I am," said George, with a jaunty pull at his new Panama hat, before carefully taking it off.

"I had nothing at all against the people I worked for," he went on, "except that they could not afford my kind. At first I did the ordering, and as is my custom, ordered only the best. Then the lady complained that the bills were too large. She ordered herself. That is how we came into conflict. I could not bring myself to use the inferior onions and celery and other vegetables which she provided. The meat, too, was just a high grade of dog meat. Of course, I didn't want the best in order to eat it myself. But it is not good for any artist to touch second-grade materials. Besides, she wanted too much to employ my spare time."

George was so speedy that he could do work in one-fifth of the time that it would take anybody else. He was efficient in housework as I was not. So the lady set George to working in the garden to take care of his extra time and use his leisure moments.

"After that I threw up the job," said George. "It was the only way to catch up on my reading and writing."

George cooked dinner for Hsun and me that evening. He took me out with him to do the marketing, and like the lady of Long Island, I was horrified by George's extravagance. He reassured me.

"An artist must have the best. But I know what I am getting and I am willing to pay the price. Always I know the difference between steak at one dollar a pound and steak at thirty cents. So don't worry. In the same way, I know the difference between a suit for thirty-five dollars and one for one hundred and ten dollars, and I never get gypped, even when I buy the suit for one hundred and ten dollars. It's hard to fool me on material. Quality pays in the long run."

After dinner George spent the evening telling Hsun how to be a good business man. Hsun, he said, economized too much. "To think and plan on a large scale, that is one of the first things an Oriental must learn in America." George was more sure of himself than ever. He gave full directions for running a large-scale tea business, and outlined some sensational advertising. Hsun never accepted his advice and it was wise not to. George had most expensive tastes. He wanted to make that office look like a Fifth Avenue one.

On the way back to Mrs. Flo's, George stopped in at his favorite bookstore and ordered some books, among others the latest novel of Sinclair Lewis, the short stories of Sherwood Anderson, and a volume of O'Neill's plays, these to be sent at once to his apartment. This was no gesture of scholarship, which George hated (with other Koreans, it might have been), but was done in token of his share in the contemporary American scene. A New Yorker must know something of everything.

A New Yorker, though, lives an expensive life. This was why George was mostly to be found in pajamas at this time. He had enough money not to work as a cook for a while, if, as he said, he economized by going to bed. In this way he needed to make very little expenditure. He would make himself coffee and toast. Mrs. Flo acted as a kind of nurse and often sent up things from her own kitchen. But two or three times a week, George got out of bed and came to Hsun's to cook. Sometimes he would send Hsun out to do the marketing, with strict orders to shop only in the best places. Hsun hated to do that. Once Hsun tried to deceive him with very good meat but bought at some other place than the store where George had ordered him. George knew at once, and was so angry that he refused to cook that time.

When he cooked he made a feast for the whole crowd. All the boys at Hsun's looked forward to George's visit, because while many of them were good cooks, nobody could duplicate George as a chef. Unlike his status at the Korean Institute, George was popular with everybody at Hsun's. He agreed with none, and did not reveal himself to them as he did to me. But it was easy to see that George enjoyed that incomparable privilege of being able to get on with others. He easily entered into the personality of a crowd, yet he never lost his own identity. He could be a shellfish by himself, but he could be a peacock before others; wherever he went, there was a chair waiting for him, and a gay audience.

2

Before long George became restless in his bedroom exile. This must herald (if I had known George better) a season of extravagance which would send him back very shortly to being a cook. He took me to the Chinese lottery several times, but we always lost even when we played in my name.

"Never mind," said George airily, "I'm getting ready to be very lucky in love."

One of the pleasures of a New Yorker, George explained to me, was to go to very expensive Broadway musical shows. He would treat me, he said, but for two reasons. One was, of course, that he was economizing, and the other was, that you must go to this kind of show alone, in order to practise winking at a favorite show-girl.

As a matter of fact, George's interests at present were engaged not on Broadway, but up in Harlem. There was a dancer whom he admired very much...a boneless girl. Night after night he went and sat in the first row.

Outside he had engaged a taximan to wait for him after the performance. Usually he went out with this boneless girl, who had finally been won by his winks, and then he expected the taximan to jump out with a deep bow and hold the door open. If respect were wanting, George would have been severe. But respect never was. George must have paid that taximan a regular salary, for afterwards he and this girl would drive around Harlem, visiting Harlem night clubs to which she had the pass.

Everybody at Hsun's was very curious as to this new girl of George's. George himself spoke in terms of 100 per cent endearment and 80 per cent mystery. He himself didn't know much about her, I think. There was even something funny about her name. She changed it as she liked. When George met her, she was known as May to her friends, but she told George now she would be June.

George described her. He said June had warm eyes.

"What do you mean? warm eyes, George?" asked little Choi.

"Eyes that have got real connection is what I mean!" snapped out George, "Even to toenails and smallest hair. When toes tremble, eyes glow. When fingers vibrate, eyes sparkle. June doesn't laugh or cry with the face alone. Dance is there as much as in her arms and legs. Not like those girls on Broadway, mechanically moving."

3

One evening George made Hsun and me go to a Harlem show at midnight, where June was dancing. The audience was quite a mixture, but there were more Negroes than whites, so that whites among the Negroes of all colors, got lost. A good representation from Harlem, and it made a responsive audience. Even the smallest babies were there, hugged to their mothers' breasts. Poor babies, trying to sleep, while their mothers laughed so vigorously—from the whole being just the way George liked—"with connection." My! those were good babies. Just a few times they would cry out, then go to sleep again.

The flashing lights though less expensive seemed more colorful than Broadway's. Nothing was sophisticated, not even those gay cheap bunches of net and tinsel on the tan-skinned dancing girls. Many were beautiful all right, but one tall black one was the star. She looked strong as a man and was mischievous. There was none of the Americans' idealization of weak and ornamental womanhood about her. She caricatured the sex appeal of this imitation white "review," made it more rowdy and more interesting, and withal more innocent somehow. She was always getting in the way of the flappery tans, calling attention to herself and them. Yet she was the best dancer of them all.... In fact, the jolly rich, highly emotional atmosphere seemed to caricature New York as George, Hsun, and I knew it...frank love, loose laughter, lack of discipline...vulgarity, good humor...sheepishness, plenty of smartness, too, and pavement cunning...everywhere a nonchalant grotesqueness (to us at least who remembered the formal traditionalism of Asia)...a veritable crazy quilt, and dizzy symphony. But the best part, that mood of freshest genius at the Lafayette, was Negro humor which found some funny side in lack of dignity, in losing face. Nobody, not the white man nor the Oriental, could laugh at himself as the Negro did. Nothing those Negroes found so funny to laugh at themselves as "niggers." Their best comedians were Negroes painted black. Eyes and lips in this race were exotic anyhow—they looked funny enough in this northern, western stream-lined civilization where the swiftest, sharpest line is the best. But still they had worked hard to make themselves much funnier.

All the actors and actresses were Negroes like the audience, except a few, such as June, acting the Negro part. George punched me when June came in. Hsun punched me, too, for he thought she was brown. She wore some warm brown stain all over the body. That was all in the nude except for a small net on breasts, and a small piece of cloth on the hips. Still she did not look very naked, for the brownness clothed her as she danced. She had the most elastic body I had ever seen...just like a rubber band. She had no bones—none, either in hip or leg or back. And she could make herself a perfect round thing by connecting her head with her feet like a rolling serpent...the stomach might be on top or at bottom, either way.

We didn't stay for the end of the show, but left after her act, as George had asked, and he went around to the back stage door. Soon he returned with June, who to our surprise was not black but white, white as chalk. So she must be a white girl unless behind that white mask lived a Negro soul. She still looked to us a strange thing and all the more for her simple dress. Her clothes were sport clothes, her face was bare of make-up, except for the poinsettia lips. As George said, she did move as if she were all alive, almost too much so, and as she walked, some thing behind stuck out and moved like a dancer. I wondered if she put something there on purpose. (But George never noticed this, for he always stood face to face, side by side, or else in front of her, never behind.)

George had not exaggerated their intimacy, for now we watched them talking lip to lip, and cheek to cheek, smiling and kidding, and June didn't care who might be there to see. She impressed Hsun and me as having been a dancing-girl from the cradle up, and she seemed the most unconventional woman, the kind George had always been waiting for. June never blushed nor was shy, which to George made a comfortable atmosphere, not like that about Oriental women. We went to a Chinese restaurant in Harlem, not far from the Lafayette. I saw Hsun was somewhat perplexed and puzzled by this June. Anyway by appearance, he seemed to be uncomfortable, for he kept tightening his necktie and pressing back his hair, which of course was flying.

June went into the washroom and there was a moment of relief and a breathing space for Hsun.

"Is she not beautiful?" George murmured happily.

"All women are beautiful if they are nicely dressed and young," Hsun said. "What do you mean by beautiful? What's that?"

"What it is," mused George raptly, "well, that is hard to say. The critic is in the same case. He can tell you what poetry is not, but he can't tell you what poetry is. The lover can tell you what love is not, but never what love is. What his girl is, man cannot know. Of course, the beauty is inside and springs from some inner covered-up place in the girl—but shining out eternally. It must be so, or there is no difference between a piece of painting and a girl. I am free to admit, you can never divorce the conception of beauty from the spiritual sight. What the Christian Bible says 'pleasant to the eye' is just a superficial conception…that only refers to visual pleasure or delight. What the truly beautiful girl gives is melody to the whole man. She brings about inner harmonization, so that the whole man dances. Sometimes this harmonization is so powerful that the man becomes re-created. That is to be in love." George considered a moment, then slapped his knee. "That is it! A beautiful girl is one that can stir man's blood and make man live and make man re-created…without which life be comes an empty shell or rather a mechanical machine…. A beautiful girl is the best Western civilization has to give for this revivification."

"Your talk of a beautiful girl is too deep for me," said Hsun. I was much interested in their conversation.

"Let me describe one to you in the language of the Western poets," I said, and quoted Swinburne whom I had been reading that afternoon while working for Hsun.

> A lady clothed like summer, with sweet hours,
> Whose beauty, fervent as a fiery moon
> Made my blood burn and swoon
> Like a flame rained upon….

Hsun laughed and laughed at this. But George exclaimed, "That's good. Write that down for me, Chungpa. Hurry before June comes back."

I set to work and George continued:

"Of course Hsun here would never understand it. You are too Oriental, Hsun. Western love is undiscovered country to you still. Ah, you don't know what it is to be sucked in by warm eyes, to be caressed by thrilling feminine tones that have no shyness, to be all melted away in Mamma tones…this is the thing you have to learn…this is the greatest discovery of the West…soul-absorbation."

I wrote George the Swinburnian passage, as nearly as I could remember it; he tucked it into his vest pocket, just as June came dancing back—for her feet were quick to move in dance even when not dancing. Like a feather for lightness she seemed, and made you feel that if you touched her skin it might make a blue bruise mark, or she might jump or squeeze up. She didn't pay attention to me and Hsun, only to George. And to George—my!

She moved her chair up close to his, squeezed his arm lightly, and said in a low private voice, "Hello, da-a-arling!"

From then on both ignored Hsun and me.

"How's the headache?" And June stroked her long white boneless hand over George's forehead. (We hadn't known any thing about a headache.) "Think you can eat a little now?" she asked as the food came. "Darling."

George snatched a kiss from June, and said he felt better. He and I ate a lot. Hsun was still too uncomfortable to eat much. And June appeared to touch only a few grains of rice. She was lefthanded, and held George's unoccupied hand all during the meal. George had ordered a number of dishes and naturally a good deal of food was left. George looked at that and said to June, significantly: "When in love hard, you can't eat much...."

June laughed heartily. She had a lazy, magnetic laugh, and appeared to be delighted and amused by all George said.

"June is beside me...in me...around me...everywhere...thoughts are in dream," murmured George, drowning, it seemed, in the new sensations of soul-absorption. "Summer nights sometimes calm nerves down, but not this one.... June excites too much the inner man...." Out came the slip of paper which I had written for George. He read it feelingly.

"Very pretty," commented June, smiling.

"You may have it," said George. "That poet must have known somebody just like June."

"I'm part-Chinese, you know," and she looked George in the eye without a flicker of the eyelash. She fed him some last tidbits of mushrooms and chicken, with chopsticks which her left hand handled very gracefully.

"See how I use chopsticks?"

Hsun and I thought she was just kidding. But George would be convinced by anything just now. Then she told us George was a very good dancer and she was taking him that night to a place where they could do some exhibition dancing.

"When I go with George, they take us for Chinese. It's more exotic."

After that she and George took a taxi and drove around Harlem some more, perhaps because they could not get drinks in that Chinese restaurant and June said she must have a drink.

Hsun remained sceptical all the way home.

"That girl June is just playing with Jum."

"Both seemed to be having a good time," I suggested.

"I can tell a butterfly girl," insisted Hsun. "George is not such a butterfly man as he acts. Good stuff in George."

"Well, it seems that George wants self-exhibition and duet dancing in the American way. With thoughts and feelings like his well-pressed dress… quite up-to-date and well-Americanized…why should George be ashamed of showing up? His only care is to dress up in the right way according to the part he plays…. Thus he gets his degree in the new soul-absorbation." I explained George to the Oriental Hsun.

4

About this time Hsun grew too poor to keep me. In fact, he had grown steadily poorer since employing me. He had made too good use of my services and the Korean directory, helping poor fellows out who sold no tea.

Hsun knew a man who knew a man named Sung. Sung, an Oriental importer, was in need of a boy to help him in his store. It was near 23rd Street in the Chelsea section. For Sung's store was too good for Chinatown. Sung, too, was unlike most Chinese merchants, who are generally easy-going and fat. He was tall, spare, and nattily dressed, with very light-colored eyes and hair smoothly combed back to leave a bald arch over both temples. Sung had a shrewd gnawing look. Altogether he impressed you that he got around fast and would be a man hard to satisfy.

But he said he would try me for a month and pay me twelve dollars for that with lunch at a Chinese-American restaurant in which he owned part share. I started in to work for Sung. I got back my old room in Chinatown, and lived very economically. One good meal a day was enough for me. I soon found I couldn't get that at Sung's restaurant—but if I wandered through the streets of Chinatown about nine o'clock at night—the dinner hour for Chinese waiters and restaurant men—some waiter was almost sure to see me and call out, "Come on—come on. Dinner time!"

Always they cooked enough to be elastic either way—five more or five less made no difference—and if I joined them, they just brought out another bowl and chopsticks. Such was the Chinese custom. They had a psychology which would seem strange to American businessmen. A spiritual treat for a material, a material for a spiritual—they saw no difference. I was recognized as a scholar who knew the classical writing, old style. Sometimes I would take them as a present a bottle of the kind of Chinese wine George drank— they all knew George. But mostly I recited poetry or produced samples of calligraphy, or wrote English letters for them, as I did once for Pak.

Neither did Sung and I get on. It was just as Mr. Wang said. For twelve dollars a month I was supposed to be working for Sung all the time. Soon Sung complained that I was taking too long for my lunch, that I was coming too late in the morning, more especially, that I was not using enough imagination in naming the price to a customer. He said, "In charging, use your own judgment. The ticket is merely to go by. Study psychology. If they are willing to pay, charge high. If not, sell some way."

This was the reason he never marked the right price in English, although it was a store only for Americans and no Oriental customers ever came there. He always used Chinese scripts scribbled on the bottom of the goods, to indicate their approximate value.

The big quarrel began when he saw me selling a shawl to a lady who had a limousine with a chauffeur. This shawl had been displayed in the window for a long time. The lady had noticed it, and having made up her mind, came in to buy it at once. She did not even ask the price until I was tying it up.

"How much?" she said then.

"$5.50," I said, which was marked on the tag in Chinese for me to tell by.

She paid that amount and went out.

Sung all the while was watching from the back of the store. He came up and his hair, so smooth usually, bristled like an angry cat's, while the little veins on his bald temples twitched.

"That is not the way to do business," he said quietly, but with glinting eyes.

He was quiet for several minutes afterwards, walking around the shop, touching this and that, though all was neat. He came back to me.

"If you don't learn American business methods, you will never do here.."

"What did I do wrong?" I said.

Then he told me I should have charged that rich lady much more for her shawl. I argued back. We had a fight. I left. I had been there three weeks, and for that received five dollars. I insisted that he owed me four dollars more. This he never paid, although like Wang, I, too, came back again and again, trying to collect. Sung argued that I must have taken some money from the store, or at least, he had lost four dollars on the shawl because I was not a good salesman.

I think *I* would make a good politician: I was not so soft spoken as Wang. Finally Sung made me a compromise because I kept coming and arguing with Sung when customers were around. He said he would send me to another big restaurant in which he was only slightly interested. I could earn six dollars a week with meals as a waiter there if I would agree to say nothing more about the four dollars he owed me.

There were nine waiters. Among these were three Ph.D.'s from Columbia, and two more to be next June; a B.A. and B.S. and one M.A. The ninth never went to college. The non-collegiate fellow happened to be the most interesting one. He was a painter in the Chinese style from Shanghai. He could not speak English well, and was a newcomer, but had a shy, ready smile. He was not liked much by the boys there, maybe because he had a strikingly distinguished look which didn't go with waiting, and was superior to the rest in many respects; but especially was Mr. Chu despised because he set no value on college degrees, and had only contempt for wages, tips, and the restaurant business in America. But Chu and I became friends. One afternoon we talked on Chinese literature and became so absorbed that we did not know when the dinner hour came, and we should have been waiting on tables.

One of the waiters, a recent Ph.D., was a real M.D. as well. He studied medicine in Peking, and had come over to take Public Health at Johns Hopkins. He had finished his work, and now preferred waiting on tables to going back to Peking. Nobody liked Chong either—but for a different reason—because he was too noisy and conceited. When he told some of the guests that he had two doctors' degrees, the others felt ashamed of him. They said that these people came to eat and to be waited on, they were not interested in how many degrees their waiters had. The headwaiter often talked of firing him, but he did his work all right in spite of his talking. That is why I saw him there still working when I was leaving the place.

At the cash register was a big fat Chinese, American-born, who had the biggest, fattest share in the restaurant's stock. Unlike the Greeks and Italians, who often suspect their partners, the Chinese never fight; I have seen Italian restaurants divide and become two, purposely occupying the same street and even both keeping the same name, which causes much confusion and soon ruins both. Chinese partners stick together. If you suspect your partner, you get it back some other way. But the richest always holds the cashbox.

Fairly good American meals were served as well as chop suey and chow mein; and since I did not like chow mein, I always took the American ones, with the addition of rice instead of bread and potatoes. The first day I worked hard to familiarize myself with the menu and all the different dishes the cook made. There seemed a lot of nuts—almond nuts, walnuts, leechee nuts, peanuts; a lot of sauce—Chinese sauce, Worcestershire sauce, tomato sauce, applesauce; a lot of creams—soup-cream, chicken-cream, vegetable-cream, ice-cream…so it impressed me strongly as a nut, sauce and cream restaurant. Not much else. But as a Chinese restaurant, it was thoroughly popularized. No electric sign for an eating-place was more brilliant than the varicolored lights outside, encircling this upstairs chop-suey place. There was a space for dancing in the middle of the floor, smooth and waxed. Once while running in to the kitchen, one of the waiters fell down with dishes and oil sauce on the floor, and even before he could wipe it up, one of the dancers fell down too, a fat man with a featherweight of a girl on top. This was in tune with the general confusion of the rush hour.

An American orchestra played constantly at that time, competing with the clatter of dishes and the roar of Broadway outside; then the place became like Grand Central Station with people hurrying from four quarters to catch trains. All sorts and conditions of people came to be fed on our hybrid food. To the dim booths lighted with Chinese lanterns came young fellows with strange girls to court—(He: "What's your name?"—and she: "Call me Dot") —Corner-nook tables were more popular with them. They asked us no questions and no questions were asked. In ceaseless procession...missionaries from China, businessmen from Malay, Harlem gangsters, Broadway actors, fat Irish policemen, country ladies from Indiana on a visit, traveling salesmen, shyster lawyers, Bronx family parties including the littlest member. When chorus girls came in groups—blond or platinum or auburn-haired, with astoundingly made-up faces, laughing and free-mannered, wearing their light-blue or yellow or red ensembles—the waiters ran faster to wait on their tables than elsewhere. They were good sports. They ate well and tipped well. And they were pleasant. They were probably making good money.

Once in a while people who wonderfully impressed did not tip well. This matter of a tip, of course, was very absorbing. Who could avoid being glad at finding a fifty-cent piece or even a dollar on the table, like picking gold up from the street or fishing for it in the sea? At first you feel ashamed to take it. Then you take it with boredom as a matter of course. Then you get caught up to speculate to yourself. Then you talk to others about it, and by and by, the first thing you look for is the tip under the soiled plate. Sometimes it is large, sometimes it is small, occasionally nothing is there. You can never calculate—unless you are very clever, like some who had their rules by which a good tipper could be recognized, or one more than usually tight. The tip has nothing to do with the amount of service rendered, it is all in the luck—like shooting craps, or playing the Chinese lottery. But it makes you size up all people in terms of the tip they will bestow.

"It is all learned from commercialized America," said Chu, the painter, in contempt. "Chinese never had these ideas before. Look at them now."

Certainly the boys made tip-getting a matter of fact. So anybody who did not tip well had to be marked. Anybody who did tip well also got marked...just as on a dean's list. That was the rule. He who does not, will not get attention, he will get his ice put in hot water. His bill will be added with good measure. One of the waiters did this on a Jewish gentleman with two very fat ladies in fur coats. Since he had been known to undertip, his waiter privately added something for the secret service. That is, he made two checks, one accurate, to give to the cashier with the customer's money, the other larger, to favor himself.

Waiting was really very hard work. And you had to have a gift for it. During rush hours it was like a combination of skating and juggling. Some could carry four or five glasses in one hand and a heavy tray in the other... with these running zk! crookedly through all the aisles made by the chairs. I did not have the gift for doing this, although I thought at the time it looked easy. I had been a good dancer at my uncle's birthday party in Song-Dune-Chi. But now when I tried to carry only two things in one hand, water and a plate of soup, some of the soup slipped into a red-haired lady's lap. But she was not a chorus girl, to laugh it off. She talked very loud, almost crying. I said nothing.

"He doesn't understand English," said her brunette friend. "Get the boss."

Yes, I understood what she said all right, but one says not much when embarrassed. "I'm sorry" is not enough.

The boss came over. Both women repeated at once what I had done. Her green satin dress had a big spot. She pointed it out, over and over again. The boss looked at it through his spectacles. In the end, she was to charge the restaurant what it would cost to have this dress dry-cleaned. Peace was made, and she calmed her temper down.

But I was fired for that. It was not my first offense. I had broken a few dishes before, too, and I had read Shakespeare and talked too much Chinese poetry. Without saying more the boss paid me off and told me I need not come tomorrow. I did not dislike him for that. He was a good man. Business is business, not charity. And he was not unfair to withhold my wages, as Sung had done. Certainly that Chinese at the cashbox never talked much. He didn't even tell me why I was fired. But I understood I did not square with American efficiency.

5

It was nearing the 1st of September. New York was still hot, close. How-ever, without a job, and with collegiate ambitions, it was plain I must make plans for the winter. So far I had failed in everything undertaken in America. Housework, clerking, waiting, in nothing was I good. It remained to be seen if I could remedy this by education.

While working for Hsun, with leisure on my hands, I had written to several New England colleges asking for a scholarship. My inquiries met with no success. But I heard from Mr. Luther, the Canadian missionary who had brought me over. Away up in Canada, he had busied himself in my behalf. A scholarship in Maritime University, his own college in Nova Scotia, was open to me. I had just about enough money to get up there; the biggest por-tion of my funds having come from Hsun, for my services before he went bankrupt.

6

For a week I stayed on, paying farewell calls to Doctor Ko and others at the Korean Institute, saying good-bye to Hsun (who was working on some vague project for a restaurant) and to the boys who used to be his salesmen. My going-away shopping was for nothing more than a few ten-cent store socks, since I had no money for any college outfit; and my packing could be done in fifteen minutes.

I said good-bye to Fifth Avenue, and my favorite walk through Central Park. How many languages you heard in Central Park between the couples walking there for pleasure! Sometimes you saw distinguished-looking people! Men with brows of thought looking like Western scholars. Girls, too, of the new Western type, bareheaded, bobbed waving chestnut hair cut in a casual tumbled style, and wearing boyish-looking Western suits; sometimes they carried soft felt hats in hand, and something—the roll of their shirtwaist collars, cut of lapel, their well-turned silken ankles, or trim brogues—bespoke sophistication and New York, in spite of those loose sport clothes proper to campus. And all this world was a closed book to me.

I said good-bye to Chinatown with its ancient ties to all I had forsaken in the East. And I cannot leave this period of my first introductory months in the New Time of America, without mentioning a trifling incident which foreshadowed later events and emotions for me. Oriental exiles in New York are always to be found in Chinese restaurants, coming back again and again. So it is not strange that even so early I encountered for a moment, and without speaking, one who was destined to take lasting place in my memories of America, to acquire almost symbolic significance for me. It was a beautiful evening, sharp, cool, worn, an evening of premature autumn and old monotone, of city mist and semi-rain blurring the lampposts, the early lights and bedraggled city corners of Manhattan. Dampness blended all odors and made the lanes of Chinatown mysterious and poignant. The muffled foghorns blew again and again. Having been for a walk across Brooklyn Bridge, I turned somewhat early into that Chinese restaurant which had been my first refuge. It was emptier than usual, for six o'clock is very early for the Chinese. Indeed, there was only one other customer in the restaurant besides myself.

He sat on the other side of the restaurant, almost across from me, before him a luxurious feast of broiled pigeons and some rare soup; but he was not eating. He was drinking, an expensive Chinese wine, it seemed, not hurriedly, but sipping. His complexion was of a faint clear olive, and quite unscored, though he must have been in the early thirties, my senior by fifteen years. His was not a typical Oriental face, impassive, static. He suggested to me that flowing, seething life reserved in Oriental painting for demoniac faces (not necessarily evil, but super-human, being allied to nature and the elements). The so-called Oriental peace he lacked. His brooding eyes of a greenish black color, unusually wide and glinting, their rippling Oriental lids, might be those of poet, prophet, or madman; but they were held in check by the gentlemanly reserve of his mouth, which was youthfully scrolled and bland. Altogether, a handsome Easterner with nameless elegance. His clothes, which by no means determine Asiatic gentlemanliness, were of an excellent texture and workmanship. This curt, harsh Western dress sat on him, too, with ease, and to it he seemed long accustomed. An Asian evidently who had been long abroad. About him I sensed the unknown thought and subtleties of knowledge I longed to make my own.

As I looked at him, so he looked at me. Perhaps he saw in me his green and hopeful self of long ago. Even after my soup came and I was busily engaged, I was conscious of his eyes upon me from time to time. The waiter removed his cup of wine and brought the rice bowl. He was being served in conventional Chinese style. But he did not lift his rice bowl to the mouth which is the Chinese custom, and he handled his chopsticks unlike a Japanese. I wondered if he could be a fellow-countryman.

While I was pursuing this line of thought, trying to pigeonhole this Eastern wanderer, who seemed a part of the cool and pensive and many-worlds-wise evening, a Korean student wandered in with whose face I was familiar. He seated himself beside me and we spoke in Korean. I glanced again at the object of my interest and curiosity, but he was preparing to take his leave. I half-waited for him to stop and speak to us. If he were a Korean surely he would. Koreans always speak when they recognize a countryman in foreign ports. But he did not. And passed out, in his raincoat and soft slouched hat. And I did not see him again for a long time.

New York, with the returning autumn, was shot through and through with vague intimations of fabulous, delicate worlds beyond my bounds of thought, of life reaching out and up in a scope unrestricted, north and south to the Poles, east, west, to a meeting place of divided hemispheres...life coiling and spiralling, intellectually rather than physically... broad, cosmopolitan, fresh, a rich spiritual emanation from material wealth. But I left by the Boston Canadian steamship line, the same route over which I had come. As I watched the skyline fade away, those vigorous spires seemed virgin-like as ever; and for all the promise of that magic enchantress, queen and gamine at the same time, harlot and little child, I was taking nothing from her away with me but endless fascination. I could point to no victory. I came away with no gain, except some poor Korean friends who had pulled me out of an outcast's starvation. And it seemed to me I had not yet known New York, or penetrated beyond the merest outskirts of her impregnable treasure, her fuller expanding life of the Machine Age.

BOOK ONE

1

TRAVELING, STILL TRAVELING...not only in space but in time...until I had come to a small Canadian village, where the houses were thinly scattered and many of the streets unpaved, and there was still a rough new pioneer spirit on the land. There were few cars— dusty-looking flivvers many seasons old, jumping up and down on narrow tires. Plainly the machine had not yet conquered all in Scottsborough, Nova Scotia. Not many miles from here was Maritime University, the college I had left the United States to attend.

In the Scottsborough depot, I was met by Mr. Luther, accompanied by his brother-in-law, with horse and buggy. My missionary friend was a large, stocky farmerlike man with a little nose, and a fringe of reddish hair around the back of his head. He greeted me in his grave, pleasant way, in words of an excellent Korean. More than my exiled countrymen, he reminded me of the country I had left. Mr. Luther would return long before the rest of us. His life, for the most part, had been spent in Korea, and he had recently buried his Canadian missionary-wife on Korean soil. The remote peace of quiet Asia mingled with the steadfast faith of the Christian missionary on Mr. Luther's brow. He was just the same, yesterday, today, and forever. The world of Canadian missionaries—like that of the Chinese in Chinatown—never changes, not for the East or the West. My teacher was a reflective, educated man, but neither Matthew Arnold nor Thomas Huxley of the nineteenth century had left any perceptible traces of their toilsome gigantic problems and doubts on him; and certainly he had never entered the century of the grandson, Aldous Huxley, and had no desire to do so. The climate of New York was not for him.

Our friendship dated back some years. Mr. Luther had been the American principal of a Korean school where I had taken some post-graduate high school courses. He became interested in me and in my desire to be educated in America—particularly after I made a debate on the subject "Does the hero make the time or does the time make the hero?" I spoke in Korean, a beautiful language for oratory, rolling down and foaming all around like mountain streams, and being a Korean boy I still believed ardently in heroes. I had no inklings of the twentieth-century nonsense of such words as:

> I am the master of my fate,
> I am the captain of my soul.

Such enthusiasm appealed to Mr. Luther, too. He was judge in the debate and he immediately singled me out as the best speaker. Afterwards he invited both debating teams to his house for tea, served in Canadian style. There were little Canadian tea cakes, which tasted to us awfully good, for Koreans eat very little sweets, none at all made out of refined white sugar with all the glutinous dark substances removed. We piled them in, and afterwards were sick. An older boy, who had read about American manners in a book, kept frowning at us, whispering, "Don't make those noises when you drink!" We were trying to show our appreciation of the tea by smacking the lips, one of the politest noises at a meal a guest can make in the Orient.

Mr. Mathews, the brother of Mr. Luther's dead wife, was a straight, silent man with a ruddy face, clean-shaven, dignified, but a person of simplicity. He was reticent and did not attempt to talk much, though he wished to put me at my ease as much as possible. My main impression was—"How different from a New York Y.M.C.A. man!"—And I felt much better with Mr. Mathews.

His house was a large new white one with a high porch. It was set in the midst of a big potato garden, a little distance out of Scottsborough. Outside and in, this house was plain and substantial. It had been built only recently, yet there was not much feel of newness about it…comfortable, old-fashioned, familylike furniture suggesting unpretentious British standards, ample space for books and potted flowers. The house was full of children. Mr. Luther and his four were visiting, and the Mathewses had several too. I was treated as one of "the children," being classed with Mr. Luther's oldest boy of twelve and Mr. Mathews' son aged fourteen. A boy of nineteen, of course, was not supposed to have reached majority, and nothing, as I remember, was talked of my ardent baptism in the tumultuous modern stream of New York. Neither the Luthers nor the Mathewses had any interest whatsoever in New York. Instead we talked a good deal about Korea. No doubt the fervent new birth of Christianity in my poor distraught and suffering country was a source of strength and inspiration to this missionary clan far away in Canada. Korea has proved far more receptive than either China or Japan to Christian proselytizing. Mr. Luther, the young Luthers, and myself—we were the Koreans, and the Mathews family were never tired of hearing about the faraway Asian continent.

I had been invited to visit the Luthers, or rather the Mathewses, until my college scholarship should begin. It was my first stay as guest with an American family in the West, and I wanted to be very goody and very nice. In the morning there was a sort of orderly crowding for the bathroom—a bathroom not outside and around the corner like that of many of the houses of Scottsborough—but on the second floor, centrally. Every one was given his allotted span there before the punctual eight o'clock breakfast. The first morning, escorted to the door of the bathroom by Mr. Mathews in his bathrobe, I parted from him with a bow. After that I took out my jackknife with which I always shaved. It was a big knife, but rather dull, and a certain flat stone I carried with me was an absolute essential. I would spit on the stone and rub my knife there hard. For finishing touch, I would stroke it gently on the palm of my hand. Then I would take the longest lock of hair on my head and cut off the very end to see if the knife were sharp enough yet to shave with. But this morning I could not find my stone. I looked and looked. Either I had forgotten to pack it, or it had dropped out on the way. I wasted many moments looking for my stone, and some more time trying to sharpen the jackknife on soap dishes and various other places. No good. It wouldn't work. Then on a convenient shelf, I saw a long straight razor very bright and shining. Just what whiskers want. But Mr. Mathews was already knocking on the door to see if I was ready to come out. I didn't want to take more than my time. Then, remembering that I had already a washstand and pitcher, I thought I would convey this razor into my own room for a moment. I slipped out unseen, bearing the long shiny blade. I was soon ready. So was everybody, except Mr. Mathews. At eight o'clock sharp we sat down to table. But Mr. Mathews was late. We had our porridge and milk. And still Mr. Mathews didn't appear. We went on to the scrambled eggs and bacon, toast, stewed apples, orange marmalade, and tea. At the very end, Mr. Mathews slipped quietly into that empty place at the head of the table— and Mrs. Mathews said in a surprised voice: "Daddy, you didn't shave this morning!"

"Never mind, dear—never mind!" said Mr. Mathews hastily.

It broke upon me! I alone knew why he hadn't shaved. *I had stolen his razor.* Yes, Mr. Mathews was too polite to explain. But oh, how embarrassed I was—that most embarrassing moment of my life! Of course, I had only meant to borrow it—I had replaced it just before coming down to breakfast. But—too late!—I had taken it during just those five minutes of the day when Mr. Mathews always shaved. I imagined his confusion in not being able to find it. He must have spent all *his* time in the bathroom looking for it—so I imagined. Then perhaps he went into his bedroom and looked there. Finally there was no more time. He had to put on his collar and tie, and hurry down. He would have to go to business directly after breakfast, with out shaving! Oh, if I had only taken Mr. Mathews' razor at any other time in the twenty-four hours!

I rose from the table and I went out with Mr. Mathews' boy. I had a purpose. We visited a store in Scottsborough. It was the only store in town, and there were many horsewhips, oil lamps, hoes, washstand sets and bundles of ginghams and lawn, and many other things for sale. But I bought a razor. I paid $1.25. Practically my first luxury purchase in the New World, and destined to last me many years. Then I went back and dug potatoes in the potato garden very hard.

2

I was enrolled soon after as a special student in Maritime University, and put with one hundred other boys in the dormitory of Green Grove. Green Grove was an L-shaped building on top of a little hill, surrounded by oaks and pines and covered by a fine meadow grass. No crows to be fed on that soft grass—nothing unclean. The boys used to go out and play ball there on beautiful sunny days. Over the hill was an arm of the sea, and salty air rushed into the nose day and night, turning white faces red. It was said to be a mild oceanic climate, but always there was a little whip to the air and a good deal of fog in the morning not unlike the rawness of Mother England.

A piece to the left of Green Grove, Seaway Park was laid out with pines and firs. These magnificent trees were very tall and fragrant; they had spread a thick matting of needles over the ground. Here were many wandering roads through the pines, making the perfect rambling walk for a philosopher—or for Milton in Il Penseroso mood. Not many people seemed to use Seaway. It was open to the public, but it was so near the college, it was more like a college campus. On fine Sundays, you might encounter a few from the city here—an old gentleman or two, with yellow kid gloves and cane in hand, strolling very leisurely. On such days, a few horse carriages might walk slowly through as well, and when one of those old gentlemen met an old lady in one of these, the horse stopped, while the gentleman spoke with a courtly mumbling—slightly confused between his cane, his kid gloves, his cigarette, and his hat. His was the aloof, suave dignity of Queen Victoria and Alfred Lord Tennyson. Plainly an "heir of all the ages in the foremost files of time" (for probably he knew his way about London—even though he had no use for crass New York). Such were the Nova Scotians, to share Seaway. But when a fine drizzling rain was sifting down, like a veil blown from the sea, you were sure to meet no one—with the exception perhaps of a lone ex-serviceman who had come back after the Great War to resume his interrupted studies in Maritime College; swinging along in his trench coat at a steady martial pace, his prematurely set and silent face showing that he wished to be disturbed no more than you did.

3

When I reported soon after arrival to the administration building and to Doctor MacMillan (a solid round British gentleman with a clerical collar), he handed me over to my two Green Grovian tutors, both studying for the ministry and both ex-servicemen. Ian was of medium height, slight, blond, very English-looking. He had a smooth, regular face, rather handsome, but closer to the feminine ideal than the masculine one. One eyebrow was always cocking up and he impressed one as being witty and ironic. Ralph on the other hand was an out-and-out Canadian, very big and masculine-looking, and of the farmer type. He was red all over, but of different shades. His face was a kind of lipstick red, but his hair and eyebrows more a sandy tint. Though he shaved with meticulous care, his cheeks and chin always suggested a stubbly field. Ralph was quiet, unhumorous, very serious, and had ladylike, minute ways of speech and action.

These two were to be my tutors and my guardians. They promptly helped me with my registration card, then guided me over to the University, where everybody had a college bulletin in hand and a number of cards. Here for the first time I was lost in a crowd of alien boys from every Canadian province around there, from professional classes, farms, factories, and even fishermen's villages. But with true British love of precedent—"not swift nor slow to change but firm"—the father's calling usually determined the son's. (In this I saw Canadians to be unlike people from the States, who love to break all precedents, where rarely does the son follow in the steps of his father.)

While I was standing, a little apart, somewhat overwhelmed by the racial, national, and religious homogeneity I sensed around me, I was approached by a narrow-faced, tender-skinned boy with dark eyebrows which looked like two strong lines drawn with a Chinese brush. He was wearing a big sweater with a letter and had a rather sneering and boisterous expression. He surveyed me arrogantly, giving vent to a long-drawn whistle, and turning on his heel I heard him say something to his companions about this "yellow dog we have to live with." His words were so wantonly contemptuous that I burned with a greater indignation than I had ever felt for all the rudeness of New York. From the frowns and severe expressions of others around him, I judged such insults were unpopular. But in the midst of reserve and silence from my future classmates I received an unforgettable impression of smugness and shut-off-ness, as if the irrepressible Leslie Robin, as his name was, had voiced what was in the back of the minds of all. From others there, as I was soon to know—though not from Leslie—there would be no lack of kindness and consideration, but the school itself was set in a rigid mold— quite unlike the colleges and universities of the United States—a mold which held the superiority of the Briton above all races created as its unquestioned dogma, which believed without a trace of modern scepticism, without a fraction of scientific aloofness or of new time-vision, "better fifty years of Europe than a cycle of Cathay"—though (being only Canadian and incontestably New-World) it, too, must cringe, before the superiority of an elder country, England.

4

—gray twilight pour'd
On dewy pastures, dewy trees,
Softer than sleep—all things in order stored,
A haunt of ancient peace.

It was strange how the ghost of elderly England was in the new air here. Green Grove overlooked the city of Halifax, a naval city on the irregular Atlantic seacoast. In certain sections—notably the large and beautiful residential district and the many outlying homes—you saw walls with beautiful flowers climbing over stone, and hedged gardens as in England. Marvellous how this noisy colonial town could still convey obliquely an Old-World pattern, reminding of the English home. The downtown section of course was not attractive by reason of the thriving industrial atmosphere—the many factories concerned with iron founding, brewing, distilling, sugar refining, tanning etc. But the first impression here, too, was of British atmosphere. Well-dressed British naval and military officers were seen everywhere. Bright red coats, bright blue jackets. And many ex-servicemen, showing how thoroughly the British Empire had been mobilized a short while ago.

This city had been one of the chief bases of British operations against the revolting Americans during the Revolution. And also the War of 1812 found the Nova Scotians active and is said to have brought much wealth to the town. During the Civil War in the United States, this harbor was the starting point for numerous blockade runners and many of the citizens now living in the beautiful residential district made their fortunes at that time. Canadian fortunes—not so large certainly as those of United States millionaires, but undoubtedly going farther, lasting longer. For like England itself Canada bespoke the tenacity, the conservatism proper to Britons, and to Tennyson's

> A land of settled government,
>   A land of just and old renown,
>   Where Freedom broadens slowly down
> From precedent to precedent.

> Where faction seldom gathers head,
>   But by degrees to fulness wrought,
>   The strength of some diffuse thought
> Hath time and space to work and spread.

5

I was studying English Literature in earnest. Tennyson and Browning, Ruskin and Carlyle. The professor at Maritime College I remember best was Doctor Donald, whom the boys called Donnie behind his back. He was a very dignified old gentleman, with Tennysonian locks and beard, and Browning personality. Sunset and evening star...the time of that looked just like him...and all is well with the world. I doubt if he would have assumed it necessary to argue the matter incessantly as Browning did...

> This world's no blot for us, nor blank.
> It means intensely and means good.

For how could it be a blot or blank to Doctor Donnie with England in the offing?

Since all had to take the Liberal Arts Course at Maritime, every freshman had Doctor Donald's *Survey of English Literature* and his classes were very large. Almost all the freshmen I knew were in my section—which contained more than one hundred students. Leslie Robin and his chums were there—and many others. Donnie was much respected. Even Leslie, always rough, wild, and insolent, dared no open rebellion before him. No high-necked sweaters, none, could enter here. At the start, Donnie had announced: "Two things I will not stand. I want nobody to chew gum here!" (Anybody with gum in the mouth promptly pressed it under the tongue, or stuck it beneath his chair.) "And I want nobody to wear sweaters in my class. When we sit down here for literary discussion, it must be done as English gentlemen." Just before Donnie's class was a busy time in lockers. It was like getting dressed for dinner. Every one had to put on that missing tie, or Donnie would not let him into the classroom.

Donnie himself always entered wearing his cap and gown. As he appeared, slowly and impressively, carrying a little bag of books for use in the classroom, there was a perfect silence, not a loud breath drawn. "Johnny Milton—Billy Shakespeare"—so one boy wrote in his theme, and Doctor Donald did not like that and commented a long time. He told the students, "Bad—bad—bad" (in a thundering voice). "You are very bad in composition.... But even so, you are better than American boys in American freshman classes," he added confidentially. (Doctor Donnie also gave courses as visiting professor in an American university.)

All the boys clapped their hands and beat their heels against the floor at that, glad to be favorite sons. In the United States, you hear very little about Canadian colleges. But Canadian colleges are very America-conscious.

But then Doctor Donald clearly was still living in England, not in America. Very proud he was to be an Englishman:

> This other Eden, demi-paradise,
>
> This fortress built of Nature for herself
>
> Against infection and the hand of war,
>
> This happy breed of men, this little world,
>
> This precious stone set in a silver sea
>
> …This blessed plot, this earth, this realm, this England!

He felt like that, with the same ecstasy and pride. To him, American colonization was the result of English enterprise; the oceanic highway was initiated and made safe during the seventeenth and eighteenth centuries owing to bold English expansion of commerce; and with Queen Victoria and the industrial revolution, then truly was the Empire most glorious of all, extending far and near, with spiderlike steel nets of communication covering the surface of all the earth.

Doctor Donald taught not only English literature—always he reflected English history, too. Somebody acted England's heroic deeds…somebody sang them at the same time. He did not agree with William Morrison, who said, "History has remembered the kings and warriors because they destroyed; art has remembered the people because they created." Doctor Donnie remembered all; warriors, kings, too, Chaucer was with Crecy and Poitiers, Shakespeare with Drake and Raleigh, Milton with Cromwell; Blake, Shelley, and Wordsworth, sandwiching Wellington with Tennyson and Browning. He would have found himself perfectly at home with his contemporary, Kipling, to whom he often referred. English literature was rightly great because it was the mirror for a great people, backed by a great moral sense, expanding over the world in a great empire. English laws, English democratic government had shocked all races into study and imitation. Behind everything worthwhile was the God-fearing, keen-thinking, liberty-loving, but decent and conservative English temperament. Day after day Doctor Donnie told how sublimation of the spirit, self-control, character, responsibility had always characterized the Britons' civilization. "Through these unacknowledged legislators of the world, the breath and finer spirit of all knowledge has come to me," said Doctor Donnie in one of his lectures.

6

English literature appealed to me more than anything else I was taking. Far more than English history, or British civilization. Day and night I read and read, until certain things that Doctor Donald was teaching were memorized unconsciously. It was the Oriental method of study. In my conversation, hardly knowing it, I used lines from Tennyson and Browning and many other poets. Sometimes the boys caught on, sometimes they did not. Tennyson was especially good, as his lines easily became prose, especially those in the long narrative poems. "Where were you yesterday? Whose child is that? What are you doing here?" It was like a conversation manual. I could say almost anything I craved to say now. But I had more trouble with the written English. I think I read too much Macaulay in studying for Doctor Donnie's class. All my written sentences began to look like the life of Johnson; long sentences, the dovetailed kind—somehow the head verb was always getting lost or tangled. Ralph, my tutor, was very patient. He would attack some ambitious sentence of mine that curled and wound around itself. He would reduce it. "This sentence is just like saying, 'I—hungry.' Now what else do you need?" Ralph was always serious, never humorous. He would explain anything *ad infinitum,* always in the lowest and simplest terms.

Ian was my humorous tutor. To know Ian a little, you would not think him serious about anything. He seemed to effuse an air of raillery. When I came into his room for tutoring, the first fifteen minutes he might sit like an English gentleman, but only for the first fifteen minutes. Then he would put his coat collar up over his head, hunch his head down into it, and look at me with eyebrow cocked, out from underneath his coat. Underneath his prankishness, Ian was very reserved. His humor was all of the active kind, a practical joking, a daily drollery which seemingly he put up as a fence to shield the real workings of his mind.

Later I found out, from Ian's mother, that all through the year he was writing religious poetry, appearing in his hometown paper. He never showed this to any one at Green Grove. But he showed his drawings to all. They were humorous drawings. Ian was a clever cartoonist, it was said. He did all the cartoons for the college paper—for instance, a man sitting on a piano, a man with a high hat and a maid coming in and dusting the hat with the man still in it. I didn't see anything very funny in that, but Western humor was hard for me to get. Ian himself had just such a tall hat. His funniest joke was to put on that high hat with a very high white collar and cravat and play the ukulele.

Ian had been studying to be an engineer, before the war, but his service in France seemed to have knocked all desire for engineering out of him. He was tired of science, he said.

"Why?" I questioned.

"Well, in times of peace, it takes away a man's job. In times of war, it takes away his life."

But Ian would never go into this deeply, only semi-humorously, so it was hard to tell what he really thought. Sometimes there were symposiums in Ian's room, in which he admitted cheerfully that the Bible could never be reconciled with itself, or with anything else. But that didn't matter.

"Anyhow, I'm only interested in composing sermons, you know. Each one a noble little essay. But there will be jokes here and there, so people won't get too bored."

The other theologues were serious, not humorous. Except Allan. And Allan was not so much humorous as frivolous. He, too, was of the age to have been overseas, and always he wore his service button prominently. Not at all studious, Allan was more society-minded. He was small, but very good-looking, with beautifully combed crisp hair, and a dimple in his cleft chin. Always he was unusually well-dressed for Green Grove. Everything he ever wore was well pressed and clean, with the exception of his trench overcoat, of which he was very fond, though it was beginning to wear out. "Are you ashamed to go out with me in this?" he used to joke with me.

All that he had from overseas he treasured. Like most of the older boys in Green Grove, he was known as a hero-volunteer. Others were shy about confessing it. Not Allan. He loved to talk of that time overseas. All the hero-volunteers were allowed to choose what courses to omit on their overseas "credit," and Allan was very pleased to cross out mathematics, natural science and psychology, which were generally considered very stiff stuff.

He loved to go to the "cinema" and often he would take me with him, paying my way. The first movie I saw made me cry—it was all Romeo and Juliet sentiment. But afterwards every movie seemed somewhat a repetition of the first one, and I didn't cry any more—unlike good poetry which can be cried over many times.

7

That autumn there was to be a track race around Seaway Park. It was the big athletic event of Green Grove that season. The town people came to look on, and even visitors from afar. Boys everywhere said to me, "You'll run, of course?" I had been a leader in sports among my childhood friends. Since then I had not had much chance to practise up. But I said, "Yes, if I knew what to wear." All the other contestants had track costumes.

Then one of the athletic stars, on the floor below mine, raced up to my room and got my extra suit of Korean underwear from its drawer, the suit in fact which George had once cut down. Everybody knew about it and had much interest in it, for they often visited me while I was dressing, and then they would question me, if I found Canada warm. They all wore their underwear long for the winter, and even when bits showed below their wrists, they didn't care. They were not Americanized like George.

We examined my underwear and I thought it seemed as modest as their track suits. When they suggested it, that solved the problem. Track day came and I went out to run in my cut-off short Korean underwear. How my Canadian schoolmates cheered when I appeared on the track! Many women were there too. A great crowd of spectators, and everybody cheered. I ran and ran. Some of my buttons burst off. Still, I did not win, for a big grain of sand got between my toes and I fell down. Two boys were ahead of me in the final spurt. But yet applause seemed all for me. I could not understand why a long write-up about me came out in the college paper next day, with a clever cartoon of me running, drawn by Ian. The write-up was very handsome, and it said that I had won, which wasn't true, owing to sand in my toe. Next night at the dinner table there were speeches and a prize, and Ralph was chairman. In the speeches I was called a good sport and a prize was made for me. (Allan alone was angry with them for allowing me to do this. He had come to watch the race with a girl, and he said it was embarrassing.) I thought it was embarrassing, myself. But I did not resent that. I knew I was considered queer and alien, but the theologues and young Clendenin were the more friendly toward me for such jokes.

Leslie Robin I could not understand. His obvious dislike for me appeared almost irrational, and after this track meet particularly, he went out of his way to emphasize his hate. In mature retrospect I believe I must have been to Leslie an irritating symbol of some sort. His sister, Miss Jean Robin, was a very nice missionary in Korea, and I think he had other relatives in missionary fields. His father, too, was a well-known Presbyterian minister.

But Leslie had elected to take dentistry. He and his gang were the wildest, most difficult students in Green Grove, always at outs with the proctors and the authorities. They lived in the Old Building, as it was called, where rooms were very large and slightly more luxurious. Some of the rooms held four roommates. The Old Building was not so staid and theological as the Main House, and it was especially noisy early in the morning owing to the boys on upper floors who fought each other for the right of way in sliding down the banisters. The struggle was to reach the dining room in the Main House just before closing time—and no earlier. All the Maritime boys slept in a one-piece garment called a nightshirt. In the morning a boy needed only to jump out of bed and stuff the ends into his trousers for the last-minute rush.

Leslie and his friends defied Green Grove traditions whenever possible. As, for instance, by drinking. Green Grove as a whole was stern on the subject of intemperance. No post-war license yet had entered here. The students kept light homemade wines in their rooms, of course, even Ian (but not Ralph), yet hard drinking at Green Grove just wasn't "done," not even in secret except by Leslie and his gang. I heard that some of the boys at these wild parties drank from skulls, for being medical or dental students mostly, it was their pride to have skulls in their rooms. One boy had a complete skeleton, with its jaw fitted up on a string so that the owner from a secret hiding place could make it move when any visitor came. Dentists, like Leslie, on the other hand decorated their rooms with teeth.

After the track meet, yellow autumn soon turned into snowy winter. Ralph left early for the holidays. By the middle of December, unexpectedly there was ice on the pond. Now the talk was not of swimming or of running but only of skating. I had no skates, but again many pairs were offered for my use. Then one day Leslie Robin burst into my room. He accused me of stealing his skates. I was very angry and said it was a lie. He snarled and struck me on the cheek. "Turn the other. You're a good Christian!" Friends of his held my arms. Then they heard steps in the corridor. They ran away.

Allan came in and found me almost in tears because I had been beaten. I wanted to get revenge, and I told Allan I must fight Robin and he must umpire. But Allan would not let me do this. He took me at once to Ian, and both talked to me, and told me that out of my love for Green Grove, I must be too proud to take any notice. I must ignore it. Fighting was against the rules of Green Grove. They made me promise not to fight with Robin. Something must have been done to Leslie, too, for after that I was unmolested. But bitterness remained in my heart. I hated Leslie Robin and didn't see why I couldn't have fought with him, with honest umpiring. In wrestling I knew I could beat and I often meditated on how I could throw him by various jujutsu tricks I knew....

I believe that my resentment against Robin—and my undignified position as the poor and humiliated protégé of the right honorable British Canadian theologues poisoned my year at Maritime University. And yet when I look back, it seems as if everybody in Green Grove, with the exception of my enemy and his followers, was very kind to me, almost too kind. I belonged to no clique, I had no chum. I was inexorably unfamiliar. And yet I was accepted by all, and hardly a boy there who did not show graciousness to me in some manner, who did not make an effort to be especially well-meaning, kind and considerate in a shy, British way. Whenever anybody received a cake from home, no matter what others might be there, Chungpa was always invited—then given two slices instead of one. I did not care much for cake, yet ate for politeness and gratitude. By and by I got sick. It was not only the cake. I was unaccustomed to the heavy substantial Canadian food—meat, bread, and potatoes. Besides, I had never had regularly so much to eat, and my stomach was too surprised. The college mother came in and took the most kindly care of me while I was sick. She was Mrs. Cummings, a tall woman, enormously large, with a red face and motherly ways. Even Doctor MacMillan came to see me, and patting me kindly on the shoulder advised me not to eat so much.

Why then did I feel myself so lonely and sad, small, lowly, and unappreciated? Why, in short, did I long once more—like a veritable Roy Gardner—for escape? The magnificent journey to America, the avid desire for Western knowledge, had it come to this?

BOOK TWO

1

IN GREEN GROVE, my relation to Ralph was closer than to the others. It was the relation of pupil to tutor or of disciple to teacher, rather than of friend to friend, though Ralph emphasized the friendship and our democracy and equality. He of all the theologues felt the greatest responsibility toward Chungpa Han, the poor boy from the Orient there on a charity scholarship. And I knew Ralph better than the rest. I spent all my vacations with him. Ralph was a missionary par excellence, although I do not know if he has ever gone to foreign fields. In fact, he felt his work to be laid out in Canada. Already when I knew him he had a small congregation among the backwoods French. I went there for the Christmas holidays, where Ralph had preceded me by several weeks.

I received many other invitations. Among them, one from Horace Thompson, the most brilliant and scholarly of the theologues, who invited me to his own home with the offer of railway fare. My friends had a meeting about it, and decided my railway fare ought not to fall on Thompson alone, and they took up a collection. They had naturally put off the problem of my holiday until the last moment, and did not know that I had already made plans to join Ralph and profit by his tutoring over the vacation. In fact, I had already bought my ticket, as per agreement between Ralph and me. They said the collection was mine anyway. But somehow I left without it. I needed only to travel for twenty hours. And with room and meals secure when I should reach my destination, I was resigned to a state of pennilessness in between. (The ticket took all of my money.)

My train left before daylight. Seated alone in an inconspicuous corner of the coach, book in hand, I had the feeling of adventure and escape again. Nobody paid any attention to me. There were other students from Maritime on the same train, some even from my own dormitory, but the responsibilities of the school year now were left behind, and one sensed the only tie that bound us was no more.

All must change trains at Moncton. Here I saw the last of my fellow students. When I boarded my train for the interior of Canada, I found the coach filled up with French boys from St. Francis Xavier of Antigonish. I was surprised at their lively interest, for at once they gathered around me, vivacious, jolly, easily laughing, their curiosity keen in their faces. We had no language contact. My school French was not good. Neither was their school English. Yet one after another they drew me into their group, asking questions, exclaiming and nudging each other eagerly. As the night progressed, we gathered into one end of the cold car and sang French songs in unison. I lost my feeling of alienness experienced earlier in the day. I was caught back again into a common humanity. As I ate one of their apples and laughed with them, I thought, "In the morning, I rode with people from the same university—people I knew by name. Some were even from the same dormitory. I had eaten beside them many times. But we seemed to be strangers. Tonight I am having a good time with these boys I have never seen before, who have no reason to be kind to me because we go to the same school."

The French boys got off, a few at a time, calling back Christmas greetings, "Adieu," "Au revoir." And all that night, the train progressed into the interior of Canada, until only a few travelers were left. I wrapped up in my overcoat as closely as I could, and drew around my neck the white silk scarf newly sent me by George Jum. Outside it was snowing heavily and the wind was strong. So much snow out there, the night seemed whitish instead of dark. The long rolling empty fields, the snow-covered forests, all showed like shadowy chalk instead of black. At widely separated stations, the train hissed out white steam. Travelers were met by natives, their hats piled high with snow.

At four o'clock in the morning I dismounted from the train, glad that the long journey was about over. Soon I would be eating breakfast with Ralph, I thought, my first meal in over twenty-four hours. I had left before breakfast on the previous day. The town I had come to was evidently very small. No automobiles were to be seen. Only one or two sleighs drawn by horses, with sleighbells that tinkled in a savage wind which whirled wildly around the little board station. The drivers were wearing hotel caps. No sleigh I saw held more than a single customer. At last even these were gone, jingle-jangling into the snowy waste. Still no Ralph. I had been there over half an hour, alone.

I concluded that Ralph had not received my letter telling of the hour of my arrival. But I had his address. I consulted it under the solitary lamp on the station platform. The stationmaster appeared to be French. I was tired of practising my French. I did not attempt to speak to him, but showed him the address, and he pointed out the direction to me, explaining with a gesture about a long hill. Snow was still falling and massing in huge drifts. In the sharp and biting wind I was almost blinded by the snow, but I did not think of the weather. Food had become an acute necessity. Since I was carrying no money, I must reach Ralph. I came to the foot of the hill the stationmaster had pointed out. I could not make out any road, so I just ploughed up the hill through the deep snow, guided by the lonely house on top—Ralph's house. I reached the porch. All around the house the snow was high, blown in by the winds. The house was dark inside...of course, who would not be asleep at such an hour? But the number was the same as that given on Ralph's address. I rang the bell. I hammered on the door. At last I heard vague sounds. That must be Ralph getting up. I grinned to think of his face when he saw me, for I was sure he was not expecting me by now. But it was not Ralph who opened the door. It was a woman. The waiting snow rushed in at the opened door. Her hair was blown out by the incoming wind, and her long nightgown too. I was thinking it was a good thing I did not throw my arms around her there in the dark, thinking it was Ralph, as I asked weakly, "Does Mr. Ralph Glenwood live here?"

I had to repeat the question many times. And when she answered, I had the same difficulty to understand her that she had to understand me. She was French. At last I got it straightened out. Mr. Glenwood was not here at all. He was in Quebec, five hundred miles away.

I walked back to the station, where at least I could be sheltered from that fierce wind on the lonely hill. And something else in the station I remembered. A restaurant. Men on night duty, it seemed, came in there for coffee, for it was still open. I stopped at the door, and heard the waitress and one of the baggage hands speaking French together. So it would be useless to try to make them understand my English. I went in and pointed out to the girl, coffee and a ham sandwich. It seemed to me I had never tasted anything so delicious as that Canadian ham sandwich and that coffee. When I got through, again I thought I would not complicate things by speaking a language she did not understand. With my head, hand, stomach, pockets, I explained I had no money and had eaten because I was hungry. I turned my pockets inside out for her to see. Nothing came of that except a few pennies. I could not understand what she said in French. But I had some idea what she meant. She meant I could not leave the restaurant unless I paid for what I had eaten. Of course, that was fair enough. And I thought, it was a wise thing that I did not mention having no money with me before eating. I wrote down on a paper napkin in English, "I do not understand French. Only English." She brought a boy from the kitchen who spoke English. Both were much amazed, and more so, because they decided at once that I was a mute. The apparition of a Chinaman, who was a mute—at four o'clock in the morning—a Chinaman and a mute—who had made use of the restaurant without money to pay...it was too much for French logic. They knew no precedent by which to act, and they argued with each other for a long time.

Presently their indignation began to change to sympathy, even awe— especially when I offered my overcoat to pay for my bill. The girl shook her head, with a glance through the window at the elements outside. Then I offered my scarf, and wrote down on paper: "I expect a friend with money. Keep this till I come back with fifteen cents." She assented. Then I wrote, and again the boy interpreted, "I want to go to a hotel. Can you direct me?"

Again they conferred. The boy called up Queen's Hotel. One of those sleighs was sent for me. I suppose they also reported that I was a mute, for when I arrived at the hotel, I found paper and pencil waiting for me to make my wants known, although at the hotel everybody spoke English as well as French. Already, too, they understood that I was expecting a friend to come and get me.

After registering for an indefinite stay at Queen's Hotel, I went into the lounge to get warm by the open fire. From the glances cast by the servants, it was evident I was an object of mystery. Growing drowsy, I went to my room, to sleep until the regular breakfast hour. I was still hungry. For three days I did not leave the hotel, but settled myself before the fire downstairs every morning with my books. Outside the heavy Canadian snowstorm did not abate. And I remained an object of mystery, not only to the hotel management, but to the handful of guests. On all sides I heard myself being discussed, both in English and in French. Guesses as to my business were of the wildest. One was that I belonged to a religious order which I had come to establish in Canada, and that silence such as mine was enforced on all the members. Another rumor ran that I was literally the silent partner of another Chinaman, soon to appear, who intended with my help to open a laundry. One man wondered if my partner had yet started from China.

I promptly sent a note to Ralph at the only address I knew, that of the house on the hill. But it looked as if I would spend the holidays in Queen's Hotel. The collection that my friends of Green Grove had taken for me would indeed be needed, I thought....

Ralph burst in at the end of the third day on Christmas Eve. Since I was before the fire in the hotel lounge as usual, our meeting was staged in public and was dramatic. We were the center of all interest. People crowded around. Not only was the mystery of the mute Chinaman being cleared up, with silence broken, but Ralph himself was known to everyone and was by way of being a local hero in that town. He said the first news of me came at the station platform, where he was told of a mute Chinaman staying at Queen's, news which at first he did not connect with me. Ralph paid my bill—he said the collection money had been forwarded to him for me, and we left the hotel arm in arm, shaking hands with everybody we met. At once we repaired to the station and redeemed my scarf. Here all warmly apologized, in English and in French, and received me like an old friend. That very boy who had directed me to Queen's Hotel was in Ralph's Sunday school class.

My first Christmas in America was a colonial Christmas, a Christmas spent on the frontier, so to speak. Ralph's house was heated only by wood fires and lighted dimly by kerosene lamps. The little town was very primitive. If one would regain again the environment of a generation ago in the States, it might be found in Canada to this day. For my experience is, Canada is some fifty years behind the United States in every way. The weather, too, had an earlier northern potency, suggesting that described by some old Yankee in speaking of his childhood.

Christmas morning came. The sparsely settled land was folded deep in snow. Looking out, one could see nothing, neither man nor bird nor ghost. But then out there a man would soon become only a bundle of snow. Looking like streamers of cotton dropping perpetually from the sky, the snow came down without end. Ralph and I went out after breakfast. We had been invited to spend the day with one of the humble families in his congregation. The sound of church bells carolling followed us as if from a distance, snow-muffled, as we plodded through the thick white banks of snow.

Over the hill and around the valley we went, until we reached a one-story house, or cabin, wooden as though made by an ax, much like Abraham Lincoln's birthplace. Inside was a single room plastered roughly in mud, with a sloping tent-shaped roof. The family was French. There was a thin dark man with a French whisker, but not in the words of Tennyson, an educated whisker, for he was a simple lumberjack, the kind wearing overalls all the year around except for Christmas and Sundays. And his red-cheeked wife, rather young-looking, stout, with dark hair. Her new percale dress of red and blue stripes had a good deal of material in it, suggesting dresses many years behind the time of those scanty short ones I had seen on the streets of New York. Into the back of her thick hair was thrust a large hefty comb. She wore besides heavy ribbed stockings, and high shoes. They had three children. The youngest—around four—like a big piece of squash, fat all over, looked like one satisfied with any condition in life—but then today was Christmas. His washed state was a marvel to see: a gleaming speckless face, undried, head watered newly, dripping still, brushed down slick with only one hair starting. He wore a tiny new red necktie, but peeked up shyly. The next boy was thin, lively, eager to show off his broken English. He was wearing new knickers and a new sweater with a letter. And then there was the big sister, old enough for a faintly blushing cheek; but her long legs were still in yard-long black ribbed stockings, and she wore a short blue serge skirt and a modest middy.

The room was fascinating. You kept discovering new things all the time. Everything done by the family was done in this one room. But everything just like the family had been shined up to receive us. Even the cowhide boots and the extra shoes in corners, the dresses, sweaters, big coats on walls, all were precisely straightened. There were two windows, one dark from looking out at the hill which sheltered one side of the house, and the other dark from looking out on the gray opaqueness of the thick-falling snow. An oil lamp was burning—a white one gay with red roses; and a great cooking stove, with pipe going up to the roof, was sending out a great glow and crackle and a savory smell of cooking things. A thick hooked-rug covered the whole of the floor. Near the entrance was a yellow dogskin with head complete. A few pictures without any frames were tacked up; one I remember, General Foch, from the colored supplement of a French newspaper. In one corner was an upright piano. Then there was the Christmas tree, of modest size, hung with some painted cardboard birds, red bells and candy canes—nothing very elaborate. Around the base of the tree waited the humble white paper parcels roughly tied. Ralph had brought some parcels for the Christmas tree too. Gifts for the children and for me. I received from Ralph the book *David Copperfield* and some knitted socks made by his mother. When it came time for dinner, mother and daughter took away the Bible from the middle of the table. A red cloth with white lines—roughly ironed but very clean—was laid, and some white napkins that did not match one another. We sat down to a large pork roast tied up with strings, mashed pumpkin, browned potatoes, home-canned green beans, and many different kinds of jellies and pickles made by the housewife. For dessert there was apple cake, and after that, tea and cheese.

Dinner over, Ralph played Christmas carols on the piano. The little girl sang obediently on request. Ralph had been her music teacher. Next he had her play the accompaniment while we sang. There and then he gave her a lesson, pointing out her mistakes patiently at the end of each hymn. Never was Ralph embarrassed to speak of mistakes. As a teacher he was most painstaking and uncompromising. You must do things his way. (I had had my arguments with Ralph. He insisted that I should say "Yes, please" or "No, thank you" on every possible occasion, such as raisins offered in his room or a book handed down for my examination. It was not that I felt the obstinacy of children against moving my tongue to form these polite phrases, but in Korea a constant succession of yes- and no-thank-you's is the sign of a yokel. Ralph was firm. To please him I compromised, making my voice as low as possible.) Ralph had the most rigid code of manners, morals, conduct. Yet he himself was the plainest and simplest of men, really living in the kingdom of God. At least, no one would ever doubt that duty, "stern Daughter of the Voice of God," was his constant companion.

Later in the afternoon a couple dropped in, a young husband and wife, in whom Ralph was especially interested. The woman was a large French-Canadian—buxom, bigger than her husband, dark, sanguine and strong-featured. She was Catholic. The man was fair, anemic, half-English, and a member of Ralph's Protestant congregation. He had caused a great scandal by marrying outside his church. And from her church, too, the woman was ostracized for the same reason. The people of this little town were intensely sectarian, somewhat like the early New Englanders. Protestants thought that the difference between going to heaven and going to hell was the difference between going to meeting and going to mass; the Catholics thought so, too, but vice versa. When Ralph first came, this poor couple had been living as social outcasts, shunned and reviled by both factions. Ralph when he saw how matters stood went straight to the Catholic Father, to talk the case over. It was one of the first things Ralph did on taking charge of that congregation. He and the priest mapped things out. After that the couple were immediately remarried in the Catholic Church. The woman was to attend mass as usual, and her husband to go to his own church but either was left free to accompany the other when he or she so desired. Acts like this endeared Ralph to the community. In spite of his youth, he shared authority there with the Catholic Father and with the British Mayor (the latter an ignorant man but a straight shooter).

That dim and dark afternoon full of falling snow, others dropped into the little one-room house. Lumbermen from Ralph's church. They came wearing huge fat boots, big black caps tied under the chin, enormous fur gloves, and as they entered from the blizzard outside, there was a great noise of stamping, the shaking of coats and the clapping of gloves. As soon as they had warmed themselves by the kitchen range, they took out whistles, flutes, harmonicas, and played ballad music, punctuating the time with stamps of their hobnailed shoes.

2

That Christmas vacation, Ralph devoted much of his spare time to reading *David Copperfield* with me, in order to improve my English. I thought he was taking too much trouble, but he said, no, he liked it. He regarded *David Copperfield* as the greatest book ever written (outside the Bible). We took turns reading aloud, and when I did so, he would correct me. He explained everything very carefully, as to a child. Sometimes I could not keep from teasing him by asking foolish questions just to get his answers, but he did not know this.

"Ralph, what does Mrs. Gummidge mean when she says 'I'm a lone, lorn crittur'?"

"She means she doesn't feel well," answered Ralph patiently, touching his hand to his heart. "Here."

Or another time:

"There is one thing I don't understand, Ralph. And I would like to know. What is romance?"

"I will explain. Suppose there is a house—like this," and as usual, he illustrated concretely, indicating four square walls with his hands. "A house that is a prison. Soldiers guard the house. And around it is a river too. Then there is a girl. A prisoner in this house. Now. If you should swim across the river, break into the house, get to the girl in spite of the soldiers, carry her away, swimming perhaps with her on your back across the river...*that,* you know, would be romance."

I showed Ralph a news item in a Canadian paper which had just come out, about an American millionairess who decided to have a baby without getting married. She wanted a baby, not a husband: she was very logical.

"Ralph, is that romance?"

George Jum, I knew, would have been much interested. His mind would have played around that like a school of porpoises. But to Ralph, it didn't even pose a question, raise an image, it didn't give the slightest incentive to discussion.

"That's not romance," he said decidedly, "that's moral blindness. You haven't understood my definition."

"But isn't that a romantic thing to do?"

"She wouldn't lose anything by getting married first. How would any child feel with that kind of start? Well, let's not waste time. Let's get back to *David Copperfield.*"

The snow kept coming down. It was hard in such surroundings to visualize New York. Outside, the Canadian countryside was just beginning to be populated, but the spiritual land of Canadians seemed fixed and set. The minds of men like Ralph Glenwood still inhabited the world of David Copperfield, made more rugged, simple, and democratic in a new continent; they lived here with the humbleness of Burns in "A Cotter's Saturday Night"; duty and the church were a sustaining part of life—you were forcibly impressed with how the colonization of America was a direct result of the Reformation of Europe, of John Calvin and John Knox. Yes, the grim, uncompromising spirit of the Puritan was upon this land, though we do not hear so much of the Scotch Presbyterian of Canada as of the dying Puritanism of New England. And the mood of this Christmas interlude with

Ralph was early transcendental, as if, with the strength of three generations ago, it still refused to rest on temporal things. This might have been the practical yet fanatical land of Whittier's "Snowbound." And more than to Keats, Ralph Glenwood must have responded to the homely simplicity of such a poem as that of the early-American John Trowbridge:

I watch the slow flakes as they fall
On bank and brier and broken wall;
Over the orchard, waste and brown,
All noiselessly they settle down,
Tipping the apple-boughs, and each
Light quivering twig of plum and peach.

The hooded beehive, small and low,
Stands like a maiden in the snow;
And the old door-slab is half-hid
Under an alabaster lid.

All day it snows: the sheeted post
Gleams in the dimness like a ghost;
All day the blasted oak has stood
A muffled wizard of the wood.

Garland and airy cap adorn
The sumach and the wayside thorn,
And clustering spangles lodge and shine
In the dark tresses of the pine.

The ragged bramble, dwarfed and old,
Shrinks like a beggar in the cold;
In surplice white the cedar stands,
And blesses him with priestly hands.

Still cheerily the chickadee

Singeth to me on fence and tree:
And in my inmost ear is heard
The music of a holier bird;
And heavenly thoughts, as soft and white
As snowflakes, on my soul alight,
Clothing with love my lonely heart,
Healing with peace each bruisèd part,
Till all my being seems to be
Transfigured by their purity.

3

And so my year in Canada passed by, my sojourn in the nineteenth century, in the Victorian age of the British Empire. At times I thought, "What am I doing here?" And still when I say Green Grove, I see pictures of my loneliness, my essential isolation and misfit. Dark days I see in the dark woodland park, dead snow and ice stretching out grayly on all sides, bright nights under the cold northern moon, as I stand facing the bitter winds, looking down on the ravening, gloomy waves. The glimmer of Green Grovian lights, which I can see from the knoll by the sea—to them I turn reluctantly, away from the wild sea and the free winds. For almost the constellations seem more friendly and warm. Up here by a solitary tower, watching the British battleships go by, somehow I feel more contact with reality than in the snug, warm, theological nooks of Green Grove, listening to the whimsical conversation of Ian with Allan or with Ralph. Away out here the destructive, hard, the brilliant syncopated rhythms of New York come back to me. And curiously enough they stab my heart with longing....

Already, like the true New Yorker, I felt impatient of the rust and mold that gather gently on the provinces. Nor could I hope to be a real Green Grover, here in Canada. I was never treated as one. For me there was always special favor, special kindliness, special protection...the white-man's-burden attitude toward dark colonies. Ralph's kindness...Leslie's brutal cruelty...I weighed them in my mind, and it seemed to me better to miss the kindness and not to have the cruelty. Yet the beauty of my surroundings could not fail to strike me in more ways than one. As you entered the big University hall, you saw written there in marble, with letters to last out the centuries, "Ora et Labora." The sons of Maritime had gone away to be soldiers in the Great War. But there was no sign that bombshells had burst here. In course of time, the students had come back. They had put away their warfare for theology; in this world all was ordered, all decided, what was right or wrong, what was noble, what was base. Great figures of the past were here in pristine authority, the vigorous voice of Carlyle still in the air, the Wordsworthian plain living and high thinking, the Miltonic conscience, symbolized by those two portraits hung facing each other in the hall, Milton at the age of twelve just before beginning to write as "the handsome Lady of Christ's"; Milton during his blindness dictating lines of *Paradise Lost* to his unloving, unwilling daughters. In the spell of this quiet atmosphere you were almost betrayed to say there is nothing wrong with the world, it is perfect, it is still intact, showing a late firm ripeness, Victorian highmindedness at the very height of Tennysonianism. Into this section, the ills, the discontent, the morbidness of the modern generation happily will not come. Missionaries will continue to go forth from Maritime, for the glory of God. "Ora et Labora."

Over the pastoral landscape, the rich late spring had come. On the green meadows by Ritchie's Pond where we had skated during wintry days, a little brook was flowing, bluets and other wild flowers waving beside its sluicy stream. I walked here under the powerful sunrays of noon, as well as under the crimson beauty of evening; sometimes a gentle mist fell on my hatless head, forming silver beads of the smallest size; sometimes in the deserted park, the new-leaved trees drooped heavily, their thick branches like plumes of mourning for their dead sire the sun. Then a black dragon hovered, a camel-shape burst, and thunder like a tiger was roaring on the wooded hills, to be echoed by the ocean, while fierce lightnings shot from heaven to earth. But after a shower the sun always came back again; then how the earth smiled in tremulous ecstasy through the late afternoon, until billows of color gorgeously rolled down to the dusky horizon, while shadows gathered, thickening at the trees! And as I saw the ever-shifting movements of this natural theatre, I mused on change in the world. I felt that nothing lasts. Where was the ancient habitation of my fathers, where were its ordered ways and everlasting laws? Gutted by time. Maritime seemed to me strangely immobilized. I had no wish to rest in another potential ruin of the age. If today I was dreaming in the warmth of the sun all about Tennyson and Dora, if this seemed a world of great rightness, gentleness and beauty, still I could not accept it as quite real, as any more than a kind of play by Barrie, such as I had seen with Clendenin in Halifax the other day. A closed-off world, far from great ports of Time, oblivious to the tune of cycles and great change, as much a back-wash of life as a village in the South Seas. Remembering Seoul and Tokyo, New York and Peking, I grew amazed:

"Can it be that only in this one corner of earth the tide of flux has not come, and all remains as if unchanged?"

And yet there were some changes even in Green Grove. Allan for instance. His engagement was broken. Now he turned to have completely opposite views upon women; and all about love which he had told me before, he must tell me again, vice versa: "Love is silly. Only distracts a man. Girls are a waste of time." No more he became with Edwin a passionate reader of Tennyson's *Maud,* or a tender admirer of *The Princess.*

And one of the boys—Horace Thompson, who had been my tutor in Greek—got a scholarship to go across to Edinburgh. He was discussed with awe, as the most fortunate of beings, for was he not going to the home of the Scots, to the mother-civilization? Who would not choose those beautiful isles where "the centuries behind repose like a fruitful land"?

And Leslie Robin no longer triumphed but was sent home in disgrace. During the final exams he did dishonest work in chemistry. In the middle of writing he asked to be excused in order to go to the washroom, where he had planted a convenient friend with a textbook. A proctor suspected. He took up Robin's question slip with the answers written out from the textbook. Robin was summoned before the pope and the cardinals, as the student-governing body was called, and expelled. Poor Leslie! A hard beginning for a boy. A long road ahead for him!

I had my moment of swelling pride, too, when Doctor MacMillan stopped me as I walked in Seaway Park. He congratulated me on my marks in Professor Donald's class—in a tone of pleased surprise. Green Grove, he said, was proud of me. He offered me my scholarship for another year, and said he hoped that I would finish up my course there.

4

As Maritime closed for the summer, my spirit sped New York-ward, but that journey was more difficult for my body. I had had no paying work during the whole school year. I must first earn my fare. So it fell out that toward the middle of June, I was trudging on foot toward Stratford, a small neighboring town, with a letter of introduction to Mr. McCann, who owned a boxmaking factory there, and was the brother of the Green Grove "pope." I had made boxes for a living once before, while going to school in the Orient.

Stratford was a sleepy little place on the river Avon, a wide, tranquil, gray stream which was always salty and had tides like the sea. The boats traveling up from Boston and Fundy Bay came in with the tide. When the tide was high, water mounted over the quay. When the tide went out, the water retreated, and the town, being left behind, promptly went to sleep again. The apple blossoms along the river were just beginning to scatter. It was a calm, gentle, peaceful land, filled with extensive fruit orchards, fertile pastures with long juicy grass interwoven with wild flowers...or else cropped short and green as a golf course by the sheep. The place was considered very historical. A little farther down the Avon, past the town, were the old willows of Evangeline and the meadows of Grand Pré. But though I looked everywhere, I saw no forest primeval with murmuring pines and the hemlocks.

Mr. McCann proved to be a tall, slouching man with a mustache, always two days behind in shaving except on Sundays. Around his factory, you could not tell him from one of his own hands. He wore grease-stained working clothes and inspected the machinery himself. His factory—a square, high three-story structure, gray, the same color as the water—was on the bank of the river Avon and appeared to me almost as sleepy as that body. From its windows you could see green trees. The noise of the sawing machinery went z-z-z-z-z-z-, even from afar, like the buzz of industrious bees. In certain sections of the lower story, a thundering roar of electric sawing issued, like a great waterfall. But on the third floor where I worked, the buzz-saws dwindled again to little more than the sound of bees, a dreamy spell to which hands worked hypnotically.

Mr. McCann promptly took me under his protection. He saw that I was installed in a comfortable boarding house. Indeed, perhaps it was the only boarding house there. Mrs. Moody, who ran it, was an old lady, very hardworking and humbly dressed. When I first met her, I remember, Mr. McCann had to call her in from her strawberry beds, where her face had got very pink and warm. She was wearing a rough farming straw hat, which she took off to hang up behind the kitchen door, smoothing down her dress to receive Mr. McCann. Her hair was black and white, but mostly white, puffed high in front and flattened by a huge comb behind. She started to smile, and she looked as if her eyes were beginning to cry because of the many wrinkles in a network around them. Big dignified eyes she had, behind glasses that magnified them, and her pink cheeks looked always shining and polished.

Mrs. Moody's house was a short, two-story one, very low to the ground, and almost covered with climbing red roses and other vines. The room she gave to me was very quiet, tidy and peaceful. It had matting. The smell of matting is associated for me with that faraway summer on the Avon with its peaceful tides. Above the matting, which completely covered the floor, were two handmade rugs, with bunches of roses at either end. I had a big double bed and a big walnut dresser, a washstand with bowl and pitcher, and a little black leather chair much worn and cracked at the arms. There was a low bench in my room with several pots of red geraniums. The roses outside were so thick and so enshading that I did not need to use any window blinds.

How good this kind and simple landlady was to me! She was rather a lonely woman, or so it seemed to me, but one not given to self-pity, or even introspection. Her husband was still living, but he was always away on a ship somewhere, for he had followed the seafaring profession. Both her son and daughter had grown up, married, and deserted Canada for the States. She saw them rarely. Mrs. Moody worked all the time. Only for a short time in the evening was she idle after the supper dishes were washed and put away. Then she would sit down in her parlor, bend back the white curtain, and just look out for a while. But not for long. Soon she would rise and go into the kitchen where were the ironing board and the mending basket. Here, if she still felt the need of recreation, she would read, standing up, her Halifax paper, or the Montgomery Ward catalogue, before settling down for the evening's work. The price I paid her—$3.50 a week—apparently included all my laundry, which she did herself, down to the mending of my threadbare shirts and socks. How carefully she darned my socks, even making them over with scraps of her own selection! And she had given me the very best room in her boarding house, although I paid no more than others did.

Every morning immediately after breakfast I went to Mr. McCann's factory, walking up the stairs (the elevator was only used for freight, for the parts of unmade boxes brought from the sawing plant below) to the third floor which held a series of garret rooms, all opening into each other, all large, well-lighted and exhaling the fresh aromatic smells of shavings and shingles. I was given the small room at the end overlooking the river, where I worked in private. I had a sewing machine which used wire instead of thread, and for the less supple strips of wood for larger boxes, a special hammer and tacks.

In the room next to mine two girls were working. One girl, Queenie, was very tall and thin, with a lively sallow, sharp-chinned face shaped just like a triangle. The other, Alice, was smaller, more refined-looking, with dark hair and a small white neck. They used to come to work as if dressed for a party, then something happened to these clothes until it was time to go home, for their owners were always seen during working hours in faded gray smocks covered with shavings. Alice and Queenie came in to see me often and were very kind, showing me many tricks for faster work. There were others, girls and boys, who worked in another room beyond, but I did not see much of them. Sometimes a little short girl, no more than fourteen, worked between Queenie and Alice, but she was not regular. I was thankful. When she was there, she made great mischief, and used to hide my hammer. She would take Queenie's big hat and put it on my head—to see if I looked like a Negro woman, she said. I guess she did not make much money. Work was done by the piece, or rather by the box. You got paid by the number of boxes built. At least this was the system by which I worked. It did not matter how much time I put in, or how much time I wasted. I could stop and study awhile, or if it was hot, go out for a swim. Light, clean work it was...monotonous— still there were ways of varying that. I wrote out poems and tacked them on the wall to read as I worked. Sometimes, on those thin, light boards like paper, I wrote out Chinese verses very beautifully. I kept them in my work drawer and, by the time I was ready to leave, had quite a book. Through the windows, a breeze was almost always stirring the sawdust smells and the shingle dust, and the low sleepy sound of the saws came up, varied now and then by the ponderous creaking movements of the freight elevator...a perfect atmosphere in which to read nineteenth-century English poetry. Tennyson's *Lotus Eaters*, for instance. But the less I dreamed, the less I studied, the more money I made, and the sooner I would get back to New York.

Alice took me home with her one night to meet her parents and her young man. We sang "Love's Old Sweet Song," which Alice played on the piano. Once or twice Mr. McCann invited me to dinner. He had a spacious beautiful countrified white house, a pleasant wife who ran all the charity organizations in the town, and two incredibly beautiful children, fair-haired and rosy-cheeked. On Sundays I usually went to hear Doctor Elton preach at the Presbyterian church. It was a help to my English and it was the only way of going to the heart of the social organization of Stratford. One time I dressed up a little bit to go. I had a stiff collar—one I had worn with my school uniform in the Orient. I had noticed that the boys in Ralph's town, when they went to parties, put on stiff collars. Mine seemed very appropriate for a church. It was straight and smooth, just like a clerical collar, with no grooves for the necktie. When I was all ready, I saw that my tie naturally wished to ride up. I must not forget to pull it down with my hands. But it was a hot Sunday, and Doctor Elton's voice affected me much like the noise of the bees and the ripple of the river. I almost went to sleep. I forgot my tie. Outside I remembered, but could not pull it down immediately, so many people were shaking hands with me and smiling.

One of these cordial people was a stranger—a large, prosperous, shiny gentleman, with something in his bustling movements and his air of peppy activity suggesting the States. Sure enough, I heard from the conversation around that he was from the States. He had come to Stratford on his way up to Boston, and it being Sunday and the boat not yet in, had paid a visit to Doctor Elton's church. He seemed to be in the book-publishing business and knew something of Maritime. At least, he said he thought Maritime a wonderful college but he was sending his son to Harvard because Harvard was much bigger. All the colleges in the States were bigger, he said, and he somehow implied that if so, they must be better. There was more business down that way too, so he mentioned. Altogether, it was the only place, one gathered—the States. Particularly Boston.

"Well, well, my boy, so you are going to college," he said to me genially.

I told him that I should probably be in the States some day, not mentioning however that I intended going to Boston that same fall. And he gave me his card which read on it "D. J. Lively…Universal Education Publishing Company."

I knew it was not unusual for men in the publishing business to be traveling into Canada on business—especially in the religious or educational publishing business—for like New England this part of Canada was not a bad bookselling field and the tastes were somewhat similar.

"D. J. Lively: There he is," went on the Stratford stranger, pointing to his card, and beaming at me. "D. J. Lively is always glad to help out a fine deserving lad. Look me up when you come to Boston. I may be able to do something for you there."

He somehow conveyed that he was very proud of D. J. Lively and the Universal Publishing Company and so any man ought to be.

I went home in a glow after this meeting, more eager than ever to leave Canada and reach the land of golden opportunity. (When I looked in the glass, I saw that all during the social amenities after Doctor Elton's sermon, my tie had been riding up. By now it was away up above my collar and around toward one ear. I hastily took it off and hurled it into the waste-paper basket—the last time I wore a stiff collar, even in Canada.)

5

I had a speaking acquaintance with all the people who went to Doctor Elton's church, but some I knew better than others. My greatest friends were Mr. and Mrs. Lovejoy, retired missionaries from the New Hebrides. Their time of active service was now over, and they had settled down in this quiet out-of-the-way spot, this New-World Stratford-on-Avon, to await the heavenly reward and immortality according to their faith. Their quiet dark well-shaded house took one on a far journey to tropical isles, for it was filled with exotic souvenirs, each with its own bizarre story. Cupboards and cases and bookshelves of beautiful shells, dresses, stones, pearls, strange native objects...years later in visiting a part of the British Museum, I recognized articles like those I had once seen in Doctor Lovejoy's collection. But each was endeared to the Lovejoys for personal reasons. And my, what tales Doctor Lovejoy had to tell! Bloodcurdling. So quietly he told them, too. You knew they were all true. Many times he and his wife had almost been killed. Twice they had been shipwrecked in strange seas. And they had lived fearlessly in the midst of jungle communities like those Oriental sages of old tales who, fortified by the wisdom of poetry, could look lions in the eye and force them to retreat. Many times he had come into conflict with the people of his savage congregation. Once Doctor Lovejoy had tried to prevent a man from burying his wife alive. He had stopped him, but the man wished for revenge. This frail, dignified, unworldly couple had lived a life of the most stirring adventure. Yet both had pink-white faces and soft peaceful expressions, as if they had never come into contact with any evil, but only good throughout their lives. Almost like sleep-walkers. Mrs. Lovejoy had snow-white hair in abundance, he none at all, except in the beard. She was a little bit taller than he, walking always very very straight, in spite of her frailness, while he was a little bit bent. They never varied their ways of dressing; she always wore long dresses touching the ground and a starched white net collar high at the neck, even in the heat of summer. He wore an old but very tidy well-brushed suit, and looked the gentleman through and through. His education indeed had been very wide, for he was one of those old-fashioned pioneer missionaries who must be a bit of everything, doctor, teacher, governor, preacher. He was a graduate of Princeton and of the Edinburgh Medical College. And he seemed to have been almost everywhere on the globe except the Far East.

On his invitation, I would often go to see Doctor Lovejoy. He was very punctual—whether he went for a walk with me along the river Avon, or waited for me in his lovely little garden for a game of croquet. If I was late, my conscience used to reproach me as if I had committed a sin. He would also have me read to him, on his cool shaded porch, where for long hours he helped me with my English, correcting my pronunciation, choosing books for me to read from his own library. Sometimes he and Mrs. Lovejoy would entertain me by playing the victrola. They had many records, all being hymns and prayers, or celestial organ music. "Greenland's Icy Mountains" too, I remember, with many voices. They had, besides, records of special prayers by famous divines, to which they listened on Sunday afternoons, and while listening Mrs. Lovejoy always bowed her head and shut her eyes, as if she had been in church, her fragile white hands crossed in her lap reminding me of the bones of white coral. They were really the most delicate and exquisite of people. Fantastic to associate them with those wild and savage tales. Doctor Lovejoy himself used to wash the cups after Sunday tea. He was as careful as a cat about not getting his hands wet at the same time. He would run the hot water from the faucet into those thin cups, then daintily and delicately turn them around without wetting even a finger–nail. Last of all, he would peer like a botanist into them, to see if any sugar were left. Such a fastidious old man to have spent his entire life with savages of the New Hebrides!

6

I remember one poem read to me by Doctor Lovejoy, read and re-read and carefully explained, not didactically as Ralph Glenwood would have done, but simply and with his own candor of spirit. It was a poem by Browning, in which these lines occur:

Therefore to whom turn I but to thee, the ineffable Name?

    Builder and maker, thou, of houses not made with hands.

What, have fear of change from thee who are ever the same?

    Doubt that thy power can fill the heart that thy power expands?

There shall never be one lost good! What was, shall live as before.

    The evil is null, is nought, is silence implying sound;

What was good shall be good, with, for evil, so much good more;

    On earth the broken arcs; in the heaven, a perfect round.

I doubt if Doctor Lovejoy got the significance of his choice of this poem for me—Chungpa Han—the very child of change—waiting impatiently here between the world of the past and the world of the future, longing eagerly to reach a great city famed like Babylon for its fleshpots and worldliness, famed so like any great city, as a complex of man. But perhaps such a quotation is the best comment I can make upon this other world, the world of the old-fashioned missionary, which has necessarily influenced my destiny profoundly, and nevertheless has reaped in me results and reactions never contemplated. The Westernized Oriental is the child of the nineteenth century, and yet a curious detachment is possible for him such as neither truculent old-timers nor their sophisticated modern children can normally expect. His own elders were neither Atheists nor Believers, Fundamentalists nor Scientists—but so widely remote as to be classical Confucians. In vast perspective he sees three different times—not only intellectually but sympathetically. Nor can the nineteenth century be either accepted as final or spurned in inevitable reaction toward the new, for in his struggle to reach the faraway boundaries of modern thought, the recapitulation of an eternal embryo is necessary for him, and the past becomes his transient stepping stone....

Many other retired clergymen besides the Lovejoys lived in this quiet little town whose waters led to Boston. And a large proportion of the town were leisured elderly people, many of whom had sons and daughters who had deserted Canada for the States. Often the daughters came back bringing children for a nice quiet summer vacation with grandparents. There were only two classes in Stratford: the leisured, and the laboring. But both were quiet and old-fashioned. The young people released from the small Stratford factories stood around on street corners after six, waiting wistfully for whatever fun might come, but it seemed quiet fun. The primitive wooden movie-house became a dancing hall on certain nights, but even then it was never noisy, and nobody seemed to get drunk. And everybody went to church on Sunday mornings, for all the sects were represented here. Restless, discontented bodies were automatically shipped down to Boston. But doubtless one needed a good deal of ambition and restlessness to break away, if one were native here. I remember the Stratford barber who boarded at Mrs. Moody's all the time. (The others were mostly transients—men working temporarily in the shipyards there, women taking courses in the Baptist normal school close by, etc.) This barber looked like a farmer and not a barber, and in fact I think he had newly become a barber, not liking the dirt of farm life. It was his ambition to get down to Boston. He was engaged to a girl who ran the only beauty shop in Stratford and who was always unusually dressed. Her clothes, though they were made at home by her dressmaker sister, seemed copies of Parisian styles. One time she would appear in a dress with long sleeves—extraordinarily long, I mean, down to the knees. Or she would wear an enormously wide flopping straw hat with streamers. Besides, she was always exceptionally decorated underneath, whether as an advertisement of her shop or just to take advantage of it, I can't say. One time she would have black hair—another dark auburn, put up in many different ways, but always very shiny and very curled, with eyelashes and eyebrows made fancy too. She, too, no doubt, was eager to get down to Boston. They never managed it. Several years later, as I drifted north once more, I saw them both in Stratford, married and settled down. Those same dresses she was wearing still, but how much faded, and under her hat she was quite natural-looking. They had a fat boy-baby now, whose ambition ultimately perhaps will be to go to Boston.

But no roots could tie me to this land. When I had earned my fare to New York and a little over, I paid my last good-byes to Doctor and Mrs. Lovejoy. How simply and affectionately they parted with me, a ghostly world of love and kindly light shining out around them! They were the perfect and celestial representatives of that fantastical mysticism which has sent Christian missionaries far and wide to the remotest pockets of the earth, face to face with all the varying puzzlements of nature, breaking ground for ruthless, blindly selfish Western forces, but they themselves all innocent and unconscious, returning at last with delicate brittleness unbroken to such quiet native spots as this—Stratford-on-Avon. The last to be seen of Doctor Lovejoy as I turned away was his bent back going up the garden path toward his small vine-clad house, one arm around Mrs. Lovejoy, clasping her hand.... The closing picture of the land of my first college year, my spiritual stopping-off place between Korea and New York.

BOOK THREE

1

I HAD NO SOONER reached the steep black streets of Boston, than the easy bread and butter of charity which I had eaten for a year seemed far behind. I was in the land of opportunity once more, and very glad to be there. But again I must attack the problem of American efficiency, American business methods. In Boston I met Hsun, by means of a memorandum from George telling me our friend would be found here. Hsun had come up on an excursion ticket to interview some Boston Orientals about a business loan to start a restaurant. He was having great trouble about the funds for this restaurant. Nobody believed that Hsun would succeed. He told me that he was still trying to get money out of Hung-Kwan Pang for the tea business the latter had taken over. Pang owed him forty dollars, but Hsun would squeeze none of this out of him. Instead, Pang told him he would make a discount, and give Hsun in payment a quantity of valuable fountain pens. To hear Pang talk, you would think he was giving Hsun a great business opportunity. Pang said he had sold these pens all over the country, and had netted $3000 with no trouble at all. After that he had bought out all the pens that this Japanese store had, but was willing to hand over his stock to Hsun on account of the friendship he felt for him. With money from the sale of pens, he gave Hsun to understand, he, Pang, had bought stocks and step by step climbed up the ladder to be a rich man. Hsun had had no luck so far in selling pens, but Pang insisted it was because he had no guts, no business method.

Hsun had brought these pens with him to Boston—a whole suitcase of them—hoping to give these as security for a loan, but nobody except Pang believed these pens were any good. We got them out and examined them. There were hundreds and thousands of them, pens with glass points. Pang had reported their wholesale price was thirty-five cents each, and that they easily sold for one dollar. Both Hsun and I were sceptical. Hsun suggested lowering the retail price, and seeing if we could sell them at once, here in Boston, before we went down to New York.

Well, the upshot was, we started out at once, with the suitcase. We sold a few the first morning, but it did not more than pay for our lunch. In the afternoon, because the suitcase was heavy, Hsun invested fifty cents with a Jewish drugstore man for permission to hold a demonstration in his window. We were given room there for the display purpose, and we stuck the pens up, using a soft sheet of cork provided by the pen company. Since Hsun could not write very well, he had me write in my best style, "Guaranteed. Come in and buy." This seemed to us like business efficiency. We drew a crowd, but they only laughed, and we hardly sold enough to pay for the space in the window. By evening we were both tired and discouraged, and Hsun was again cursing Pang.

Next morning, we tried again, each going in a different direction. I took part of the pens in a Corona typewriter case, lent me by a Chinese restaurant man. I had the idea of trying business offices. But many of these buildings had "No Canvassing" signs. Then an office caught my eye with familiar letters written upon the window. "The Universal Education Publishing Company." Perhaps I might find D. J. Lively there. Maybe he would not kick me out, even if I were trying to sell him worthless pens. But I was unprepared for the hearty welcome which awaited me. At the end of the office, behind a fence and surrounded by typewriters and stenographers, the good-looking shiny gentleman I had already encountered once in Stratford was leaning back in his swivel chair and he caught my eye almost instantly, leaning forward with a beaming smile. I stepped up, still with misgivings.

"May I talk to you a moment, sir? That is, if you are not too busy."

"Why of course! I am never too busy to talk. You know, my boy, people who run up and down with papers in their hands all the time—these people who seem very busy and never talk to others and never try to help others—these are the kind that never get much done. No, my lad, D. J. is never too busy to talk," (here he gave me a sly wink), "but he makes investment and profit out of his talks. Sit down, sit down."

Having shaken hands with him and seated myself in a straight chair by his side, I hardly knew how to begin.

"Well, my boy, I see you lost no time in looking me up. And you are interested in selling, that is it?"

I almost jumped. He seemed to have read my mind.

"Well—I want to make some money for the coming college year. I must have it if I am to stay in Boston," I began, hesitating.

"Out with it! Straight from the shoulder! Don't beat around the bush. You knew that D. J. Lively is your man. College—yes, very fine, very fine. Do you see that man over there in the far corner of the room?" he lowered his voice. "I pay that man a college president's salary every year. Yes sir! I never had a college education myself, but then I know by heart our great educational work—*Universal Education,* in three volumes. And I have been of untold service to countless boys going to college."

I was still too bashful to mention the pens. And anyhow, Mr. Lively kept right on.

"How I do like to see manly independence! The spirit that inspired Abraham Lincoln and George Washington. The spirit back of these United States of America. Nothing is too small by which to make honest money. George Washington, the father of his country, was only a poor bookseller once. Did you know that, my boy? Yes, a poor bookseller." He made an impressive pause. "And the man you see before you, too. D. J. Lively. That's how he got his start. The selling business. Have you ever tried it before?"

"Not in Boston, sir.—Er—I have these pens," I brought them out, mumbling.

"What? So you are a salesman!" Mr. Lively leaned back in his swivel chair and laughed heartily.

"But I'm afraid they're not much good...."

"Here, here! That's not the way to sell anything, boy," sputtered Mr. Lively. "You're going against the first law of salesmanship!" His round eyes protruded. He looked shocked. "Dear, dear. But give me those pens. I think I can use a couple." And he winked, with twinkling eyes.

I handed the Corona case over to him. He selected six. I was overwhelmed.

"Why—why do you want so many," I stammered, "when you already have a good one?" For I saw it on his desk.

"You see, I have plans for you, my boy. I want to give you confidence in your first venture. But that isn't the point. Let this be a lesson to you. You have sold yourself to me already. I stand before you favorably impressed. So your pens have sold themselves. But see here, my boy, between you and me, you should be selling something better than this." He examined the pens with a thoughtful frown, much to my humiliation. "Don't you think so?"

I said that it was very hard for an Oriental to learn American salesmanship.

"Come, come, my boy, that isn't the spirit of American optimism. Your background may be a good thing. Only you must reap advantage out of that. You must select some field where that will help. New England, now. An Oriental salesman for books. H'm!" Mr. Lively paused, and looked at me inquiringly. "A fine clean Christian young Oriental earning his way through college." Lowering his voice he asked my views on life under two headings, whether I ever smoked or drank. I replied, "No."

"That's right," said Mr. Lively with relief. "Now, my boy, everything's all right. I wouldn't smoke. I have never smoked because I think smoking is morally wrong. As for drink, I wouldn't associate with anybody who touches it."

I was thinking that Mr. Lively looked just the kind of man who would enjoy a good cigar. His was also the energetic temperament, I was almost sure, that would like to swear sometimes, but observing his big, morally shiny face, I was sure he was speaking the truth and that he never did.

"Good. And you are very much in earnest, eh...about this education?"

"Yes sir. I came to the West especially to study Shakespeare. I have already read all his plays that have been translated into the Japanese."

"Shakespeare? Good, good." Here Mr. Lively clapped me on the shoulder and remarked to the air with boundless magnanimity. "H'm, this fine boy seems the genuine article. Why, nobody could doubt it. Everybody in New England will want to help you. D. J. Lively is a man hard to fool. Certainly *I* could never doubt a fine, earnest Christian lad." Then he said to me with beaming eye, "How would you like to sell our *Universal Education,* my boy, and earn the money to put yourself through college?"

"Great!" I exclaimed. (I wished George could have been there to see him!... It was just what I had always thought...so the American man did business...such a generous man, his charity shining out to every corner of the earth—even to the interior of Asia—you could see it in the good-looking Y.M.C.A. building in Seoul, or in the Educational Institutions in Peking. So many schools and hospitals—all, I thought, coming from the charitable feelings of a man like this.)

"But look here, Han, you must learn something of salesmanship. Your approach in selling me these pens was very very poor. My boy, you evidently have no notion of the veriest fundamentals. I was startled, I was almost discouraged when I heard what you said about those pens being no good. I was your prospective customer, you know. But you'll learn. I can see that. Cultivate your faith in yourself. And in the goods you are selling. Did you ever stop to think what a noble calling for any man—that of selling books? selling *Universal Education* to all men?"

"Almost like a missionary," I was thinking. While Mr. Lively went on in inspired tones, like a man cupping his ear to the Muse.

"Yes, just north of Boston. We will let you monopolize that field, I think. Never forget the fine earnestness of one who is seeking help to educate himself. Never swerve from the straight, the narrow path.... And in salesmanship, just as in Life, you must have Faith. Faith in all the finer, nobler things—in yourself, in the goods you are selling...."

We parted with the understanding that I should come in tomorrow and learn about this business opportunity.

2

When I reported my interview with Mr. Lively to Hsun in glowing terms, he agreed that it was for me a business opportunity, and he advised me to stay in Boston for a while until it materialized, rather than come to New York where he himself found it so hard to make a living. He saw now that the pens were no good. And Hsun was right. Anybody who was such a fool as to buy our pens would tell others not to buy, and if he saw us again would try to get his money back. In a sense, it was like begging, taking money away from people for nothing, and not from rich people but from poor—for people who had money would never buy such pens. The poor who could not afford a decent pen were the only possible customers. So it was not even Robin Hood heroism. We were both disgusted with the pen business. And that very night Hsun took the boat for New York.

But my future did not look so rosy to me, either, after calling on Mr. Lively the following morning. For first I found that I was required to buy a Prospectus—a fat, handsome volume, bound in leather, and containing the most telling extracts from those three superlative volumes, *Universal Education*. But this prospectus cost ten dollars—as much as a copy of the work itself. In other words, each of Mr. Lively's salesmen automatically became a customer to him before earning any money at all. I would have been discouraged, if Mr. Lively had not taken me around with his hand on my shoulder and introduced me to all the office force as his future salesman. They greeted me with "Very glad to meet you," which was a lot. Thus I was persuaded. I invested my ten dollars. And Mr. Lively gave me a business-like receipt and the prospectus, together with a number of papers, sales talks of various kinds to be memorized. Some were as long as twelve pages, others only eight or six, and a few, as short as three. But there was still a contract to be signed with the company. Mr. Lively refused to sign this contract with me yet.

"We must do nothing hastily," said Mr. Lively, and he broke it to me that I would need to take a long course of training in his school for salesmanship. Then I was indeed discouraged and explained that I had no means of getting along while learning to be a star salesman.

"Oh, I'll fix that," said Mr. Lively, who radiated optimism. "You are my boy from now on. Why, I'm going to take you out and show you what a real American home looks like from the inside. You can live in my home with my own children scot-free while you are memorizing these talks. I'll give you some private lessons, too. After that, you can attend some of the meetings in my office and brush up a little on the finer points of sales-manship, and then I think you'll make good."

Then he told me to be at his office at five o'clock and he would take me out to his home in the suburbs. "Be prompt, my dear boy. This is the first lesson for the future business man."

At five o'clock, I found Mr. D. J. singularly fresh and unexhausted, as full of good will as ever, after pumping it out all day.

"Sit down, my boy. Be with you in a minute." He took down the receiver of his desk telephone. "Mildred, Mildred, is that you, Mildred? This is Daddy talking. What can I get?" Then I heard a shrill woman's voice at the other end of the wire sounding mad and nervous. "I don't care! You get anything you want to." And Bang! She hung up while Mr. Lively was still talking.

D. J. turned around to me. Gently he beamed, like a bald mountain with sunshine. He winked, conveying to me an air of conspiracy.

"I'll fix it. I know how to handle Mrs. D. J."

We stepped into Mr. Lively's big Cadillac car, as expansive, good-looking and morally shiny as its owner. "We'll take Mother out a real good steak," he chuckled, winking again, as he drove around to a large clean shiny meat shop in the city, and purchased an exceptionally big, tender, thick cut of beefsteak. "With her that ought to close the deal. We'll put this one over."

And not losing his good humor for a moment, he went on talking about Mrs. Lively, telling me what a good cook she was, how she was a college graduate, and a distant relative of a New England poet, as we drove out of Boston.

"A superior wife and mother," Mr. Lively summed up in the same tones of hearty eulogy which he used toward *Universal Education.* "A noble example of womankind. Tender heart—boundless energy. High-strung...but a real helpmate. Makes fine lemon pies. Yes, sir, I knew the stuff of Mrs. Lively as soon as I saw it. None of your bob-haired type for me. So the sale was cinched, you might say—well," Mr. Lively looked at me with solemn gravity. "I stepped another rung up the great American ladder of Success when I married Mrs. Lively." Then he went on in his hearty optimistic way, "My boy, Mrs. Lively is going to be a mother to you. You'll be Mrs. Lively's boy as well as mine."

He talked more about boys he and Mrs. Lively had raised, on the selling of *Universal Education,* until today they were big successes, making large incomes. One or two schoolteachers he had saved from their fates... now they had large cars, like this one—he pointed to the long shiny hood of the one we were riding in—and much bank stock.

"You and I are going to get on well," reiterated Mr. Lively confidently. "I know the value of Shakespeare, though I am a practical man and not a college graduate. Between you and me, the best business men are not college graduates. But I always say, give me Shakespeare and the Bible...and the three volumes of *Universal Education.* 'Speak the speech, I pray thee'... you know that quotation?... Oh, you must work hard to memorize these sales talks, my boy.... You will have plenty of time to study them out here with Mrs. Lively, even though you help Mother a little about the house... um...I don't suppose you drive a car, my boy?" Mr. Lively glanced at me appraisingly, almost as if he were measuring me for a suit.

"Well, I have not had much experience," I murmured modestly. But evidently not modestly enough, for he seemed to be hopeful. He said it would be a fine thing if I could take him in and out of the city after a hard day's work sometime. And he let me take the wheel in hand. It was the first time I had ever handled the steering wheel of an automobile. My experience, I had meant, was with bicycles.

"For mercy's sake, boy, that's not the way to drive." His big florid face became quite faded as he snatched the wheel just in time to save us from the ditch. The car tottered a moment on two wheels.

"Whew! Whew!" sputtered Mr. Lively, wiping his face with his handkerchief. "I see you're the go-ahead, no-stopping kind. But this lesson of yours—my boy—this lesson of yours—it almost cost me $7000."

He repeated the price several times, as he got out and rubbed the fenders with a dust cloth on the ditch side.

"My boy," he resumed, when we were driving safely once more, "I know you've got the stuff from which good salesmen are made. I can't be fooled on your personality. But I don't believe you'll ever be able to drive a car—if you take my advice, you'll keep away from machinery!—a car—don't forget—worth $7000!"

We came into a small suburban town also of a morally shiny character, with trees, big shiny houses, and beautifully shiny lawns, hedges, and flower beds. Mr. Lively stopped before a handsome, tall three-story house built neatly of yellow bricks. Its back was on a large park.

"Do you see that park?" said Mr. Lively, pointing it out. "It's my back yard—and I don't pay a cent for it!" He chuckled, and this joke seemed to please him very much.

Mrs. D. J. opened the door herself with a bounce, before Mr. D. J. could bring out his key. She snatched the meat from Mr. Lively's hand.

"Mother, this is one of my boys!"

Mrs. Lively answered with a loud sniff. She was a little, shrivelled, domestic-looking woman with an aggrieved expression, all wrapped about in a huge bungalow apron.

"You know I've got no time for talking now," she screamed, as she ran away.

"Mrs. Lively, you see, does all her own work," said Mr. Lively, not at all taken aback. "This house believes that the way to be happy is to work. Mrs. Lively is my treasure. I would not be where I am today without the help of Mrs. Lively. A girl of true blue."

This seemed to be said for the benefit of the speeding Mrs. Lively. But she took no notice.

Now two children came running to meet their father. Mr. Lively introduced them as Martin and Elsie, aged six and ten respectively. They were really lovely-looking children. Elsie seemed shy and sensitive. She followed her mother into the kitchen and I could hear her semi-whispering voice plead as the swinging door swung violently. "But Mother, Daddy says he's come to help you. Let's be nice to him."

As for Martin, he entertained me while his father was off washing his hands, by telling me how much money he and his sister would have from insurance when Mr. D. J. died. Of course, in the Orient this would have been shocking manners, but it just showed Martin's practical upbringing. I'm sure he was very fond of both parents.

"Come to dinner," screamed Mrs. Lively, popping in at the living-room door again.

"Yes, my dear. The queen of cooks, the cream of wives!" said the cheerful Mr. Lively, who had returned and was patting Martin approvingly on the head for remembering the rate of interest on some parental bonds. But Mrs. Lively was gone again. She seemed to be always running up and down, in and out. She slammed the dishes down upon the table and ran out very quickly to the kitchen, where we could hear her opening and shutting the oven with a bang.

"Is it a lemon pie night?" asked D. J., keeping up his loud and conciliatory tone. "Surely I smell lemon pie."

"Yes!" shouted Martin and Elsie together. "Lemon pie night. You're right!"

"I was telling Chungpa" (Mr. Lively had already inquired my given name on the way out) "about Mother's famous lemon pies. And I was reminiscing. O well I recollect the time she came to me to get a job. A job—would you believe it?" Mr. Lively snickered, "Selling—ha ha!—books. That was before your time, Martin and Elsie. I looked her over and I said, 'No, my dear, I can never give you that sort of job. It's not your line. But I can—and I assure you I will—give you—Myself!' " He beamed fondly on his rather too jumpy and frowny partner of bed and board. "I am a great judge of character, as you have already sensed, Chungpa. I recognized the artist of the lemon pie. Wasn't that the way of it, Mother? Didn't you marry me because I wouldn't give you any other job but my self?"

"How can you be so ridiculous, D. J.!" frowned and pouted Mrs. Lively. But he affably squeezed her and gave her a loud, benevolent kiss on the forehead, until Mrs. Lively began to melt with unwilling smiles. Now indeed she was nicer to me, and heaped my plate many times full. That steak was wonderful.

<h2 style="text-align:center">3</h2>

Of course, the whole Lively family was very human and very nice to me, except that I could not memorize the sales talk very quickly while being a help to Mrs. D. J. There had been no definite understanding about this. Being a help evidently meant washing all the dishes and cleaning the fourteen-room house, and wringing out the clothes for Mrs. Lively, and if she went out under the porte-cochere and began washing the windows of the $7000 car—as I noticed she did once or twice when I was getting ready to study and looking out of the living-room window—naturally I must go down and help her there, too. But she didn't treat me like a servant, there was no yes-madame about it, and Mrs. D. J. was very nice at times.

She had the same repertoire as Mr. Lively about the poor boys or poor girls whom they had helped to get through some tough spot…and she, too, preferred some successful young salesman who now owned a beautiful home, who was prominent in clubs and who possessed a handsome car.

Mrs. Lively was rather an indulgent mother. But she was always working very hard when at home. She did everything herself in running that big house, except that once a week a washwoman came to do the big things. But next day Mrs. Lively ironed everything herself. It was my job to bring things in from the line in the back yard, and to wring out the things she did not give to the laundress. Of course, she cooked all her own meals, ordering from stores by telephone, except the meat or something special which Mr. Lively loved to get on the way home. She cooked many pies, biscuits, and muffins. When she burned them, she would cry. I never saw anybody crying so much over unimportant things! When Mr. Lively came home, he usually found her angry, or in tears. She was as perpetually flustered and aggrieved as he was beaming and assured. Then he would get her out of this by kissing. Gradually she would recover…speak a little, cry a little, finish the sentence. A good cryer. A good laugher. And Mr. Lively said she was a good woman and a good wife—and very tenderhearted. Mr. Lively always said to me that I was lucky to come into a beautiful American home and see the inside and know how things were running inside.

"It's a great pity that many Oriental students never have a chance to see American home life before they return. The Americans are models of family life, and you have a lot to learn."

They all went to bed rather early, and I was left alone with good lights and a good chair for reading, and a fairly large number of books which at least made a beautiful decoration for the living room. I examined all these books while I was there, and I think Mrs. Lively thought I should help more, because I burned so much electric light. They had Dickens, Scott, Kipling, Stevenson, Mark Twain, Shakespeare, Longfellow—mostly with pages uncut. Elsie was the only reader among them, and she hadn't got around to all the books yet. As for contemporary writers, the Livelys did not have any except Henry van Dyke, Robert Service, and Edgar Guest. *Edgar Guest's Poems* was their most recent book. It was autographed. Mr. Guest had lectured in one of the Y.M.C.A.'s where Mr. Lively also spoke. When Mr. Lively told me about it, he said, "Mr. Guest is a grand fellow—because he makes a lot of money with his writing and he is a good moral man; he is well known." I think Mr. Lively wanted an endorsed statement from him on the *Universal Education* work to be used in selling.

4

The classes in advanced salesmanship for which I had been waiting were beginning. I had to go into the city for them, since they took place in Mr. Lively's private office. Here were comfortable chairs all right, and a big desk for Mr. Lively, with a blackboard to one side of the desk. We did not pray, though I somewhat missed that. Mr. Lively opened the meeting by asking in Sunday-school voice: "Our company—what does it stand for? What has been its motto for twenty-five years? What is it known for?"

Silence from all the students, whom Mr. Lively held with his hypnotic eye. A lady who sat in the back spoke up in ringing tones: "I think it's— Service, Mr. Lively."

"Yes, Service," beamed Mr. Lively. "Our company lives to give service. Doing good is the secret of how it makes money. We are famed for service to customer, to salesman, to home, church, country throughout this great magnificent United States of America. The point I will make then is— Service, beginning with a capital S. We'll just put that down to remember." And he drew a large expansive capital S on the board, running from top to bottom, and at the very top finished out the word in small letters.

"Now I think of something else this company has plenty of— something beginning with S. Can anybody suggest it? Well, I will tell you," pursued Mr. Lively. "It is—STUFF!" and he clapped one hand on the palm of the other to emphasize. "And with Service and the right Stuff—what else? Come, what is needed to make sales?"

The same lady from the back of the room said, "Sticking, I *think*, Mr. Lively."

"Right! The difference between a good salesman and a poor salesman is sticking to it. Now—we add up Service, Stuff, Sticking—what does that come to?"

"Sales!" sings out the voice from the back of the room.

"Sales, of course! And it's sales that make the successful man or woman in business.

<pre>
                            Success
                      Sales
                Sticking
            Stuff
        Service
</pre>

(And we mount the ladder.) But it takes all four S's to make the big S in Success! Now—if we draw a line like this through all the S's" (our teacher playfully suited the action to the word), "what do we get, folks? Why, yes! The American dollar!"

Everybody laughed. I thought Mr. Lively would surely approve of the Chinese character for Buddha, which is man with a dollar sign after it (so: 佛).

"The successful salesman *is* a success. Remembering my little table. An invaluable aid. Apply it. In matrimony, for example. When you want to clinch the deal!" Mr. Lively winked, and continued to beam inspiringly into our eyes. "Cultivate the personality of the successful salesman. Active, positive, alert, aggressive." And certainly he seemed the epitome of every word. I listened receptively. Was I not being admitted into the Holy of Holies of the American civilization? This was just the very baptism I needed.

"Now I'll turn you over to our teacher, Miss Fulton, who has come all the way from Cincinnati to teach you." (She with the voice in the back came forward modestly rubbing her hands and smiling.) "Miss Fulton started as a saleswoman. Soon she was selling fifteen copies of our work a day. She went up, up, up. There was no stopping the lady. Today she has a beautiful home in Cincinnati and a country-house in Michigan. She has her own car, her chauffeur, and stocks and bonds in the bank as security."

Miss Fulton was about forty-five and quite stylishly dressed. She had black hair, curled and marcelled, with white and red colors on her face that moved rather stiffly when she smiled. Gold teeth gleamed in her successful smile.

"I'm sure it's very nice of Mr. Lively to say all this about me. But— why—the only way to make good is to go ahead. I know I am addressing a picked class. That is a help. All before me have the fortunate gift of a positive personality. A lot of people do not have this. But because you have—each and every one of you—Mr. Lively has picked you out to be his salesmen. I would say, from my experience, Mr. Lively is a very careful man when he picks. Isn't that so, Mr. Lively?"

I looked around at the class that Mr. Lively had picked. There were several ex-ministers, a widowed mother who had brought her little girl of seven to attend the class with her, a group of college boys on vacation, etc.

"To begin with, salesmanship is an art. It is not easy. Few things in this life sell themselves. Or look at it this way. If you are able to sell the customer something he wants, we can hardly call that salesmanship, can we?

The good salesman makes the customer want the unwanted article."

To me this was novel to hear, and the opposite of Confucius's saying, "Serve as you wish to be served." How would you like to be forced to buy something you did not want? But Miss Fulton was hurrying on to the next point.

"When you begin to understand this other side—the creative side—of salesmanship, it may mean your entrance into a new life. It may revolutionize your personality. But first a few rules of common sense. Get up early. Start the day right. Have a good breakfast (not just grapefruit and coffee). Never try to sell on an empty stomach. (The anemic person, the person with no vitality does not make a good salesman.) Never try to sell on a full stomach—you may not take full advantage of a situation. Remember, you are training as for an athletic event. Salesmanship is a contest. You must be vital, dynamic, for constantly you will have to overcome sales resistance. No customer willingly buys. He struggles against buying though it may be for his own good.... Be vital, dynamic," Miss Fulton consulted her notes again. "Well, just be sensible. Be good to yourself. You are your own asset or liability. Go to bed early. Lie down a few minutes after each meal for a rest or a snooze. You will be surprised at the surplus vitality you can accumulate this way." Now I understood why Mr. Lively lay down always after eating. He was recharging his vitality for some more profits and good investments.

"Then, as a salesman, you must take special pains with your appearance. (But let me remind you, have nothing conspicuous in your dress. You want all your customer's attention centered on what you have to say, not on your red necktie.) See that your teeth are well cleaned, mouth well washed, fingernails immaculate, hair neat. Make yourself an attractive human being. But when you are selling, you must dress rather humbly—plainly, avoiding all that is gay or expensive-looking."

Miss Fulton paused just a moment for breath, then continued. "And now a few words about technique." She held up the sales-talk manual, which I had been memorizing now for several weeks. "This is your sales-Bible. You must not question it, or try any innovations until you have first tried out all that is contained here. This manual holds the cream of what all great salesmen and saleswomen have found most practical. We know these talks to be successful, they come from men and women who are Successes.... 'And by their fruits shall ye know them....' Do not talk about anything that has nothing to do with business. Let every word you use be planned to put the deal over. Never forget why you are there, and that you are fighting for time, time to convince the customer. Now you know it takes twelve minutes to give the main sales talk. If you think you have succeeded after the first five minutes, get out that sales form. For heaven's sake don't waste time then!" Miss Fulton spoke in such tones of admonitory horror, that there was a general laugh, and a bright smile from Miss Fulton herself. "But if you feel you have not sold your article, keep the sales form in the background. Don't hesitate. Go on to the second talk, to the third. You are not likely to run out of material, for you have an hour's talk prepared for you in this manual. After that, you can scrap the manual and try your own resources. Anyhow, keep at it, until you are forced to leave or have convinced the customer. Perhaps you may see her looking confused. (I say she, for most of your customers will be women.) Confusion is the first sign of weakening. You must seize on it. Take out your sales form now and say softly, 'Just sign here, under your neighbor, Mrs. Smith....' Or if you can't say that, because Mrs. Smith hasn't bought yet, say, 'Sign here, leaving room for Mrs. Smith. She is my *next* customer.' If once you have a signature, you are safe. The form is a contract saying she will pay. Some women sign without knowing exactly what they are signing. But people never withdraw from the written contract. After that you must say in a gentle, firm voice, 'Now in order to meet certain regulations, the company asks for a five-dollar deposit'—say the amount very low. (Always quote prices in a low, soft voice.)

"At this point she is likely to say, 'But I have no money right now.' Don't hesitate. Suggest some way to get the money. Or offer to lend her the money. It will appear as a generous gesture. People in a house or an apartment are not likely to run away. Say, 'I happen to have this five-dollar bill in my purse.' (And you must always have it.) 'I am going to lend it to you, as I see you want these books so much. The company does not authorize me to do this, but I will deposit my own five dollars in your name.' Then you give her the bill, and let her place it in your hands. When the books are sent

C.O.D. with her signature underneath and a bill for the full amount, including your loan, you will find she always pays."

I began to feel rather tired and sleepy, and to wonder how many more minutes of sales talk Miss Fulton herself had. But now she folded up her notes and placed them on the desk, so she seemed to be nearing some conclusion.

"Just a word about the different bindings. Always begin with an ambition to sell the most expensive. It is the most beautiful and the best (and of course you know you are making more money for yourself as well as your company when you sell the most expensive binding). So take it for granted that she will want the most expensive binding. If you see you are failing, come down to the cheaper, and only at the last, the cheapest of all. That is better than nothing. If you see she never had any intention of taking anything else, you might even add, in the interest of selling, that you find her very wise."

Miss Fulton ended the first lesson with the advice to sleep with the Bible on a table beside us and the sales talk under our pillow, for she said: "But never forget the motto of our company—Service, service to others. We all know that we are not only helping ourselves and the company in placing *Universal Education* in all American homes, but we are making the customer do what we know is good for her. We are spreading the light of knowledge and a true foundation of good Christian character."

I began to understand better and better the seemingly divided policies of Western missionaries and Western business men. It all depended on which side you were on, the salesman or the customer, to get the rightness of this point of view.

5

The park which Mr. Lively boasted of as his back yard was very large, with streams and a small lake, woods, paths, and wild flowers. Of course it was open to the public as well as to the Livelys. One Sunday afternoon while I was walking there, I was much surprised to see George Jum coming toward me with his usual demure grin, and June beside him. George had dropped some hints in a letter that he might be coming to Boston, as June had a dancing engagement there. But I was unprepared to meet him quite so soon. We took a walk together around the park and George pointed out some nice nooks. He said next time he would bring a clean sheet to spread out on the grass, so no grass stains would spoil June's white dress, and there they could sit or snooze and be comfortable. I felt slightly embarrassed until I remembered that it really wasn't Mr. Lively's back yard. We stopped before the Lively house for a moment and shook hands all around, but Jum refused to come in and meet my benefactors, as June had to get back to town for some engagement. He promised to come again at the earliest opportunity, however, and as George and June moved off arm in arm and very chummy, I looked up and saw Mrs. Lively peering at them out of one of the upstairs windows. Mrs. Lively promptly asked me about them. I told her it was my friend from New York and his fiancée, and did not understand why she still appeared so shocked. But her mouth closed tight and she said nothing.

Next day George came out alone, and spent some time in my room with me. He wanted to take me back with him to Boston, so I told Mrs. Lively I was going away for dinner. Again she said nothing, though I thought her expression looked somewhat surprised and aggrieved. In Boston after an early dinner we went to see June dance in one of the vaudeville circuits, with a Boston Korean in business there, who owned a car. Afterwards we got June and took an automobile drive. George urged me to come to New York for a visit and I thought it was a good idea. I had intended to come all along before settling down for the winter. He had to get another job and couldn't do much for me, but I could stay at Mrs. Flo's in his room and read his books. What decided me was that the Korean who owned a car was ready to drive us all back to New York. I got back to the Livelys' very late that night—or rather, in the small hours of the morning. The Livelys had given me a key, and I went up very quietly. But next morning when I came down, Mrs. Lively put her handkerchief to her eyes and whenever she looked at me, she sniffed, with deep reproachful sighs. I was mystified, but began to make out that my fault was being away since yesterday afternoon. When Mr. Lively came, he said as much. I had left Mother with all those dishes to do. I seemed the combination of prodigal son and erring housemaid. There seemed to me no legal grounds for this. Nothing had been said about my having a job at the Livelys and no money had passed between us, except my ten dollars for the prospectus. And still the faultfinding was not over. After Mr. Lively was through, Mrs. Lively came to me alone, and bravely winking back the tears, she complained, "How is it? Daddy and I have been so wonderful to you, yet you cannot have any gratitude for us. This is very bad taste in you." I did not know what to say. So I said nothing. My silence inspired her to say more. I had not only been out too late the night before, I had been out with that bad Korean boy. Neither Mr. Lively nor Mrs. Lively, I found, had any use for George.

"You ought not to associate with such a boy as that, Chungpa—a boy who smokes, drinks, swears. You are a good Christian boy. You have been taken into a good Christian family and treated like a son here. And I am sure that boy is not a good Christian boy."

I could not truthfully say that George was. Of course, he had been very wonderful to me. However, his charity was not of their kind. I saw no way of making them understand each other. It was plain that George and Mrs. Lively ought never to have met, as being totally incompatible. To say nothing of June, the boneless dancer.

"George is Americanized," I said. "Most Koreans are not like that. My friend has not much education, but he has a good heart."

Mrs. Lively added at this point that she didn't approve of my friend's attitude toward girls. I wondered where she could have learned so much about him. Then I realized that when George was in my room talking, Mrs. Lively must have overheard. The anecdote George had been telling was entirely innocent, though perhaps George had made it sound otherwise. He had gone to call on a Korean girl who lived in a girls' dormitory in Boston. This was like George, who was always very sociable. She was at least forty years old and very serious, a sincere Christian studying to go back to Korea and work there with the missionaries. George's interest had been purely that of a compatriot. But because there was a rule on the wall saying that lights must not be switched on and off by the girls entertaining visitors, and that curtains of the alcove where they sat must not be drawn, George had amused himself by doing both. He spoke with great contempt of an institution with such rules on walls. Mrs. Lively had overheard some of this, for now she said:

"It's all right for a boy to go with girls—not many; but with all girls you should speak decently, act nicely. When you visit a girl, you must always have somebody around. And always the door should be opened wide—so older people can see what is going on in there and certainly there should be a *light* in that room !"

George had not sold himself to Mrs. Lively. I saw that he had left a very bad impression.

"And I can tell you," she burst out again, "it is not wise for an Oriental boy to go round with an American girl. He should marry his own kind, and she should marry hers."

Elsie had followed us into the library and was listening to all this.

"Oh-h!" she cried, her mouth wide open in surprise. "Mother, if a Chinaman marries an American girl, what kind of baby would they have?" Elsie giggled. "Mother, wouldn't that be funny? I should like to see it."

Mrs. Lively went off at once and talked the whole thing over with Mr. Lively. Then Mr. Lively, too, had something more to say. With eyes unusually round and staring and face excited as when I had taken the wheel of the Cadillac car, Mr. Lively told me, "My dear boy, see here, I love you just as much as if you were my own boy. But you are getting wrong ideas. I don't want to see you marry an American girl. Neither would I want to see Elsie marrying an Oriental. And all decent people are like that. It is not as the Lord intended."

I was very solemn and silent and unable to open my mouth to say anything.

BOOK FOUR

1

AGAIN I HAD the Great City to wander in. Again I breathed the air of the Machine Age. Again I was buffeted by the waves of an amorphous tide, a tide of such confused racial components that it became traditionless, new, almost naive, ready for anything, with confused unlimited potentialities both of good and bad. I never entered New York without feeling that anything might happen here.

One of my favorite routes was along Broadway around 42nd Street where Broadway is democratic, not to say vulgar. But it has New York personality, plenty of it, and its own individuality. "What a sight!" I kept thinking. "Is it not the greatest pageant in the history of the world?" Pedestrians tried to cut in the way automobiles did, and I tried the same, pretending I was in some awful hurry. "Watch the red, when crossing, if you want to enjoy that chop-suey tonight," the policeman called to me with a broad grin. He, too, felt at one with his crowds; he breathed, was a part with the seething mass, of good and bad, and hell and heaven and limbo—mostly limbo. And my mind raced on. Yes, you have to measure your distance carefully here, even if you have no dinner tonight. Just to talk takes every effort and faculty. A training in itself. It doesn't pay to try to cut in. Least resistance is to walk straight. Let me try to be in the American line....

And all the while, revolving the experiences of the past year, I was soliloquizing inside myself somewhat like this:

"To be a New Yorker among New Yorkers means a totally new experience from being Japanese or Chinese or Korean—a changed character. New Yorkers all seem to have some aim in every movement they make. (Some frantic aim.) They are like guns shooting off. How unlike Asiatics in an Oriental village, who drift up and down aimlessly and leisurely! But these people have no time, even for gossiping, even for staring. To be thrown among New Yorkers—yes, it means to have a new interpretation of life never conceived before. The business interpretation. Even the man who only goes to a show and is making arrangements about it has a business air. His every action decisive, orderly, purposeful...he must know exactly what he wants to do in his mind. Just to move in New York and not be ploughed under, man must prevision and plan out. Free, factual, man is reasoning from cause to effect here all the time—not so much thinking. It is intelligence measuring, rather than intellect's solution. Prophets of hereafter, poets of vision...maybe the American is not so much these. But he is a good salesman, amidst scientific tools. His mind is like Grand Central Station. It is definite, it is timed, it has mathematical precision on clearcut stone foundation. There may be monotonous dull repetition, but all is accurate and conscious. Stupid routine sometimes, but behind it, duty in the very look. Every angle and line has been measured. How solid the steel frame-work of this Western civilization is!"

2

And yet I was soon to meet a man who was to challenge my complacent view of America and the civilization I was so eager to learn from. That very evening, I went alone to Chinatown, to treat myself to some dinner. I had no sooner entered my favorite restaurant than I recognized the man sitting in the corner. In fact, he was sitting at the very same table where I had seen him a year before, a well-dressed, refined-looking Oriental, with thoughtful face and interesting features. He was alone, and I got a sense of immense solitariness in his cool aloofness, and in his dark, melancholy gaze. I met his eyes and I bowed to him, as I saw a look of recognition flash into them. For some reason, as I had remembered him, so he, too, remembered me. He came over at once to my table and sat down.

"How do you do?" he said, in a refined and careful English, with a smile which warmed his rather somber and reserved face. "I have not seen you here for a long time."

"You are a Korean?"

"I was...but I have been away so long I do not feel one any longer."

"But you will be going back...."

(All Koreans with incomes returned to the homeland, I thought, in spite of the difficulties there.)

"I don't think so."

"You like it here?"

"No," he hesitated. "I can't tell where this civilization is going. Can you?"

"Korea may soon be freed from the Japanese," I said for argument's sake. "You would go back then...wouldn't you?"

"What's freedom?" he asked quickly. "No one is free. We are all chained."

Then he asked me how I liked it. I replied in a flood of words, in which I tried to tell of my pursuit of life, life, more abundant life, and my feeling that America was the country of the present and the near future.

"You have arrived much prejudiced in favor of New York City.... I wonder why?"

"I may be said to have smelled it many miles away," I boasted, "like the cedars of the Palace Peh Liang T'ai, as the legend tells."

"I would say it was more like Si Yuan," he replied promptly. "Pleasure resort of the tyrant Yang Ti, where when life went, the trees were decked out in artificial leaves of silk.... And why did you think life would be here, instead of on the European continent? When I was leaving, most serious students went to Europe."

"Yes. When I was leaving, too. But I always wanted to come to America."

"I went to Europe. I was in Europe for twelve years."

"Do you think I would like Europe better?"

"No…. Still, Europeans are more like Orientals. The hysterical shouts of the people here get on my nerves. But the West is much the same everywhere. Everywhere troubled and uncertain. Very much like Asia. Educated people everywhere no longer believe much in their own culture, religion, or civilization."

"Well—New York gets me! Here I do not feel that hopelessness you speak of. Here you can think anything, see anything, learn anything! I feel like the men of Chinling marching into the capital…."

(I referred to a Chinese classical poem:

> Changnan is a beautiful place!
> Chinling is a majestic city!
> On and on waddle the green waters,
> And up rise the vermilion towers.
> Flying gables lean over the riding path:
> Weeping willows shadow the imperial canals.
> By tall canopies the solemn bugle shrills:
> Repeating drums speed off the flowery carriages.
> The great shall be in the Hall of Fame,
> And the hero reap every deserving reward.

And of course I wrote on the menu—the only paper there—certain characters of my quotation.)

He looked at those quaint, beautiful signs dubiously.

"You are a funny fellow. You can't like New York—and this at the same time!"

"Why not?"

He laughed. For a moment he said nothing. I watched him lift the clumsy, thick cup filled with ordinary Chinatown tea, in his graceful hand, a hand which, compared to the Western man's, looked more flowing, more supple, yet also more anciently formed as if whittled to the bone and seasoned before he was born. It was a hand built for deft Korean chopsticks and the slender brush pen, a hand never to be entirely at home in the West, I thought. I glanced at my own hands: they were broad and square, padded firmly and thick, the hands of some archaic generation close to the antique plough, though my dear dead grandmother had scrupulously kept me away from all these practical things, cultivating the scholar...still, in spite of her, my hands looked like those of a person of action, his far removed from any activity—except that of the lightning-stroked pen.

Then he, too, took the menu and covered it with lines of characters, saying as he handed them to me, "Of course, we both know this is a kind of madness." But an eager look of understanding and sympathy passed between us, and we wrote back and forth, one quotation suggesting another. He showed me many I had never heard, gems from lesser-known poets of the great Tang and Sung dynasties, metaphysical poems of Taoist poets hard to understand, rare lines from the great masters which until now had escaped my notice. One or two poems I fancied were the stranger's own—couched in the same bold antique characters, spontaneous, alive as the characters of a master calligrapher, these had a somewhat wider span in time, an application to the occasion and our meeting as if composed on the spur of the moment. In my childhood, before I had realized the passing of the old Korean order, I had dreamed of meeting learned gentlemen like this in the capital of Seoul, of passing my days in the joyous communion of ancient scholarship with brilliant minds like his. How times can change! We had come half way around the world to meet in New York's slumlike Chinatown. And though we abandoned ourselves irresistibly to the old poetry, it seemed almost with a sense of shame. More than once, too, it crossed my mind that I was wasting time. This was not what I must learn from him. For he gave the impression of one who had soaked in the complexities of Western civilization.

It grew late. Chinese customers, a few Americans, thronged in to eat. The place grew hot with fumes and steam. The garish Chinese-American electrical lighting was the last possible extreme from an emperor's golden candelabra used to light poets home through dim and tinkling streets, past overhanging gables and curious towers, as mentioned in the ancient Chinese poetry. We had harked back to a spiritual realm more remote from New York than the world of Horace or Catullus. My companion looked around, disturbed. "The wrong smell for poetry is here. Come to my place. There we can talk."

3

Outside the restaurant a heavy rain like black ink was pouring. Like beetles called up by the rain, the shiny taxis twisted and turned cumbrously, seemed bound to collide in their narrow quarters. These dim light-splashed allies, as sinuous as dragon tails, clanked and honked hideously. My host hailed a taxi. Very luxurious it appeared to me. We sank back in deep upholstered cushions. I stared at the thick tasselled rope to hold by, the built-in tray for the cigarette, as with a swift slicing movement, far different from swaying sedan or white mule chariot, the car churred through the slanting black night rain.

"This is the Village," said my new-found friend with a laugh, as the taxi stopped. "But it has neither mountain nor stream." And he quoted ironically, "If a home has not a garden and an old tree, I see not whence the every-day joys of life are to come!... Mine has neither garden nor old tree... but village...cozy name, *ne*?"

This section was very dark and secret-looking. You could not decide if it were merely informal or only a slum. The shadows here were blue and silent. That street lamp far away was pale. There were many big studio windows in neighboring houses, some with a muffled beam of low lights behind drawn curtains rough and fantastic. And outside on the streets dejected cats and ash cans. Going down instead of up, we stepped into a narrow hall lit by a dim electric lantern. "I live on the second floor." We went up soft-carpeted stairs. On the white door before us was a place for a card. I read in simple engraving: TO WAN KIM. "Is it a nom-de-plume?" I asked.

The words in Korean had a very mysterious sound. To Wan means "Garden Isle," but this, by Asian connotation, suggested at once some dreamy subjective realm far removed from life—such as "Castles in Spain."

"It is a name proper to a Korean ghost," he said. "Enter."

He unlocked the door and we stood in a small foyer painted in a clear Chinese red, the molding in white. It contained nothing but a modernistic mirror on the wall and a stand with an umbrella and a few continental canes. He showed me into another room. The room itself was not large, but most compactly arranged. The furniture was low, modernistic. But he had an old bronze Chinese bowl and a vase of antique Korean pottery, the latter a considerable art treasure. In a narrow rectangular black vase a glistening lily, its golden stamens moist with bright yellow pollen, suggested his love of perfection, and the Oriental's preference for one flower over many. Its fragrance wafted through the room, anachronistic to the early autumn rain outside. But it made the room seem further isolated, exotic, unreal, with a hint of the artificiality of New York. The streamlined utility of all the furniture gave out a pleasing repose and a sort of dreaminess, in hybrid adaptation to the strange creature it harbored. A cozy hearth invited one to sit in a low rough-fabricked chair and take out a near-by book. I saw brass andirons and all sorts of tools for kindling and keeping a wood fire. But most attractive to my sight were the high bookcases which seemed to fill the room, and were its keynote.

When Mr. Kim left for a moment, I examined the titles of books. About equally mixed, Eastern and Western, I noted with approval. I went to the Eastern books first. And they might have been those of my poet uncle, though not so primitively bound. Several rare books were there, which my uncle had never fingered—no, not in all his journeys to China, nor into the most scholarly provinces of Korea. There was also a modern section from contemporary Korea, China, and Japan, the chaotic unmade new literature, which seemed to have exhausted inspiration by its wild leap into novelty, into borrowed modes. I turned to the Western books and was slightly puzzled. Late books, esoteric, far removed from Maritime College or even the interest of George. Then whole shelves of English poets, many of whose names at least I knew. And not only English. I saw German and French, Italian and Spanish, and in small sober Oxford bindings, Latin and Greek. There were also a number of books on art, both Eastern and Western, among them bound facsimiles of Korean paintings, a portfolio of seventh-

and eighth-century things, and another of the fifteenth and sixteenth.

Mr. Kim returned, bringing a black glass tray and some black glasses filled with ice. He asked me what I would drink. I had no taste for American liquors at that time. I said, "Do you have ginger ale?"

"Surely. I see you are not yet baptized into American drink and it's just as well."

I put back, reluctantly, the rare portfolios containing examples of an art which I myself had never seen. Again I glanced curiously around the room. Three pictures were hung on the light clear walls…all Oriental, but each, I thought, of a different culture. That one of cats was plainly Japanese …the black pine branch painted on silk was Korean, and the landscape triptych on bamboo—that was probably Chinese. The contents of the room were evidently very carefully assembled by one of some means, one acutely sensitive to mood and surroundings…even that lampshade, of a fine raw silk which lent itself well to the Chinese brush—both to the heavy powerful strokes and the soft delicate musical ones like rain or drifting wind.

Mr. Kim came back with bottles. I still was looking earnestly at the lamp. "That is good writing." I referred to the decorative calligraphy on one side, which, roughly translated, read, "The Exile, Man." The other faces of the lamp showed black brush drawings, fish, pines, a world of wind and water, a lonely boat, with that vital fine economy from the Orient which inspired Whistler. "The drawing too. That is excellent!"

My host said nothing. He placed before me ginger ale. He sank into a chair and raised his glass. He, I saw, was drinking something different.

"What is American drink?"

"Gin." He lighted the fire already laid. No heat comes on in apartments at this time, and the evening was slightly chill. "Gin." Then he said deliberately, pointing to the lampshade, "You like it? Yes, I designed that. And my own textiles…. Wait…. Here are more by the same hand." He opened a drawer and brought out rolls of silk, which I undid one by one. They contained his signatures, the delicate characters—three—for To Wan Kim.

4

We talked until the fire sank down to ashes. I had met in Kim a deep and reflective modernized mind, mature now, while mine was just beginning to stretch—but in his art he was a rigid traditionalist, untouched by any Western influence. He used the tools, the technique of a thousand years ago, in line with those poet-painters who held that characters were paintings, and paintings the decorative accompaniment to literature...symbolic strokes so closely joined to picture-words (and the words themselves set in ancient classical molds as rich and stiff and jewelled as the Elizabethan sonnet) that neither was complete without the other. Here in New York, divorced from other poets of his kind, Kim's classical artistic life went on as if in a vacuum. It was a curious revelation. He was in mood and outlook probably of the Oriental generation just preceding mine, but even then the classics were being discarded. Kim was tragically aware of this. When I spoke my admiration—my sincere admiration for remarkable work—he replied brusquely and with a scathing irony:

"Why? You and I know that such writing—unlike the worthier phonetic systems—retards the progress of man. It should have died out long ago like Egyptian hieroglyphics. Why doesn't it die out in me? Is it because I studied only Chinese classics when I was young? Is this the reason my brain is alive with this script rooted in the history of Asia and the dim past of man? How absurd! What incredible childishness! With seventeen flying brush-strokes to make with such care that monosyllabic sound—Lung—meaning dragon! Then with what fine glow and fondness the calligrapher looks at his work! And there is no dragon, any more than an angel or devil. How can man waste his brains on such a thing?"

"I don't feel it is wasted when I see such work as yours!" I said honestly.

"But who cares for such stuff nowadays? The old literary language is doomed. Or it is clear that if the Chinese keep on learning their classical systems, they will have no time to fight with the Japanese. And then there will be no more China and no more Chinese. Chinese of original minds nowadays all turn to write in the Pei-hua. Much is to be said for the able emperor Shi Whang Ti who ordered all classical books to be burned." He seemed to want to change the subject.

He asked me again about myself. As I told him more concerning my escape to America, he nodded. "Yes, you and I both come from conservative pre-Christian families. My father has been more indulgent…or is it that he has many other sons? In you I see myself some fifteen years ago."

He was much interested in my desire to go to college in Boston that coming winter. He knew something of Boston. In Boston he had taken a post-graduate degree in philosophy he said. But he spoke in ironic belittling manner of American civilization there as elsewhere.

"You will study a little of everything and not much of anything, and you will have no time to think until you come out. The educational method is that of acquiring superficial factual knowledge. Ranging and shallow, rather than searching and deep. It is just like going into a New York subway. They try to educate too many. You can see the same in the Dearborn assembling plants: It is the business method. It works to turn out Fords…but not to turn out scholars. A dry, mechanical, tedious atmosphere! Most of the college boys go to college not because they want it, but because there is nothing better to do at this age. If they found something better, certainly they would do it. But then they are like their teachers, who only hold the job till something better turns up. It is merry-go-round. Teachers and boys—both drag themselves into lecture halls with artificial show of interest. You will find it is sham. The teacher gets his job by the rubber stamp, not by what he really knows or how well he can teach. And the students graduate by credit hours and not by their mastery over anything. No wonder the scholar's high position in the Orient is reversed in this country. Here you will find he is despised and mocked."

"Well, it seems I can do nothing until I go to college and learn something," I complained. "Not even cooking or waiting or dishwashing. When I get out of college, then I may begin to master American civilization, American culture."

"You think it is worth mastering?" Kim laughed. He set down his glass. He raked out the dying coals of wood in the grate. "Come on. We will go to the party. I will show you some American culture. Tonight."

5

We did not need to walk very far. "The party" seemed to be just down the street. We rang and walked up many steep flights of stairs. A tall, young American man, with tortoise-shell glasses, face flushed and hair touselled— still plainly an intellectual type, I thought—was standing on the top landing, swaying toward us in a friendly way. He seemed very frank, very informal, very nice. That drink made his speech rather fast and foolish, though. He led us into a studio apartment.

At first it seemed as if all the noises of Broadway were enclosed in that room. From time to time there were raps from overhead and underneath as well, from irate fellow lodgers. The ceiling was somewhat crooked, like the streets outside, and a big skylight sloped down. On the walls were the oddest of paintings, looking crooked also. It was in the days when every drawing of a certain style seemed slightly distorted. In mood, however, all seemed to chime in well with a pair of African idols in gleaming black wood trimmed rather obscenely with shells. Our host, whose name was Bill, with drunken solemnity introduced them to me as "the eternal and primeval Ma" and "Pa." The room looked rather bare, for furniture had been moved out, rugs taken up for dancing, and chairs stationed against the wall. Toward one end of the big room was a long table with all kinds of drinks…different sizes of bottles with different colored labels. Everybody was to help himself and anybody who knew how mixed some new kind of drink. To one side was a grand piano and here one of the men was banging jazz, which never stopped as long as I was there. When that man grew tired or needed more drink, another took his place. It might have been some kind of temple in which to worship African jazz. But this jazz was not so lazy, deep and blue as some jazz I had heard; it was hard, staccato, sounding mechanized and artificial. We sat down near the table.

Somebody gave me a drink. I tasted it and shuddered. It didn't seem possible to drink that. Kim was already on his second glass, besides what he had taken at his own fireside. So he seemed to like it all right. But it did not have the same effect on him as on the others. Drinking, they became like little kids.

One young fellow when first I looked was on the floor turning somersaults, and next he was lying on his back with a banjo on his stomach, playing, and with his lips singing a different tune. This young fellow maintained that he was a Yale man—but never went to Yale. He boasted how he had the choice between going to Yale and going to Paris and he chose Paris, which he said he never regretted. He said he knew the Yale yell. Now, with his drunken body, he stood up and, getting one man and two girls, he made a ring, his own arm on the man's shoulder, his other on the girl's, and his forehead against the girl opposite, sounding out the Yale yell.

Brek ek ek ex
Koak koax
Brek ek ek ex
Koak koax
O-op parabaloo
Yale! Yale! Yale!

"Oh God!" said a man beside me, in tones of loud disgust, looking at his neighbors. "I ask you! I am going to Paris from Yale; he is coming to Yale from Paris. William Wilson! Isn't this terrible?"

"Perhaps the influence of dadaism?" spoke up a sardonic slight young man with pointed eyebrows.

"He never heard of it."

"I haven't either," said a thin childlike young girl with a soft voice.

"Sally, you don't need to.... It comes natural."

"He behaves too adolescently to understand dadaism where one tries to get back to the mental age of four," drawled a tall black boy, gracefully draped on a straight chair and speaking with an Oxford accent.

"I want to dance," said Sally plaintively. She rose. "But don't you like it?" she pointed to my glass, in much the same way as you would in asking a child, "What! not like ice-cream?" She had a piquant face and big brown serious eyes which she blinked and focused carefully to see me better—for I imagine that her head was going round.

"Come on, Sally, I'll dance," interrupted a taller girl, with spectacles and a pompadour of bright red hair cut in a boyish bob.

"Wait.... I want to see" (to me) "—what's-your-name—is happy?"

"He just came over, he hasn't acquired the taste for American drink," Kim said, as he changed my glass for purest ginger ale. "He is here to make research..." he smiled, with a light flicker of the eyes indicating that room and the party, "I brought him here to show him some Western civilization...."

"He is studying Western civilization?... Ha ha!" giggled the girls, "Hahaha...how cute!"

"You have read Spengler?" asked the taller girl, sententiously. "*Der Untergang des Abendlandes?*"

Kim nodded.

"And what do you think?"

But the softer and more groggy young lady, Sally, clinging to her friend, was already pulling her on. Now they came to a halt before the young Negro.

"You don't look so happy either, Alfred. Aw, come, cheer up," Sally pleaded in a coaxing drunken lisp, "Why don't you be happy, Alfred? I want everybody to be happy at Bill's party."

"Can't I be happy and keep still?" he answered with a too sober smile.

"No—you have to a-a-act like a child to be happy. Throw away in-in-in-hibitions. D-dance and sing—and be-be a Negro."

"Sally, you're drunk!" laughed her friend, dragging her on. They waltzed around the outskirts of the bare space in the center, where many others already were dancing, singly or in twos and threes. Now another girl seized the stage. All the rest dropped out to clap her. The man at the piano, half-turning round to look, also played the jazz louder and with more accent to encourage. She was large, tall and well formed. Rouge stood out in pirouette circles on her cheeks, and her mouth was painted like a poppy. She must have been completely drunk, but the drink helped her to make that kind of dance-step better. There seemed no muscle that she did not use, especially hips. I considered the difference between her and the Korean geisha girl, who is very slow and sedate, with a long skirt. This girl was good, so they all said, clapping and beating time. She almost equalled the masters of this dance up in Harlem.

Kim lifted his glass only once in a while now. His face was flushed and his eyes shone across at me in some kind of sarcastic humor. But he kept his own counsel and spoke only when spoken to. I gathered that he was well known in this group and a privileged character, without having ever been truly known. In becoming Americanized, Kim was not so frank as George. Kim, the black boy and I seemed the only quiet members of the party. The young Negro drank little and in all things, including dress and speech, seemed more formal than the rest, more like a foreigner. Doubtless he drank more, I concluded, up in Harlem. Or else the "zeitgeist" for his race was something different from jazz and freedom and Africanism. I turned to listen with interest to him speaking.

"Obscene? Oh, no. I don't see anything obscene about them *per se*," he was saying to his white neighbor, nodding coolly toward the African idols. "Not in their own jungle shrine, certainly. Obscenity is really relative...."

"How's the master?" one young man spoke to Kim with real enthusiasm about his work, "I'm going over and see some more of your brushwork soon. May I?"

They began to talk about recent exhibitions in New York art galleries. I heard the names, Matisse, Cézanne. Symbolism; and "Significant Form"; Millay, Eugene O'Neill, and Katharine Mansfield.

Platters of meat, cheese, olives, hors d'oeuvres, were brought in for guests to help themselves (those who were not being sick in the bathroom or bedroom by now). The Yale man who wasn't a Yale man created a real sensation. He had been out in the kitchen helping and had taken his own hand for part of a roast to be cut. It was really a serious wound, they said, and he was hustled off to a doctor around the corner.

We got up to go. Bill was very nice. He was full of cordiality to me just because I had come there with Kim. When we came out, my head was spinning, as if I too had drunk a lot. Strange to find air not thick with cigarette smoke.

"How did you like the poet-scholars of America?" Kim was saying.

"Are they really the poet-scholars? Those—little boys and girls?"

"All behave like that. So who can say? And the greater are even worse. In this country, in this age, art becomes the instinct for self-advertisement."

We walked back to Kim's apartment. And Kim spoke still more on the same subject: "Americans are said to be only a young race. Nobody claims that they are very superior yet. But I call these particular friends of mine 'the pygmies.' There is a fascination in watching them. (That is why I once wanted to go to the Congo....) They all work hard to give a book or painting—some piece of art—to the world, to get renown and notoriety. In thousands of studios over the city tonight you could see them...for there are many more of this same kind—more than all the students in New York University or Columbia, which have their ten thousands.... Hordes and hordes...the twentieth-century poets and artists of America.... I should say they are gnats rather than pygmies. Yes, gnats. Then I must be the ass...to be annoyed. Gnats always come swarming around an ass. He kicks; they fly. A silly way of doing—there are so many gnats in the world, an ass could never escape...." (I thought he did not like his Village neighbors very much.) "But Oriental poets and artists were never like these...it is a different species."

"We do not come to the West for poetry," I hinted, "but for man's new way of mastering Nature. With the scientific outlook, man gains more success...."

"Science has destroyed diseases and superstitions and sent away mysticism...that is true. It has improved the material condition of human life. But even so, I see the soul everywhere is sunk in melancholy discontentment.... Man is no happier, as he loses mystery.... Where now is the old magic, which, as legend tells, transported even dogs and chickens to heaven by a draft from Lao Tze's cup? Once man felt about himself and all the creatures a Wordsworthian glow of immortality."

"You have been in the West for sixteen years and you see nothing to it?" I exclaimed incredulously.

"Nothing to root man, nothing to anchor him.... I have not been idle. For sixteen years I have wrestled, in Germany, Italy, France, England, America, leading myself into a Kantian labyrinth, into an Hegelian logomachy, into a scholastic inferno (yet not through any Protestantism nor Catholicism), into the geometric abstractions of Einstein...and I can find nothing."

I felt subdued and saddened to hear these words from a man I admired so much. The dawn was lightening over the Village, but it now brought sagging and depression. We still stood before Kim's apartment house, while Kim concluded in serious and earnest tones:

"You and I came to the West to find a new beauty, a new life, a new religion. But is there any? Alas! we have come at the wrong time. It is too late. Too late to be saved by Dante's Beatrice, too late to love like Shakespeare in the sonnets, too late to be with Shelley a Plato-republican, too late even to be a Browning individualist or a Tennysonian sentimentalist. The next act is unnamed—"

"Napoleon in hell?" I suggested.

Kim smiled. "Well, I have nothing to do with Napoleon...in former life I was an Eastern poet...but tell me, what now is to be our fate? being unable to go back to that previous existence, being unable to label ourselves in this new world...becoming lost within another lost world?" He held out his hand. "Good night. Good luck!"

BOOK FIVE

1

ARRIVING IN BOSTON on a beautiful September day, I immediately engaged a room on Trowbridge Street for $1.50 a week. It was a little attic room with not much in it but a large double iron bed which took up about all the space. And it was very uncomfortable besides, as I found out that night...being lumpy and uneven...and I had to be very careful to choose the region in it where I lay, or when I got up in the morning too eagerly, I would hit the ceiling a star-raising blow with my head. It only remained to get some kind of scholarship in the University and to start out to earn my way through college by expert salesmanship in between intervals of studying.

Mr. Lively drew up a handsome contract for me. I was overwhelmed when I read that. It was not like business at all, but was testimony to my outstanding abilities in studies and to my Christian character, adding in a special clause that I did not drink or smoke. And it summed up the whole situation, too, how I was working my way through college. Something there encouraged me considerably—it said that Mr. Lively's company intended to give me a free scholarship if I could sell the minimum requirement. I had not known of that.

"Now, my boy, if you have any difficulty in selling," said Mr. Lively heartily, "just show the customer your contract. Don't be bashful. Make him read this. And say, 'Just one more order, please. It will help me so much!'... Wait a minute. That necktie won't do. I'm glad, my lad, you're not a dandy, but that tie looks like a string!" He opened the long box which was in his office and was, when closed, just like a seat. I saw it was filled with neckties, handkerchiefs, and all sorts of accessories. He selected a quiet, but vigorous-looking tie, and taking my own off, threw it into the waste basket. "There. That shows more Christian neatness. Look the part. Have faith. And remember," said Mr. Lively, "speak the speech...." (It was the only quotation that he knew from Shakespeare. Whenever I mentioned Shakespeare to Mr. Lively, he always gave me that. "Speak the speech....")

2

I received word in Mr. Lively's office that Kim had come to Boston at this time. I found him stopping in the Copley Square Hotel.

"You seem comfortable, here," I said, looking around the neat dark bedroom with its easy chairs and spacious writing desk.

"Yes, but I chose it for the Boston atmosphere," said Kim, "not for the comfort." And he pointed out to me the buildings around the hotel, the romanesque-styled granite church with its dark sandstone trimmings, that other church, New South Church in Italian Gothic style, and the gray stone public library which Kim said was Italian Renaissance built to resemble a Florentine palace. Then the college buildings of Boston University all around. "So you see all of Boston is represented here. The churches show the religious side. (They are very exclusive. As in some religious orders of Tibet.) The colleges stand for the educational aspect. And this hotel, staid and substantial, is the dignified commercial side."

He asked me what I thought of Boston. I hesitated. "There seems to be an intellectual breathing all over." (I did not add, except where Mr. Lively was concerned. Though even he appeared to approve Shakespeare.)

"Yes, here one is conscious of morals and dignity, as if a copy of *The Evening Transcript* were in everybody's overcoat pocket."

"And sharper air is here, under a bluer, radiant sky.... September wind and autumn sun are equally piercing...but so far the air does not intoxicate me so as to absorb me in it. Not like New York. It must be a sectional patriotism for Boston that I lack."

Kim laughed. But he insisted that it was an interesting city. "Not very genial perhaps.... This is the land of Puritanism which only three hundred years ago was engaged in hanging old women for witches and torturing little children by telling them to confess their faith and so be saved from the devil and the flames in hell."

He paused to point out the more enlightened example of the Chinese, as expressed in the Ch'un Ch'iu or Spring-and-Autumn Annals, concerning customs from the year 722 to 484 B.C.

"Do you remember? A certain duke wished to burn a witch as causing a great drought, but his ministers would not allow him, saying, 'What have witches to do with the matter? If Heaven wishes her to be killed, it would have been better not to allow her to be born. If she can cause a drought, burning her will only make things worse.' "

Nonetheless Boston seemed to have some kind of fascination for Kim. "If there is any true dignity and sincerity in American democracy one would expect to find it here, where people once would die for their ideals. It is like Peking—guarded by invisible traditions. All except Bostonian natives are foreign here, you know. But now we will go to see some of the representatives of education."

Kim took me to call on a professor on Kirkland Street, Doctor Alexander Campbell.

"I suppose he is almost a native now. He came here as a young man to deliver the commemoration address on the death of Tennyson in 1892. He liked this country so well, he said he would like to stay. When a young man, he used to write poetry, which has appeared recently in *The Boston Transcript* and in other periodicals. Now he does not write much poetry, for he believes that when a man is young, he writes poetry. In Boston, a man becomes older, and soon a philosopher. But in Professor Campbell, you will find one of the best professors Boston has. He is all made of blood-jumping Utopian stuff."

We went to one of those quiet-looking houses on Kirkland Street. Kim had previously called up, and Doctor Campbell himself answered the door. He took us into a room with a big brick fireplace, a room lined with books. It was lighter here than in the hall, and I could see a tall, slender man, as fiery as Mercutio in his look, and with hair the blackest of the black—a little bald on top it was, but combed over from the side. He had a small black moustache and brilliant, fire-darting, black eyes. For the rest, he was very lean, with lean white fingers and a lean, impulsive jaw. I liked him from the start.

He settled us in comfortable chairs, took a cigar and offered another to Kim.

"I think you are a little young to smoke, eh?" he said to me. "Cigars, at least."

I said I did not smoke.

"Neither does my boy. My boy's seventeen."

"He's already a college instructor though," Kim said to me. "Isn't that so, Professor Campbell? The youngest instructor in the University, if I am not mistaken."

"Yes, yes. The youngest instructor, so I understand. But then he has big feet. He has such big feet, he had to do something, and big feet are just the thing for standing on in a classroom."

"Well, this young man was an instructor at sixteen," Kim said, pointing to me. "He taught Japanese. He also taught mathematics."

"Well, well, you don't say. That's very extraordinary!"

Then Professor Campbell told of his respect for the Oriental students he had had, and of his lifelong admiration for Lafcadio Hearn. Hearn, as I was to find out in his course later, was one of Doctor Campbell's great enthusiasms.

"Altogether," the professor told us, "you mustn't be surprised to see me become a Buddhist any day. I already have a Buddha," and he pointed to it in one corner of his room.

Now a neat and quiet maid brought in the tea tray, and Doctor

Campbell poured tea; and into his own cup and into Kim's he put something out of a bottle that he said was rum. "I like it," he said. "I'm very bad. I like to drink and to smoke—and to swear." But to me he gave plain tea.

"Mr. Kim tells me you are from Edinburgh, Doctor Campbell," I said.

"Oh yes, but that was very long ago. I came here, met Mrs. Campbell—she comes from Canada—and here I settled down. America is my home."

Next day Kim made an engagement for us to lunch with another professor whom he said it was very important for me to see, as Doctor John Lewis Wellington was on the committee for giving university scholarships. He lived in Wellesley Farms, which was in the very region to be monopolized according to the contract drawn up by the Universal Education Company with me. So when I jumped out of bed in the morning—as usual cracking my head—it was to reach for my harness with my clothes. (I had made up my mind that after lunch I would start out to make some money for the coming year.) As I dressed, I realized for the first time what a neat little invention Mr. Lively's was, for carrying the prospectus. With it, I could start out as a salesman and still be disguised. Each of his salesmen had been outfitted with one of these. It was a kind of sling which strapped to the vest and hung down between the arm and the side. There were two pockets, one for the sales form, one for the prospectus, and both slipped in and out with maximum ease. Thus equipped, I started my double life of scholarship and business that morning.

We rode on the train and got off in a white, shining village, typical of this part of New England, where some Utopian university atmosphere seemed to penetrate. No dirt, no hidden evils anywhere, no slums. There were winding village streets and many branching trees, mostly elms. In general, houses were of two styles—white frame, simple and staunch, with tidy lawns and white picket fences, or weathered brick houses with wine-colored ivy and shady, cloistered porches behind a berry hedge. One felt that inside each was ordered spaciousness, leisure and many beloved books collected through the years, a gentle, self-sufficient, disciplined life. The air was country air, and full already of autumnal peace.

Doctor Wellington lived in a brown-shingle house and he seemed to live alone, but I think he had a son somewhere and perhaps other children, from what Kim said. Although so intellectual, Doctor Wellington seemed well balanced emotionally, and most human and unsophisticated in all things. He was in the garden when we found him, a stooped old gentle man with a trowel in his hand. He was wearing a navy-blue serge that was beginning to be pale and seemed only to last him because it was made of such good material. The lapels were smeared with Boston baked beans and his necktie was a string. Although he was over seventy years old, he gave the impression still of a choice maturity rather than of age. His blond skin was eternally smooth and childlike with faint polished pink on the fragile cheekbones. His hair, too, was of the sandy kind that doesn't change much, even when it goes gray. He had a pointed nose, pointed chin, and wore glasses on a shrinking string. One soon saw that if he did not have that string, he would have lost his glasses. The pipe he had lighted a few minutes ago he could not find until Kim reached into the professor's pocket and fished it out for him, just as the cloth was smoking. Yes, he seemed a most forgetful sort of man, because his mind was on such intellectual things as why the American turkey is called turkey, and the origin of the word "score."

3

Professor Wellington, Kim, and I ate an early lunch in a pleasant, airy New England inn—early, because the professor had to rush off to keep an engagement in Boston. I saw him and Kim on the train, but said I would look around and observe the country out there a little more. I lingered in the station after the train had gone, wondering who was to be my first customer. I hated to begin without knowing anybody. Mr. Lively had recommended spy-work first. A man's picture caught my eye. He was on posters all around the station waiting room. "Vote for Lawyer Eliot Norton as next Senator." Pointing to the posters, I questioned the man at the ticket window. The ticket man was surprised I had not heard of Mr. Eliot Norton, the town's leading citizen, a famous lawyer, and important politician. "Oh, Mr. Norton is a wonderful man!" I consulted the phone book in the station. Both home and business addresses of Mr. Norton were given there. I wrote down his office number and set out.

I had no trouble gaining an interview—but then, of course, the prospectus was concealed. And just by moving my straight chair around his desk, I got him in the right light. Mr. Norton was a fine-looking man, of tall, athletic build and thin, keen face, with luxuriant, waving gray hair. I launched upon my sales talk with spirit. He kept interrupting to ask me questions which were off the subject. They were questions about me. But I parried them and got out the prospectus, trying to make that memorized lecture sound as inspired as possible. Again he cut me short—saying he would take an order. He let me put him down for the most expensive binding too. The sale was too abrupt to be quite sporting. Either he bought to help me or to get rid of me quickly. I was more inclined to think he bought to help me, for he asked to see my contract, and drew me on to talk about myself. This would have been a pleasant occupation, but I knew his time was valuable, and so was mine. "Don't waste it," so Miss Fulton had said. So I came back to business and asked him if he had any other customers to recommend.

"Yes," he said smiling. "You might try Mrs. Norton, my sister-in-law. I'll give you her address. She's been to your country and would be interested, I suspect, to meet you."

The house I had been directed to was on the outskirts of the town. There were many acres of gardens and lawns around it, and many elms and beech groves. More like a palace, it seemed, than a house. There was even an artificial lake with swans and a big tennis court. With alert, aggressive, American step, I advanced and rang the bell. A big Negro in a white coat answered it. He took it for granted that I had come to call, and ushered me in very politely. "Is Mrs. Norton at home?"

"Just a moment."

I sat down in the rich and spacious living room. An aristocratic lady with a beautiful, smooth, pink face and waving gray hair piled high, sailed in, holding out her hand.

"How do you do? I'm so glad to see you. I don't know you yet, but you were sent by a friend of mine, weren't you? Let me think. Who could it be?"

I explained that her brother, Lawyer Norton, had sent me.

"Ah! He knows how interested I am in students from the Far East. I have lived some time in the East myself."

She went on, talking fast and asking me questions, until I was so embarrassed I could not bring out the prospectus, even though I knew we were wasting time. The Negro butler came back in. He came to announce luncheon.

"And, of course, you'll stay," exclaimed Mrs. Norton, rising, and leading me toward the dining room by the arm. "I'm so glad you came to look me up. I feel as if I knew you already."

I didn't know what to do. I told her I had just had my lunch—I had lunched with Professor Wellington.

"Oh, you know him, too? Isn't he the most delightful man?"

By this time she had seated me at a luxurious luncheon table, and I was being introduced to Mr. William Norton, her husband, the elder brother of Lawyer Eliot Norton, and to Miss Elizabeth Norton, the youthful image of her mother. Miss Norton, I was told, had just finished her studies at Wellesley. Mrs. Norton announced that I was a Korean student, and her daughter asked me what studies I was interested in most. She herself she said had majored in French. Then the talk turned on how hard it was for Americans to speak foreign languages, and on the Oriental languages I knew, Japanese, Chinese, and Korean.

After luncheon, Mr. Norton had to go back to his office (his business, it seemed, had something to do with ships) and I was left alone with Mrs. Norton again, as her special guest. She showed me her Japanese prints and her lacquerware, and asked me questions about them. She said she had started her collections in the Orient, and what did I think of them? I translated some Japanese words for her, and it was all very chummy, but the more she talked, the more difficult it was for me to begin, as to a stranger, to make her want to buy the unwanted article. Mrs. Norton seemed to sense my discomfiture.

"Now I know there is something I can do for you," she said gently, pressing my fingers. "Don't be shy. You came to the house intending to ask me a favor?"

I thought, this is an opening Miss Fulton has not listed. Even Mr. Lively had given no rules how to take advantage of that.

"Come, tell me what it is. I know how proud you Oriental students are. But you must let me be your friend as long as you are here. I know how lonely you must feel, to land in our vast foreign country."

At last I stammered that I was intending to work my way through college, and did she know any people who might be interested in three big volumes called *Universal Education*.

"Oh, I have heaps of friends. We'll make them all buy that. Let me see...(be sure to use my name in getting in)." She got out pencil and pad to make a list. "I'd buy one myself, but we already have it. Brother Eliot—you know, the one who is *your* friend—bought those books only last year. Not having any use for them, he left them here with me. Such a nice boy was selling them."

So now I saw that it was not my good salesmanship at all! My sales talk had in no way convinced Lawyer Norton. He had bought *Universal Education* in the handsomest binding, just out of charity. Perhaps he bought one of that kind every year. I realized that Mr. Lively had sent me out to beg for his company. This seemed little better than selling bad fountain pens. Already I had "lost faith in the goods."

4

I kept up selling all that week, before college opened. (I knew by now that I was really going to college. A half-scholarship had been secured—the kind that gave the applicant $250, but out of that he must pay a $300 tuition fee, leaving him $50 in debt to the college.) My success in selling was very uneven. Outside of Mrs. Norton's list I was not able to sell at all, though I walked all day and stopped at every door. Mrs. Norton's list was soon exhausted. Even my success there was not always in the nature of sales.

Once I went to solicit a certain Mrs. Ward. She was very very wealthy. Even with Mrs. Norton's name, I had to get through about ten secretaries. She was an amazing-looking woman with dyed red hair and masculine dress. Six or seven bird dogs were moving about in that room.

"Well, what do *you* want?" Mrs. Ward greeted me, her hand on the head of one of those dogs.

For an answer I began on Mr. Lively's prepared sales talk.

"Bosh!" snapped Mrs. Ward. "I'm not interested in hearing that. Let's talk about horses."

We talked on for some time, but whenever I tried to get back to *Universal Education,* she cut me off, saying she was bored too much. At last I said I would have to be going.

"Wait. How much is your commission on that thing?"

I stammered something. "Oh, not much."

"Well? Five dollars? Ten dollars? Will ten dollars cover it?"

I told her how much the commission was, but the check she handed me was far more than that, even when I sold the most expensive binding.

"Take it and cash it quick. Before I change my mind. But don't put me down for a customer. I won't accept."

She saw the hesitation in my face.

"You're afraid I'll call up the bank and countermand the check, when I get to thinking it over? All right, young man, if you'd rather have the cash. Give me the check. I'll cash it for you. I always write checks even to myself. It's the only way I can keep track of where the money goes. No, don't hesitate. I like you. And I give you my word, I can afford it."

After classes started, I became even more discouraged about bookselling. There was nothing certain about it as a means of livelihood, it took up an enormous amount of time, and a good deal of carfare. I felt that I could never make the minimum requirement to give me that free scholarship my contract spoke of, even if I stopped college and devoted all my time to it. I envied now the boys who had some simple menial job like washing dishes.

5

I had craved a more cosmopolitan environment than Green Grove and Maritime, and I had found it. I was lost among a host of students ranging from extreme wealth to penury such as mine, and of all classes and all nationalities. Those in my Monday morning class on Greek and Roman civilization (I had promptly scrapped the Greek verbs of Maritime for some thing more general) seemed to be mostly native Americans, so far as I could judge. But just behind me was sitting a neat, short, well-dressed Oriental, with a very dark complexion. I could not place him. The professor had not yet entered. I turned around eagerly in my chair and accosted the other Oriental. "Where are you from?"

"Boston," he said frigidly.

I thought one of my neighbors was about to explode. He was a tall, good-looking American boy with ruddy face, blue eyes and thick dark hair parted on the side. All during the first short meeting, he kept poking me in the ribs and grinning, with sly looks at the Bostonian behind who had snubbed me. We left the classroom together, and went into the Square Cafeteria. Charles Evans—for so he introduced himself—was still chuckling.

"Your friend is really from Siam," he volunteered. "I know him. He's a friend of the Siamese prince."

I was charmed with my companion and he seemed to have taken an immediate liking for me. I was soon telling all about myself, and he about himself. Over the porcelain arms of our cafeteria chairs, we swapped stories of our financial difficulties. Of course he was not so hard up as I. He had a scholarship but it was a better kind than mine. And his family lived in a near-by town so that he could go home for week-ends, and recuperate from the midweek starvation. He too had tried selling books, but only during the summer. He did not think it was practicable for the winter, while going to college. He tried to think of various things to help me out. On the advice of Charles Evans, I decided to let my contract with *Universal Education* lapse for a while. The Korean businessman who was a friend to George said he knew the steward of a big hotel in Boston, and he was in need of an extra boy there. We went around for an interview. The job was that of standing in the pantry and cleaning off the plates, handing out supplies to the waiters, and things like that. I engaged it at once.

Only a small number of Koreans were in Boston that year. None were in any of my classes. They were mostly taking engineering or medicine. All—with the exception of the theological students who rated a soft berth—were having a hard time. There were a number of Chinese students and these were all kinds, rich and poor. Some of the rich received enormous allowances from home, which in spite of the rate of exchange enabled them to fool around and take their education as they pleased. So it was often noticed, rich Chinese boys were seldom very serious.

But of all the Orientals the Siamese were the most well off. There were four of them in Boston at this time. All were wealthy, all friends of the prince, they lived in style. The prince was such a publicity stunt man that some doubted if he really was a prince. Always reporters were hanging around him, and my, how he adored that! He was always dressing up to have his picture taken. The reporters took him, playing golf and tennis, and also on the ballroom floor. One reason the Siamese were so prosperous was their country did not need to spend money on armaments, and by the political accident of location was free from all international worries such as the other countries had. It made them rather soft though. Only one of the four had much stuff. Now Vidol, the Siamese in my Greek class, was particularly stupid. Never, never, never would he grasp any sense of the West—so I used to think. But then the professor was not very elastic either. He was an old hard-up bachelor with long, slightly graying hair standing up all over his head, and scholarly untidy clothes. Nothing existed in the world for him but Greek civilization. He had a dry sense of humor which used to crackle about the head of Vidol. But soon the professor would grow genuinely angry— sarcasm became inadequate. Some painful scenes were staged between them in that class. For Vidol would never admit that he had not read an assignment. Others said as a matter of course, "Today we have not read"—or "We read so far and no farther"...and that was all there was to it, the professor would pass on. Vidol preferred to provoke fires of cross-examination. The professor would bait him, would raise his answer to a moral issue between them. And even then, with the fact shamelessly apparent, Vidol would not admit that he lied.

"Yes, I read, but I do not remember."

"Vidol, you are lying!"

"No, I read...."

With dark unyielding dignity Vidol stared back at the professor. And before such alien falsehood, the professor lost all control; he would grow white and shake with fury. It was an obsession with him to break down Vidol, to force him to confess he was not telling the truth. A drama of East and West was staged before us.... "Never the twain shall meet," one might say after seeing it—providing each was as stubborn and inelastic as these two. A crazy battle of wills, the unconquerable water of Vidol's will insisting softly, "Yes, Professor, I read..." saving face by some obscure logic of his own, and the professor's savage rage, seeking to smash that self-possession by his moral hate, to make Vidol own up in the name of truth. We never knew who won, whether Vidol couldn't stand it any more and dropped out, or whether the Greek professor told him he had to leave. Anyway, he died out, too near the beginning of the term to have flunked naturally. Charles missed him very much. He used to call him the "scholar from Boston."

Yes, Vidol always "read" everything in that professor's class, whose assignments were prodigious, unreasonably hard. Even Charles, one of the best students there, could not cover them from day to day. Charles would have to go somewhere and laugh after each class.

"Why does he lie? I can't understand. He knows he's not getting away with anything."

"Of course, the East does not put the same emphasis upon the words of fact as the West," I tried to explain. "A gentleman says what is respectable and decent to say. No doubt Vidol really means 'I ought to have read.' He may be very humble. In the Orient a teacher would know that he had not read, from his answers, and would not seek to humiliate him like that. There would be no loss of face, either way. Vidol would not be forced to say that he had neglected his duties and his proper obedience to a teacher, and the teacher would not be forced to say that Vidol lied."

This interested Charles very much. We had a great deal to talk about. I had much to tell him, he much to tell me. And we were able to talk—with real communication and understanding, I mean. Certainly in Charles I found all I had missed in Maritime University. We held discussions on just when the truth of the fact became so important in the West. (This of course was long before the coming of science, although science has done much to sharpen that factual sincerity known to the West as truth.) Perhaps with Socrates.

"Of course," I said to Charles, "there is the saying of Confucius, 'A *man* without truth—I know not how that can be,' but we in the Far East had Confucius instead of Socrates. As thinkers, they were somewhat different."

"Yes, and Confucius I suppose was a stickler for form," suggested Charles.

"Yes, indeed!"

6

My first winter in Boston comes back in feverish kaleidoscope. A thousand bits of existence I seemed to lead without connection. One moment I would be sitting in Doctor Campbell's class, in a utopian world of the spirit where nothing mattered but high thoughts and the integrity of the mind....

He was perhaps my favorite professor. I admired his teaching methods exceedingly. He always attacked his class with a fiery rush. If he failed to inspire them and make their eyes shine, he considered that day a failure. Alexander Campbell was a born actor. The stage would be set for his entrance. Rushing into the classroom, his tall, lean body darting like a rapier, he would always arrive ten or fifteen minutes late, the half of a cigar in his mouth. "Oh, I must leave this outside of the classroom, mustn't I?" he would remember at the last moment. "Just a minute," and flicking away the fire, he would drop the cigar gracefully into his pocket. "Now we will say our 'grace.'" And walking like an actor strutting his lines, up and down, with long leaping stride, he would quote some favorite lines from Shakespeare, Carlyle, some old Chaucerian quatrain, or Browning stanza, with vibrating voice, magnetic personality, rolling and savoring the words in his mouth. Then he would have the class stand up and repeat after him his chosen grace for the day. This they would do, many purposefully trying to imitate the thunderous roll of Doctor Campbell's famous voice with smiles and smirks. These "graces," when we had repeated them many mornings after Doctor Campbell, were bound to stick, and as soon as we had mastered one, he gave us another. At the end of his course, one couldn't help knowing some of Doctor Campbell's pet quotations, whether one went to the trouble of memorizing them outside the classroom or not.

After Doctor Campbell's class, I would sink down in the Boston Library, in a kind of spell, but I had hardly begun to finger some of the pages in his long, rich assignments than one of my other existences would begin calling, and I must rush to my bread line, to drudge in the New Hotel. From Doctor Campbell to the grossest world of Harpies' feet and soiled mountains of plates. My mind would be torn back from a platonic world of pure and radiant ideas of food and the curious sanitary methods of the West....

Coming in at the back door of the New Hotel I would report to a fat man sitting by the punch clock. I was admitted to the supply room, where I struggled into a white coat. (The hotel was very proud of its sanitation and always invited inspection.) Long before the business for the evening started up, I would be surrounded by tables of butter, sugar, salt, celery, olives, cherries to be put into grapefruits, grapefruits to be cut, and pyramid on pyramid of cans. I handed things out to the waiters dressed up in their tuxedo coats, and took in return each man's number, for no article went out of the storeroom without being signed for. At the creation of dinners, every hair was numbered, every robin was counted; how different from the after-math and judgment day of plates! But all proceeded with high-class business efficiency and the most modern sanitary methods.

I was on duty from four in the afternoon until around eleven at night. My wages were fifteen cents an hour and a free meal in the helper's kitchen. There was plenty to eat there, but the meat was tainted, the fish smelly, and the helpers' kitchen used no materials fit to be served upstairs to the guests. It didn't matter much, for all the helpers were eating perpetually, just to relieve the monotony of the work. The chief steward never appeared among us without chewing something he had found in the special dining room upstairs, or between bites, smoking a big cigar. It seemed to agree with him. He, too, was fat. Everybody working here was fat. This was the kingdom of food, like the kingdom of the Drunk Land immortalized by Chinese poets. The chief steward, who had engaged me, was always kind and easy and in a teasing mood. But I had little to do with the chief steward. The man directly over me was Belcher, just out of business college. He was not so good-natured as the head steward and held his employees strictly to account in matters of time. Neither was he so fat, since he had not been in the hotel business long, but he was fattening fast as he, too, wandered from kitchen to kitchen picking up bites. There was another helper, a boy about twenty, who was always chasing to and from the refrigerators a girl who worked in another department. At the refrigerators, he would get to hug the girl and could also snatch a bite of white chicken or cold meat. Even the kissing here, I thought, had to be done in the presence of lobster and mayonnaise! In my department, too, where there was not much chance for anything substantial, one did a fair amount of nibbling. In cutting grapefruits a good deal of juice could be caught in a cup and you always had the centers to suck. Cherries went on the grapefruits, and a lot of cherries I ate. As for melons, they provided much without giving cost to anybody, for what was left from fixing those generous portions had to be thrown out anyhow.

Every once in a while at the hotel there would be a banquet. A banquet it was indeed, even for those lined up at the back door, the extra helps. Sometimes as many as twenty additional hands were called in. I noticed that at a banquet—behind the scenes at least—nobody seemed to get tired of eating, ever. At the beginning we were idle for a few minutes sometimes. Then each contrived to get a handful of nuts or a swallow of coffee…taking out last course first. I could see why the extra helpers ate. They all looked so thin and underfed. I think they had no other job. Day after day just waiting for banquets. Maybe they called at all the big hotels. Maybe they hunted garbage, I don't know. Sometimes, of course, there would be two or even three banquets a week during the height of the season. But then there would come long stretches of vacant days. Nothing doing. I know they made calls every day at the New Hotel where I served, to find if by any chance banquets were going on. Still, even when the great occasion came, Belcher had to turn many away. A great many more extras always applied than there was any need for.

We worked by the service door to receive the plates before passing them on to the dishwashing machines. Sometimes the dishes came out from the banquet with whole half-chickens and big pieces of steak or legs of duck intact. By rights these must pass in steady stream into the garbage can. Oh, how that garbage can was buttered! Butter on practically everything, even on fat steak or creamy vegetables. How rich and juicy and luxurious the French cook had made all these to feed the garbage can! Not that the hotel wanted them for the garbage can—but they had been paid for, and the management was proud of its A-grade class and its fine system of sanitation. So the foreman would shout out for stealing the hotel's paid time if any snatched at the left-overs. You should have seen how those extras watched out of the corner of the eye! The rule was against stealing time, not food, and it was still possible to grab a piece of that chicken on the march to the garbage can if it could go in the mouth all at once. (No rule there about chewing while on the job!) Or sometimes, with lightning speed, half-a-chicken with only the breast taken off is slipped into the coat pocket to wait for the leisured moment.

Now come the ice-cream plates, half-untouched, still semi-solid. These cannot go into the pocket...for all would be melted away in a few minutes! Sorrow! But some clever helpers were able to pick up ice-cream, even ice-cream already watery, and whisk it by the fingers quickly into the mouth. Even if cigarette ashes were sprinkled there, who would mind? If your only chance for ice-cream, month in, month out, is at a banquet, you must seize it.

Back-door banquets impressed me deeply, and I could never cease wondering. All that food passing along through hungry hands to feed the garbage pail...it was so wasteful, so fantastic, so American!... Food that would never be the same again...and just at that moment looking so savory. The hungry applicants for the banquet, turned away (who perhaps waited outside to lift up stealthily the banquet garbage lid), would find by that time the chicken legs had been all mixed up with broken dishes and salad refuse. Once in the garbage pail, the food was hardly fit even for the pigs.... I always felt unusually depressed after a banquet. Not because I had to stay up until three or four in the morning. I was glad of that, because then I received extra pay. But there seemed some hitch in American business methods. Why, you could feed more people with the waste food than those who had already been fed!

At the end of the banquet, all the helpers, except the regulars like myself, were again dismissed with pay. They were not even needed to wash up the dishes, for the hotel had the latest, most modern dishwashing machines and these could easily take care of even the enormous number of dishes used in a hotel banquet. It always paid the hotel to invest in the best mechanical devices for decreasing hands. Perhaps in another fifty years the New Hotel can give even choicer banquets—delicacies brought from the North Pole and the South Sea Isles—and by that time there will be some machine, some endless caterpillar thing that will make the connection between tables and garbage pails complete without human intermediaries. There will be no more back-door banquets then.

At about eleven o'clock on nights that were not banquet nights, I was relieved from my slavery in the world of food, and could return to the utopian realm of pure thought. But going back to my little unheated room in the attic on Trowbridge Street, I faced again the physical weakness of man. I drew out my books and tried to get back to the mind's exhilarating world, but ocean winds outside my unguarded window panes buffetted my lonely perch, and a numbing cold, hostile to life, soon overpowered me. There was nothing for me to do then but go to sleep, spreading my overcoat and clothes over the bed, for that room became as cold as if I had been camping outside exposed to the Boston elements.

I partially solved the problem of a place to study by fleeing to the big public libraries, living there all my free waking hours. But the public libraries closed at ten o'clock. Later on, I thought of the station waiting rooms, and next I lingered in there, sometimes until two and three in the morning, fingering my books chaotically, always catching glimpses, meager glimpses, and a million suggestions I never had the time to follow up. My efforts at study were like those of a student the night before examination, slipping over some book of 500 pages in half an hour, turning to another required book, another and another, and so on through the long, hectic night...a vast impossible feeding without digestion!...

When I say Boston cold, I recall one of the Siamese—not Vidol but Mahidia—because he shivered so. Mahidia was the nicest of the Siamese group, the most sensitive and the most intelligent. Mahidia was not his real name, for that had innumerable syllables and nobody could pronounce them, but everybody, including professors, called him for short Mahidia. He was very shy. His locker was next to mine in the student cloak room; for a long time we met there without speaking. Then one day he pulled out two long, expensive cigars and offered me one. I refused, but said I would walk with him while he smoked.

"It's too cold to walk," said Mahidia shivering. And he invited me to his room. He roomed, I found, with the Siamese prince, the very good-looking, short little fellow with a handsome sport coupe. Mahidia would never accept invitations from Westerners. Charles told me that, and I noticed it was the case. He would accept invitations from me because I was an Oriental, and we often went to Chinatown together, to eat Chinese food.

I have wondered sometimes if Mahidia's shrinking to cold was not partly psychological. Boston cold is not the same as New York cold. It is a cold not only physical but spiritual. I am not referring to the University world, which is a hothouse, a world of theory, and good will, and internationalism. I refer to the feeling that emanates from a common Boston crowd. Often I thought, as I walked among them, going to and from my place of work, "Is it because the mayflower is so sensitive to the fierce frost that the people of the mayflower country, too, are critical and hostile?" And so I believe the sensitive Mahidia sensed alienness and a temper vastly foreign to the Asian. The Asian, too, is self-controlled, repressed, but not with that profound unshakable distrust of Nature inherited by these people from the time of Milton's *Paradise Lost*.

Mahidia was a brilliant and conscientious student. His professor was Doctor Burton, who considered him one of the best in his class. It was Mahidia's genius for physics that had brought him to this land of ice and snow and tortuous thought—him who was soft and lazy in gesture, in manner, in look, with his slow, slender catlike walk and his quiet, slow habits of speaking. One of Nature's satin people, Emily Dickinson would have said. All that dark appearance and suave sveltness proclaimed the tropics. So he was like some South Indian monkey transported to a cold northern zoo. He told me privately that he would not live in New England for $100,000. The only thing that kept him alive was the thought of home to go back to— Siam, beautiful Siam, with its monsoon climate. Oh, how he went around shivering, under his heavy fur coat! Even in his steam-heated apartment, shared by a prince, he shivered perpetually. And I think that unconsciously he shivered in the New England coldness of temperament just as he feared and shivered in the biting climate.

7

One day in late spring, near the end of the college term, I was lingering before the New Hotel, reluctant to go in, even five or ten minutes before my time. Just then a familiar figure sauntered out the front door where guests alone issued. It was To Wan Kim, fastidiously dressed as usual in clothes made in London, and with that characteristic air about him of an aloof and gloomy wanderer among men.

"Hey there! *Pyun-an-hasimnika?*" I called excitedly in Korean, a greeting which ironically enough means, "Have you Peace!"

I was very glad to see him. He seemed pleased, too. He told me he had intended looking me up. Whether this was the case, I do not know. I did not know at this time why he ever made trips to Boston. It was his general restlessness, I supposed.

We went for a walk on the Boston Common, and I ignored my call to duty at the New Hotel.

"And how is college?" he questioned. "Do you like your studies?"

"I have not been able to find out," I said bitterly. "Oh, if only I had the time to read some of those books they talk about in class! Or even to review my notes of the professors' lectures!"

Kim laughed. "Of course that's just what they want you to do. And I believe all the best students do. But it is a wonder to me how I could have eaten up all those dogmatic statements once. I must have, since I got good marks. But I learned very little, nothing that really counts."

"Making a living and going to school are absolutely useless!" I bemoaned.

"Well, you need never accuse yourself—you are just loafing. In this way you will have a saner viewpoint." Kim seemed to be speaking in earnest. But I felt these cold and unsympathetic words.

"I often think people are not sincere in saying as you say. You cannot know. You never had my difficulties."

"I sometimes wish I had," Kim answered somberly. "I could hardly know less about life than now I do.... But don't be so despairing," Kim argued more gently. "A college education isn't only in the textbooks. Most of life anyway, is in absorbing various viewpoints. I would not worry, even if I learned nothing. Many, you know, don't."

"It has often seemed to me I could do more if I didn't attend any lectures."

"It may be a good thing to attend those lectures. I would keep on."

"Yes, since I am already in debt to the college fifty dollars and cannot pay, I may as well keep on."

"That's my advice.... I do not know how it is, Chungpa—I expect you to get something out of the West, something that I have missed."

It was spoken suavely and lightly but with the lofty significance that often clung to his simplest words. I, too, had this faith in myself. And suddenly I felt I loved him very much, though I knew so little of this man's life and he of mine. How much more intimate George and I were on an everyday plane! And that charming and frank and close-thinking Yankee, Charles...he and I could philosophize and joke like boys of the same age. But with Kim all was serious, warped by the subjective view...he was both arrogant and secretive. Yet his words plumbed deep. When I was with him the universe stretched out unfathomably wide. We seemed to inhabit worlds of somewhat the same dimensions. At least the echoes that passed were unique in kind.

We returned to Kim's room in the New Hotel and he ordered some ice and two glasses of fresh limeade. For his own drink he took out a small silver flask from his suitcase. When a boy came up with ice, I knew the boy and I knew where that ice came from. It was from where I worked, and it was just the kind that I sent out of the ice room for other people. I knew all the steps by which that ice left the refrigerator, all other times to serve other people, this time to serve me. I did not much like ice, but purposely I took a piece and put it in my glass and watched it melt. Strange! Kim wouldn't appreciate how many hands that ice passed through on its round-about journey—I broke off my reflections, remembering that I was long overdue down there. I left Kim suddenly. I went down by the elevator and walked out of the hotel like a gentleman. I went around to the servants' entrance and punched the clock and put on my white coat. Belcher had harsh words for me, since I was late.

8

As I contemplated the year just past, it seemed to me I had not grown at all—no—not any part of me. Yet mind and body were tired and cramped from work. What had I to show for it? Nothing but pages and pages of notes, for I had not missed many lectures. These notes were curious in shape. Nobody could read them except me. They were in English, Japanese, Chinese, and Korean. Much could be said for the Chinese as an excellent system of shorthand. Man, perpendicular, one straight line, then a curve, takes less time than the writing of the English A. Or mountain: that is a long word in English. How simple in Chinese—like the roman numeral III. And yet I would not recommend the complicated signs for dragon or tortoise or soul. Tortoise for instance is a complex and mystical picture requiring twenty-six strokes. There is nothing so simple in any language as the English sign for "I." Outside of these notes, which, having a good memory, I knew almost by heart, I had learned almost nothing. I had had no time. The poor marks I made in some of my courses were probably more than I deserved, yet they humiliated me. And confronted with masses of material which I had no time to read, I wondered sometimes if it would have helped me to lose myself in there, even with more time. Each professor saw his own field as a feast, and an end in itself. They all had the bookworm's point of view. I felt I was not interested in muddling around with first one thing and then another, just for the joy contained in the doing. And caught between my two worlds, I felt a like revulsion for the kingdom of bookworms as for the kingdom of food.

I resented particularly the professor in Roman culture. I wanted to say, "You are the professor of Latin, and I believe you can conjugate Latin, nominatives and accusatives, very well. But I am here challenging you. How much Catullus have you in your blood?" Of course, these Greek and Latin courses in English weren't so bad, not so bad as taking Latin and Greek. But how little I came out with! Just as from the dean's lecture on Life—which was no life—no more than that bombastic lecture to tourists on a bus... saying Arlington, Buckley, Clarendon, Dartmouth, Exeter, Fairfield, Gloucester, Hereford, and so on all the way to Massachusetts Avenue; then coming back to rhyme up "ton" with "don"—Boylston, Clinton, etc.— Boston on a bus, which certainly gave the tourist not much of Boston.

My bewilderment and rebellion before American education were enhanced by looking back to Chinese models. Confucian education never required the study of anything but poetry, and it approached that mostly by being a poet. All scholars were poets. There was no division between the critical and the creative. None but the poets were scholars and none but poets attempted to write on poetry. It did not make for Aristotelian analysis, but it vitalized the whole field of knowledge to the creatively minded. This was the way I wanted to approach Western knowledge. And found it would not work, for there was no tradition like that in American education. I was distressed at the lack of unifying principles. I could build no bridge from one classroom to another, just as I could build no bridge from the New Hotel into the mental Utopia. I wanted to relive imaginatively, emotionally, Greek, Roman, Judaic cultures.... but only briefly like a kind of gestational recapitulation...thence to pass onward to the Renaissance—first on the continent, then in England, and from there to America...America, the child of the Renaissance, wrested from the Redskins by this new spirit of rebellion, inquiry, science, and individualism. The Renaissance, that was the period that thrilled me most. Here I saw the eternal workings of some natural law and yet a miracle like Aaron's dry and sapless rod blossoming. I was never too tired to speculate on why the continent of Asia had fallen behind, while the West went on to triumphant rebirth again. Asia's backwardness seemed the demonstration that Nature abhors separateness and inviolability. How much had Kubla Khan, the invasion of the Huns, the Moors, the Crusades and its Arab wars contributed to Western development? I absorbed, too, at this time the views of Doctor Campbell, who believed firmly in the merging of cultures.

"Why was Hearn so great and vital?" he was fond of saying, "Because he had four distinct races and their heritage in his blood."

(Hearn was one of his enthusiasms. He called him the man most misunderstood, and he was never tired of praising Hearn's attempt to marry another culture.)

More and more I intellectualized my instinctive purpose in coming to the West. On my own cultural heritage, I wanted to ingraft the already ancient tree of the Renaissance, to make from that something different, something new...my own rebirth. Thus, in approaching the West I was eager to feel its life in an unbroken stream pass through my heart-blood.... Homer, Æschylus, Plato, Christ, Augustine, Dante, Chaucer, Shakespeare... lives that were born and that died and yet were linked in continuous process of ever-revivified life with its vast onward momentum and exalted, unknown function. Seen in this way, history becomes not history, but poetry and creative life in process, its background the life that lived and decayed, yet itself is not subject to the common laws of mortality.... In short, I wanted the whole Western hemisphere in one block. And there was no course of study in college so general, so comprehensive as to give it to me.

BOOK SIX

1

MY FRIEND, CHARLES EVANS, told me that he was going that summer to Cape Cod to work on a farm. I envied him. It seemed just the right antidote for a winter in Boston. As it turned out, I, too, did work on a farm, but in that region north of Boston which I was supposed to monopolize as a salesman for *Universal Education*. In fact, I started out to sell books there. I had rather avoided Mr. Lively during the winter months, and when I looked him up again, I received many reproaches and expressions of disappointment. I had not made good!

"It looks as if you have no stick-to-itiveness, my boy!"

I told him I was ready to begin again, and then he repeated that he still had hopes. All that I needed to begin selling right away was determination and an up-to-date prospectus. I shied away a little from a new prospectus, for I was very short of funds. But Mr. Lively showed beaming generosity coupled with shrewdness.

"I tell you what I will do. I will give you a new one for the old one," Mr. Lively said, when he saw my hesitation.

Again he took me out with him to his home, where I was welcomed boisterously by Martin and Elsie. The whole family was so nice to me and seemed to be so genuinely affectionate that I was ashamed of myself for my doubts of Mr. Lively's sincerity in the kind of contract he had once drawn up. He really believed that business and altruism should go hand in hand, I am quite sure. But my, those volumes were very hard to sell, once you had lost faith in the goods.

I had no more names to try on my lists of wealthy patrons. I thought I would go to those little communities farther out in the country where education had not much penetrated. By chance I carried in my address book the name of Farmer Higgins, given me by Mrs. Moody, my kind landlady in Stratford-on-Avon; Mr. Higgins was some relative of hers by marriage. The Higginses received me with the utmost kindness, and though they kept no other boarders at this time, I engaged a nice room with them very cheaply. They thought I was just there on a vacation.

I kept trying to sell around the neighborhood for over a week. Several copies I sold to farmers' wives with children, but perhaps the sales talk intoxicated them—farmers as a rule do not talk much. Oh, I did my best with the speech, which I must say came out at times very eloquently. So a few were convinced. I made enough in commissions to pay for my first week's rent and to eat frugally in the restaurants of near-by towns. There were many small towns like a network in this region and street car fare was cheap. One day in the middle of the second week, after having lunch as Miss Fulton recommended (not too much), I went to a house, a good-looking one on a hill not far from a fair-sized factory town. A woman answered my knock and said she did not need anything. There had been long steps to climb to that front door, and it was hot weather, and having climbed them, I politely insisted on getting in, without mentioning that I was a salesman canvassing.

When I entered, there was a man—a big rough-looking man in shirt sleeves, and he was eating lunch. Of course it was a bad time to call. I realized that now. How I wished he had not been there, so that I could talk to the lady in private, but she said, "Here is my husband." So I braced myself and thrust out my chest as aggressively as Mr. Lively had taught us to do, and advanced to overcome his sales resistance. I said to the woman's husband I wanted to have a talk on something educational. It was going to be a hard contest, I knew. All this time he had been looking at me rudely. He said, "Get out or I will kick you out." But I paid no attention. I knew no American would kick an innocent stranger out that way. He swore...and when I insisted on talking, he kicked me out. I rolled down those long steps. I was bruised, but not much hurt. I stood up at once, and called, "My hat— my hat! " For I had left inside my straw hat, for which I had paid sixty-five cents in the Raymond store in Boston. I wanted it at once, in order to run away before I got more kicks, but I couldn't run away without it because it had cost sixty-five cents. The man picked it up and put his foot in it, and his shoe came out at the top of the hat. Then he kicked hard, as if he were revenging himself on the hat. It dropped in the middle of the steps and I ran up to meet it and lifted it off the steps. But I saw it was no good now. So I got mad too. I finished it up right there and walked away. Loud laughter followed me. Some children and girls were in the yard playing. They had watched the whole business, and they giggled in ecstasy as I walked away fast.

I did not have the nerve to do any more selling that afternoon, though the day was long unfinished. At last I got back to the room in the Higgins farmhouse, walking all the way to calm my feelings, and I lay down on my bed. The sun was shining in through the windows. It was hot. It was too hot for comfort, but I just lay there with my feet on the bed, doing nothing. Mrs. Higgins thought I was sick. She came in and sat by me, seeing me so flushed, and asked me what was the matter. At last I told her the whole story. I had to tell somebody, so I confessed that I had tried and tried to be a star salesman, and my salesmanship did not work. Mrs. Higgins was very sympathetic. She went out and brought me in some grape juice, very cold, from her icebox. She consoled me, saying with a sigh, "It's so hard to make a living, particularly in a foreign country. You poor boy!" I roused up to state firmly that it wasn't because I was in a foreign country (for that sounded too much like I couldn't make good, as Mr. Lively had said). "Any other would have the same difficulty in selling *those* awful books...."

After Mrs. Higgins had left me, I began wondering what I would do next. One thing was plain to me, I was not going to sell any more *Universal Education*. Perhaps I might start out and walk to Canada, there to work in Mr. McCann's boxmaking factory. I thought and thought, and nothing else came into my mind—except that man who had kicked me. And he was right, I thought. He too was probably working hard for a living, perhaps in one of those shoe factories I had seen in the neighboring town. When the whistle blew, hundreds of hands rushed out of the gate into the streets, a little pale, a little weary, all in a hurry to get something to eat and some coffee to drink, a little leisure and a little peace. No wonder he was angry at me for breaking in on that, trying to sell the unwanted article.

I grew tired of being in the house. I walked out through the flower garden and I came to the vegetable patch where Mr. Higgins was working. I watched him. It was a pleasure to put my mind on that. I took a hoe and did the way he did. He seemed surprised, but pleased, to have somebody there to talk to. After a couple of hours, he said, jokingly, "You ought to stay here and work for us!" I said, "Oh, I would be delighted." And I worked beside him until it was time to stop. That was not until his wife called him in to supper. She invited me too. How good her supper seemed! I was tired and relaxed and hungry from my hoeing. There was so much to eat, a lot of vegetables from the garden, a lot of cold meat, a lot of tea, a lot of jam, and fresh butter and home-canned fruits. And almost all there was, we ate. I always thought that in eating I was an expert. That is, my stomach would always receive a lot without saying there is no more room, and also without making any complaint afterwards. But with Farmer Higgins in eating I could not compete. I never saw him hurrying in anything except that. For in eating he was very fast—a whole chunk of bread in the mouth, a whole potato, and before either was all gone a big piece of meat. After supper, I thanked them and went up to my room to read as usual. My mood of crushed despondency was almost played out.

Another half hour, and Mr. Higgins called me down again. He said he and Mrs. Higgins had talked it over, and he proposed that I stay there and help him on the farm during that summer. "Fine!" I shouted, "Fine!" (Oh, what a relief that was, not to go on selling *Universal Education*—no longer to express my courage and determination to succeed, by earning a kick!) There was no contract, but I was to work by the week as long as Farmer Higgins needed me. I was to have my room and board and three dollars besides, every Saturday.

It proved to be a wholly satisfactory arrangement. Life here for me was simple, sound, wholesome, and primitive. The typical Oriental is all of these—a view the West has yet to form of him, it seems, since as a stock character he is either a cruel and brutish heathen with horrid outlandish customs, or a subtle and crafty gentleman of inscrutable sophistications. In reality he is a troubled little child, at least in contact with the West, to which he is introduced straight from his own antique and outmoded culture. Really in the West the most salient virtue of the Confucian heritage (among its many faults) seems to have escaped notice, that virtue which strikes a peculiarly harmonious balance between being a wholesome animal and a dignified human, and which has grown up in the most persistently agricultural region of the world since remote ages. At any rate, I—as an Oriental, bewildered before Western "knowledge"—was well content now to be in the country again.

The Higgins farm was set amidst the stony Massachusetts hills. Here Farmer Higgins had come when he got married and here he had cleared off his fields as his ancestors before him who first wrested soil from the Redskins. The soil was fairly fertile, though rocky. Well, at least those bare rocks in the pasturelands were supposed to be a bad feature, but I think Mr. Higgins had an affection for them. They were an unavoidable part of nature, like winter snow and summer sun, like thundershower and willow shade, and they had their own beauty and tranquillity. Out of these acres and this landscape Farmer Higgins' substance came. Mrs. Higgins did her part too, baking, cooking, canning, laundrying, breeding chickens and packing away their eggs.

I gained new insight into a farmer's existence. In fact, though I came from a purely agricultural civilization, this was my first time to farm actually, or to know what farming means. I could see Mr. Higgins' days backward and forward. When the cold disappeared as the winter snow began to melt, his mind would be bent on planting beans, peas, corn, and other vegetables; as soon as the smell of the fresh earth rose from the ground blown up by the early spring thaw, long before the small birds and little chickens roused from the egg to a playful mood, his work would begin. From then on he was busy every hour. Only during the long deadly winter hours could a farmer loaf, and sit dreaming before the kitchen stove.

There was an awkward plow that for many months rusted in the winter storehouse, a conservative yet faithful instrument with a personality resembling Farmer Higgins' own, or those slow cows or that big dog or horse. And, oh, what uphill, tedious work with that! I know, for I helped Mr. Higgins to plant the late vegetables, while, like his plow, he worked, slowly and surely. He was a big, rather gangling man, always placid and friendly. He would tell me stories as we worked, stories out of his own experiences or from his biblical readings. He loved to repeat the scriptural allegory as he sowed: "Some seeds are eaten by wild birds, some cast upon rocks to wither away, but the seed sown in sound soil increases a hundredfold." (I inspired him to such talks whenever he looked at me, for to him I was the confirmation of his spiritual life, that bread upon the waters coming home.)

Mr. Higgins had simple thoughts and simple aspirations. I do not think he ever felt any ambitions away from farming. And though commerce and industry took over the neighboring towns year by year, with stores and factories ever on the increase, Mr. Higgins remained a farmer just the same. He was ignorant of what was going on in the world, in politics or business or economics, except what concerned him in his farming—farming on a small scale, for his was a small place, a small family enterprise. His narrow, upright life was as simple as his home and business. He was not a member of any club, such as the Rotary, Elks, or Kiwanis—he was not sophisticated enough. And he was so very conservative in politics, he even did not know if he disliked or if he approved of labor unions, socialism or anything like that. Such things he did not understand. He understood the Bible, the only book he ever read with concentration, and he took pride that the early biblical people were farmers like himself. He was narrow in all lines, just as he was conservative in his religious views, but ever unpretentious. He and his wife were good church members of a local Baptist congregation, going not to the nearest town (there was no church of their denomination there) but to the next nearest town, for which they hitched up the old farm horse to the buggy. Each thing was rigidly right or wrong for them, even the difference between sprinkling and immersion. Sectarian rivalry was strong in that little farming community where men and women read the Bible and little else. To them the Christian Gospels still had a lot of heat to warm them up. The Higginses were just the kind of people staunchly back of missions in the Orient. Humble and hard-working...supporting, out of meager incomes, missionaries in foreign fields, getting their romance that way and in attending eagerly to the pastor of the little Baptist church, who preached, to serve God always and to fight against sin.

Life was almost harshly simple. And it was not easy. For instance, I did not have much time for studying, no more than an hour a day, although often I goaded myself to work from two to four hours after supper before going to bed, while all the time I nodded in heavy lethargy. And next day it was very hard to get up in the morning. One appreciated as never before conditions in the Orient where scholars, however unfairly, were exempted from physical labor. The summer mornings were burning hot, but Farmer Higgins took no account of that. I never saw a busier man than he was in the field! There was always haying to do. Timothy and clover grew on the meadows and high tall grasses, to be piled into those haystacks by the big barn. Mr. Higgins would swing the scythe with a full round stroke. He was very good at haying. He worked like an artist at it and I often thought his great gangling body at such moments had beauty and rhythm and peace in its every movement; but he never knew it himself. My work most of the time was hoeing, hoeing the corn, the potatoes and other crops in the garden. It must be done about 11 or 12 in the morning when the sun was high and hot, and it seemed to me the hardest work of all. Those weeds...I felt a kind of pity for them as I worked. They were just as good-looking as the crops, sometimes much better, for many meadow flowers grew among them. I could not hate them except that they did not give fruits, and still they tried to compete. Poor weeds! poor golden daisies! And as soon as I had cut them off from their cool roots in the earth, the hot sun dried them up. That sun was merciless. Farmer Higgins and I and even Mrs. Higgins, we all had faces baked like cake with little cracks. Yes, farming, if you do it only a few hours a day, is a wholesome pleasure. But if you do it all the day long, getting up very early and not stopping until sundown, then it is very hard work. There are so many elements to watch, the sky, the insect-breeding land, the weeds, the fruit that must be picked when exactly ripe. Then the bird enemies constantly to chase away. With his old clothes Farmer Higgins made another Farmer Higgins and stood him up in the fields as sentinel for the crows. Always one must be watching, and working, every minute.

Mr. Higgins kept saying with satisfaction that this year was going to be a good one. A full year meant a farmer could make a small nest egg for the shoes, hats, and winter clothes needed, perhaps store a little surplus in that local bank account, hoarding it up for the lean years. But even so I saw that Farmer Higgins on his small farm could never make anything like prosperity or luxury. And though the Higginses were master and mistress, they worked harder than I who was the hired man. There were never any loafing days, not even Saturday or Sunday. Well, Sundays were free for me, but not for Farmer Higgins or Mrs. Higgins. There were the milking, the feeding of chickens, horses, pigs, and cows…all seeming to occur on a farm very often. Besides the house chores, Mrs. Higgins went, all other days but Sundays, to the woods and waste patches, to gather the wild fruits and berries, or out to the vegetable plots, to pick beans and peas; for all that was not eaten or sold right away must be put in jars for the winter. Mr. Higgins himself arose the earliest, to make his milk deliveries in the near-by villages. When he came back, we had the big breakfast, cereals, hot breads, coffee, eggs, and pie. After that I worked beside him all day, without skill perhaps but with my utmost energy. Before he had always hired skilled laborers like himself, and it did not take me long to find out that farm work requires skill and experience as well as any other trade. But he had also paid them more money. Still, with my unskilled work and the aid of machinery, Farmer Higgins could do very well with just us two. I thought of him often in connection with the farmers of Asia. No doubt in Asia he might have been accounted a prosperous man, and many others would be working for him. At least, he was never in danger of famine or starvation, and he by himself was able to produce more than a hundred Chinese farmers could produce. This was because of his labor-saving devices, though he did not even know that he was living in the Machine Age....

When the summer was over, the Higginses said good-bye to me as to a son. They had become much interested in me over the summer, and I'm afraid they even hoped I would do something grand in the way of glorifying God and the Baptist missionaries. I had thirty dollars to take away with me, all rolled up in one-dollar bills and put away in an old wallet given me by Farmer Higgins. Many weeks it took to accumulate so much, made by sweating under the burning noon. My wages had amounted to slightly more, but I had bought some books and shirts and other things. Mrs. Higgins fixed me up an abundant lunch and put it into a large paper box, enough to last for days. I started out, suitcase in one hand, lunch box in the other. I walked until I came to the street-car line. Then I got in and rode toward Boston. The long street-car ride took half a day.

2

I had decided that I wouldn't enroll as a student that year. I would use the libraries for my own reading. And I would try to support myself more adequately. Useless, I thought, to work and to prepare for examinations at the same time. For a week or two, without going to the dean, I read assiduously, attacking many of the books I had not been able to read during my courses last winter, especially the books on Greek culture which had interested me. Then I became alarmed by inroads into my thirty-dollar capital. I stopped reading at the library and began to walk the streets again, looking for a job. The season at the New Hotel had not yet opened. Up and down I went, in and out, over the crooked hilly streets of Boston. No work anywhere, no work for me. (How the commercial people looked at me with cold and alien stares! Oh, how many thousand years would it take to have that Bostonian air with congealed pride all its own!)

While walking around, I encountered Charles Evans. We sat on a bench on the Common and talked. Charles was enrolled, of course, and taking classes. He was much disappointed when I told him of my decision to drop out for a year; he disapproved. A few days later, owing to this meeting with Charles, I received a note from Professor Burton (in charge of the foreign students) asking me to call at his office. Professor Burton expostulated with me and urged me to enroll at once, offering me again the part-time scholarship and the fifty-dollar debt (now increased to $100 by addition to last year's). I hesitated. I asked if instead of taking a half-scholarship for a year, I could take a whole scholarship for six months. We went to see the president and the dean. My plan was all right with the president, but not with the dean, who said if I was having a hard time in Boston, I should go back to Maritime from which I had transferred. Again I refused the half-scholarship and said I would go on reading in my own way. Professor Burton would not let me do this. He talked to me very seriously, said in his opinion I was making a grave mistake. At all costs I must struggle on in the conventional way and gain my college diploma. Of course he was right. But there it was, as Kim remarked, the importance of the rubber stamp.

So against my better judgment, I embarked the second year on that ghastly business of studying on an undernourished stomach. There were distinct advantages, though, in not having a job. At least, one could get some studying done that way, by the use of libraries and borrowed books. I went without meals often, but a loaf of bread sufficed for a few days. My stomach shrank and became meek.

While the weather was fair, it must be confessed, in spite of attending classes in college like a gentleman, I lived like a hobo. I slept on park benches in the daytime, and dozed in a chair in waiting rooms at night. But as the weather grew colder, I had a stroke of luck. I met again a Mr. Rhinehart who had visited Green Grove while I was there. He made me a kind of errand boy for him, licking postage stamps, etc. And he did me a real service by letting me sleep on the couch in his office at night. The first night I moved in, it caused some excitement to the night watchman, whom Mr. Rhinehart had forgotten to inform. The watchman found me in that bed, with sheets and all—provided by kind Mr. Rhinehart—and the watchman wanted to call up the Police Department at once. It was a dark, conservative-looking office building not far from the Back Bay section. I was given a key. From five o'clock on I could study there in solitude. Being heated during the day, this office was not cold at night, and made a most comfortable lodging.

I knew many other students who were as hard up as I. One, Cortesi, I met in the chemistry laboratory. He was the son of a poor Italian farmer from the country thereabouts, one of eleven children, and with nothing but his own brains and ambitions to help him on. Chemistry was Cortesi's passion, his greatest source of pleasure, his romance. He was a slender, frail fellow, with light brown hair and no beard, so that he never needed shaving. His hands were very white and delicate, as if he had never done any manual labor in his life. Both his hands and his brains were very quick. He seemed very shy. But in laboratory work, if nobody else was around, we had much mirth and laughter. He was more at home in a laboratory than anywhere else. Cheerful and quick, working always with a great enthusiasm, like a cat who has got a rat.

I sometimes went to see him in his little room, just such a little room as I had had on Trowbridge Street. Somewhere he had procured a small battered victrola, but it was his only luxury. He liked music, especially Italian operas, and he liked to dance suavely by himself to his victrola when only I was there to watch. Cortesi made vegetable soup with hot water out of a spigot, and invited me to share it with him. He had put himself through college by living mostly on raisins, raw carrots, and figs.

One night in his room—I don't know how it happened—we spent hours on hell, heaven and purgatory, comparing the Buddhistic system with the Catholic. But Cortesi was really not much interested. He said he did not believe that mystical systems were any good. "I have no use for people like Dante and Christ. What lunatics!" According to Cortesi, the emotional life of a poet, the religious sacrifice of a martyr, the ecstasy of a mystic—such dreams and fancies were good for no one; he meant to give them as wide a berth as possible. If you get hungry for such things, chemistry could take their place. A man could become quite mystical enough over chemistry. But as a matter of fact, Cortesi was the most sensible, sober and rational of beings.

BOOK SEVEN

1

THAT EASTER VACATION I wanted to go to New York. Some students showed me how to hitchhike (part of my college education which was to prove an asset later on). Seven of us took up our station along the Boston Post Road. We were finally picked up by an ex-college man, who revived his college memories all the way down talking with us. Arriving in New York, none the poorer, we had a hilarious dinner in a cheap little lunchroom. I heard the others laying plans for a room, but of course I was going round to George Jum's place. They divided the night into three parts and drew lots. Two were sent out to engage one double room in a modest hotel toward which all contributed. Those who drew lot number one were to sleep from 10 P.M. to 2 A.M. At two, this pair vacated for the next couple, who were allowed to sleep from 2 to 6. The last couple in the third lot must spend the whole first night in seeing New York, but they could sleep from 6 to 10. Then all would meet outside around the corner and use the day in sightseeing. The hotel would never know that it had rented a room to six boys instead of two. My classmates intended to stay in

New York like this as long as their money and strength held out, as none of the six had ever been in this city before.

2

As soon as possible I set out to call on Kim. And I had difficulty finding his place again. This part of the city was a maze. It was hard to tell the streets from the funny little lanes and alleys and blind ends. Here and there by some dark doorway stood small groups of young men and women in casual attire, smoking cigarettes and wearing no hats. The Villagers, I thought. For some time, I realized, all the bright young people of America had been collecting here, all eager to be poets, sculptors, artists, anything in fact to get away from Main Street and to burn the candle at both ends away from the gossipy neighbors.... I entered that quiet sunken doorway at last. Kim was expecting me, for I had telephoned, and he came to meet me in comfortable heelless Chinese slippers and a short quilted sack coat of red silk; this suited admirably his dark low-molded face and black hair with its complicated Western cut. I realized then that Kim was a part of this pageant, he was one of the Villagers, though he might not have liked it if I had told him so. No, he was not ashamed to step out in that exotic dress to buy cigarettes around the corner (how different from Boston), and the people on the street and at the corners and in that dark drugstore greeted him carelessly as if he were well known.

We returned indoors. Kim had been painting upon the floor, Korean style. There was his black ink-stone, where the powdered ink was crushed to be mixed with water; a round Korean cushion too, and several brush pens of the finest quality. The faint bitter herblike smell which I associated with good Chinese ink and the mysteries of the calligrapher's art permeated the room. And the stale American cigarette smoke as well. But Kim gathered up his work and, when I attempted to examine it, waved me aside. He showed me a new book he had recently acquired. It was a beautifully bound and illustrated copy of *Don Quixote*.

"I think I am a Don Quixote out of the East," said Kim thoughtfully, "with my sweetest Dulcinea the old-fashioned muse. But there is good stuff in this book. Who knows? He might be better for you than Shakespeare, my friend. You and I, we should be sceptical when we have seen so much, laugh at ourselves, and at the same time laugh a little to ourselves. Yes, this man has the originality of Shakespeare, but he writes not of bloom but decay."

I liked the idea of talking about Shakespeare, of course, so Kim got drink for himself and settled down. "You are right as far as you go," he said. "The Orient has not had Shakespeare yet. We had Confucius. Yes. But we had no Æschylus. That is why we never had Shakespeare. Only Li Toi-kei."

It was good, I thought, to be with him again. Two hemispheres opened out before me once more, not just the world of collegiating. We talked and talked. Kim too seemed to enjoy it.

"My, this banquet of talk is a treat I don't often have," I exclaimed at last.

And Kim rose and got more drink. "Well, here I am, keeping on drinking more and more. I must be afraid of being dry-mouthed this evening. But fools must drink like fish. He who doesn't know what he is after in this Western world is a fool. He is worse off than a poor fish—they stay forever in their own realm. And drink water. I this." (He did so.) "Marcus Aurelius, when tired of Greek philosophy, sent for some Eastern wisdom. It is my turn. So here I come, out of the East to the West—of the West and of the East...as far as Manhattan...to this Village where fools live, nay, pygmies creep, cockroaches crawl. I came to get Western wisdom. I was too much in a hurry...unlike Marcus Aurelius. So I could not send anybody for it. When I get here—ha ha! I see that the Western wisdom is as valueless to me as those old German marks and only good for wallpaper as being cheaper than paper. Yes, here I am (may you not be the same!). This is Western wisdom," he lifted his glass and stared at its contents. "You won't get it in college. This is it."

After that we had some Chinese poetry. After a certain number of drinks, Kim always turned to Chinese poetry. Out came the brushes and the ink again. (And modern typing paper.) "Chang Hsu, after three cups, writes inspired characters...strokes of his long-haired writing brush drop on the paper like clouds of driving mist." It was like that with Kim.

Before I left, Kim said to me, "While you are here, I will take you to see a Marcus Aurelius in America. Yes. I have an American friend who thinks there is nothing good except out of the East. You will hear him talk a great deal about the Chow dynasty, its philosophy and art. But you can't expand for him your new views on Greek culture. It is not ignorance; his formal education in college was based on Greek civilization. Even in his studies of science, philosophy, psychology, astronomy, he could hardly forget those Greeks. They bore him, that is all. He is not like Goethe to say, 'Beside the great Attic poets, I am nothing.' But perhaps the time when Goethe lived was more slavish than this time of my friend Brown. His eyes grow blank when I mention the changes in ideology when Christianity invaded the Western world. But they burn with enthusiasm when he talks of the time that Buddhism entered China during the Han period. Truly, he is never tired of talking on Buddhism, its effect on Chinese art; but the Western religious art leaves him cold. He speaks with veneration of Confucius. Not so of Plato...to him the modern East is being Westernized and spoiled."

"Isn't it fine!" I exclaimed. "The West is meeting us halfway. As we Westernize, they orientalize!"

"Well, it is so with Brown. He is always thinking of the long Chinese wall and the court of Kubla Khan, instead of the luxury palace with frescoed walls from that island empire of Crete. He is thinking of the Tai Shan, and the Yang-tze Valley, instead of the Macedonians moving with their herds down the Vardan. Is he some transmigration of a Taoist priest moved to Park Avenue?"

3

Kim had asked me to drop around whenever possible. The next time I called, I found that he had company, an unusual thing for him. His visitor was a man from the East like himself—a thing still rarer. Hsu Tsimou was the name, a famous name in China, where he was a well-known poet and an ardent supporter of the new literary movement under Hu Shih. You were not with him two minutes before you felt that here was a man as different from Kim as day from night. Kim remained in all things an observer, especially toward the West. He might be as familiar as Tsimou with

Browning, Shelley, and Keats, but he did not swim, breathe and have his being in exuberant romantic waters. Hsu Tsimou did. He was a romanticist pure and simple, a child of the Western nineteenth century.

Educated in America, where he had taken in fact a degree in economics, commerce and banking, he had returned only to keep his business desk full of manuscripts and poetry. His father, a wealthy Chinese businessman, finally allowed him to leave the bank, and from there he went straight to study Western literature in Cambridge, England. Kim had met him in London. Afterwards Hsu Tsimou went to Italy and studied Dante. Grasping the significance of Dante in founding the Italian literature, he became a passionate convert to Hu Shih's new movement of the Pei-hua or literature in the spoken language. (This cropped up first in the matter of translation; the argument of Hu Shih was, ridiculous to put the vulgarities of Western novels and plays into the formal stilted elegance of a purely classical and literary writing. All translations, at least of Western prose, should obviously be made in the Pei-hua or spoken tongue. The corollary was soon evident— the spirit of modern China could best be expressed in unliterary language too.) Well, like Hu Shih, Hsu Tsimou made a vow never to write again for publication in the literary language. He was devoted to all movements emancipating China from tradition, and was unconventional in all things.

When I came in, Kim and his guest were having an argument—not on literature, but on love, a favorite topic with Hsu Tsimou, I found.... He was a Chinese of average height, not so tall as Kim, and rather slighter, with a very handsome oval face, and black eyes full of fire, and an unconquerable zest for life. Hsu Tsimou was so handsome, indeed, that he looked like a character out of an old Chinese novel—such as *Dream of the Red Chamber.* His whole personality reflected radiance and enthusiasm, very different from Kim's somber nature. Tsimou had just brought out a picture of his second Chinese wife whom after many vicissitudes he had married romantically, in despite of conventions, and he was saying: "Love is my inspiration, as Death to François Villon, as the wine to Li Tai Po. I always wanted to dedicate my life to love. And so I married it. The world is full of rain, wind, and bitter air, but that does not matter, so long as I have love. With love I can sleep in the moonlight without food or bed."

"To most men peach blossoms seem to last for a short time of the year. To you all the year round, always peach blossoms?" Kim said in a joking manner.

Tsimou would have no irony. He had taken love over whole from the West, like a sun that sets in one hemisphere to rise in another. To him, love was life itself, his god, his truth, his beauty, and religion, as he expounded.

"It is only while being drunk," said Kim, "that I can agree with what you are saying." (But I thought they were both drunk, each having a glass nearly emptied of white Chinese wine.)

"Becoming sober," Kim went on, "there appears to me an illusion. I feel you may be somehow deceived.... The man who has felt many currents, finally he comes to stand still...he returns to the Taoistic view." (Kim got out his sketchbook of ink drawings.) "See that man in his boat? His eyes are on the far horizon, because that is the infinite...where the infinite sky, the infinite water, the infinite blue are one. That is the goal that this man dreams of, that is the hope. Rowing on fast as he dreams, this meeting place of sky and sea seems to him always so near...always it is in sight (is it not, we agree?)... Yet it is so far to measure with a boat for this man. True, it is the nature of this man to travel toward some goal. He may have no other thought night and day, panting and struggling.... But will that goal ever be reached? Is he not like Ulysses? Each success makes some newer obstacle. Always he must go on, the sport of the sea. He who has faith in travel gets shipwrecked, as well as he who has doubt. He who works hard succeeds no better than he who is drifting...for no one has ever reached the place where the sky meets the sea. How many we find on the sea, trying to get where the end ends...somewhere along the way, the ship is wrecked, while the traveler, unable to find even a stone to cling to, sinks forever into the vast ocean of oblivion.... Toward a hopeless goal and fatal adversity! Is it dignified to be deceived?"

"Poor man! Poor man!" murmured Hsu Tsimou, never losing his childlike radiance, his sparkling simplicity. "What foreign disease have you caught here? Is it metaphysics? Are you seeking for God?"

He said it incredulously, for the Chinese are usually satisfied in agnosticism; Koreans too. They are philosophical, but not religious or meta-physical. Missionaries have said this: We will not understand God. It is the practical in Christian ethics that has most appealed to the converts in the Far East.... And I heard Hsu Tsimou trying to persuade Kim to return with him to Shanghai, to join with him in new movements, new ideals, the task of revivifying the East. "The East, my friend, is where we belong! And this East is not dead as you say. The desert is soon going to bloom. When all the bad old ways are cut off and thrown away—underneath the roots are still green —grafting of new life will take place. The best of the West upon the undy-ing roots of the East. That is the world for us. There we have some part to play. What is it that Lu Hsün says? First there is no road always: the feet of many people put one there."

But Kim showed no enthusiasm for going back. It looked as if the Orient meant no more to him than last year's leaves in the wasteland. "I fear that death lies at our roots. You must cut off the roots. And then man might as well be here as there."

It was very interesting to see these two together, for they were in great contrast. Hsu Tsimou was simple in all things. He had only arrived from Europe that day, and had come straight to Kim's place, suitcase in hand. In that one suitcase he could travel all over the world and had done so many times. And even it was full of books. I saw, when he opened it to bring them out to show Kim. He looked as if he never needed much cleaning; for Tsimou remained Oriental. His haircut was simple too, slightly long black hair parted in the middle and falling into his eyes now and then; while Kim's went up from his forehead and all around in complicated ways. Tsimou's shirt was a simple white, his tie a solid green; Kim's Western shirts were checked or striped, his necktie was always of some complicated pattern. It was so of all Kim's Westernization—he was detailed and subtle; Hsu Tsimou, simple and swift. Impossible for Kim, I thought, to select one simple trend like Hsu Tsimou, such as anti-traditionalism or romantic love—one simple color to be his banner and make him an enthusiastic, energetic man. And yet my friend was not so narrow as to be consistent, even in his assumption of Taoistic drifting and passivity.

Kim went out to get cigarettes around the corner, and Hsu Tsimou and I were left alone. Tsimou sighed and shook his head. "What will be-come of Kim?" he questioned softly. "He can't go on like this. Either he must get that American girl he is in love with—or take up communism...for he stands now at the road with a blind ending."

"What girl?" I exclaimed in intense surprise. The thought of Kim in love had never entered my head. George, yes...he was always in love. But Kim!

But Hsu Tsimou had no more to say about it. Perhaps he knew no more. And Kim was many-sided and a person of mystery. I realized I knew few things about him.

4

Kim had arranged for me to meet Mr. Arthur Brown, his friend who was interested in Asian civilization. We drove to Park Avenue. The doorman of the house where our taxi stopped saluted Kim as if he had seen him frequently. So did the elevator boy. Kim rang at an apartment on a high floor, and a neat maid in uniform answered the door. I saw that even in the dim hallways were many Chinese paintings. I had no time to examine them. Mr. Brown came in just then and received us with a hearty handshake. "Let us go into the Chinese room...and we will have a tea ceremony in the Japanese room later."

Our host seemed about forty years old, a man of medium height, of plain but interesting features and a fierce hawklike nose. I would not have taken him for a scholar or an art connoisseur. He looked more like a banker. Really he had been an engineer once; or at least he had studied engineering in college but I don't know if he ever practised it.

We entered the Chinese room, the walls of which were hung with bamboo paintings, storied tapestries, embroidered pictures. It was of enor-mous length. There was heavy furniture brought from China, made of Nan-mu wood in Canton style and decorated with marble slabs in red and gray clouds, a solid square table looking as calm and immovable as any mountain and several deep Chinese sofas to lie or rest on, showing strong fat carvings that must have come out of Peking. On the floor were large Chinese carpets, and to one side of the softly burning fire, an opulent Chinese screen.

One's mood was subtly changed by these physical objects. Taxis outside were forgotten. One returned for the moment to that leisured tranquil world of yesterday, to the relaxation of harmonious fatalism. As we walked slowly through the whole extent, I felt that Kim must love to wander here.... The Young Girls at a Chinese Window...the Panther in the Grass...the Dragon of the Peaks...and many more. Kim stopped longest by the landscapes, mountain ravines like visions—high summits among the clouds with groups of scholars holding symposium oblivious of the coming storm—a vigorous storm caused by a raving dragon as the artist had portrayed, yet somehow even the dragon was included in their fellowship. One was caught up into a sublime pantheistic composure before nature and life, warmer, softer, tenderer, simpler than stoicism, yet of such lofty resignation that tempest and destruction became no more frightful than "the crying of a little child."

Mr. Brown said, "Wonderful, aren't they? No race has perfected the effect of color and composition along decorative lines as these Chinese artists and their Korean brothers." (And he pointed out one there as a prized Korean painting.) Then just as Kim had warned, Brown gave us to understand that he was not interested in Western art of any kind. It had gone off down false trails. As for Christian art...

"I can't stand contorted human emotions...the strained anthropomorphic viewpoint. Crucifixions, mater dolorosas...Botticelli for instance... or the passionate Primitives.... As a young man, I used to collect such things. When I became interested in the art of the Orient, I got rid of them all."

Now Brown got out his books of study in Chinese calligraphy. Already he could write the 600 fundamental characters which form the foundation of the written language; and the 214 radicals he had written down separately in a beautifully bound blank book. His calligraphy was painstaking and neat, but rather lifeless, and in the strokes, as was natural, he had small sense of the sweeping demonic style which is the soul of the art. What Brown lacked in feeling, however, he made up in intellectual grasp. Always he tried to rationalize the word pictures through the evolutional process, and I saw he was learning more logically than we who were brought up in it. A fine mind he had.

Kim said of me to Brown, "Here is a young Korean, one of those few last men with the classical background. He comes from a remote Northern province not much touched by the West. He improvises in the old style, and is better than I am in the handwriting."

Of course it was untrue…. Kim was so much better than I that it was foolish to say it—for he had already levelled to a definite style, which reflected his own personality no matter what he wrote, whether fast or wildly; mine somewhat changed with the mood and the occasion and was always better when I took time and thought. The personal rhythm is important in calligraphy as in verse, and it was always striking in Kim's work.

Brown went out of the room to bring in something else to show. Kim said: "Such private collections no longer exist in the Orient. Do you realize that to study Oriental art, man is now obliged to come to the West? But with Arthur Brown this is genuinely his passion. He has read most of the books and articles written on the subject in the Western languages, including related topics by such authorities as Laufer, Pelliot, Maspero, etc. Every important collection in Europe and America he knows. He has a good library of his own, and his comments are original, suggestive and interesting."

"You must feel very congenial here."

Kim smiled: "Mr. Brown and I are alike but different. He is accepting the East in the spirit of blind optimism while I am accepting the West in the spirit of sane pessimism. But this makes him the happier man. I have given up one world and cannot accept another. But Arthur has no such conflict. He seems well satisfied with Oriental art as a substitute."

Brown came back with illuminated manuscripts from a Buddhist Korean monastery. We examined these, and also the gravely chaste Korean chest—Greek in simplicity—in one corner of the room. Mr. Brown had assembled his Chinese and Korean pieces together (even in museum cataloguing I have found, this is often done). Last of all, we went into the Japanese room, where Brown said the "tea ceremony" was to be held. In here were sliding windows, and walls papered with Japanese paper of the best quality and design. There were stools, no chairs, and a Japanese table, but slightly too long-legged, and behind the table, a long seat with Japanese covering against the wall. This room was quite dark, being lighted only with Japanese lanterns. There were Japanese games, including Japanese chess (which Brown played sometimes with a Japanese). Now we had the tea ceremony. But it was not tea, but the American cocktail that was served.

5

Would not a man with such excellent taste in art hunger for the same kind of thing in food? Eight-jewelled cakes, tiger boned wine, 300-year-aged eggs?... Shark's Fin soup in one of those Koryu bowls he had, or at least Chinese lobster making necessary the use of those carved ivory chopsticks from the emperor Kang-hsi? I followed him into the dining room with a lively spirit of anticipation, thinking on various passages about food in the Chinese classics. "Nine times must the soup be boiled and exposed to the scorching heat; a hundred times it must rise and fall in bubbling effervescence. Taste a slice of meat from the nape of the neck; take a bite of the claws of a crab before the coming of the hoarfrost; break open the fruit of crystallized pearl-cherry, a delicious morsel. Allow the almond gruel with its steamed lamb to boil up into clouds of vapor. The clams must be half-cooked, and steeped in wine; the crabs slightly underdone and soaked in grain...all tender and savory foods must be gathered in to feed my old Gourmand!" And although I had not drunk, I felt I could gobble up the spirits and demons of fish and dragon.

It was a prim room of early colonial furniture with tall white candles in pewter candlesticks on a glistening white tablecloth. Two American ladies were there. One was young, being introduced to me as Miss Hancock. She was of that type of person who looks as if she has been immaculate from the cradle up and constantly scrubbed with soap. Her light-brown hair seemed never to have been bobbed. It waved, showing now and then sparks of old gold, but it was very soberly put back, keeping its place without the spirit of mischief. She was dressed in a russet velvet dress with lace at the throat and an old-fashioned amethyst brooch. In her taut rather boyish figure was a hint of the North, although there was nothing boyish—at least tom-boyish—in Mr. Brown's young cousin, Helen Hancock; she was all old-fashioned mannered, dignified, serious, modest. Her face in repose held a sensitive and wistful shadow almost of Hawthornesque melancholy. No mystery, no sophistication was visible in her. She showed the direct honest primness of New England architecture, a white house with apple trees in blossom before it. I don't suppose she would have been considered beautiful by Hollywood standards. That is, I believe she was not much pursued by American men as a star, possessing the "it" of those times. But I got the impression that Kim considered her very beautiful, that to his eyes, her young slender figure was in a springtime of bloom, favored with sunshine and rain without knowing storm or violent wind, scorched desert or burning heat-tide. Mrs. Brown had seated them side by side at the table, and Brown seemed to look with genial eye upon their obvious friendship.

Mrs. Brown, I thought, appeared somewhat older than her husband. She had iron-gray hair, gray eyes, a pale face not at all beautiful, and a stout full figure. She showed, however, a quiet feminine charm of poise and repose and one fancied that Brown, in his choice of a wife, had Chinese taste. (But not in dinner, I regret to say. One had to be contented with the wife.) Later I learned that she had been a trained nurse, married unexpectedly to Brown in middle life after attending him in an illness. Very practical she seemed, well satisfied to rest on earth. She made no attempt to keep up the tradition of American ladies to whom conversation is an art, and where ladies' charm is understood to be the product of that plus gesture. Mrs. Brown had neither talk nor gesture. I doubt even if she had much appreciation of her husband's Oriental collection. It must be told, however, that when dinner was over, I felt I knew Mrs. Brown better than Mr. Brown, who talked most of the time.

Mr. Brown had a loud, vibrating, metallic voice, aggressive in his quest for knowledge, yet whenever he spoke it had always dogmatic tones. He never made any questioning remark in the mood of wonder or doubt, but everything he said was meant for 100 per cent sure. I noticed Mr. Brown seemed to have some hidden fault to find with his young cousin, Helen. I suppose it was that obviously she could never be Chinized! No more than a white meetinghouse. She was quiet, but lacked the feminine stodginess of Mrs. Brown. Helen Hancock did not seem a young woman of intellect, exactly, but she moved from the higher centers and she had the temperament if not the talent for the realm of high ideas. She had recently graduated from one of the Eastern women's colleges and was very fond of European travel, I gathered.

"Well, To Wan, this young lady stole one of your drawings from me the other day," said Mr. Brown. Kim slightly colored and looked mutely at our host. "You may keep it, Helen, with Kim's permission."

"May I, To Wan?"

Kim nodded. "And any more you like. But what was it?"

"Your pen-and-ink drawing of the Clem below Karmesh...I adore it, so wild, so German, so mystic."

"It is very Oriental. Certain places in Diamond Mountains are like that, on a still grander scale. (And Helen murmured, "How magnificent!") "I did it on the spot, something I don't often do, without composing my mind. I did not do it well, and I meant to destroy it. It got mixed up with some other things I brought over to show...."

"No, it wasn't so good," agreed Brown, his great voice booming out across the table. "Too romantic...much too tragic, too Western for Kim.... What got into you, Kim?"

"I don't know. I think all mixtures are horrible. There is a Japanese artist living not far from me in the Village. He is always engaged in trying to make an acceptable bust of Lincoln—or something like that."

Brown had rich, hearty laughter; it vibrated the whole air.

"Oh, but he is making big money with that kind of stuff," returned Kim.

"So do bootleggers. Nothing is easier...one can in New York." (I wondered how, but did not interrupt.) And it was easy to see that such remarks endeared Brown to Kim.

"Susan, he has taken all my rucksack trips. Isn't it exciting?" Helen was saying, a nostalgic light in her blue eyes.

"Like Kim, Helen is something of a globe-trotter," Brown remarked slyly. "But she remains a Bostonian all the same. Aunt Helen, you know, was a globe-trotter, too, at your age."

"How horrid of you, Arthur!" said Helen and looked vexed.

"Are you homesick for Europe again?" asked Kim. "That is why you wanted the Clem?"

"Aren't you? What can you see in this noisy country of ours?"

Kim looked as if he might have answered, "You." But he replied instead, "I never travel any more. I am losing the desire. I never find peace, so the travel itself seems futile. And I remember, too late, the story of a Chinese emperor who employed 10,000 magicians to set out for him in search of the heavenly flower, but he found it at last growing in his own yard. No. I have no homesickness for Europe...nor for my own country. The world seems my country, such as it is.... Perhaps it would have been better for me to dream away life to the sweet music of Rossini, drinking the mild capri bianco or verona suave. But really I somewhat prefer now American cocktails."

"And I don't like cocktails!" Helen confessed, shuddering.

"Nor New York," murmured Kim with a teasing smile.

"I like Brookline better than New York, and Germany better than Brookline."

"I can see why a man of my race might not like New York. But why a woman of yours?"

"And why don't *you* like New York?"

"The only goal for a man here is money and power. But money and power in New York are not for men of my race. Even if we succeeded, we would not be admired for that, but only hated and feared."

"Why hated and feared?"

"Pagans, coming over to spoil good manners and respectable morals. When powerless, pagans are more tolerable, isn't that so? Pagans are not so much to be feared."

"Our neighbor, Miss Lowell, in Brookline, spends all her time in translating Chinese poetry. I only know what I have read of hers. I don't feel such poets are pagans. Nobody does."

"Oh, come, Kim," Brown interrupted, "We are all pagans here—except Helen. Susan, aren't you a pagan? You know you're a pagan." Mrs. Brown merely smiled indulgently without committing herself.

And now Brown took my arm and drew me toward the Chinese

room, where he said cigarettes and more drinks were waiting. Mrs. Brown prepared to withdraw through another door, and Helen with her, but Kim interposed. "Aren't you coming?" he said to Helen.

She hesitated. "Then there is to be no Chinese lesson tonight?"

"No, none."

And Helen came with us.

As we strolled about the Chinese room once more, to let me look at the paintings, Brown was singing to me the praises of Kim: "A most unusual person. And a great artist. Some day, like Wu Taotze, he will disappear within one of his own paintings. I wish I could do something for To Wan. But he won't let me. He gives me pieces for which I ought to be paying a handsome sum. He won't hear of money. It was he who made a catalogue of all these things for me, with English captions and verse translations...."

Behind us, Kim was talking to Helen. "A famous Chinese philosopher was asked what he would do with a useless tree. He said, 'Why not plant it in the land of non-existence and yourself lie in a state of bliss beneath it, inactive by its side? No ax nor other harm could touch it, and being useless, it would be safe from danger.' This has been my philosophy, in utilitarian civilizations where I and my muse are not wanted. My life is the useless tree. I try to plant my tree in the land of non-existence. It is the same land we see in Arthur's collections over these walls here."

"Tell me more about Oriental art," said Helen. "I am so ignorant about it."

"Its simplicity sometimes escapes the Western eye. The inspiration is usually nature. That the artist admires with primitive simplicity. It was said of Yu-K'o that when he painted bamboos, he forgot his own body and became transformed into bamboo, he saw bamboos, not mankind. So when you paint a horse, a cat, a butterfly, a stream, you must become all these, not see them in terms of utility to man, nor as part of some mystical scheme to human advantage (not like the praying cows of Italian primitives, that is). He who succeeds in setting down the soul of bamboo, of stone, of old trees, that man must feel serene and divine (he is in union with nature, as they say). Some things in Wordsworth, Shelley, Coleridge, Blake, and other poets you know will suggest what I mean. Keats has said, 'A poet has no identity; he is continually in, for, and filling some other body.' This is the spirit of the Orient, at the same time mystic and sensuous. Like the German word, *Seele*...so simple.... As when you are happy, and can't say anything, you talk on flowers, trees, birds, clouds and streams." And Kim's face looked happy for the moment. "And then you meet your friend through the medium of nature more universal than the human face or individuality."

Helen met his eyes, then turned hers away. "What an amazing dragon," she quickly commented. "Where did they ever get the models for such things?"

"You must say good-bye to the Oriental muse, if you paint as Western artists do from models."

"Do you never paint from models?"

"Well, a Chinese poet-artist says, 'Art produces something beyond the form of things, though its importance lies in preserving the form of things.' A craftsman may be able to represent form, but genius is something else. So always the Oriental artists aim to interpret the inner spirit rather than the outer look. If an artist draws a rose, it is not the color or the form he is trying to get, but its blooming fragrant grace. To him the mystery and beauty of the rose are more significant than shape. Always it is suggestiveness he is creating; not show." He interpreted a poem for Helen from the great T'ang poet, Li Po, one of Kim's heroes:

> Ch'uang ch'ien ming yüeh kuang
> I shih ti shang shuang
> Chü tou wang ming yüeh
> Ti tou ssū ku hsiang

> Moonlight before my bed—
> Or is it hoar frost spread?
> To the moon, I raise my eyes.
> With thoughts of home, I bow my head.

Afterwards we sat down in the symposium circle, and Brown and Kim had glasses filled with drink and cigarettes to smoke. Helen and I had neither the smoke nor the drink, and so we had few words for which drink always seems the medicine. It was mostly Kim who talked; not, as before dinner, Brown. I had never seen Kim so stimulated. A question from Helen, a hint from Brown was enough to set him off. What tales he had to tell, and what a variety of people and scenes he remembered! In the Far East, he had wandered through the heart of storms, amidst guns and fires, battles and revolutions. He had lived long in Europe, he had visited in the Near East, even in Africa...one moment drinking the famous beer of Heidelberg, the next eating fettucini at Alfredo's in Rome, sauntering by the bookstalls in Paris, Shanghai, Tokyo, and now recalling everything over a glass of American gin in New York City. His suave irony came out as never before in delicate humor, and he kept Helen and Brown in gales of laughter softened immediately afterwards to a touched gravity. The Oriental exile of Kim's generation is really a new character in history. His break with his kind is so profound, by reason of the abnormal expansion of his knowledge and experience; he is at the same time so outside the alien worlds he travels in, so isolated and apart, he gives a new interpretation of the solitariness of the human soul, its essential curiosity and dauntlessness.

It grew later and later. Time to go. I said good night to Brown. Kim was talking to Helen about an exhibition in New York of some modern French art he was going to see, and I heard him ask, "Would you like to see it?"

"I'd love to."

"May I come for you here?"

Helen's face clouded in perplexity. She hesitated. "I'm not staying here. Tomorrow I will be with my aunt, and from then on, until I return to Boston."

"Aunt Helen?" asked Kim quickly, with a smile.

"How did you guess?" she held out her hand impulsively, clasping his warmly, as if asking forgiveness for circumstances outside her power to change, as she said, "Will you let me meet you at the gallery?"

6

Kim invited me to come to his place once more, before I returned to Boston that Easter vacation. For tea, he said. When I got there, to my surprise, I found Helen Hancock. There were only we three. I believe Kim asked me out of a sensitive tact that would err always on the side of formality rather than give Miss Hancock, who was rather old-fashioned, the slightest reason for uncomfortableness. Helen was sitting near a bowl of roses and Kim was walking up and down before her, smoking. They seemed very cozy. I interrupted some argument when I came in, and Kim immediately resumed it.

"No, Helen, what you were saying is wrong. How can there be an absolute—for truth or morals? Nothing I see so relative as morality. To illustrate my meaning, if you had to choose between being burned in hell-fire and walking naked down Fifth Avenue, you would probably choose the former, though the latter is no more than a question of social etiquette."

"You think I am no Lady Godiva?" Helen laughed.

"I think you are an extremely conventional Western woman. And you see you are blushing—that is symbolic." (Helen contradicted him.) "Today in certain parts of Africa or in the South Sea Islands and else-where, young girls and women bathe naked in a natural pool with men. And if you were there, you would be accustomed to this daily practice although at first sight you might be shocked. In some countries nakedness has actually been prescribed by laws and clothes are immoral. For instance, in Rohl all women who are not Arabic are forbidden to wear clothes. And the king of Mandingo commits a sin if he allows a woman, even a princess, to approach him otherwise than naked."

"There! And you still argue we are no better off than to be in Africa!"

"Not morally," Kim was insisting stubbornly. "Morality can never be judged outside its own environment. You speak of the evolution of morality. I do not see it. Education, invention, and progress all help to satisfy our savage natures far more than primitive society. Why, primitive man had to work hard to conquer one enemy—he had to give all his might, and risk life against life. Now a slight touch on a button—like pressing an electric light—

this will defeat thousands of men. Savageness of man to man, isn't that what we mean by immorality? Or should mean. Progress has not removed the motive to kill—but only extends it, complicates it, just as warfare is expanded by new engines. Don't be deluded by modern civilization, electrified advertisement, press a button and you see a wonder-lighted land!"

So they went on, while one gathered from the few soft words of Helen that the grand question of life is moral, and the big problem of the universe is truth, and Kim kept repeating like some man who must save face, "In my experience, the pagan is no more savage than the so-called modern; no, he is only much simpler, much closer to natural laws. Man grows more unsure of his part in nature and more artificial, the farther his stage..."

Till Kim said, "The water is boiling." And Helen, "Let me make the tea." How warm and nice it was to be in here with them where some subtle excitement reigned in the atmosphere! At least, knowing Kim, I felt that he was moved by something, though he had not had his usual drink, only tea. And Helen—who mostly suggested that she was bred in an old-fashioned Christian home with nineteenth-century New England morality which forgot that Adam was ever naked with his wife and not ashamed in the Garden of Eden—unconsciously looked as relaxed, smiling, shyly receptive as the opening buds among the roses in the Chinese bowl. The tea was rare. It had been sent Kim from home. It was almost colorless, but some little flowers opened themselves frailly there. A delicate bouquet came forth, yet the tea was not sweet; it had nothing of honey-cloy nor jasmine-taste, only a faintly buoyant bitterness stealing through and refining all the senses.

We sat around Kim's nest of small tea tables. Though somewhat higher they seemed quite in keeping with Korean style. The smallness of the room and its unusual crowding with the tea things drew us closely together. Helen, it seemed, was going to Europe again next summer. Talk turned on that. Kim said: "You must think of me on some of those Alpine walks. Promise. When you see green grasses and running gushing streams. Then you will glance in imagination at the unhappy savage, Kim...a kicking rebel in your march of civilization."

Helen looked at Kim as if in a playful perplexity. Quite unlike the girls at the Village party, she never smoked nor drank gin, but sipped tea and ate tiny sandwiches, so small that I could put three in the mouth at one time and speak understandably. But Helen took three bites to each instead of three to one bite. "And you are so truly a civilized person, To Wan. But why are you here? Not in civilization, I mean, but in New York."

"It is the human restlessness in life. Oh, this ambition of man's to conquer everything! How great! How magnificent! I think so. Because of it, Ulysses wandered to unknown lands across the seas. Man must go beyond the deserts of burning sands, through the unexplored forests and over the ice-glued poles—what for? Nobody knows. But what a man! forever homesick, forever lonely, forever unsatisfied! What romance in his insatiable activities! The Columbian navigation, the journeys of Livingstone and Stanley...and so on over the snow-capped peaks of Himalaya, across the plain of Mongolia, past the deserts of Araby to the shore of the yellow sea. It has always been so. There was Alexander. He tried to marry Asia and Europe—but at that time he was like a wasp making a fight with a caterpillar. Genghis Khan in his day invaded half the world. And today what is he? Only a shadowy figure in legend. The Roman Empire existed once and is no more. Behind it, many more empires lost in the dim past. Once the highest culture of the world was passing through Korea, unknown to the contemporary West of Charlemagne. Where are all these empires now and what were they for? Only to become splintered into fragments? And still man tries and tries again. Man, man! the strangest animal! He alone feels the romance of conquest, the glamor of commerce and exchange, the divine thrill of the religious search! And he alone so badly wants his face saved, more than all other creatures. Then what other animal so active as he? For him there is no mating season...winter as well as spring, far into autumn, deep into summer, all year round a lover and maker forever...."

Helen said nothing to this, but merely consulted her tea, so Kim continued, "But I mean it. I agree with Lao Tze. Civilization is life's mistake. Man thinks.... The more he thinks, the more thinking kills in him all natural instincts. Even the instinct for death. Here in the West those who logically conceived death, and were willing to wait for it, long ago became disillusioned. They had to build up superstitious conceptions of immortality of the soul...or the even more deluded idea of resurrection of the body. As man develops his brain power more, as he enters into the evolution of higher organisms, so he becomes more sensitive and more nervous, his problems are more complicated, his sorrows are increased. I have seen it. My country has many sorrows. But they are more natural ones, such as not having enough to eat, or the premature dying of children, or failure to have any children at all   something like that. And now, the Japanese oppression and the hint of race-death for all. But just see the sorrows Westerners can create. Romeo and Juliet. Do you know, I have heard Orientals laugh at Romeo and Juliet. Too silly, they said; they never heard of love till they saw that. The tragedy of individual love is something foreign still to their viewpoint."

Helen looked a little offended about the Orient. "Strange, to think of a whole hemisphere without our complicated Christian views on love...a Western woman would not be very happy there."

"You value that?"

"I suppose I do." Helen paused. "I have always unconsciously believed in it, as the only happiness, power, and security possible to women. Perhaps I am wrong." Helen said a few more hesitating words on that. She was reserved, yet candid and sincere. Not a great talker, but when she got through I felt she was one to make love a profession and romance an occupation, and that when it did not come, she had become a wanderer in homesickness and a traveler in distress. As Kim believed in art for art's sake, she believed in love for love's sake. Napoleon is remembered because he was a great general in battle, Michelangelo because he was a great creator in art. Helen, it would seem, if she fulfilled logically her aspirations, would choose to be remembered only as an ardent lover. Helen Hancock, in short, was rather nineteenth-century, with a slight veneer of twentieth-century education, travel, culture...and the freedom given the American girl in a prosperous Boston family, cautiously used. At the same time I saw as no Westerner could that she was just the type to appeal to Kim. He would not like a revolting, tortured spirit like himself. Helen's character and principles had irresistible fascination for the man of lost patterns, the man with a deep Confucian love of ordered life. Nor did they cause him the irritation of one who was brought up on those. (Arthur Brown, for instance.) Her difference of ideas was thrilling stimulation, yet his own innate simplicity of soul—an

Eastern quality—found an echo in hers from New England. I suddenly agreed with Hsu Tsimou…it was a consummation devoutly to be hoped for. Helen might save Kim if she only would.

"I like what you say. It is a beautiful sentiment. But I think that for you the ways of other cultures remain heathen ways, cruel, barbaric and unspeakable…" Kim said to her with a twinkle in his eyes.

"Oh, it's not that. It's a matter of roots and environment."

"But you do have racial prejudice?"

"I don't think I have."

"Don't you feel always with me 'To Wan Kim is a man of another race'? I sense that in you."

Helen hesitated. I felt she was weighing her own feelings, determined to give them as honestly as she could. "I don't know how I feel about you, To Wan," she said, crossing her legs and putting her hands behind her head, regarding the fire reflectively. "I enjoy you very much. I think I am always happy with you. As with Nature."

Kim flushed with pleasure. "And you…to me are sunshine on gray mountain slopes. The difference between a frowning cold day and a jolly and sparkling one. I cease to be a lonely exile in your company. I return to the world of men and I leave the realm of ghosts. I feel the joy and grace of humanity again…. But you, what did you mean, in what you said just now?"

"It is hard to express, To Wan…there is a restfulness with you I do not feel with other men. Perhaps Oriental art—if I knew it and loved it as Arthur does—might give me the same feeling. Or is it that we must agree somewhere, very fundamentally?… Yes, I am much more natural and simple with you than with men of my own race, that is the only difference."

But Kim looked dissatisfied with this. "Is it not because you would make an invisible wall between us as man and woman? A wall of all the shortcomings of East as West sees them?… Isn't it unfair to look into another society, seeking only specialized virtues…in their absence finding only specialized vices?"

"I don't understand you."

"Your measuring rod is depth or shallowness in the love relation, for instance."

"It is part of my upbringing and philosophy perhaps."

"Yes. The Oriental coming West brings his measuring rod too."

"What is it? Now we will understand each other," exclaimed Helen with vivacity. She was always at home in absolutes, it seemed.

"From the fourth century B.C. comes a story. A man saw a little child crying hard for the loss of its parents. He said to his teacher, a Confucian scholar, 'I could never understand the rites of mourners. Here in this child we have an honest expression of feeling, and that is all there should ever be.' The teacher rebuked him. 'The mourning ceremonial with all its accompaniments is at once a check upon undue emotion and a guarantee against any lack of proper respect. Simply to give vent to the feelings is the way of barbarians. That is not our way.' Well, this little child crying is the way of Western love."

"Yes," said Helen doubtfully.

I wondered, would Kim try to show next that he worshipped not Woman even if he did? Of course he was not one for a genuine Romeo-Julietting, and he had too much pride to be as cheap as George. But George would say 'It is better to worship women than ancestors. It is more sincere, more natural and more beautiful. One is living to inspire you, the other dead to be forgotten.' Yet I wished Kim would not show this pride with Helen. George might get on with better success there, if he had Kim's talents in other directions.

Kim continued, "Choice, and surrender to love…this in the West is heroism in the lover. 'Love is the most beautiful phenomenon in all animated nature, the mightiest magnet of the spiritual world, the source of all veneration and the sublimest virtue'—that is Schiller. But you cannot guess the shock of these words to the poor Confucian pagan, with his measuring rod of discipline, by which love is regarded as the barbaric emotion, for love brings forgetfulness of pride, decorum, dignity, and family duties toward others. This Oriental looks around bewildered on your civilized world of civilized wives and civilized husbands. And out of your most sublime virtue do come the most involved vices. Oh, the beginning seems to be very fine. But then after the thrill of the honeymoon they get bored. They want separation, divorce, surrender to love over again. Sometimes, if I read aright the newspapers, they go back to the savage custom of murdering. Yes. This sublime sentiment gets them united. This heroic rebellion gets them separated. This noble and inspiring passion gets them murdered.... But then the murder is logical. How could we have Romeo without Othello? With love the highest virtue, jealousy should be elevated too. Love, it is said, is impossible without some degree of hatred and jealousy and some difficulty. If one says he has none of these on the stage of rival's competition or these difficulties, certainly he has no love, he is no lover, just a pass-a-day-together, week-end companion. Many people I know here say there are freedom and charm in the week-end marriage...and would like to change all marriage to the freedom and charm of that. To me that kind of freedom would be to be a fish still alive in cold water in the frying-pan, and that kind of charm only make-up-face-and-falsetto. But I am neither Confucian nor a Western man. Better to accept Western love wholly or not at all, I should say. Even so, in Western love we do not know the ending. While in Chinese poetry the last line always is written first."

"And being narrow, I'm still pretty sure I'm better off in New England than in New York, Asia, or Africa," said Helen with an innocent laugh.

"Why not stay there, then?" Kim asked. "Why go to Europe?"

"Oh, I'm always ready to come back. Maybe Arthur is right.... Do you think I am a typical Yankee puritan?"

Kim thought a bit. "No, not exactly. You are a product of this dominant West—Europe as well as America. Out of Christianity of 2000 years, out of the Renaissance of 500, out of the Victorian expansion of the nineteenth century. You are still very conscious of the transcendental philosophy of Emerson. Goethe helped. And Tennyson and Browning. It took all these centuries to make you what you are. And now you have just the right pattern and are satisfied, the pattern of all that is beautiful, graceful and charming."

Helen flushed. "Oh, To Wan...sarcasm again...Oriental irony?"

"Irony? My irony? It has no more tail to sting. I am tired of irony—too tired even to laugh with irony. I might yawn with irony, but never laugh. I can only laugh with you. Never, at you. When tonight I could give you my life on a nickel, and buy an ice-cream cone and find the entrance to the graveyard?"

"Do you mind if I say something?" said Helen.

"I always like to hear what Helen says."

"Always you have seemed to me overexcited, moody and nervous, and it has a good deal to do with drinking, late hours and cigarettes."

"What is one more cocktail in New York after all I have sucked? What is one more cigarette after ten thousand? Why should I fear a little thing like this?" He held up a fresh cigarette. "Keep your fright and horror for something bigger than that. Suppose I smoked opium like De Quincey. Still, you can't buy opium in New York, it is too expensive. Besides, more than the drink, it is illegal. When one can't get De Quincey's medicine for the moments of depression, what have you against this cheaper substitute? This dose is not a stimulant but a sedative to me. And with enough drink, all the affairs of the world become no more than duckweeds on a pond, so a Chinese philosopher says. I have to have them, in this risky game, in this rotten air, in this lonely city. No, I will keep my cigarettes and cocktail a while longer. I need civilized vices in order to compete with civilization."

Then Kim added, "But do not say I am a pessimist or unbeliever. Though I deny the values of two hemispheres. I am still not civilized enough for a real cynic. And I believe in two things. In Helen and in Death." And he reached to his book case and showed Helen a poem which read:

> C'est la mort qui console, hélas! et qui fait vivre;
> C'est le but de la vie, et c'est le seul espoir,
> Qui, comme un elixir, nous monte et nous enivre,
> Et nous donne le cœur de marcher jusqu'au soir.

And after that his whole mood seemed to change. Kim's face brightened, he was happy now, and gay and sparkling. "All live for the moment in the present hour. When that hour comes to perfect bloom, it is a lot. Who cares then whether time is going to see fruits, or the flower turn to seed, or wither in the desert sun—or be blighted in the winter cold? Yes. This is good. Over a cup of tea in a warm room with you. Just to bloom for an hour—and not to be a Faust in the anxious search through philosophy and history."

7

I left New York at the latest possible moment—Sunday afternoon. Hitch-hiking alone, I was picked up by a young man in a new, sporty roadster. That is, he told me it was new, and he said, "Let's see how fast we can go." We saw several cops, but he boasted that he could outrun all cops. This seemed to be true. We saw a number of cops on motorcycles, but he went faster than any of them. He told me he intended to sleep in Boston that night, and he would need a good long rest, as he had been up late the night before. We passed Marlboro but we were still a good ways short of Framingham when a traffic officer dropped down the railroad gate in front of us. (He had received a telephone message from one of the disappointed cops far behind.) Now my driver got into trouble. For this gave them the break, and all the motorcycle cops we had outrun came up with us. My driver didn't even have his license with him! He was informed that he would have to go to jail for the night. But he was in very good spirits and he said, pointing to me, "Let my buddy go. He has to get back in time for an early morning class and he's only a hitchhiker." So he was taken and I was left. It was too far to get to Framingham for the night, on foot, and too far back to walk to Marlboro. Since it was nearing eleven o'clock, I knew everybody on the road would be afraid to pick up hitchhikers, for fear they might be robbers or gangsters. I stood a long time at the crossing, talking to the cop who had dropped down the railroad gates. It was a busy section and continually he whirled his stick and blew his whistle. He was a big, good-natured Irishman, and I explained to him again about my class in Boston.

"You see, I have to get back. Or I'll get on probation. And maybe flunk."

"Well, son, I don't see how I can help you."

"Oh yes, you can, sir, if you wouldn't mind."

Then I begged him to lend me his cap and whistle. Just for a moment. The cop grinned. He saw my scheme. "Can't do that exactly. But I will help you out." He blew his whistle a mighty blast. He stepped out in front of the cars heading in the Boston direction and held up his hand. My! how all those cars grated and stopped. They thought they were being stopped to find some criminal, or else that they were going to be searched for bootleg whiskey.

"What car is going to Boston?"

"Here! Here! Here, Officer, I'm going there."

Each thought he must carry in some important message and everybody was excited, just as when the chief of police rolls by with all his bells ringing.

"Take your choice!" the cop waved me toward the cars.

I picked out a very handsome one and finished my trip to Boston in a roomy limousine.

BOOK EIGHT

1

JUNE HAD ALMOST COME. Time to make plans for the summer. Boston already grew hot and stifling on some days. Before the college term was over, a prospect turned up that looked very advantageous for me. It came through Richard Chai, a Korean medical student interning in one of the Boston hospitals. My prospect was a position answering phone calls in a doctor's house on Beacon Street while the family went to Marblehead from the middle of June until the 1st of October. Chai took me around to meet Doctor Dimassi in his office. I liked the doctor very much, and he was cordial to me. So my summer was settled. A great load off my mind. The work would not be arduous and I could get a lot of reading done.

Richard Chai had been kind to me all that winter. Poor in the beginning, like the rest of us, Chai had done very well in Boston. In his medical studies he was a *cum laude*. He was given a blood-chemistry course to teach in the medical school, and now he moved in a circle of influential American friends. He was ready to help out any Koreans who behaved themselves.

Chai was really one generation removed from Korea; he was Hawaiian-bred—a slim, small, delicately built person with hair rather fine, brushed high from his forehead. He was always scrupulously neat, fastidious, soigné. A born society man, he yet had tact and well-meaning for everybody—an unusual combination obviously destined to success in a professional line. George Jum maintained that Chai tried too hard to be "white," but then Jum was prejudiced against him, and he against Jum; they were too different. Besides, ever since coming to Boston, Chai had been in love with an American girl, Martha Wright, confidential secretary to Doctor Morrison. Chai was very circumspect in this and did not talk much until he saw how it was going to turn out. He courted Miss Wright first through his high grades and their meetings over scholarships. (She handled scholarships, just that kind Chai was always carrying away.) And grades would naturally mean a lot to her, for she was wearing a Phi Beta Kappa key. Miss Martha Wright was a handsome, imposing girl with golden hair always beautifully marcelled, and was very popular in the university circles where she moved; she was intelligent and efficient in everything, even in the good appearance where often Phi Beta Kappa keys do not help.

Chai bided his time, but was playing every love-card skillfully, avoiding both the crassness of George and the gloomy confusion of Kim. By this time he had Martha Wright and Doctor Morrison both singing his praises, one to the other. Chai was not much interested in my line—philosophy and literature—but in his own field he knew what he was doing.

No Korean anyhow was much interested in my line. Nobody except Kim and George. For instance, there was the Korean Eulchoon Chang. Chang was studying to be an engineer—and unlike Guru, the Hindu, he overcame all theosophical temptations—he stuck to engineering. Chang's mind was clear and practical; in personality, he was amiable, alert, but quiet, tending strictly to his own business. All Koreans I have known had a good word for Chang and for his gentle shrewdness. Even George, who did not care much for the student type. George's respect for him might be measured by the fact that he predicted to me: "Chang will some day be a millionaire because he knows the value of money." To know the value of money was with George almost a mystical phrase. It did not signify either spending or hoarding—but it meant cleverness with a tool, a necessary tool which would fit you into the American environment. Chang had done many kinds of work at first. But now he had a very successful job, which began in Jordan Marsh's where he sold Ma Jong sets. Chang knew how to play Ma Jong very well, for he had learned in China, where he lived for a time on his way to America. He quietly expanded his salesmanship job into that of teaching Ma Jong. His appointments came through the store. Ma Jong was at the height of its popularity. During the summer he sold Ma Jong sets, and during the winter he studied in college and gave Ma Jong lessons in his leisure hours. Ten and twenty dollars a night he would make for instructing a party, and as a teacher Chang was very popular. He had self-possession and tact and he got on beautifully with wealthy Americans.

Chang had known George for a long time, having also done some studying in New York. Each had a tolerance and respect for the other's personality, though they were not exactly chums, being too different. Chang told me he had in mind to get George a good job in Boston through one of his wealthy patrons. I said, "Oh, George will never leave June." Chang said, "Didn't you know? They fight all the time."

Chang had been in New York more recently than I. And Chang said she would send George wires to visit her in Philadelphia. When he got there, she received him in a sumptuous millionaire's apartment. She had the same kind in several cities. It was strange. "There isn't much money in dancing unless you are a Broadway star," Chang said. Also she would sometimes break their date in the midst and send George away suddenly, if she received a telephone call.

"I believe she is June to George, but May to some one else," Chang said. And he said thoughtfully, it would be a good thing to bring Jum to Boston. Anyhow he meant to offer him a good job, as soon as he could pick one out.

Chulmo Chu was also very anxious for George to come to Boston. Chu was not exactly a student, though originally he had come to Boston to study. He had already spent three years at a college in the South. He thought he was ready to be a senior in a college in Boston. But in Boston he was degraded to the rank of a freshman. Then at the end of the first semester, he was made a special student because of his poor grades in English composition. This completely discouraged him in education. At the same time he had the offer of a very good butlering job with a wealthy real-estate man, Morris Reynolds. "Four years in college and nothing to show for it," argued Chulmo Chu. "Why should I go on being a starving student when I can get a good job like this one?"

And nobody could deny that of its kind it was a very fine job. By the middle of May, the Reynolds family had all gone to Europe for the summer, and Chu was left in charge, with their great, luxurious house all to himself. He got his usual wages while they were gone, and he had the use of a Ford car as his own. When the car was turned over, his employer never suspected that Chu was anything but an accomplished driver, and as a matter of fact Chu had learned how to drive it in a few hours. In spite of inexperience he never had had an accident. And now he had been driving this car for several months. He was very clever always with his hands. He boasted that he could do things simultaneously, such as driving and taking pictures at the same time, a cigar in his mouth.

At last George came up to Boston. But it turned out, June came along, too. However, she was staying with friends and we did not see her much. George stayed with Chulmo Chu. Saturday, Chulmo wanted to take the car out, and I felt I should drive up to the Higginses and tell them I was not coming back that summer to work on the farm. We started out, Chai, Chu, George, Chang, and I. Then George insisted on stopping for June. We picked her up at a downtown drugstore. She and George seemed as thick as ever, though George did say rather sarcastically, "It's good you did not make me wait this time"…and she, as sweet as anything, "No, darling." I think she was fond of George and his lovemaking, but not quite fond enough to be sincere. I was a little uncomfortable as to how they would behave before the Higginses. June's skirts, of course, were very short and her mouth very red. Otherwise she was all right, for she always dressed simply. Humble, kindly, sincere, the Higginses came out to meet my friends. George did most of the talking, while June did some of the interpreting. June was good at acting. She told Mrs. Higgins that she was half-Chinese, that she and George were engaged and were going to Hawaii to live. Mrs. Higgins put down any shortcomings that she saw in them to heathen ignorance. But she told me they would make a wonderful pair, and you could see her thinking that perhaps they might even do something for the church. Mrs. Higgins took June off with her and made her a gorgeous bouquet from flowers in the garden. June and George seemed in a very good humor with one another until they got back to Boston. Then June had another engagement.

George began running down Boston, after that. So it didn't look as if we would get him there after all. "Oh, what a hell of a town! No good whisky, no good shows, women all homely, cold intelligentsia! Boston hasn't even a decent magazine."

"*The Atlantic Monthly,*" said Chai, sharply. (Always he was irritated by George.)

"That I can't stand!"

"I read it regularly. And everything there is very well written..." Chai insisted coldly.

"Well done...I know...well done! You may like steak well done. I like mine rare. This is according to taste." And George shut up sulkily. He wouldn't argue any more on Boston.

But soon he and Chai plunged into argument again, this time on love. Chai was very reserved on love, but he had decided opinions. "Love is having a wife that is well chosen. All else is fool's play. A wife can make or ruin a man. That is clear."

George snorted at this. "Well, love, like poetry or like life, has a thousand definitions. Many are brilliant, suggestive, clever and enlightening. Love...I can't tell what it is. But it is only real to those who have experienced it. It is as the breathing air that gives life to all living creatures; the bird that was put in a cage without ventilation died. (It is divorced from logic and has nothing to do with acquiring a respectable wife and four or five children.) But just as with life, nobody can define it except by living, so nobody can talk on love except by loving. And I have loved a thousand different ways, some ardently, others half-heartedly, and still again reluctantly, and now I have come to the conclusion, to love is loving and is nothing else."

"Yes, the man who loves many wastes time and energy," said Chai. "In the end he is left with nothing to show." ("Like four years in college and

not even the diploma in hand," commented Chu with personal reminis-
cence.) "Never love wastefully. That is my advice to you." (Chai meant to
be very disapproving of any show-girl.)

"Hell, you are wrong!" cried George the romantic and the anti-
Confucian. "Love has to be wasteful, or it is no more love. Yes, it is wasteful, but it is not losing anything. You, Chai, are not saving anything up...
only to miss the radiance of the tender morning and the grandeur of the
setting sun. Even when the love is gone—and in this life nothing is sure—
the picture of the lost world, the memory of yesterday's love, gives the
strength for tomorrow."

George went on talking about various aspects of love, and Chai
equally contradicting. He said a kiss could not possibly last as long as George
said. George said, "Well, I need every bit of the time allowed." They made a
bet. George said he would carry it out as soon as he could get June up to
Chulmo's. So she did come up, late one night. While Chu was making
cooksoo in the kitchen, George said to Chai to get out his watch. June was
sitting on the Morris Reynolds table smoking a cigarette lazily, and she
agreed George ought not to lose his bet. George began just as the minute
hand reached a certain point, and Chai said, "Go." Chai stood right there
looking at his watch as if he were watching an egg boiling in water. Chai lost
his bet. George won. A kiss from George did take as long as George had said
it would.

2

Even before George had left, Kim came to Boston on one of those obscure
errands of his. I received a note asking me to meet him at the Boston Public
Library. Arriving there, I found Kim in the lobby, seemingly engrossed in
the works of Sargent. We went into the Bates Hall and to my surprise found
Helen Hancock. She was in white sweater and skirt and without a hat. She
rose at once, and we tiptoed out.

When we arrived on the street outside, she said with a bright smile,
nodding at Kim, "We're playing truant from New York."

"Boston too, *nicht*?" said Kim.

Her car was waiting. She was a good driver. We drove to Riverside, and Kim rented a canoe. It was a beautiful day, a little bit warm but not too warm. Under the shade at Riverside, heat did not penetrate much. This place was new to me, but they both seemed to know it. Oh, it was wonderful to be in the country again, just at this time, when the college year was closing! We had left Boston behind, Boston where the accumulation of puritanic dirt made me uneasy. I would have liked to jump at once into the river, wash off all dirts and send them down to the sea, becoming a child again as I was in Korea. These were not actually the dirts that could be washed off in the bathtub at all. *They* are only the outside kind. But oh, to wash off the dirts from the inside, something of dullness and discouragement, disillusion and weary lethargy, those dirts of futility that the winter brought to the weary struggler in Boston! Ah yes, the sunshine was good, and not too warm! It was so good that you feared it might not last long. Far away the blue banked-up clouds showed a vapor of pearly whiteness. The pure, exhilarating New England wind blew my hair and touched my shirt sleeves vigorously, but sunshine was encircling all, and wherever the wind touched, the sunshine touched too, with a golden, gentle, all pervading pressure. The soil was green-clothed all over, trees luxuriously blooming, branches spreading out, leaves spotlessly clean and large, as if new overnight. All was green, not the green of one color but the green of many greens—of dark, bright, light, even whitish greens…indeed I noticed some of the leaves were tinted yellow, with tenderest russet, too. You felt that the whole year, all eternity, was here wrapped up in a package and waiting to be unfastened just for you. What tranquil relaxation, cheerfulness, serenity was in that atmosphere! The sun slipped into the moistened earth with poignant odor. The distant hills sent up a mystic haze, and the winding, pleasant river ran zigzagging on its healthy errand to the sea. There were bees and many flimsy flies roaming over the blooms of the common shrubs. We heard a multitude of sounds, yet the landscape had one voice, softly singing.

The canoe glided down like a floating fish. Kim and I paddled at either end. Helen sat in the middle of the boat, stretching out slim silk-covered legs. I thought she looked rather like an escaped nun out of a convent. But Kim was a wild man of the desert coming to a blooming oasis out of the Sahara. On and on we glided, not working, always moving. Now we passed a deep crystal pool where the morning mists, it seemed, still gathered, yet clear, to the bottom, like a looking glass. Now we reached the changing, rippling currents, we went fast. How clean, clean the running sparkling water! How cold it felt to the hand! Like that wine described in an old poem I knew by heart, rich-bodied as with spring, yet chill as fall winds, warm sunshine and ice mingling in its breath. I thought of melting snow-fields higher up, mountain torrents, faraway brooks and valley streams, all combined and verging toward the sea, bearing our boat onward...yes, everything moving, drifting seaward, but with a flowing motion, making no rushing sound.

What varied banks we passed, sprinkled with rushes, meadow-sweet and bluets. Now we glided around wooded islands in their young dress of rich, tender green. One island was so enchanting that we drew in to the shore. Jumping out, we tethered the canoe and sat in a pine grove, resting carelessly on the new grass and last year's pine needles. We gazed up at the bright sky through the tender leaves and lacquered needles, and all the while there came the murmur of striped bees, and the chirruping of pastel-green insects.

Kim was lying comfortably at ease. His body merged into the earth like the curves in Oriental pictures, like a dog or a cat or a fox that nestles down; he had none of the gingery abruptness, the temporary unhingement of the Western figure flinging itself down on the lap of nature from the accustomed chair. Helen of course sat upright, her knees folded under her in a delicate angularity, her whole body poised in the Gothic brittle lines to be associated with New England. Kim was recalling a poem by Su Tung P'o.

"In this poem a friend tells Su Tung P'o: 'You and I have fished and gathered fuel on the river islets. We have consorted with the fish and the prawns, we have befriended the deer. Together we have sailed our skiff, frail as a leaf; in close companionship we have drunk wine from the gourd. We pass through this world like two gnats in a husk of millet on a boundless ocean. I grieve that life is but a moment in time, and envy the endless current of the Great River....' Listen what Su Tung P'o replied, 'Do you understand the water and the moon? The former passes by, but has never gone. The latter waxes and wanes but does not really increase or diminish. For, if we regard this question as one of impermanence, then the universe cannot last for a twinkling of an eye. If, on the other hand, we consider it from the aspect of permanence, then you and I, together with all matter, are imperishable. Why, then, this yearning?'"

"To Wan, how beautiful that is," exclaimed Helen, thinking it over. "How stimulating and suggestive!"

"That was written in the year one thousand and something," said Kim lazily. "But still I see nothing in the West to compare with the reasonableness of such a mood."

Helen hitched herself forward a little as if beginning conversation in earnest now, though Kim still had the lazy attitude. "Why did you give me T. S. Eliot's poems to read?"

> ...What are the roots that clutch, what branches grow
> Out of this stony rubbish? Son of man,
> You cannot say or guess, for you know only
> A heap of broken images, where the sun beats,
> And the dead tree gives no shelter, the cricket no relief,
> And the dry stone no sound of water.

Kim quoted. "Well, did the book touch you emotionally, Helen?"

"But he is intellect *vs.* emotion, is he not?"

"There is no such thing. A poet is always emotion *vs.* intellect... although he never ceases to defend the intellect against the emotions. And Spencer has said, 'Were it fully understood that the emotions are the masters and the intellect the servant, it would seem that little can be done by improving the servant, while the master remains unimproved....' Then you were not touched emotionally by him?"

"My main emotion," said Helen honestly, "was that I was sorry for Mr. Eliot. But I don't think I understood him very well."

"Why feel sorry? He will go back to Christianity...whereas I am in the same predicament but worse. All my roads cut off. Nor can I possibly go back. Nature is sterner with me than with Mr. Eliot." Kim settled himself more comfortably. "And perhaps it is just as well."

"Then you yourself don't like Mr. Eliot much?"

"He has given me some headache. But many Western phenomena have done that. His influence will undoubtedly live a few more years. Then that, too, will vanish just like morning dew from these green leaves, since we mortals are more interested in life than in death. (Even more interested in life than in art.) Of course I am not minimizing. *The Waste Land* is a great poem and its creator is great. He has seen beyond most. Death and the something that once was, greater than the death that is now. How hauntingly he conveys his seriousness! But it takes a greater to see more than that. What inconsistency in going back! Christianity! Buddhism! Confucianism! All are like milestones on a road that is past. How impossible for me to go back, more impossible than to see how many angels can dance on the point of the needle without being jostled. And I, too, am inconsistent. I myself do not know whether Westerners like Eliot are more to be envied or pitied. I envy one moment, I pity another moment. And I myself am probably the more pitiable spectacle. My emotions are strong enough, but my intellect seems a sick, disobedient servant. I am tired of the Western learning and all it implies. Yet one thing I know. To us Easterners, until our vitality becomes all exhausted—this Western death is a luxury we can't afford!"

And death indeed did not seem in the atmosphere. I thought, where now are the suffering ghosts of Abelard and Heloise? Dante does not mourn for Beatrice here, neither Petrarch for Laura. Nor does Othello walk here with Iago. Here only are blooming trees and fragrant grasses, the sounds of human merriment from rowing boats. A good many of the canoes hold just two. Romeo and Juliet—I thought. And the sky's hues and the earth's tints were mingled before us on the flowing water. We made a further stop to get some lunch, and all that we ate seemed a part with our happy drifting through nature.

By mid-afternoon, the temperature already seemed to have acquired the summer gesture. Some we saw that afternoon were swimming in the river. And we saw others in their bathing suits playing along the edge. Yet I knew the water was cold, from the touch of it. Perhaps the girls and boys were there, having in mind to show off their legs rather than white sport dresses. But the bright, shining flesh fitted in like beautiful poetry to the jolly pastoral scene. As for the many others seeking pleasure like us in the canoe trip, their presence was no more disturbing than the rest of nature. Some were already landing, others just setting out. Laughter, a lot of banjo, a lot of song were heard. New England seemed to be meeting now the summer isles. We drifted out into the wide part of the river, which seemed a vast boatyard full of movement. All the silent water was made alive by boats and canoes. Under the bright afternoon sun, every stroke of the paddle became a gleam. Happily I glanced at my friend. His face was not so pale and heavy as in the wintertime when I knew him before. The glowing sun was already getting into his skin to mellow it. But the spiritual change was greater than the physical. He had become light, lazy and playful; he was more natural, more Korean. Romantic despairs of the fantastic West seemed to have left his eyes, which were now lazily blinking. He was more alert, at the same time more receptive, and the whole man had gained elasticity, ease.

As we drifted down and down superbly with the day, we found the river divided into two branches—one left and the other right. The left side was crowded with more canoes, and the water there was smoother, but the right had more currents, no canoes; it seemed straight and looked promising. We took the swifter right. The canoe slid down without any paddling. By and by we came to a mill under which the river ran. Before us was a bridge to the mill, a bridge with four feet making three tunnels between. We thought we could go through one of those arches. We steered the canoe straight there. But we could not get through. Now the canoe was turning broadside, it was placing itself against the bridge between the arch and the river currents. We could not paddle back upstream because the current was too strong. Nor could we go on through the opening and escape it. Now the end of the canoe was cracking, water was leaking in. Things floated out…. So many things from the boat, light overcoats, books, bottles of cool drinks—these, once released, went through the channel, there to be lost, it would seem, in the current forever. But we could not think of them now. For now we, too, were in the water. The water was trying its best to push us under. We grasped the foot of the bridge. Looking at that hole now we did not want to go through. Helen was struggling in the water. Even her hair was wet. Kim leaped to the bank and managed to pull Helen out with my help, and together we all three rescued the poor cracked canoe. Then we ran downstream, each trying separately to rescue the overcoats, the rented cushions, even those well-soaked books including *The Waste Land*. Helen was the first to give in. She sank down on the grass. We ran back to her, our arms full of drenched salvaged articles. She did not cry, but laughed. Helen laughed and laughed. And we laughed too. "Poor Ophelia, too much water," I said.

We went into the mill and tried to get dry. It was a very dirty place with old rags lying around over the place, but it was very hot, for there was some kind of steam machinery that moved the water round and round. Helen disappeared behind a big mound of old rags. She tried to wring out all her clothes upon her. We did the same on the other side. Presently an old man came in, who was, I believe, the watchman. He was scandalized and kept saying that the mill was private and no one had the right to enter the place to get dried. He fussed and stuttered. Then he swore at us. We got out then. Finally we took canoes rented by other people, who paddled us back to the boathouse, each one in a different boat. We told the whole story, and Kim offered at once to pay for the canoe. But the boatman said it was all right, and took Kim's address, and said he would deal squarely with us for we brought back the canoe instead of leaving it on the bank and running away, as others sometimes did. Upsetting by the mill-stream was a well-known accident.

Now we had the problem of getting dried before we could go back to Boston. There was a small town near-by. Here we separated. Kim and I went to the police station, where we were given prison nightgowns and we dried our clothes amidst huge laughs, fat spits and the smell of cheap cigars. Those policemen were very nice. Helen drove into the town to get dried in a friend's house. But she came back to the police station in her car for us, and we all returned to Boston and had dinner in a Chinatown restaurant. We separated early, tired and glowing. Helen went back to Brookline, and Kim and I to our own rooms to sleep.

3

Doctor Dimassi's house faced the Esplanade, a beautiful paved walk parallel with the River Charles. It was of brick, tall and substantial. Gorgeous suave sunshine fell quietly through the Back Bay street; always a cool sea breeze fluttered the vines. There were small plots of grass on each side of the house looking more mossy than New York grass, and arching trees that seemed older than New York trees. Behind the house were a large garden, a big tree, and many flowers. A great silence lay on this street and all the tall, dignified houses seemed to be empty...most of the Back Bay people went to Nahant and Marblehead at this time of the year. But even when winter came, the same air reigned, a dreamy tranquillity, and Old-World stateliness, for it was a back bay truly, where the tide of modern business had not yet come in.

Inside Doctor Dimassi's house was a cool, dark, rather sacred feeling, which may have been due to the general tone of Back Bay or to the professional dignity of the doctor's office, to which the ground floor was devoted, with its scientific incense of formaldehyde. The living room was on the second floor, a big, leisurely room with low, comfortable divans, opulent footstools (seats in themselves) and great deep chairs. This room held a baby grand piano, a victrola and a radio, and also a big drum which was played by the doctor himself. There was a commodious fireplace for burning logs, a large table holding magazines taken by the family, *Harpers, Scribner's, The Atlantic Monthly, The Mentor,* and certain Roman Catholic magazines. Doctor Dimassi was a Roman Catholic. A tall, athletic, handsome gentleman about thirty-eight, with golden brown hair, strong white teeth, and a warm smile, he was the blend of a Sicilian-Puritan marriage, a generation or so behind. Now he was firmly ensconced in Boston society, though his Italian ancestry still gave him a rich Renaissance look and an air of cosmopolitan distinction. He knew Europe very well, but he himself was a prosperous citizen of Boston, with his season ticket at the Symphony.

The great dark staircase went up and up; the carpeted steps rippled gradually, so that they seemed almost flat. My room was on the third floor, the children's floor, on the other side of the hall from the big playroom, which had a floor mapped out with all kinds of games, big toys waiting on low shelves and many many windows through which the sunlight poured. Above was still another floor, the servants', when Doctor Dimassi's family was at home. My room had a double bed, a luxurious couch, and a door that opened into a smaller room with a cute little bed there for a child. A little desk was in this little room opposite the little bed, and I often studied in here, raising my eyes from my books to look out over the Charles River.

Every day the Negro janitor came to dust about a bit. All his life he had been with Doctor Dimassi's mother-in-law, who was an old-timer in Boston. John was his name. He was a tall, fine-figured black man about fifty. He was always very dignified and never had any sense of humor, which was unusual in a Negro. As janitor he had one specialty—it was really his profession—shining the brass on the doorplate.

Doctor Dimassi and his partner, Doctor Starr, were away all day, only returning in the evening to sleep, for they kept bachelor quarters together, in the absence of children and wives. Sometimes they came home for lunch; then they ate nothing but great round crackers, imported, crumbled into capacious bowls holding double A grade milk. Whenever they ate at home they always invited me to sit down and eat with them in the big, cool, still dining room with the curtains drawn to keep out the summery sun. Our relations were ever friendly. My job was an easy one: to be always on hand, sleep there, answer telephone calls and take down messages; my wages were six dollars a week and my room. By and by the doctors conceived the idea of eating dinner at home sometimes with me. The Club they said was very expensive—especially, added Doctor Starr, cigars!—and it was far more pleasant and cheaper to eat at home. Coming in about six o'clock, the first thing they did was to change to gymnasium suits—trunks, nothing else. Doctor Starr would mix them both a small cocktail while Doctor Dimassi and I did the cooking. Our dinners were very simple. Thick, juicy steak of the quality George would appreciate, or a big fish fresh from the sea. And rice. The rice was my charge. Doctor Starr then made the salad, and everything was placed on the dumbwaiter, while I ran ahead to the dining room to pull it up. Afterwards we sat down in style, but startlingly nudist, for all three were naked from the waist up, since I imitated the doctors to avoid the summer heat. The two doctors talked like college boys. They had a good time in kidding each other. Everything was a joke except the Catholic religion. Like many Catholics, Doctor Dimassi was devout without ever going to church. I heard his view about it. He said he accepted his faith not for a future salvation but for a present one. It was a pattern or tune needed to make life ordered and harmonious. Many Americans missed that. He preached to me one day on the dangers of becoming Americanized and losing all sense of values. I asked the doctors if they had ever read William James' *Varieties of Religious Experience*—which happened to be the book I was reading just then. Then Doctor Starr laughed, and said that happened to be the only book he had not read.

All during the summer months, I was like a hungry cow eating grass in a valley. There was a public library within five minutes' walk, and also I could use the various college and university libraries of Boston and Cambridge. I browsed from shelf to shelf—sociology, philosophy, poetry, anything that took my fancy. I consulted only my appetite. Shaw, Gibbon, Wells, Sinclair Lewis, Thackeray, Thomas Hardy, everything in odd assortment...the Brontës, the works of Jane Austen...the Americans, Hawthorne, Cooper, Poe, Melville, Whitman. I read translations of Plato and Aristotle. Besides what I read thoroughly, I touched scattered pages of thousands of books. I began to gather roughly what this man stood for, that man preached, as I picked out the general configuration of Western literature and the heads that had bobbed on the crest of its cultural waves. In the morning I walked and got books for the afternoon; I did not need to be on duty at Doctor Dimassi's until four o'clock. Even after that, I was not confined to the office, for there were telephone extensions on every floor.

Toward the end of the summer, I had a short note from Kim, telling me to be sure to look him up if I came to New York, as he had heard of some remunerative work in translation I might be able to do while studying in Boston. I thought this was worth going to New York to see about. So I engaged a Chinese student to take my place at Doctor Dimassi's, and went down on the boat.

4

Kim was glad to see me, and had me stop with him. I found him in a curious state of up and down moods. Helen was of course back of this turmoil. He had been seeing a good deal of her lately. She had returned from Europe and was visiting in New York. When she was with the Browns, he could see her freely, and when she was with her aunt, they must meet clandestinely. Her aunt, it seemed, did not approve of her friendship with Kim and was at sword's point with the Browns about that. Helen had begun at her aunt's and ended up at the Browns'. The next move appeared uncertain. I felt that their relationship was rapidly nearing a climax. I could say nothing to help my friend, indeed I could only guess at what was taking place now. Kim had no defense against Helen's conservative background. It intensified the feeling he had had all along, that he was an unwanted guest in the house of Western culture. Yet through the West (for the present, at least) he had reached the intellectual frontier of humanity. And however much Kim spoke of himself as drifting, his sense of time and tide had been the force carrying him to New York, depositing him here in unwilling attendance upon the Machine Age. From my own case, I knew that well. His emotions were deeply involved with Helen Hancock and there was nothing he could do but wait until she made up her mind. Useless to preach George's doctrine, "Do not take life too seriously." Kim would have said, "What could a fish living way down in a lower well know about the superior regions of air up above?" Yet both were Westernized. Each in his own way seemed to accept the existence of romantic love which could not be analyzed in the philosophical teakettle or in that artistic liquid tube in which Kim washed his ink brushes. George had all the animalism of the pagan, the lust of the world, the flesh of the twentieth century...while Kim's love was the voice of an unseen bird in agony in some mountain solitude, a man of another world, good for nothing in this one. One moment I thought what a pity they could not get on together, this Sancho Panza and Don Quixote of mine, and the next I saw it could never be.

Kim was not too absorbed in his own life not to take up my interests with alacrity, and the same morning I arrived he took Brown and me and a friend of Brown's to luncheon in a luxurious French restaurant. Brown's friend wanted translations done of some commercial advertising to be used in Chinese movies. As Kim had foreseen, here was some easy work for me, that could easily be forwarded from Boston to New York. Having been introduced by Kim, I was commissioned at once. So my business in New York was practically over. Kim said to wait a day or two and he would be going to Boston himself. We could go together. Helen, he hinted, might make one of the party. He said we would ask her at dinner that night. I looked forward to our trip with pleasurable anticipation, but by the middle of the afternoon, Kim was again in the depths of depression.

We took a long walk over Brooklyn Bridge and back. We paused on the bridge. I was thinking, "What a picture! The arched City Hall against the afternoon sunset, these long columns and these high towers. What different rhythm from the Grand Canal of Venice or the Hankang of Hanyang! How much more crowded and more vast! This city...this bridge. It links humanity to the world of mechanism, the world of mass production, this magnanimous gigantic structure.... All is the work of a short time, in a small space. It would have taken men in different ages hundreds of years to accomplish this. See what man has done, the changes made, here. Could nature herself with all her sweeping storms above and bursting volcanoes below affect earth so much? And what this bridge contains in people and things, spirit and matter! Where could you find that elsewhere over half a continent? The craftsman may have worked in deadening monotony, the engineer may have planned in routine formation. But the product emerges with individual creativeness, a monument to the American age. Precise, exact, swift, poignant, and powerful. It is like the swoop of the high falcon, like winged horses galloping down."

While Kim looked down into the water as upon wounded marks in his own soul, "This island," he muttered, "is rockbound. It can't grow any more. Yet the inhabitants in it increase more and more. Probably it is no longer than the span of a century since the New York of today emerged, from rural farmlands where a few simple, contented people worked, out of green pastures which once fed innocent crows to cry 'caw'! Now all the depraved creatures and exiled souls in humanity gather to help the big city's growth and add to the radical scare. Harlem is no more a forest to walk in. The Battery is no more a bathing beach. How much has the salty water down there increased its salty volume through human tears? Probably not much…most New Yorkers are not like Kim to come out here and cry in it, they are too busy. This too is called evolution. Well, science that tries to explain the how-and-where of truth, from simple to complex, from particular to general, is no help to me. As for religion and philosophy, they bring us these headaches. Is man an image of heavenly pattern, vitalized with divine breath? Bless Helen, who would seem to think so. Is he a monkey developed to the higher level with added links? Bless Darwin, who enlightened us so much…and if so where could there be that dignified soul any more than in the crow whose wing I once broke? It doesn't matter how we come here…the fact is, we are here. As for God, good, holy, infinite, the personification of highest aim and purest virtues…isn't Helen all these to me?… But what is a drop of water in that mighty river which itself is eaten up and swelled by the ocean in that shadow of Lady Liberty? Why not cut the hearts and livers of fools out and feed them to some monster the way I eat chicken livers? That way, no more fools and no more heartbreak. Here, toss them to Lady Liberty."

But when Helen came that night, Kim had changed again. He was subdued, tranquil, and joyous again. We all three took a taxi and went to some street, just where I can't remember. It seemed that it was somewhere east of Sixth Avenue, maybe on 12th Street, or perhaps it was nearer to Fifth Avenue. As we came in from the outside, down a long dim corridor, we knocked with a little brass stick, and a man's eye looked out through a narrow hole just the size of a slit in the posting box for letters. He immediately opened the door, so he must have known Kim by sight. The man was talking to Kim in some foreign language. Then we were led in and there was an imposing lady, stout and tall, in a black sequa-trimmed evening dress. She saluted Kim in a familiar voice:

"Buona sera, Signor…. Lei va bene, Signor?"

She spoke English too. She was talking English with other men who came in. She wore a perpetually easy and affable smile with frequent strong laughter. She appeared the good friend to everybody, and everybody in turn called her "Mumsey." What Mumsey meant, I did not know. It may have meant Fat Lady, or the feminine master of the house. All looked at us. Helen's arms were full of roses—Kim always had flowers for her, procured from a special Korean shop that he knew. Her face, gold red on white, appeared radiantly fresh here, among more artificial women. She was eager and simple like a freshman college girl, yet with that stand-offish attitude which to Kim was a great attraction. She and Kim looked an unusual pair. People there smiled, not at us but with us, everybody in a happy-go-lucky mood. Kim chose a table, took the roses, called by name to a waiter he knew to bring a vase of water. But we were not ready to sit down yet. Kim said, "This way we go and have some drinks."

He led the way down a narrow stairway rather dark. The upper room I saw was meant for dining, although the waiters were bringing in drinks constantly there from that place below, too. Kim stepped down first, Helen followed him, and I followed her. She didn't seem to have been in the place before, but she was quite at home. This was to me strange in view of New England morality and American prohibition. So I concluded that it was not bad etiquette, even among the puritanical, to dine at speakeasies, well-conducted ones as this appeared to be. Custom always can smooth out all inconsistencies, and generally it is custom rather than moral law that sways, as Kim earlier explained. Certainly Helen showed no sign of being inconsistent. Her slender form, which habitually had rapid movement always accompanied with a smile, moved proudly through, and one was proud to be seen with her there.

Now we were in a large basement room. It had an exit in front of an iron gate going up steps, but nobody came in that way, though a few were going out. A man employed by the speakeasy was working the door, letting people out. There were also several tables scattered over this room, and seats with tall black backs, and a few men and women drinking in happy and jolly topsy-turvy mood, some singly and some doubly, and others triadly or fourly, fively. There was a long bar running at one end, and some ladies and men standing there and drinking. A good-looking, sociable young man waited on the bar. Behind him back of the bar were pictures of Jimmy Walker, many movie actresses, actors, fighters, etc., all autographed. Around the room were signs written in several languages, meaning, it seems, "Your health." Kim asked what we wanted. Helen said reluctantly, "Beer." And I, "Ginger ale." The man at the bar looked surprised at me and asked, "Ginger ale with what?" So I said, "With water." Everybody around us laughed. Helen said, "You'd better have this," and pointed to her beer runner. I said, "Yes." For himself, Kim ordered a smaller glass, something yellowish-white with a red cherry dangling on top. This was the first beer I was to taste. Kim and Helen took up their glasses, so I took mine, and we all touched glasses, and Kim and Helen said, "Prosit." We drank. The beer was awfully bitter—vile stuff, I thought. It was not even so good as tasteless water, and certainly worse than argyrol in the nose, which I had had once, up in Green Grove while sick. I almost spit that first mouthful out of my mouth. But I pretended to drink, and sipped in each time in quantity about the size of the tiniest bead—then more—and a little more. We stood there, and Helen and Kim amused themselves by reading the signs in different languages over the walls. Kim seemed to know them all, Helen only English, German, and French. Then he taught her how to say "Prosit" in Chinese, Japanese and Korean, which three, however, were not there.

Kim finished his small glass quickly, and ordered another. At last Helen finished hers, and Kim ordered that repeated too. Then they looked at my glass and asked me what was the matter. I said it was bitter and not like the rice wine in the Orient. But I knew it must have been the same kind that Helen drank, because it came out of the same spigot, and she seemed to like it. So I restored my courage and took a big mouthful and shut my eyes and swallowed, as if I were taking cod-liver oil. Kim and Helen laughed. But the method worked. And beer didn't taste so bitter now. I tried once more and it was not at all bitter—rather it was the bitter taste that is mellow and suave, with echoes of sweet. Now my beer was all gone. Kim promptly got me another. I drank that much more quickly. It made my tongue more elastic, my eyes more visionary, my head more dreamy. I began to see how Kim could make such good soliloquies. With drink it was not hard to be Shakespearean. I, too, felt ready to see "Helen's beauty in a brow of Egypt."

"It's very strong beer," Helen said. "Something is added." She left most of her second glass, but I drank mine.

My stomach was a bit full. But I knew I was not sick. Oh, I had the brain to think, but I could not stand up by myself. I grasped the edge of a stool and waited. I knew what I was doing, but my legs did not seem to know what they were doing. I tried to move them, and they did not support my body very well. I was thinking how I would be able to carry myself upstairs without any embarrassment. I still held to the stool tightly for fear that I might fall. I guess the other two did not know how I was feeling. Kim said, "We will have dinner now." So I thought I should not have taken so many pretzels while beering my stomach. But we started up. Helen went ahead. Kim led me, to follow. My lord, it was going to be hard! I grasped the edge of the bar from my stool and I measured from the bar to the wall, then from the wall to the stairway. Well, it was not so hard as I at first supposed. And luckily the table was not far from the stairway, back in a little corner quite secluded. Here the roses were waiting. On our table was a dim lamplight, and against the wall beside the lamp, the roses. We sat in a triangular way, no one facing the other but semi-facing, all in profile.

Helen took out a little case from her bag and smoothed her neatly pointed nose. I think she was not drunk, for she was just the same, speaking neither more nor less. Only Kim and I seemed to be drunk, he on his yellow-white stuff, I on beer. He was a changeable personality. One must think of him as a complete pessimist, except that on certain occasions he could become as inwardly joyous as a little child. Tonight it looked as if he did not know whether he were happy or miserable.

It got late, but we were still eating dinner, there were so many courses. Afterwards, we had coffee, and then Kim ordered for us all three liqueurs too. Over the liqueurs, he talked: "This time tomorrow night, we will be upon the sea. Under us, all around us, there will be nothing...no nationality, no civilization, only sea...out of the human world, into the mermaids' world.... Yes, I always wanted to see mermaids singing and combing their green hair down underneath on blue rocks.... Perhaps I have let the crashing waves and perilous rocks disillusion me as to those mermaids, fancies only on the lips of outlived poets. Yet I know well what they should look like.... Mermaids are dressed in beautiful dress and carry silk fans of fish fins. They wear necklaces of pearls still wet and living out of oyster shells.

They never feel cold. They think it is fun to leap out like the flying fish through rain showers, then they wring themselves out again under the sea. If ever you got their coat, it would be good material for your raincoat. Better than synthetic rubber. Better than Korean straw. Mermaids swim better than they walk. They can sing better than Whitman. They eat crabs and lobsters. But not chickens and steaks. Sometimes I wish to go to the mermaid universe…marry a mermaid…and learn to sing her song. Won't I miss chickens? Chickens such as we ate just now? Never mind, there is sure to be drink…. I wonder if she has good drink…as good as your Western whisky and martini…. Mermaid's drink…I will look it up on this drink-card…. By God, it is not here! though I see everything else…. I ask your advice, shall I take my Korean silver cup-bowl and candlesticks to the sea? They might be rare down there, that realm knows no East or West…. No, I will not pack up my lofty objects…. I will give them to my old charwoman, with my heavy German books by Spengler and Kant…. Has she any use for them, I wonder? Well, I have none, for I will enter the mermaid universe…one good in poetry would not be barren there, their muses have a swifter wing…" and on and on he spoke, nonsense like this.

Every now and then a waiter ran up from downstairs carrying little trays with glasses. The place was not crowded, but still there was a good number of people, drinking and talking and laughing at their different tables. Mumsey was a member of many of these parties. Finally she came over to us and apologized in a whisper for the room being noisy. She looked at one man, rather elderly with bald head, drinking and singing and staying a long time.

"*Far niente*. It makes no difference. Your place is very nice," Kim said in Italian. "But tell me," he continued in English, "Who is that gentleman making his night home here lately all the time?"

Mumsey said: "That is Professor X, a very well-known writer, who was an editor." (She mentioned a very proper woman's periodical.) "You know professional men—businessmen—if married, are very happy when their wives' vacation comes. Mrs. X is visiting some relatives in Boston, where she goes home every year. She and her husband come here sometimes together, but then he never gets to go downstairs, and has to return home early. It is she who keeps him quiet, and makes him go away early to bed, so miserably. But now that he's alone, he's having such a good time here! Look at his innocent pleasure! That, you see, is the married man's vacation. Some do lots worse. The whole trouble is, she tries to make him be a nice gentleman and he has to go through the whole thing, even not swear, except on the golf links on Saturday afternoons. But every year he makes it up like this. See! That she objects to. Well, she may be back any time now, and he will be so different."

That old man was really very funny. He quoted Virgil in Latin and Sophocles in Greek and Shakespeare in English. He was a friend of the waiters, of Mumsey, and of the man at the bar. He was going around, talking to everybody, sitting now here, now there, as if he were the host. And now he tried to wrestle with the waiter.

We took Helen back about midnight and set her down at the Browns' door without going in. Then Kim dismissed the taxi and we walked back. I saw Kim's mood had changed again. Joy and hope had abandoned him as if forever. A taxi skidded by us holding two amorous people clasped in each other's arms. "Taxi love!" exclaimed Kim, with hollow laugh. "Why not taxi birth and death? Does it read like the legends of Chin, the myths of Arabia or the fables of Greece? But all twentieth-century matter of fact in New York City."

I tried to cheer him up with thoughts of our trip on the boat next night, though I wondered what he intended to do in Boston when he got Helen there. Kim was not to be moved from despondency, and answered my optimism, "Yes, why does not God give me a pair of rosy-colored glasses, too? The ones that Alice in Wonderland wore, for instance! Maybe Alice's glasses were operated by English angels, mine by heathen devils.... Christians say angels are happy in heaven and devils breathe out the cry of hellish anguish, heart-sick and mind out of order. Even a beautiful September night seems to me like an ominous gloomy one. Serene moonlight above is a flatterer. Aha, Macbeth and King John reign in this night air for me! And yet I don't know that I want Alice looking glasses. It takes a greater eye to see the irony of the world. I prefer the noble Don Quixote's history. When this noble knight charges through ghosts and clouds to sure defeat, how could one retain the innocent heart of Alice in Wonderland?"

By the time we reached his apartment, Kim seemed back in the don't-care mood of the Buddhist, everything one. "Well, in the long run of history, what does this heartache matter? Life—'like a dream, like a vision, like a bubble, like a shadow, like dew, like lightning,' as the Lady Chou, dying, said. We'll light candles, and try to warm ourselves in ghostly flame. Buddhism and I both died in the land that gave us birth. Still its candles, so many candles (he pointed) burn here over the shrines of strangers.... Well, well, a mighty dream of life to him who found it once.... To Asoka and Wu Ti. O yes, enlightened Sakamuni! Let us not doubt: once under that pippala branch and morning star, the mystic dawn did come to that ascetic Gautama. But that was long ago. In the twentieth century on the cold hard pavement, worlds and centuries away, what of it? Here we are in the agony of the dreadful night, dream-haunted, solitary, as the babe that has never smiled, yet filled with the lonely experience of weary old age. Empty grumblings, rhythmic rumblings. Sight may not come again. Old man, poor man…dawn is too far ahead. But bow. We should bow to our ancestral candles.... Nami Abitapool! Boundless grace! All love! All humanity!... Oh, to the man in dreary darkness, will there come a star?"

5

So the tickets for Boston were bought. Helen came in a taxi with bags, having left the Browns as if she were boarding the evening train for Boston. Apparently she and Kim had not taken even the Browns into their confidence about this trip to Boston. Her aunt in New York had made a great deal of trouble about Kim, and except the Browns everybody in Helen's family was passionately stirred up. This had happened only recently. Now Helen was going home to face the trouble and try to persuade them to have a different attitude toward Kim. Kim had no such illusion. But he could not bear to wait in New York, and I think he had some idea of getting her to fly off to Europe with him, or somewhere far away from their grasp.

The boat was not at all crowded. The holiday people had all returned. And Labor Day's rush was over. Neither had the students started back in a body for the college campus. All others but ourselves on the boat looked like business people. In the bow of the boat, alien and isolated, Helen and Kim stood, arm in arm like two people walking intimately down a country lane together, suddenly frozen immobile. I left them to themselves, and stood apart watching the sunset which was painting on the sea canvas a lake of fire. Colors became ever more brilliant, yellows and Aztec scarlets making the universe strange. Sea birds wove toward us and away. The boat glided through waves of gold and blood, as if travelling out in sacrifice to a cruel god. I took a walk and came back again. The sky and sea had softened and grown tender. A blue hour with the lilacs of New England, and the pearly luster of an Autumn moon. Helen and Kim stood as before. They were not saying much, only a word now and then. All that I got was pantomime. Helen's eyes seemed to be full of tears. I know, for Kim put his finger to her cheek and showed her the moisture which came off on his finger, gently shaking his head.

Later, Kim and I sat on the writing balcony waiting for Helen to come from her stateroom and go in to dinner. We watched a play going on. A woman sat at a desk. She wore the kind of velvet hat that is mysterious and obscure, so that you could not see the face very well. A man sat on the other side of her desk, writing, though there were empty desks, too, all around. He was not writing very arduously. Mostly he was making self-introductory remarks, it seemed. He was expensively dressed and had a big mouth and glasses. He was smoking a big fat cigar. Now he had to look around for the cuspidor in which to throw his ashes. He flecked his ashes, but he missed.

"Oh, I beg your pardon!"

"It's not my carpet," the lady looked up smiling.

"Well, some people call that the cleanest kind of dirt," he said, flourishing his cigar, with rosy cone, "but I hardly think so."

The lady shrugged. "Not clean? Well—why not? I like the smell of good cigars."

"Chemically speaking, there is an alkaline in ashes damaging to fabrics," he explained. (Obviously, create your own topic and conclude with your own expert knowledge, that was his kind. Perhaps he belonged to some commercial chemical company, I thought. Probably a travelling salesman.) Now he was talking of Baltimore, about the dinners that were so darn cheap there. Only $1.50, with all sorts of fresh sea foods. Where else could you get such a bargain? "I always plunk down five or six bucks for anything decent at the Pennsylvania Hotel in New York." From the prices of food in New York, he went on to talk about the prices of entertainment, giving proof by figures that he was no piker. She seemed to be well up on musical shows, too, and he said they ought to take in one together some time. This made progress, and by the time Helen joined us, they were very chummy and went into the dining room as man and wife to sit down not far from our table. Helen and Kim were much disgusted by them, especially when the man took out his wallet at the end of the meal, and flourishing a roll of bills about, handed the waiter in payment a $50 note, to show he had nothing smaller.

After dinner we went out on deck again. Helen and Kim seemed content to walk up and down and watch the water together. They had forgotten long ago the couple who had played the pick-up game. Even I scarcely existed for them in their absorption. And my friends' faces became lost in darkness. Only their figures stood or walked apart; figures they were to me only, allegorical figures, lovers sailing on a grave and uncertain errand over the sea, while the space became all space, the time all time. I looked toward them tenderly, and inwardly I cried: "O Helen and Kim, you may love all you want, there is plenty of time!" (As if I might soothe their imminent fear of tomorrow, their gravity on a sea so calm and dark that none could see in that mirror victory and triumph, as none could prophesy certainly storms and defeat.) Time for victory as time for failure. So much time no man can use it all. But his sighs tire him, his pain eats him, his sorrows bury him, before he sees space exhausted or time finished. Sail on and on, Helen and Kim. Where? Why to the uttermost horizon, to the farthest rim, on—on—on. Yes, forever there space extends, forever time holds all, and the bird of life is flying, invisible ghost in an invisible immortality. I looked into the sky...unbroken continuity stretching forever, embracing the stars and the sun and the sun's sun in its bosom, around in a ring to the smallest atom again. I looked into the sea...imperishable beauty, indestructible energy. As the serenity, as the freedom of the sea and sky tonight, so was time, its yesterdays, its tomorrows all there just the same as its todays.

Confucius by the Shantung, Sophocles by the Ægean, Jesus by the sea of Galilee...and that Fall River line as beautiful to me as the ship of the Achæans that journeyed over the mighty globe—shaken in search of a former Helen ages ago. O time! Your magic hues have dyed the Arabs' seven seas...the green of the Indian Ocean, the violet of the Mediterranean, the black of the Euxine, the blue of the Persian, the yellow of the Yellow Ocean...and the Red Sea, the Dead Sea, the Caspian rocking the cradle of Islam. On your bosom, O time, dreamers must dream, thinkers must think, the lonely isles must be explored and charted, and lovers there are waiting to be loved.

6

Kim and I were up early before Helen appeared from her stateroom. We waited for Boston to come into view. It was a morning of cool blue mist, full of a sceptical and mournful Autumn. My exalted mood during mystical night was all gone. Like Kim, I regarded the future dubiously.

"I am hating to get back to Boston from New York," I put our mutual disquiet into words. And because I could not bear his impassivity, as of a man already condemned awaiting execution, I went on in practical words. "I may have another month at the doctors', but after that I don't know where anything is coming from."

"You will get along somehow," said Kim, as if glad to attack with me some simpler difficulty than his own. "Boston has treated you well on the whole. You must not expect a full theological scholarship, for you are not a theologue. But professors in Boston have great sympathy for any adopted Oriental child. As long as you are willing to be docile and obedient."

"That's just it!" I agreed indignantly, and Kim smiled. "I hate being nicey-nice."

"Well, I'm afraid we cannot do much against Boston," said Kim. "Morals and manners are greater strongholds than fortifications. They are more unyielding. That is the Oriental conviction. But all insularity defeats itself in the end, if that's a comfort."

Then Kim looked me over, and he said to me some things I long remembered, for they were my own conclusions, too. "And after college," Kim began, "what are you going to do?"

"I don't know," I said. "I want to see all America. Not just the intellectual centers. But if I remain in America, I must come back to them, I suppose."

"There is a great future for Oriental scholarship in the West. Have you ever thought of that? Nowadays in the West we see a definite trend. People begin to be interested in the Orient scientifically and esthetically. Before they thought in terms of Christianity and Western institutions. They are going deeper now, and this interest will increase year by year. I have come at a very unfortunate time. There has been little room for an Oriental intellectual in the West. But you have all your life before you and for you clouds may gradually clear and an easier spiritual climate come for you. Let me give you advice. You will be thrown of course into uneven competition. Generations of a different mental training you have to span in one. But remember. African cats and Asian rats have managed to survive in Europe, and from Europe to emigrate to America. Cats you know got in at the beginning of the Christian Era from Egypt. How they have thrived during all these years in Rome, though in Rome you would think life for them would be hard. I understand that the rats arrived with the Huns from Asia. Nothing has been able to kill them, not even the pied piper of science. They survive to this day in New York's tenements. Now you are better off than cats and rats. You are not so objectionable and you have much to contribute. But your problem is the same. You have to eat. And to eat, you must enter into the economic life of Americans. Listen then. First you should get a good Western foundation in education. But—and here is your difference from the majority of students who come to the West from the Orient—don't lose touch with your own classical traditions. By chance you came here from an old-fashioned community. You arrived with an unusual training and inclination for the ancient classics. You complain that you find it hard to learn the American efficiency and to find in that a means of livelihood.

Don't set too much store on American efficiency. In making a living, Oriental scholarship may help you more than your American education, though this seems strange to contemplate now. But in such a field, you would have the advantage. There would be less competition. Read on the Orient, all that is written from the Eastern and the Western points of view. As you read, analyze. You must be now like a Western man approaching Asia. Buddhism, Taoism, Confucianism have not been much analyzed scientifically. Oriental history, above all, we know it has not been written with regard for the truth at times. I suppose, like myself, you can see without trying to do so the exaggerations and prejudices of the West. But by keeping a well-balanced mind, you will see, too, the exaggerations and prejudices of the Orient. The field I suggest is not small. It is mostly uncharted. But the more you study of the art, religion and literature of both hemispheres, the broader and more elastic as a living being you will become. As a transplanted scholar, this is the only road I could point to, for your happy surviving."

We were silent then for a time. And suddenly Kim asked me what I thought of Helen. He did it dispassionately like a detached mind from the clouds, looking down philosophically on his own emotions. And I tried to reply in kind.

"I think she has a very beautiful spirit, inherited from an older generation," I said. "Of course she has no fault to find with her own environment. Only her loneliness."

"You are thinking she would make a wonderful wife for a Boston professor?"

"I think so. But I think you would be happy with her too."

"You are right," Kim said. "I know she has lots of faults, but she is the only one I really care about. And there is no substitute. If there were any substitute, there would be no broken heart at this time."

Kim at least was expecting the trouble that was to come from Helen's family. He said he would probably not have time to see me much in Boston this time. He was expecting some day soon to sail for Europe. But he would communicate with me again before that happened.

BOOK NINE

1

NOT FAR FROM Doctor Dimassi's, just by the Harvard Bridge, stood a handsome house of bright red brick trimmed with white stucco. I often sauntered by this house when I went for a walk. Sometimes I would see coming out of this house a large fine-looking gentleman with a healthy pink and white face, who carried a cane and led a fat little spaniel. The dog really made our acquaintance. It was a very friendly little dog with extremely short legs and long silky ears almost sweeping the ground. One day the dog stopped to smell me as I stood by Harvard Bridge. Since the dog was on a leash the master, too, was obliged to stop. The obvious thing was to say, "Good morning," and I added, "This is a cute little dog."

"A very inquisitive one," he responded.

Then he asked me whether I came from China or from Japan. It took quite a time to explain all that, and we strolled along together. I told him I was a self-supporting student, and was looking for something to do. Particularly I needed some cheap heated room to study in.

"You can't do much and study," he mused reflectively, which seemed an unusually sympathetic remark. He hesitated, then at the end of our walk, he said, "I believe I have something for you." There was a little room on his top floor which was empty, and it had a good bed and plenty of heat. He had wanted his library indexed for a long time.

This was good luck. Doctor Dimassi's family were just about to return from Marblehead. When the time came, I moved my belongings just across the street, a little way up toward the Mount Vernon way. My new employer's name was Mr. Schmitt. The red and white brick house was even bigger than Doctor Dimassi's; I suppose it cost about the same amount, but the Schmitts had more taste for display. Everywhere varnished gleaming furniture, rosewood and silver, and everywhere draperies bending many times. The chairs were lustrous and so cushiony that you sank into them several feet. It was the kind of house with beautifully colored Persian rugs stretching down glassy halls, big front rooms, middle rooms, and back rooms, all with fireplaces and marble mantelpieces, and a winding staircase.

Again my room looked over the Charles River from an exclusive section of Boston. The window sill was so wide that I could keep books and papers there and use it like a table. The room had a three-quarter size white iron bed, very comfortable, a chest for clothes and an elastic reading lamp. There was only one other room in the tower, a much larger one, and this was occupied by the Schmitts' Negro cook. Laurenzo was his name, at least it was his first name and I never knew his other. In his rich negroid way, he was amazingly good-looking, very large and black with a magnificent physique, and hair not kinked but crinked, rather like a much rippled permanent wave. Laurenzo had soft regular features more broad and massive than a white man's and unusually thin lips. He was always polite, too polite in fact. I was used to greater freedom and frankness with my housemates. The washstand with running water stood just outside my door. It was practically private to me, for I never saw Laurenzo using it either to wash or to shave. Once I asked him if he ever did these things. But he only smiled broadly and said with diffidence, as if he didn't know how to take me, "Oh, ah keeps clean...hands always in the water."

Laurenzo was a remarkable cook. I know, because sometimes the

Schmitts invited me to eat with them. And yet he cooked without meat. The Schmitts were vegetarians. They belonged to a religion which did not believe in eating meat of any kind. Mr. Schmitt maintained that meat was unhealthy. Every bite of meat eaten, he preached, robbed a man of part of his natural longevity. Thus if a man's destiny was to live to eighty years, eating meat, he would automatically cut life down to seventy, and so on. "Alas! too many modern men have degenerated because they cannot live on vegetable food," I quoted the Chinese poet-philosopher Chu Hsi, and Mr. Schmitt was much pleased. I think I would not mind a diet of vegetables if I could eat them always as Laurenzo cooked. Great soft sweet potatoes, the color of apricots and with a curl of smoke arising from the center; green vegetables like landscapes after a rain. Once or twice a week too they had chicken, which they argued somehow inconsistently belonged to the vegetable kingdom. At other times they had something on a meat platter—it cut like steak or roast—but was made entirely of nuts.

The Schmitts belonged to an anti-vivisectionist society. Just the word vivisection made Mrs. Schmitt cry. She was much younger than Mr. Schmitt, very plump and affectionate, with a turned-up nose and blooming face. Every morning she would wait at the foot of the winding stairs for Mr. Schmitt to come down and when he did she gave him an affectionate bouncing kiss. Mrs. Schmitt was English-Canadian. Mr. Schmitt was of German parentage, but long transplanted to Boston, so that now he was practically Bostonian. They belonged to a school of New Thought called the House Omnipotent. This was no church really, as they did not believe in church, only in a spiritual force of the invisible powers and the brotherhood of man communicating simultaneously with all the world. Mr. Schmitt was rather a busy man. He was the editor of a New Thought paper using very mysterious sentences always hard for me to understand. So he worked hard on his small Corona typewriter, which usually accompanied him on his frequent railway journeys. He also gave several lectures every year on the cruelty of those who ate animals. Yet Mr. Schmitt was not a missionary. At least only for animals. He had no use for the other kind of missionaries. He said he hoped I had never been influenced by any missionaries, for they were full of dogma and contradiction. They contradicted the Bible, Mr. Schmitt said. And every time I saw him that winter, he preached to me against the devilishness of missionaries. When I still said I had some use for some missionaries, Mr. Schmitt kept on, trying to convert me not to have any use for any missionaries since none, he said, understood the brotherhood of Man and of God.

Before Mr. Schmitt became an editor for that paper *New Thought,* he must have been in the postcard business, for in his library was a large cupboard with glass doors containing many different kinds of postcards—stacks and stacks—with quotations from Emerson, Ruskin, Browning, Tennyson—all the heroes of the nineteenth century. These, being very beautifully and expensively printed, were the kind one pays fifty cents for at Christmas time. Mr. Schmitt had a curious library. It was almost all religious, philosophical, mystical and theosophical. No science book was there, only Christian Science. He was very sympathetic toward Christian Science. And yet with the exception of the scientific fields, his library was rather broad. He had Kant, Emerson, Carlyle, Poe, even Whitman and Melville, Goethe, Mullner, Schiller, Schopenhauer, Lessing, Klopstock, Schleiermacher. He read German as much as English, and several times offered to help me with my college German. Mr. Schmitt got me a card catalogue, and I set to work arranging his books. The Schmitts were rarely seen and I had the library all to myself to work and dream in.

A period of unusual isolation for me—these two months before Christmas. In addition to my studies, I was occupied with indexing, and with the translations Kim had obtained for me to do. I discouraged visitors, for I knew the Schmitts were quiet people, and would not want college boys rushing in and rushing out, disturbing their musings on the House Omnipotent. I speculated some about Laurenzo. The first chance I had had to observe any one like him. All revelations about Laurenzo came at week-ends. Sunday was his day off. On Saturday he would work very hard, cooking a lot of things for Mrs. Schmitt to warm up over Sunday. But Saturday evening, as soon as he had finished up the dishes, he left the house, dressed up in his best clothes and shiniest tie. He carried then an enormous suitcase, as if he were leaving for some kind of trip. I said he must be strong to carry such a suitcase. He agreed. Yes, he was strong, he said. But when I picked up his suitcase, I found it wasn't heavy after all. It felt like an empty suitcase.

Late Sunday night, I would hear Laurenzo returning. Usually he was very quiet. But now he came, banging his way upstairs, tripping over steps, dragging after him some heavy object. It was that huge suitcase. I left my room to see what was happening. At the top of the stairs, Laurenzo set the suitcase down, very carefully, rubbed his hands together, chuckled to himself, and waited a moment to get his breath. As he picked up the suitcase again, a faint clink of glass responded from the inside. He put his ear down and listened with satisfaction, rolled his eyes at me, winked, and clapped me familiarly on the back, inviting me into his room. I followed him. He carefully shut the door, then tipsily opened the suitcase. It was completely full of slightly flattened bottles of a brown color, and others larger, full of white liquor. He uncorked one of the smaller bottles and handed it to me, telling me to sample it. I tasted. It was awfully strong. He himself took another, and let the drops flow down his throat with ecstasy. After that, he never noticed that I wasn't drinking. He began to laugh for joy.

"Ah, my God, now I'se happy!" he cried, and he took another stiff swallow. "Happy, O boy! And it's because I'se drunk. O yes, I know I'se drunk, devil-drunk. I feel like a king.... Sh! *She* won't like it," and he pointed downstairs, to indicate Mrs. Schmitt. "No, she won't like it. But a man has got to do something." The next moment he was mopping his eyes. "It's the only way for a niggerman in this world."

He began to walk up and down the room declaiming.

"Do you see me? I'se a college man. I'se been to Williams College, and to Washington, and then I come up here to go to Harvard. I'se studied medicine four years...." (I think Laurenzo was exaggerating a little.) "But how's that going to help me? Here I am chockfull of education. Still a niggerman.... That old devil down there (he meant Mr. Schmitt), he got everything. What he know about medicine? But a niggerman's only good to cook and wait, that's all."

He continued on this subject for some time. Then he drew near to me and became confidential, dropping his voice and rolling his eyes. "I guess I'se good at something else. Women like me. I make all women wild. You wouldn't believe it, how they like Laurenzo. Not in open. Uhnt! But in secret. Because I'se big and strong and black. I knows it. Street-cars, parks, anywhere…where I find 'em…" he gave a kind of singsong formula. "Smile, talk, hold hands, kiss 'em, do 'em, leave 'em…. I'se got some kind of secret, white man don't know…."

"How is that, Laurenzo?"

"White man don't know nothing about his women…. But me, I got that secret…. I don't bother going round with no nigger gals…not me! They don't like me neither because of my education." Here right after chuckle and leer, Laurenzo began to weep uncontrollably again, and to go on about how a colored man hadn't a chance. He alternated self-pity with boasting and obscenity, and abuse of kind, dignified Mr. Schmitt: much of this was incoherent, but some at least sounded like the language of sincere hell coming out. At last he dropped down on his bed, weeping into the pillows. "Not good for anything much…that's niggerman." The next moment he was snoring heavily.

In the morning, there was subdued confusion in the air. When Mr. Schmitt came downstairs to be kissed affectionately by Mrs. Schmitt, he found her almost in tears. And there was no breakfast waiting on the table. "Again?" said Mr. Schmitt.

"Again."

"Laurenzo must go," said Mr. Schmitt.

"Laurenzo must go," echoed Mrs. Schmitt.

But as soon as Laurenzo sobered up, he was a changed man. He was not obscene any more. He wasn't loud. He stepped aside for me when we met in the hall. I would hear him pleading down on the second floor, pleading with tears, with terror, remorse in his voice. "One last chance, Mrs. Schmitt. Just give me my last chance. I hate the stuff. I'll never touch it again. No more, no more, no more…"

He sounded so sincere in confessing, so earnest in promising, so abject in abasement, that Mrs. Schmitt would forgive. That was Mrs. Schmitt's weakness, just like crying at the word vivisection. She would always forgive. Then I waited to see how well Laurenzo was going to reform. The Sunday after, he drank, but his job was on his mind. It took two or three week-ends before he forgot again. Then he came home drunk as before, and stumbled into my room noisily without knocking. "Hullo, hullo! Now I'm going to tell you something! Show you another thing, this nigger, he's good for." He drew me out on the landing and pointed to the regions below where the Schmitts were having a musical evening. Downstairs Mrs. Schmitt was playing the piano, and a lady guest was singing. "Listen. Can that woman sing? I ask you, can *she* sing?"

"You don't like her singing?"

"Man, you don't know! Look-a-here, *I can sing!*" He opened his mouth right then and there. I pushed him into my room. "Sh! Wait a moment, Laurenzo," and I closed the door. But Laurenzo had already opened his mouth to sing. Volumes of sound rolled out. It was magnificent. He really could sing. I don't know where he had learned, but he was, as he said, better than the lady guest downstairs. "Let me go down and show those people how to sing." And I almost had to fight with Laurenzo to keep him upstairs with me. I followed him to his very door, where in spite of me he turned and yelled, "Listen to me, you white people down there. You ought to hear me sing Brahms. Lordy, Lordy! Hear that woman flat. I knows that song. Ought to get me down there, white woman. I knows how to sing."

Still Mrs. Schmitt didn't fire him. Not that time. I think she hated to let him go because he was such a marvellous vegetarian cook whom she had got by special order, and besides she felt sorry for him. Mr. Schmitt said anyway he shouldn't be coming there when drunk. And Mrs. Schmitt said yes, when drunk she was afraid of him. Next week-end they chained the inner door, so that it would open just a little, and Laurenzo could not get in Sunday night after twelve, unless he woke them up. They slept away the night in peace. Laurenzo did not ring the bell, nor make any noise outside to rouse anybody. Next morning he was found sprawled out on the doorstep, with moisture all around him and a strong smell of spirits. One arm was stretched out over that big suitcase. When he fell down on the home-step to sleep, he had set down the suitcase too hard, and some of the bottles had broken and the liquor had seeped out.

Poor Laurenzo! And he was so nice when he wasn't drunk! Too nice! With all his faults I got to know him better when intoxicated. He might utter the language of hell, but some of his true thoughts came out then. At other times, never. He may not have been very truthful even when drunk. Mrs. Schmitt said it wasn't his nature to be truthful. But he was frank. He was ready to show the world then that he stood on his own two feet—but he couldn't stand on them.

2

I did not hear from Kim. So I presumed he was still in America. About Christmas time I went down to New York to see how he was getting along and to have an interview with Mr. Brown's friend about some more commercial advertising in Chinese translation. Then I found out what had occurred in Boston previously between Helen and Kim. Her family had been very nice to Kim, polite but distant. And he felt bitterly that they had not been honest with Helen about their inflexible stand. Helen had been sent off on a round-the-world cruise with the promise exacted that she defer her decision until after a long separation. But Helen had told Kim that she would never change. Nothing had been said about their not writing to each other. Yet not long after that, Kim got a letter from Helen's father. 'If you love her as we love her," the letter said, "the only way you can show it is bravely to keep away. Barriers have been passed that were never meant to be broken." The letter urged Kim not to write, not to force himself upon her "sisterly affection and Christian charity" in any way.

"So many words," said Kim, "to say in plain language, 'No trespassing.'" It worried him that he had not heard much from Helen. He feared she had not been receiving his letters. Of course it was the ebb of the year. I noticed that Kim seemed without a spark of youthful gaiety. He made soliloquy to his mirror in the hall: "Helen used to look into my mirror. And now there is no trace. I look. But nothing is there. Only an insane man in whose eyes is the image of Helen." And again: "What becomes of the dreams dreamt, the hopes hoped, unrealized? Dreams are fools' night fancies. The product of the idler's imagination. For no one has entered the cloud castle through the rainbow gates of dreams. All are words, written on the fading memory book, where it sticks on the eyes' visionary image, the mirror that lies. Everything, everything in this West, is said to be 'hope so.'

Yes, hope hops here like a grasshopper? What is this hope, Western-manu-factured? An invisible drug that keeps the sick man alive till tomorrow. Wait till the morning sun rises. So says hope. What does tomorrow bring? What can tomorrow bring? That same hope only. More hopes and tomorrow's tomorrows will see that sun also rise. Yes, hope, and again hope—and always month after month, hope.... It is a fine consolation."

We walked the cold Manhattan streets and Kim told me how he had gone to Helen's church in Boston, where her family had owned pews for many generations. It was a house of God but exclusive. People didn't flatter or smile when you came out. They stared and whispered. Then his mind seemed attracted by the holly wreaths and Christmas trees in the windows we were passing. Kim pointed and said, "What is the meaning of all this pine, holly, spruce, mistletoe, ivy; this decoration of fragile balloons and lifeless glass birds; of ringless bells and imitation stars, and rich-colored baubles that break into dust when you touch them? What fantastic ritual! Well, man is a mythmaker and creator of superstition. You can make your own Christmas tree and be a child under it. What make-believe time of a week! What play-happiness. And twelve days later all to be burned in the fire. Well, that is life. But I do not care much for the Western Christmas tree."

I came back to Boston and had the flu. Everybody was having it just then. Even Laurenzo. He had been rushed to the hospital, and I was alone on the Schmitts' fifth floor. No one knew I was sick. I lay on the bed too weak to move, without even the energy to walk down those five flights of stairs and enter the nearest cafeteria for food. Sometimes I slept and other times I couldn't. My head ached. My throat ached. So did my chest with hard incessant painful coughing. I think I was partly delirious, and I kept seeing Kim, and imagining I was sailing with him on a bleak uncomfortable sea. Rocks were ahead and we seemed sure to be wrecked, and no one was with us. He and I were sailing entirely alone. Then the thought came into my head that I had the flu and was going to die up here on the Schmitts' fifth floor. Nobody would know the moment when I died and nobody would care. Many Oriental students had died like this on foreign soil. I cried to myself in despair, then gave up in exhaustion. Hope and ambition seemed to have vanished from me. Only the tictock of the alarm clock in the room, the sound of the cold Boston wind whistling at the windowpane, the beating of my own heart, how I disliked to hear all these! I hated them so much that I dragged myself out of bed. I stuffed pencils and papers, towels, shirts into the window cracks, trying to shut out the snuffling of the wind, and tottering, I put the clock outside the door. But still I could hear my own heart beating, and that sound was unpleasant to me, there in my silent world that made no noises. Truly "I felt a funeral in my brain and mourners to and fro," for I think I have never had such an attack of the nerves. All my senses, except that of the nose, were keener than senses ought to be. But my nose refused to aid me, either for smelling or breathing. All my handkerchiefs were soaked. Now I was beginning to use anything I could get. Shirts, socks, yes, anything. I lay like this for three days and without a morsel of food or of any liquid except water. That of course was one reason I felt so morbid and saw the earth only as my grave of death. I did not put anything into my stomach with which to fight off those germs. Just a bowl of soup—even just hot salt water—might have made the whole world brighter. At the end of that time, my will to live reasserted itself. I dressed myself feebly in anything that came to hand, lurched down those five flights and out into the street, seeking the nearest cafeteria for food.

3

By the middle of May that year, I was again installed with the doctors, since their families had left early for Marblehead. From this point on, the hardship of working my way through college was over for good. The next winter, I received a full scholarship, not from my college, but from an anonymous friend whose name I have never learned. I also studied during this summer and the next, in the graduate school, doing further studies. Professor Campbell and the president of the University both wrote me letters to the graduate school, letters in which I think I was five or ten times exaggerated. Anyhow my hard-luck days in the Boston environment were now behind me, and this easier time made me more sociable.

I was no sooner established once more with Doctor Dimassi than I began to have visitors. Charles Evans of course came frequently. Often he stayed for dinner and cooked with me and the doctors. He was much liked by the doctors and such parties were a round of laughter and conversation. Afterwards the doctors went out for other engagements, and Charles and I read aloud together in the spacious living room, listened to chamber music on the victrola, discussed philosophy and other matters. Early twenty is an earnest age when philosophy much appeals. Charles came from liberal-minded Christian parents who never attempted to dogmatize with him, but even so their conceptions failed to satisfy him. A perfectly balanced, natively moral Yankee, he shared in the bewilderment of our generation—a bewilderment, I think, world-wide and not yet passed away—in a search for values with no values anywhere very obvious, intellectually speaking. The incredible Scopes trial in Tennessee must come to mind as a kind of landmark to this period in America. And in Boston, this friendship of Charles Evans for me was a subtler graft of the earthquaking needle, of the new age of broad communication, cross-fertilization, and the shaking of boundaries. Our combined efforts of East and West were unable to find an honest argument for God in our philosophical courses, though this was not the fault of our professor, a very kind gentleman with a great fund of knowledge, who interpreted everything ultimately in terms of Christian ideology and an ex-clergyman atmosphere, so that we made a neat sightseeing tour through philosophy and arrived right back at where we, or rather right-minded people, necessarily started from, a nice Christian monotheism. I think Charles was more avid in this search for God than I was. It was in his Yankee blood, whereas in the Orient mystery has always been accepted for what it is. The Western mind is more abstract, too, than the Oriental. Language has had much to do with that. Chinese philosophers even in their most abstruse moods write in picture characters, and use parables. I always insisted to Charles that I got more out of Western poetry than Western philosophy, in the study of Western thought, since one poet can do ten times as much as one philosopher, whether in conveying scepticism or mysticism. It can hardly be said that we two solved any problems during these long debates, since values are natural monuments upheaved by emotions and it is almost fruitless to build them with the intellectual chisel and bricks of air. But an

Eastern and a Western mind came close together, and the mood we generally ended up in was that of a pragmatic Taoism, or a Taoistic pragmatism, if such a thing is conceivable.

My Italian friend, Cortesi, often came to see me at Doctor Dimassi's and sometimes he would spend the night. He enjoyed playing the large victrola and the radio, and sitting in the big comfortable chairs. But Cortesi always moved around on tiptoe here and a straw in the wind would make more noise than he. When he spent the night with me, he didn't bring pyjamas. In fact, he never seemed to have any personal belongings except one suit, one shirt, one necktie, and one pair of shoes. In this he was like me. But on that suit, that shirt, that necktie, he had no spot—in this he was unlike me. He used his shirt for a pyjama, but it never seemed to get wrinkled like mine. As he was getting into bed, his necktie disappeared. I believe he put it under his pillow—for you could never see it until it came back suddenly again next morning. One moment you looked at Cortesi without his necktie—the next moment, the tie was on, neatly tied. He was very circumspect in dressing and I never caught him at the moment of change. I don't suppose he put the necktie on under the sheets, but he always managed to find that instant's space when the roommate's eyes were turned somewhere else. And never, never would he take off the trousers when anybody was looking—girls wouldn't be so shy. He always watched the occasion when you were wiping your nose or were away off somewhere in the bathroom. Shoes, too. Magically they left Cortesi's feet, tucking themselves away carefully under the bed. Magically they slipped back on when nobody was looking. I could never persuade Cortesi to stay on in the morning and have breakfast with the doctors. And he never seemed at home when Charles Evans was there.

I saw a good deal of a Japanese at this time, Wadanabe. He was studying theology, but really it was for the purpose of investigating psychology and philosophy. By calling it in name, theology, he had the privilege of a good scholarship and a place in the theological dormitory. Wadanabe was both agreeable and intelligent. We got along very well in spite of the great political antagonism between my land and his. The average Japanese does not understand the Korean situation anyhow. Wadanabe did not seem to reason with the more ruthless nationalists, "Anything is right that's for our country." He had a good knowledge of classical Japanese *Haiku* and he wrote Haiku himself. He was a frail boy, hollow-chested and pale, and his teeth gave him a good deal of trouble. Since there was a bitter quarrel always between Japan and China, he liked to have me go with him to the Chinese restaurants on Tyler Street to do the ordering. But always he ate soup or more soft things like that, holding his hurting teeth. He attributed his dental disorders to Western food in the theological dormitory.

Westernization was giving him other troubles, too. At present, Wadanabe's mind was mostly taken up with a Japanese girl student. Kiki Harada was a willow-slight, plainly dressed girl, good-looking enough to have been married long ago in Western style, but her only joy in life was Kant and Hume. She, too, was a student in philosophy. Her mother was well known as an educational pioneer for women in Japan, and the administrator of a Japanese college for women in Tokyo. Kiki, with that continuity often found in the Orient, was utterly loyal to her mother and only interested to follow in her footsteps. In other respects she was Oriental and conservative— shy, proper, self-contained, with absolutely no frivolous glance in the direction of men. She very much complicated for Wadanabe his perplexities on the subject of love. Love to him now was a sad, wistful, complicated theme. Why should one follow in the approved way of arranged marriages? Why should not love and engagement follow on one's own initiative? How could one make a conservative Japanese girl be radical? But to hear him talk, you would think there was between them some overwhelming question. However, I met Miss Harada later at an international tea, and when I mentioned to her Wadanabe, she hardly seemed to know who he was. Wadanabe? Wadanabe? Finally she recalled that they had talked together once at a party, and he had perhaps been in one or two of her classes. I began to suspect that romantic love was a lonely pilgrimage to an unearthly country, where you had with you possibly the Western gods and poets, but no human companionship.

Doctor Dimassi and Doctor Starr planned to do housekeeping regularly, so they asked me to look around for a friend who could cook. This turned out to be Eugene Chung, who joined me just before the college term ended. Eugene was a good deal older than I and we had not much in common. An American, active in missionary fields, had adopted him at one time, and had helped him to get through Peking University. He still called this man "Father" and received many presents from him, including a typewriter and checks to help out his American education. But Eugene was terribly homesick for China, and he was rapidly Chinizing instead of Westernizing. He had come to the West expecting oceans of brotherly love and Santa Claus. Certain bitter experiences convinced him now for the first time of a definite race prejudice. He began to lose all interest in Y.M.C.A. activities. His one thought was to get back to China and his own kind. In China, he was already married and had two children. He had been married without choice in the old style, but separation now had the strange effect of making him as love-sick as Wadanabe. He thought about his Chinese wife constantly, and no Western lover could have been more pitiful and more sincere in missing the loved one. His love, of which he had first grown conscious in the West, made him speculate a good deal on that subject. No wonder, he told me mournfully, Westerners were such ardent lovers. He saw it all now. Longing and abstinence created love, but in a way that was a very good thing. It made the wife more important. In China a man never knew what it was to be without a wife; almost before man realized natural longing, woman was placed in his arms. "Never can we know truth without knowing error. Never can we know light without knowing darkness. Never can we know the Chinese woman until she is not there. So by wandering, we know the value of home," said Eugene. And he was going to make the most of his new discovery, so he said. He meant to have a new house for himself and his wife away from the grandparents. "Yes," said Chung with all the ardor of a bridegroom. "And in my house there will be separate rooms. She shall be herself. I, myself. That is the Western custom. This way husband and wife will not have too much of each other. When I was at home with my dear wife, we had too much of each other. Not a night did we pass apart. No, not since I was eighteen. Every night we did as man and wife. That is too much. Too much of a wife is not to have a wife. Oh, I am sorry to be so long from home! Oh, how we miss each other! Absence increases longing, longing increases love. Oh, how much I have come to love my dear, dear wife!"

Eugene was very solemn in this and never thought there was anything funny in his explanation of love. He was artless and sincere, but we could not kick or play together and could only discuss Chinese history. Indeed, his new devotion and his new typewriter took up all his spare time. For when he was not writing long letters to his wife in Chinese, he was practising with his typewriter the touch method, spending hours and hours on just his name. How I pitied him for not enjoying himself in something else! But his only regret was, he could not combine his two interests, write his wife and at the same time use that machine. This he could not do because she knew no English.

I had met so many different kinds of students during my period of isolation that I planned to bring a small number together for an international party of my own. One of these people was Lopez, a Filipino. Lopez had been a Roman Catholic when he arrived in Boston two years before. Before he left, he had been everything, ending up as a Baptist fundamentalist, believing word for word that Adam walked in the garden with Eve, his wife, that Joshua stopped the sun and that Jonah slept in the whale. By this time he had given up dancing, shiny dressing and all frivolity. Probably it was not so hard for him to give up dancing, for that had made him very unhappy anyhow. At one time he went regularly to the Y.W.C.A. dances in Mechanics Hall, for he loved dancing. There was much race prejudice felt at these international dances, and no girl would dance with him. Oh, how miserable and restless he was, chewing gum, one stick after another, going out to spit it away, coming in to ask once more, "May I dance with you?" Now the world of the flesh was over with Lopez and he was going back to teach fundamentalism to the other Filipinos.

Another whom I asked was a Negro student, Wagstaff. Wagstaff was very different from the Schmitts' Laurenzo. He was sober and industrious, and had reached Boston and its universities with an unswerving purpose and concentrated willpower. Originally he came from the South. His life had been varied and broad, but always poor and struggling. He had been a porter on trains. He had played the cornet in a minstrel show. He still played the cornet, and when he came to see me at Doctor Dimassi's he usually carried his instrument with him in a little bag and played for me. He even gave me a few lessons. I blew and puffed just as he did, but the music didn't come for me. Wagstaff had been an elevator man in New York and in Cleveland. Now he was an elevator man in Boston while he studied. In fact, he said pessimistically, he expected all his life to be an elevator man. "What room is there in America for an educated Negro? There is not much else but the 'yessuh' job. And either way, I shall hardly be assured of a decent living way." Yet all his life, as he ironically commented, he had been working like hell to get degrees and a higher education. "And the more American culture I absorb, the more Whitman, Emerson, Lincoln I read, I give you my word, the more hatred and revengeful spirit I have...." At first Wagstaff had been very quiet with me. And with others he was always extremely sensitive, shrinking from racial snubs. But later, the one subject he wanted to discuss with me was the subject at the back of every educated Negro's thoughts, his shadowy existence as an outcast in the white man's world, and all the legal as well as illegal discrimination practised against him there. One time he and I were walking late at night. We passed a Child's on Boylston Street near the Public Garden. I invited Wagstaff to go in and have some flapjacks of the kind those good-looking young waitresses in green coats were making in the windows. He didn't want to, but I overcame his objections. There were few customers, for it was late. The waiters were standing around idle. We waited a long time and still no waiter came to us. I got all ready to go up and raise a row. Wagstaff wouldn't let me. "Come on. I don't want the cakes anyhow. I'm used to this situation. I face it every day. I can't get up heat on it any more."

This wasn't exactly true, for it was the great emotion back of his existence. I tried to compare the Oriental's position, and his. But he would not see it that way, I was outside the two sharp worlds of color in the American environment. It was, in a way, true. Through Wagstaff I was having my first introduction to a crystallized caste system, comparable only to India, here in the greatest democratic country of the world. It was seemingly beyond the power of individuals to break through. Thinking about it, I did not see what he could do. I suggested that like Kim he leave it. France, they said, was a good country for the educated Negro.

"If I save up money for the steamer ticket, how will I earn my bacon when I'm there? This is the only elevator country. No. I was born here. This is my land. But it's a two-faced world, I'm the one that knows."

His experiences—and I did not see how any Negro could avoid them—had given him the psychology of Guru, the Hindu: get what you can. That may have been why he liked law. He was a law student in the university. Most of his other reading was upon the Negro question. Any book, any poem, any play written by a Negro writer, he had read. And he said, "They say that Negroes always lie. Why shouldn't they? They must lie to exist. They see around them a world of lies, a cruel unfriendly world from birth, where they are gyped because of color. There is only one philosophy that can come from that. It will not be 'honesty is the best policy' or any lie like that. Learn the language of gyp, learn to gyp too. Confess honestly that right isn't might, but might is right, always since the world began. That's the perspective that only a Negro gets." But if any white man were within hearing distance Wagstaff shut up at once.

Charles Evans I invited to my party. And my Italian friend Cortesi. And Wadanabe came too. Eugene, the Chinese student, was naturally there. Lopez, Wagstaff, Charles, Cortesi, Wadanabe, and Eugene...oh, my party was a terrible flop. Even Charles' free and easy spirit could not pull it off. Each one there had been friendly to me and, on occasion, a sincere, pleasant companion. But no two got together, except the Italians who were friends before I knew them...each pair were like oil and water. In fact they would have nothing to do with one another.

4

In his final year Charles Evans became engaged to Ruth Bachelor, the niece of Professor Burton. It was a most fitting union. Even in appearance they went well together. Charles was a tall, raw-boned fellow with a shock of dark hair, strong black brows and blue eyes. His warm, dynamic temperament suggested the South rather than the North, but his mental approach to all things, his caution of extremes, and his puritan probity were of New England. Ruth was rather tall, slender and unusually pale. She was a daughter of the same race as Emerson and Thoreau. You hardly needed to be told that her father was a gentleman farmer on a fairly large estate outside of Boston, with a typical New England white house laid out with fine lawns, pastures and woods. Of course it was reflected in her that the earth was wholesome, the sky blue, life sweet, and work a blessing. Yet I never heard her asserting any of these views. She resembled the gentle and orderly landscapes of her own native region, harmonious and mild even in a semi-wild state…and of a pleasant, even temper, practical, active yet serene. She was graduating that same year from a college in the city, but her heart was ever in the country in her own spot of ground where she knew all the walks, tree by tree and stone by stone. One suspected her of being a quietist, since it appeared as if from childhood she had mastered the art of living. Then if so, she must have shaped and formed her own philosophy. If so we never heard. When all other girls told theirs, or even their personal tastes and smallest viewpoint, Ruth kept still. She seemed ever ready to listen and laugh, to catch the humor in all things but not to talk back. So probably she was peaceful by nature rather than by conviction. But this quiet assurance was just what Charles needed, and I noticed that getting engaged to Ruth did more for my friend than any amount of philosophical talking. He now ceased most of his gloomier doubts and questionings. He directed faculties and energies to definite purpose.

They were married that summer after a short engagement. I attended the wedding. In fact, I was Charles' best man. I suppose he was the first American ever to have a Korean in that capacity. They were married in Ruth's New England home by a Unitarian minister who officiated not because either Ruth or Charles was a church-goer, but because Ruth had known him from the time she was a little girl and had always told him that when and if she got married, he must marry her. Charles already had a position engaged for that winter, teaching in a boys' school. He and Ruth left in Ruth's car for a summer honeymoon on the coast of Maine.

That same summer I attended another engagement party. And this time it was for Chai, the Hawaiian student. His Bostonian courtship had flowered in success. But then Chai had received a very lucky break. Just that spring Miss Martha Wright got sick. She was taken to that hospital where he was interning. Chai couldn't have made a better opportunity. There she was for six weeks, removed from the other candidates. As doctor and lover, he reaped a double advantage. She could see Chai in either role—he was ever at her side—always in the best light, and nobody could complain either, when Chai looked after a patient. Courtship was business now and business courtship. So every morning she received from his hands the *Boston Herald* and every evening the *Boston Evening Transcript*. He remembered her taste in books, of course, and the flowers which surprised her each day put in their tender word. In short, spring, convalescence, innocent flowers in dark Boston...and a wistful young foreign doctor giving from morning until night exhibitions of professional talent and lover's unfailing devotion...the thing clicked. They were engaged soon after she came out. Doctor Morrison, to whom she was the confidential secretary, received the news with the greatest cordiality and took the young people under his wing. So they were married, the same year that Kim fled to Europe. The news of their marriage came out in Boston papers with pictures of both and long complimentary write-ups as if here was a wonder in the world. They were going immediately to Hawaii to live. Tropic and exotic isles were to be their home.

BOOK ONE

1

MY PERIOD OF conventional education was over, my self-teaching days had not begun...and now my life shifted for a time to Philadelphia. I was happy to leave Boston. I looked back upon that period, shaking my head. Four years I had kept on existing with difficulty as a student. I had received a diploma from one university in Boston and one more from another. I got by somehow on partial scholarships, the college loan funds, my friends' help and jobs that were given me mostly out of sympathy. In a way I might have starved if I had not been a student. It was a kind of racket. Just by being a student, I had got fed, clothed, sheltered, as guest in the house of Western civilization. And I thought to myself cynically, now I understand why there are so many quasi-professional students here from the Orient, like Mr. Ok.

The scholar of the West is an introvertish creature, happy in inner worlds of thought, irritated, bored and out of place when he is forced to see too much of his ordinary fellow humans. Mine seemed not really the temperament of the Western scholar, while, unlike Kim, who was pure poet and intellectual of the East, I had some baser elements in me of George Jum. I understood very well George's passion for the "diplomatic service," or for the exhibitionist world of the American stage. One of my selfish thoughts about the passing of Korea often was, that without a country there seemed no way for a man to take some active part in the human affairs of his time. And like George Jum I really like to walk the earth with people. I got on well with them. I did not become suffering and ironic like Kim before tastes, interests, attitudes that were not mine.

So it really pained me at times to keep on, getting more collegiate up in Boston without getting more educated. I could not help seeing that concentration on one subject makes nobody any real specialist, and minoring by distribution of hours makes no man liberally cultured. Latin and Greek fail to make anybody classical. Neither can the modern language department make one erudite. Sometimes, indeed, college education seemed to me only a curious convention…the specialty supposed to specialize, the minoring to broaden, the scraps of mathematics, science, and psychology supposed to develop higher reasoning powers, lastly the physical training supposed to finish off the rounded man. Aha, there he is! the cap and gown gentleman with a sheepskin under his arm. How suave his functioning mind! How sound his body! He has met all the requirements that college has measured to him.

I had my qualms. George Jum already had done more toward acclimatizing himself in America than I had done. He had had more of the three great L's in living, not just existing.… Leisure, Love, Luxury. He was not a guest in the house. He felt himself quite at home. And certainly he had acquired better the popular social requirements of American youth, while outside, than I while inside, college. Flirting, necking, drinking, telling anecdotes, I had none of these which George already had, even though these are thought to be specialties of the successful college boy. Of course the I.Q. had not X-rayed George and diagnosed him all over. But it wasn't with entire complacence that I compared myself with him. George was so free and independent, and he could still make his own dogmatisms on everything.

George remained a carefree and slovenly generalizer. But I saw it was up to me to become a professional specialist—not just the specialist of the major in college—since I could not cook for the wealthy nor aspire to Hollywood. Something in me all the while opposed such specialization. I thought to myself, "There are many here who specialize in certain things—it is almost the law of this American civilization…like the man who helps to make machines, by working on a particular detail, say, driving a nail. So his life work means that he repeats that single routine work in one narrow channel. He is not a magnanimous creator of that gigantic machine, no, for he has lost the plan of it, he has been absorbed by it, he is the servant of it, not it of him…how has he any vision to see to the far horizon? He has henceforth no destined goal except to drive that nail." And it seemed to me that the life of the specialist became utilized in an ever narrower groove, and did not reach the embracing whole of life. "Poor soul," I thought, "Poor modern soul, he is tortured in his confined prison, never to get out…he must handle his specialty, never the infinite. He rides in his automobile over miles of paved space, but he does not leave the car he is riding in. He flies, but he never enters the air of the universe. He submarines, but never sinks himself to the heart of the ocean, he tunnels mountains, yet he never feels the spirit of earth, as Shelley or the Taoist poets did." And what was I to specialize upon? I had intended at one time to study medicine. But I found out very soon that I was no medicine man. Before the accumulation of facts necessary for that my soul seemed to dry up, becoming parched like a desert. I would have to run quickly and read over Shelley's *Ode to the West Wind*,

Oh! lift me as a wave, a leaf, a cloud!
I fall upon the thorns of life! I bleed!
A heavy weight of hours has chain'd and bow'd
One too like thee—tameless, and swift, and proud
Make me thy lyre, ev'n as the forest is:
What if my leaves are falling like its own!
The tumult of thy mighty harmonies
Will take from both a deep autumnal tone,
Sweet though in sadness. Be thou, Spirit fierce,
My spirit! be thou me, impetuous one!
Drive my dead thoughts over the universe,

Like wither'd leaves, to quicken a new birth;

And, by the incantation of this verse,

Scatter as from an unextinguish'd hearth

Ashes and sparks, my words among mankind!

Be through my lips to unawaken'd earth

The trumpet of prophecy! O Wind,

If Winter comes, can Spring be far behind?

In that I seemed to receive some kind of nourishment, escape from the vast machine. But I felt, too, about literature...here, too, is specialization, of the worst kind. I saw how literature muddles away from life, and without life what is literature? Just as without touching all the affairs and problems of human existence, what is education? But because of my pleasure in that, I came back to literature, and I sought my specialization in that field. I studied the presentation of literature as made by the lecturer in the classroom. I took courses in pedagogy and in comparative literatures, courses in the dissection of literature. And still the thought remained in the back of my head of Kim's advice. But I had done little on that, as yet.

All that summer after Charles Evans had married and gone, I hung on in Boston, like the man without money in a restaurant who must keep eating until somebody he knows turns up to pay for him. I had college debts, and I could find no job. Already more than satiated, I was saved from the intellectual banquet by Mr. Wu, a Chinese acquaintance. He was a very short, very frail man whose bones looked eggshell-thin. And he was all a bundle of intellect. A true scholar. He was a government student, taking now his doctor's degree in philosophy. Everything was so easy for him, that while taking it, he wrote a book on the side. This was his third. The others were on sociology and economics respectively. Naturally, he considered the average American undergraduate just like straw. Mr. Wu was a great admirer of Sun Yat Sen and was thoroughly saturated with the spirit of the first revolution. Like Hsu Tsimou, he was full of hope for the future, and he urged me to come back with him to China. He was the dean of a well-known government college in Shanghai and he promised me a teaching position. But I could not make up my mind to that, still feeling like Kim that

I could watch world forces better in the West. By the time Mr. Wu got back, there had been another revolution and he himself was out of a job.

One day Mr. Wu introduced me casually to some Chinese in charge of the Chinese section of the Sesquicentennial Exposition in Philadelphia. I was much interested in that. They needed another man in their department and after a few interviews took me in at a good salary. In Philadelphia I got along well in this work, which consisted in much talking and some polite selling, and in meeting many people. Among those whom I met were executives of Boshnack Brothers. I even met Mr. Boshnack, in charge of one of the biggest department store businesses in the world. Mr. Boshnack talked with me, and invited me to a private conference. He asked me how I would like to work in his store in Philadelphia. How would I like to equip myself to become a buyer for Oriental goods? I thought to myself, here is the opening in the actual world which I have waited for. Indeed, I had known all along that I could not put the world of business efficiency and Mr. Lively behind me. I had only escaped for a time during college education. So I agreed to come and work for Mr. Boshnack, at first as a clerk, until I could find out more about the business, but with the ultimate hope of being made a buyer.

Boshnack Brothers had two stores in New York, one in Chicago, a whole block of stores in Philadelphia, and a branch in Paris and one in Tokyo. I now had the opportunity to see something of how a department store ran. At the head of course, with luxurious offices high in the building, were the reigning members of the Boshnack firm—two fabulously wealthy brothers. Then came the buyers, thousands of them, drawing from $10,000 to $15,000 a year, every one. A tidy salary. (So it was a bright hope that was held out to me.) To be a buyer is the dream of every clerk in every department store in America. And I was in almost the biggest one of all. Boshnack's sold the littlest thing as well as the biggest. There were buyers for needles, for rugs, for books, for china, for airplanes. Each buyer was given so many inches of space in the big store. This was his kingdom. Just like a small proprietor, he paid for all that went into his space, and kept track through his clerks of all that went out...except that he made no profits. In his department he was looked up to almost as much as Mr. Boshnack himself. When he passed, the underlings said in a hushed voice, "The Buyer!"

Below the buyer—and that means far below—was the assistant buyer. He was somewhat in the position of vice-president but without any opportunity ever to become president. When a buyer died, the assistant buyer was never promoted to his place. For the buyer occupies a very important, high and mysterious position. Like prophets and like college presidents, buyers always come from the outside, and sooner a salesman will go from an obscure place to be buyer in a totally new store, than those immediately under the buyer rise to his station in life. Once an assistant buyer, always an assistant buyer.

Below the assistant buyer came the aisle man, a still greater drop in fame and in fortune: The aisle man was a $25-a-week man, and not much above a common salesman, but he got dressed very cleanly, and tried to point out the faults of all those below him. His work was in O.K.-ing checks, C.O.D.'s, exchanges, returned goods, and in verifying complaints against his department. But besides these complaints from outside, he must be very active making his own complaints. He watched if any man or girl came in late, and bawled these out. He had to go and peep in the women's washrooms from time to time, to see that no girl clerks were lingering there. Some girls he accused of keeping change from customers. Some he accused of making off with stockings. Poor devil! he worked hard! But there was not much chance for him. Great as the gulf between the buyer and the assistant buyer, even greater was the gulf between them and him. I wonder how he could ever hope to be a buyer. But he did. Men must dream.

You could have as many aisle men and clerks as you wanted. After that came so many experienced saleswomen at $20 a week—and so many girls at $12 or $13 a week. Twenty dollars a week was considered quite good pay. One of two even got $25, but you had to have been in the same store seven or eight years for that. The men in the store liked to say how the girls on $12 a week made a side-living by prostitution, since it was impossible to live on that in a big city. I don't know if this was true or not. But then everybody there—except the fortunate, princely and snobbish buyers—worried about how to live, and among so many poorly paid employees, many got caught in tricks and were fired.

Of course, in this system only the owners made any profits. Still, the pretense was kept up of profit-sharing in the earnings of the store. Every clerk got one half per cent of all he sold. That meant one penny on every two-dollar purchase. By the end of the week, he hardly totaled more than fifty cents or one dollar, and this couldn't be bettered even in the shoe department or department of women's clothes. (The saleswomen and salesmen were put on a lower wage there.) Still, like tips, even fifty cents or one dollar a week was something to work for, and everybody tallied up eagerly at the end of the day to see how the day had gone for him. It was enough to make him side with the store in doing business, and have the true salesman spirit.

The store was full of psychologists, psychiatrists, and other trainers in salesmanship, and the ambitious were allowed an hour off every day in order to attend this school; most newcomers were ambitious enough to take that hour off. In the school a saucy young bachelor lady of thirty-five would give lessons on how to sell…lessons which were all theoretical, making me doubt if she ever sold anything in her life. I was reminded of Miss Fulton and Mr. Lively's training corps, but that was amateur work compared to this. One of the lessons featured suggestiveness. For instance, if the customer came into a house-furnishing department, you should approach her like this, "What a beautiful day!" Waiting a while, you added casually, "A beautiful day to be out in a country house." When that had got in its work, you continued, "No country house is complete without…blankety blank"…you could fill in with anything Boshnack Brothers had to sell.

The point of another lesson was human interest. Scene, the toy department. When the mother and baby came in *together,* if they left the store without having bought something, it is because the clerks have been lacking in human interest. What more legitimate object for human interest than a baby? No harm in displaying that. All the world loves a baby. Make for that baby then. If possible, get hold of Baby's hand, win Baby's confidence. Nobody—not even a mother—could possibly blame you for being interested in babies. If you aren't, you ought to be ashamed of yourself. Make that baby happy to be in Boshnack Brothers'. Show it things. Let it play with things. Don't be afraid it will hurt them. Mother will see that it doesn't, or if it does, she can pay for them. Wind up the mechanical toys for it. Down on your knees. Get it absorbed. Yes, put it in the little auto, clear the way. Let it ride as far as it wants to go. It's good for Baby, for you, for Boshnack Brothers, for everybody, And this is the one time in salesmanship you don't need to say anything. A baby of four or five can talk for itself.

As can be seen, a good deal was made out of human psychology. For instance, when husband and wife come in together to buy. The instinct of the woman clerk may be to address the husband. This is wrong. Do not ignore the husband, but concentrate your eyes on the eyes of the wife. If the wife's eyes tell you "yes," it doesn't much matter whether the husband's eyes or mouth say "yes" or "no." There is just one other thing to remember. If the wife's eyes say "no," don't try to sell to the husband. It won't work. The goods will come back, and you will lose your pains.

There were some very special lessons for those selling in the woman's dress department. The buyers there had to be very well up indeed. Always there must be more beautiful rugs on the floor here than anywhere else, everywhere an atmosphere of luxury. The reason is that women are very susceptible to the luxurious suggestion, especially when it comes to clothes, and if they see themselves in a mirror standing on soft velvety rugs in a setting of opulence, the effect is irresistible. Another thing, the buyers must look after the mirrors. Special mirrors are provided, although they cost more than ordinary mirrors. These special mirrors are not the faithful kind at all. No matter how bad-looking you are, you'll find a better-looking person in them than when you looked elsewhere. The customer cannot fail to be pleased, and will generally attribute it to the Boshnack Brothers' dresses. Sunlight and shadow and false lights must also be arranged as artfully as in a sculptor's studio, and all of this the buyers, and even the saleswomen in the woman's dress department, must thoroughly understand. An artist's course in complementary colors was also given to any one interested.

A few of these points could be applied to the men's clothing department, but not so much, for men were harder to fool and not so luxurious. In fact, some American men were so economical that when buying dress suits, they returned them after a night or two, to have the money refunded. Aisle men were especially educated to be shrewd here, and to argue that they had found a piece of paper or a match.

Well, it was a sparrow-jabbering sound, this sales-training talk, much like the sound of Ma Jong pieces falling on the table, and I thought I had never listened to anything more boring in my life. But no love of God entered here. Only warm human interest. And I had left Boston for good. And of course I ought to believe in selling Oriental works of art....

In spite of the warm human interest, in Boshnack's I saw the blindest, deafest, dumbest collection of human beings I had yet seen, though many were college graduates. Miss Stein, manager in the chinaware department, was a Vassar girl who had been there about ten years. She was, I suppose, "educated." Certainly she was capable enough. But she had no interest outside her own store space. Success in her line absorbed her every thought. Others I saw weren't so fortunate as to have any success to care for. An old woman with trembling hands wrapped dishes in excelsior all day, drawing for that $14 a week. All her life from 8 o'clock until 5:30 she had been doing that. The young girls were probably just working until they could get married, and without much ambition for a career, but some married women were here for an indefinite period—mostly elderly and hardworking, either widows or divorced or with invalid husbands. Poor Mrs. McGee I remember especially, very big, very fat—who couldn't see except through glasses and who sometimes lost them...always running fast, for the assistant buyer who treated all like dogs or little kids. But for everybody it was very rushing. Much of the action of moving on and on was futile besides. Aisle managers, floormen and buyers were always watching. When life wasn't a scramble, you had to scramble it a bit purposely.

It did not take me long to form an opinion that life in a department store was a horrible life for all people. What appalled me was the regimentation. You could never go out to eat when you felt like it, but must be assigned a regular lunch hour. Some went at eleven, others at twelve, still others at one and at two. And of course you were obliged to drop into some place just around the store. There were lunchrooms for employees in the store indeed, but these were very bad, and served only the leftovers from the regular customers' restaurant, so most employees preferred to eat outside, even if they paid a little more for it. Horn and Hardart was a popular place, for it was quick. You dropped a nickel in the automat, pulled a lever, and down dropped a cup of coffee for you, or for ten cents you took out a ham sandwich. Every morning the employees trouped in through an awful basement door. You couldn't take anything in or out with you, but had to be examined each time as if you were suspected of being a thief. Each employee had a ticket or voucher for admission, so that no unemployed pickpocket could squeeze in at the same time, and if you forgot the voucher you were not admitted without a lot of red tape. Every employee had not a name but a number. His number was on his card on the wall, lined up with many other numbered cards. The first thing he did before taking off hat or coat was to punch that card by the automatic clock, showing the hour and minute when he reported to work. After punching, he wasn't so eager. He lingered around in the washroom as long as possible, keeping out of the way until 8:30 or 8:45. But everybody had to dust and order his goods before the store opened. Even afterwards, in order to show up well, you had to keep dusting and ordering and keeping busy when there was no customer in sight. You never could look as if you were taking life easy, as in an Oriental store. And four times a day you had to punch that clock, as a number coming in and going out.

I was placed first in the chinaware department, where the capable Miss Stein was my section manager. Everywhere were aisles, a whole floor's length, tables piled high with dishes and glassware. The cards above gave advertisement as well as cost.... "Tea set complete with 23 pieces, now $3.75"...and some additional caption like, WHILE THEY LAST! These same tea sets filled up the stock rooms, but only one or two of a kind were displayed at a time, to make them seem rare. Later I was put into the adjoining department for antiques, which included Oriental objects, where the "Ming" vases sold for $50, $70, $100, and where there were many cases of real jades bought directly from China. I got into trouble over teakwood stands. They could not have been teakwood stands because they warped. They must have been cherrywood stands. Real teakwood I knew never looked like that. But I mustn't call them anything but teakwood stands, for nothing but teakwood stands would sell in that department. Mostly Boshnack Brothers were honest, when it was a matter of dollars and cents or living up to the label price. Having an eye out for big business makes a man honest in small things. That is the trouble with small shopkeepers in Italy… they have not yet learned about big business, so they try to cheat the customer in small things instead of concentrating on big deals. Boshnack Brothers never did that. When sets of dishes were bought, no one could be more careful in packing, and in not leaving anything out. And they were generous in making exchanges, or in otherwise satisfying complaints through the complaint department. But Oriental art, they seemed to think, would be despoiled by taking away the word teakwood even from the cheaper grade of stands. I protested and Miss Stein tried to do something about it with the head buyer, but nothing was gained. Teakwood the stands were advertised, teakwood they must stay, even if hewn in Connecticut. But I could have no faith in any of these stands. Even the better grade, where the wood really came from China, were all broken up into small pieces when imported, in order to escape heavy customs duty, though joining is one of the most important features in a teakwood stand, and one for which Chinese craftsmen were ever famed. Once in America, they were fitted together any old way.

Everybody had constantly before him the standard of shrewdness, shrewdness for profit as measured in dollars and cents. A petty limiting atmosphere lay upon all one's thoughts and acts from the moment one entered Boshnack Brothers' store. If in honest indignation I went to discuss with Miss Stein those teakwood stands, she would whisper, "Sh! Come a little later. Mr. Boshnack is right up there looking down. I want to do things like that when Mr. Boshnack isn't looking." Then I would look high up at the great balcony running all around the store, and there sure enough would be big stout Mr. Boshnack, looking down on the clerks and the customers, and to me, for all his Benjamin Franklin spirit, he was almost like a great spider in the midst of his web.

If Miss Stein seemed to me dumb, it must be said that the men in Boshnack's seemed even dumber. Of course, I had more opportunity to observe the men. But it must be true—men feel restriction of freedom even more than women do. And these were sorry examples. In Quaker House Hotel—there was a Boshnack men's club. Not all the men in Boshnack's could belong. So it was something like a college fraternity. The ordinary salesmen were debarred; but nearly everybody else was there, and it made so many that the dues—one dollar a year—were enough to pay for the rent of a grand room. The hotel was very glad to have the club on its premises, in one of its best rooms, for that way, many people were seen coming in and going out, smoking cigars, loafing around, laughing and having a good time, and they made the hotel appear popular. The clubroom was very luxurious with plenty of lamps and comfortable chairs, and rich thick carpet. There were chess and checkers, cards and poker chips. Sometimes forty would gather in this room, sometimes two...sometimes one was there all night entirely alone, and at such times I really enjoyed membership.

When the clubroom was filled up, there was a good deal of talk. Five per cent was on business management; 70 per cent was on sex; 25 per cent was about Rudy Vallee, Gene Tunney, Jack Dempsey, and Babe Ruth. The main recreation and great hobby was the talk on sex. Most were poor struggling family men whose lives were in the inescapable rut, but in them was seen nostalgic longing to be as free as George Jum; and the easiest way to sneak out of bondage was by way of some illicit sexuality. There were two around whom the rest generally gathered for the laughs and talk. Daugherty, the man who hired and fired, a tall fair man with well-slicked hair, slightly bald, clothes very neat as men in his profession have to have, but beyond them no distinction at all. And MacMann, a big fat fellow, entirely bald, who had been working for Boshnack Brothers twenty-five years. MacMann had several grandsons, and a Baptist missionary daughter working in China, but among "the boys" you would never know about MacMann's background. Daugherty and MacMann got together over the checkerboard, and while the game was in progress, they wouldn't say much, no more than, "Well, is there time for another game?" But when there wasn't time, they would talk.

"Well, how do you find nigger gals, Daugherty?" the fat man would ask Daugherty. And others then would look around, snicker, and come to listen.

"A-aaaaaa! Can't stand niggers."

"What! Not even to sleep with?"

"A-aaaaaa! Nauseate me."

"Why, nigger girls are just as good as any others!"

"A-aaaaaa! I'd lose my virility."

"Fact!" interposed another man. "Lot of that depends on the looks of the woman you sleep with."

"Rot!" from MacMann. "Pretty faces don't mean a thing...nor pretty clothes neither. A woman's a woman. If face don't strike you, cover it up with a bath towel. Let me tell you, nigger girls are the best, in my experience."

MacMann asked Daugherty then, had he virility, and the fastidious Daugherty boasted that as for white women, he could use twenty-five in a night. MacMann wheezed and exploded with red laughter. "Aw, come off. You're just kidding. I tried that. After three or four I was through. I had to kick them all out."

So conversation went. Once it was started, others would chime in and keep it up. All evening they could make talk like this, seven nights a week. They brought out many heroic deeds with prostitutes and near-prostitutes. A popular brand of story was that which dealt with someone's efforts to get with a loose woman in a respectable boardinghouse, how many times he tiptoed out in his stocking feet, how many times he had to turn and run back. Once these men got started, like bad boys, it was a contest to see who could be most unashamed in talk. One made the boast he could go through every love motion in a car, without taking off his hat or removing his lighted cigar. Another, by recounting details of a seduction he had carried out, made the *Plastic Age* seem purely academic. And yet I suppose all were fairly decent average American citizens. But they had no superiority, neither in virtue nor vices, neither in talk nor reserve. Always the license they took was of the most petty kind, cautious, shrewd, timid and secret, as this kind of rebellion was. Here in the escapist mood to which Boshnack Brothers' Men's Club was devoted, wives, too, dropped from their place of grim importance. As the burden and the reward of secure jobs in Boshnack Brothers—the link to duty and badge of the treadmill chain—they became subject for snickering talk like any other woman. One clean-cut young fellow, rather good-looking in the Arrow-collar style but with nothing behind, took everybody into the joke by telling how his bride raised the hotel by screaming on their wedding night.

This, then, was the atmosphere. This was the substitute for what the romantic George called Mystery. I guess they were not as barbaric as he was. But for a man not to be talking as they were was to be out of place in Boshnack Brothers' Men's Club. Campbell, assistant-buyer in the chinaware department, tried to draw me out. Whenever he could, he would talk with me before others to make them laugh. He used to lecture me on how to swear. But he was a very well-meaning, rather earnest fellow. I began to express myself once on the department store business. Horrible, isn't it? I said. He couldn't believe that I meant it. What! No good in building up a big department store business like Boshnack's? Campbell could not see good in anything else! He thought I was crazy. "Yes," I said gloomily wlth sincere dogmatism, "it costs too much in soul-destroying energy. A store is worse than a factory. The aim is always money, things, sales…never life, never creation of anything. It turns away from life. It makes humanity into just a stuff-handling machine."

That got under Campbell's skin. I had assailed his loyalties. Boshnack Brothers', he argued, was for the good of man actually. It didn't matter to him, he said, that he wasn't a Boshnack. If you didn't have capital yourself, then work for him who has. And why—why—for ages to come, this monument would last, made by the initiative and brains of Boshnacks, to be handed on down to more Boshnacks and their sons. (Campbell was a sincerely loyal employee, like many there….) What! Boshnack not public-spirited, not humanitarian? Look at those endowment funds for keeping up historical houses in Philadelphia (Boshnack's most recent publicity stunt). Look at the gifts to charity every year. Didn't I know that if any other department store gave $1000, Mr. Boshnack made out his check for $10,000?

George wrote, congratulating me on having so good a job. He said he was glad I had the guts to go into big business, and he, too, wished he could get out of housework and place himself with a firm like mine where a man could climb. I wondered if George was right and I was wrong. Well, this must be the lesson I must learn, of American life. This *is* American life, I said stubbornly. All day long the moving multitudes of humanity, with busy legs, constantly darting false smiles to cover their depressed facial expression, the worn-out machine bodies turning round in the aisles of unmoving glass and china sets, slowly figuring with shaking hands—haste and moving too many heavy things made them so—now over the tally they go, recording 50 cents. Chasing after the dumb aisle man to O.K. a charge account, a C.O.D. sale... two eyes to look at the customer, two hands to count the change...then to make a sale check, to carry the goods to the packing room, then to run with the legs' tottering strength after a new customer, for fear of losing that sale to another salesman (there is a half per cent commission on that sale), at last the dead-tired body moving from the cloakroom to breathe the air—the street air, the dusty, respectable, stale air of staid Philadelphia. But where were all the enchantment and romance, the glorious vision, which I had seen in my dreams of America as a boy?

2

I met Miss Churchill through Mr. and Mrs. Winters, with whom I had attended classes in a Boston graduate school. I always thought of Miss Churchill as very old. She was a tall, gentle lady, slightly stooped, with a head of luxuriant iron-gray hair very simply arranged, and she always wore black sweeping skirts, and knitted shawls around her shoulders. Very plain and hearty she was in all she said and did. Whatever formality she had was that which was natural to the heart and never put on from the outside. Her companion, Mrs. Hopkins, an old friend of Miss Churchill's, was a thin, fragile little woman as delicate as an old silver spoon. Because her chin came out slightly and her nose turned up, she gave the impression of being a saucy talker, more so than she was. Everything in that cool dark house seemed thin, antique and old-fashioned. The furniture was early American, very plain but polished and rubbed soberly by time. The chairs were substantial, esthetic, too, in their simplicity, but they were not chairs to lounge in, but to sit straight in, thoughtful and prim. Miss Churchill was active in the Friends' Society in Philadelphia, which supported relief work in Belgium, also famine sufferers in China and Armenia, and which raised scholarship funds for Japanese scholars in America in order to console them for the exclusion laws. She was a Free Quaker, quite free, and somewhat of a rebel in her way. A niece of hers had married a well-known Japanese some years before, which had created a scandal in the family. Miss Churchill, both before and after the marriage, had always given her encouragement and sympathy to the young couple. In a beautiful old Philadelphia house on Clinton Street, which had been in her family for a long time, she used to entertain in a quiet way all kinds of people, particularly young people and many of them from foreign lands, such as India, Japan, or China.

At first I went to Miss Churchill's only as one of many, with the Winters, or with the Hindu student Senzar, or the Japanese Miyamori. Miyamori had been specially selected on a scholarship given by the Friends' Society. But he was already a mature man—thirty-eight or forty, with home ties firmly established in Japan. He had the rosiest, most uncritical view of American civilization of any Oriental I have ever seen. He frankly envied me as a more or less permanent exile, and advised me never to go home, since all was primitive and barbaric hell back there. Tall buildings, subways, autos, universal sanitation, great department stores like Boshnack Brothers, these seemed like Utopia to Miyamori. He was a small, dainty man with a tiny moustache. He seemed like a feather, very childlike and ungrown. And he had a habit of writing bad poetry to all his American friends and signing his name "Very respectably." He was invited by Miss Churchill less and less. As for the Hindu Senzar, I well remember the time he, too, was eliminated.

It was at a dinner party given for some English actors. Miss Churchill had a young girl art student living with her that winter, by name, Miss Laura James. She was a tall, slender, frail girl of English ancestry, two generations back. Laura had abundant fair hair covering her ears and caressing her cheeks, and done in a large knot behind. Her face was very thin and rather long, her large eyes were of a slaty dark blue, and she had full, wistful lips which pursed themselves sometimes as if in a small, and lonely contemplation. I considered her very attractive, and whenever I looked at her, I thought of a certain poem by Rossetti called "The Blessed Damosel." Laura had an uncle who was a successful actor, and I believe the guests that night were friends of his. Anyway, they were a young English couple, very refined and superior. The Winters were there, and Senzar and I, so it was quite a large dinner party, of international blend.

Senzar was an Indo-Oxford product, and was now in America studying engineering. Of course, he was a fanatic patriot, but his words were so much in the clouds, you could not make out whether he intended to go back to India or not. So long as he kept silent, Senzar looked handsome, poetic and sad. And at first he kept silent, rolling around the splendid melancholy of his great dark eyes, so silent that everybody was sympathetic, thinking him shy. But with Senzar it was not shyness. His idea of conversation was the firebrand, elemental attack, mortal combat. On any subject he was ready to die. He was just looking around for an opponent. I do not know if English domination has made Hindus that way—I suppose so—for most of them are ready to go off at a moment's notice. Anyhow, Hindus and Far-Easterners did not get along well together in Boston schools. It is thought by some Orientals that Hindus lack humor and proportion. What Hindus think of other Orientals, I do not know. But Senzar soon fastened on me as his opponent. Suddenly he began questioning me about my college.

"Well," he laughed shortly, "I wouldn't come to America for an undergraduate education, not if you paid me. For I must have the best!"

"Man, you ought to have come to America before this, then!"

"America hasn't anything. Oxford has everything."

"America certainly is best for engineering and physics, which is your line," I argued.

"No," he contradicted flatly. "I am the best-trained of anybody in my line. America for practice. Oxford for theory. Oxford is best for engineering, best for physics, best for electricity, best for medicine, best for dentistry, best for mechanics, best for everything. Oxford, where I went, is best for all. Anybody who goes to an American university isn't educated. That's what I mean."

The others had been listening attentively to this, with sly glances of amusement and surprise.

"Ha ha! You think you're educated. You don't know how to talk English!" laughed Senzar. "You say it this way—I say it that. Ha ha!" And he drew comparisons between my American and his English accent. "Then, Americans are not sound," Senzar kept on, and the Americans and the English began to get very uncomfortable. He was unconsciously parodying the English-felt superiority of the English university man. This in itself was painful to that young English couple, both university people, who were there with open minds and much good will toward America. With coolness and irony, the English actor, who was an Oxford man, tried to take Senzar down. He said good words for American ways, even American speech, and criticized his own country, tolerantly and semi-humorously. Suddenly Senzar writhed and turned on him.

"Why do you speak these lies? Englishmen are hypocrites. Englishmen despise all others but themselves. They are the most conceited and boastful race. They despise Americans even more than Hindus. I know, for I have heard them speak. But the English don't speak this before Americans. Liars, crooks, hypocrites, devils! O what people you English are."

This was making it worse and worse. Miss Churchill was flushing. As hostess, she was in a bad jam.

"Aren't you wording it a little bit strong, Mr. Senzar?" hinted Miss Churchill, nervously twisting her hands.

"Strong?" demanded Senzar incredulously.

"Naturally your national views blind—"

"Blind? Not a bit of it. It is you who are blind. I know all about England and the English. You don't!" he stated rudely and emphatically. "I have lived among them, visited in their homes. All my life I went to English schools. I went to an English school in India. Even there in four months I could learn what it takes English boys four years to learn—for I am more intelligent than English boys. Even the English see it. I am a genius." Senzar's face trembled like dark flowing water. His dark eyes glittered hard and bright with hate, as he looked around him with a haughty challenge. "That is why they try to win me to their side (hypocrites!). In England they treat me better than they treat Americans. They do not like to own it, but before Indian genius they are uneasy. They do not understand my vitality. I was five years in Oxford. (Naturally I have learned all there is to learn. Nothing to get from their education anyway. Only mechanical things.) So you think you know the English? No! This cold-blooded, thieving, wooden, two-faced race? Oh, no!"

Those polite people were just gasping. No Japanese and Chinese with their countries at war would have made such a scene at a party. It wasn't over yet. Senzar gave a leap. His lithe body sprang into the chair directly in front of the English actor. Miss Churchill shivered. He shook his fist wildly. "Soon we will drive you English out. When we get guns, we will shoot. We are not afraid of death. We despise it. Because we do not believe in it. I know *I* am immortal!" Senzar slapped his chest. "That is my Indian teaching. I do not learn that in any English school. We rebel, you see, without guns. Girl students stand up to be shot down. You shoot us, hundreds, thousands, when we shoot one Englishman. We do not care. You English are afraid, with guns. We are not afraid, without guns. If you were in India you could not sleep for thinking about this. In India, every Englishman wears a bullet-proof vest under his clothes. He is afraid for his life. We face bullets with bared breast. We are the unquenchable fire in India. It is you English who will die, for you believe in death!"

Mrs. Hopkins tried to talk about the theatre. He waved his hand for silence. He went straight on, like a crazy man, telling what shameful things the English did in India. Senzar had forgotten me. This Englishman as it happened was wholly in sympathy with home rule. But Senzar did not wait to find that out. I jumped back into the fray. I interrupted Senzar to tell what the Japanese did in Korea. "You Hindus are better off under the English than we are under the Japanese." He shook his head, waved me aside. But I would not be waved aside. Since he contradicted everybody now who opened his mouth, I kept on. I deflected his words and his wrath toward me. Not without enjoyment, too, I sought to stem that lava which Miss Churchill felt to be such a social catastrophe. Westerners do not talk with the whole body and heart as Asians do. It was furious debate. We were talking on different subjects, but our words clashed in a battle of the elements. It was a stirring evening. But I got Senzar back at last to be my opponent again, away from the Englishman. When Senzar left—he never stayed late, because he got up every morning according to some Hindu ritual to greet the dawn with study—I was almost decorated for merit by the exhausted Westerners.

"Poor Mr. Han! You were trying to stop him, weren't you? Wasn't it awful?"

Senzar, for want of tact, was never invited by Miss Churchill again. I became a regular guest now, for dinner and the evening, every Wednesday.

BOOK TWO

1

THE HIGH-LIGHT OF MY WEEK was
Wednesday night, when all was as far as possible removed from Boshnack
Brothers', the world of dollars and of daily bread. The two gentle old ladies,
Miss Churchill and Mrs. Hopkins, had sharp, youthful minds. They were
interested in the latest books, plays, politics, current events. But my real
pleasure on Wednesday nights came from the companionship of Laura, a
Western girl of my own age. Laura was a good talker and a good listener.
She was gay and always had a fund of small adventures to relate. We got on
so well together, that Mrs. Hopkins of the saucy chin, and quiet Miss
Churchill with the hands like Whistler's mother's, often withdrew to write
letters, leaving Laura and me to sit by the fire and talk. The polished floors
gleamed around us, the brass answered back, the high old ceilings receded
overhead, and to the faint clicking of Laura's knitting needles—she was
always making a sweater from balls of soft wooly yarn—we exchanged
reminiscences of college and our student days in Boston. Laura had been
graduated from a woman's college not far from there. It had a beautiful lake

and wide grounds, very different from the dust and clangor of Cambridge. I had always looked on it with interest as being just like the world of Tennyson's *Princess*.

I found myself being introduced by way of Laura's memories into these magic scenes, which were peopled, to my great surprise, with Bobbies and Timmies and Tommies and Vans and Jims. Each name brought a nostalgic light to Laura's eyes, and when she continued with "she," I might have thought she didn't know her English grammar, just like Miyamori sometimes, except that I was aware no boys could graduate from there. Sometimes on lonely walks in that vicinity, I had dreamed of disguising myself as a girl student and getting smuggled in, but fear of detection had prevented that. So I had to wait for this—for Wednesday nights and cozy chats with Laura, who was not loath to take me by way of talk in there. Aside from their names—which were like boys' or puppies'—everything seemed in order and just as I had imagined to myself. Like the sexless beings of Hudson's *Crystal Age* they had lived a utopian life (far from anything so gross as department stores or hotels), roaming over green fields, breakfasting on sunny slopes, reading, writing, discussing, curtailed only when it came to moonlight by fast dormitory laws. Everything took place to the accompaniment of Keats and Swinburne—whether they canoed through realms of gold upon the lake, or leaped the boulder by the pine-forest stream (a peak in Darien) or rolled in long grasses to the rhythm of Hertha (varied with much giggling over bits of college gossip or tales of eccentricity about their women professors, whom, unlike the students in men's colleges and their queer professors, they usually adored). As Socrates discussed philosophy informally walking barefoot up an Athens street, so their green and juicy minds caught tenuously at this and that, while they rambled through wildwood, until all the poetic landscape beyond the campus held emotional memories of new thought-horizons, and New England nature, like nature in Shelley's *Prometheus Unbound,* became a ballet in which the feminine personalities of Laura and her young friends blended.

Just like their eccentric professors, some girls lent themselves more than others to Laura's tongue, which relished eccentricities. Two I soon picked out as constantly recurring, Van and Trip. Van was short for

Evangeline, but Trip had tripped at the wrong moment and fallen down. So much I gathered. Trip, I declared, was a name that sounded like dancing. Laura laughingly disagreed. Trip trotted, Van lolloped. Both were crazy girls—absolutely mad! They were direct opposites and inseparable friends. Van, it seemed, was tall and blonde. Trip was short and dark. Van was the soul of neatness. Trip was a legend of untidiness. Van was scientific, competent, and practical. Trip was impractical, not competent, and in college wrote poetry. This year they were living together in New York, while Van studied medicine.

Another Wednesday night when Trip and Van as usual joined us, as shadows out of Laura's college years, I recognized them and was glad. Laura had some of Trip's poems in college magazines, and in manuscript. She brought these out. As Laura explained, Trip was exceedingly serious. The only thing light about her was her nickname. One of the typical poems ran:

> There are some thoughts with an eternal face
> Bright with a light outshining earthly sun,
> True with more truth than anything in space,
> Sure, and by such all surety is won.
> When the white blazing thought approaches near
> It strikes an anguish all the mortal heart.
> It comes as earthly love and doubly dear
> Now since immortal. But it may depart
> Not finding us formed perfectly to serve,
> Too dull, too coarsely made, too slow, too blind,
> Not fine enough, in hand or heart or nerve,
> May leave us aching in an empty mind.
> Thoughts of eternal light, wearing like love
> Immortal raiment, swiftly then remove.

Every Wednesday night now they appeared, that couple Van and Trip, writing gay letters from New York, about funny adventures, mad alluring encounters with people and streets, such as two girls from apartments in downtown New York always find—and two emotions stood out in me all of a sudden, my longing, my nostalgia for the magical city, and my lunatic desire to meet this Trip, the poetic and impractical one so different from Miss Stein in Boshnack Brothers'. Laura fed my flame unconsciously, as she rambled whimsically on. "Sometimes, I'm afraid I am not serious. Serious, you know, with the big S. It's a great handicap in art. Seriousness always scares me a little. And I can't see it as worth-while. Not but that I admire those people who are, even when they give to the saner ones hysterics. Now, you, Mr. Han, are very serious. Aren't you? You would like Trip." Laura counted stitches and purled once. And did not know what she was knitting into her pattern.

Anybody with this kind of obsession sooner or later reveals it to the world. Nor is there anything inconsistent with Western emotion in falling in love with a shadow. As Kim had quoted, Don Quixote is a classic example. I had never been in love before. (Except with Katharine Mansfield.) All day I was moving mechanically, passing through that great luxurious department store with everything to sell that was a thing and nothing intangible. Thank God there were nights, long lonely hours to think, to become *me* again, to try to recapture the magic and mystery with which I had first dreamed America. I could find it no longer in books, the books I had brought from college (which were mostly English literature), though I read them again and again. How often I had swum into the depths of Browning's spiritual sea, resting myself under Tennysonian sunsets, diving in again, through frothy Swinburnian waves, sitting on the Rossetti borderland of this seen bank and the unseen yonder horizon, meditating in Arnold's academic cloister, finding relaxation in Morris' earthy paradise and utopian vision! I had not so much tasted critically as *gesmäckt*. But somehow I could not recite Thomas Carlyle and John Ruskin with quite the old satisfaction in my drab little room in the Quaker House Hotel, several floors above the Boshnack Brothers' Men's Club. "Work, work, work, there is a perennial nobleness, even sacredness in work.... Blessed is he who has found his work, let him ask no other blessedness..." How did that fit in with selling cherrywood for teakwood stands? As for Ruskin, "Magnanimous, magnanimous, magnanimous is life."... I had always liked that adjective magnanimous, but Ruskin now sickened me. And Tennyson, whom I had never had so much use for as the ones with great pomp and thunder...I read once more about Maude and Madelaine, then threw the book from one end of the room to the other. Even Browning was English fog in the lungs. And when I came to

How the world is made for each of us!
How all we perceive and know in it
Tends to some moment's product thus,
When a soul declares itself—to wit,
By its fruit—the thing it does!

I wanted to say, "Well, prove it."

2

I suggested to Laura James that I must go to New York on business soon... business as to which I was a little vague. I couldn't just say New York was calling, nor that I had a date with my ideal. I asked her if there was any message she would like me to leave with her friends, Van and Trip. And Laura was surprised and said it wasn't necessary. But I kept up, until finally Laura said, well, she would write and tell them I was coming. As a matter of fact Laura was a good friend to me here. Having got used to the idea of my looking up Van and Trip, and at the same time fearing I might receive an ambiguous or a mocking welcome, she had championed me in her letter with some heat. "I am sending you a true gentleman," she wrote. "Be nice to him." Van and Trip had their little joke about what Mr. Han, true gentleman, could possibly be like, then forgot all about him. But it gave me an excuse for calling. It was spring when I bought my ticket to New York— about the middle of May. O that suave urbane spring! It was Sunday, for Boshnack occupied my time on Saturdays. The train was singing to me the American gypsy message, time, time to wander again, time to be starting, to be shaking off the past, beginning to start out to go and find something. (Just what it is nobody quite knows, but something.... Oh, yes, something big!) Miles are so easy to cover, mileage is short. But it's long to find the some-thing all want to find. Spring...and the porters standing by Pullman cars, the porters like Wagstaff...while all the network of rails, the shiny new rails sprawled out on a vast continent, and all the succulent greased cogs and unaccountable wheels seemed built only to accommodate man's free lurching spirit, as he rides, rides at time in swift flight, into the unknown future over insignificant space, still seeking that something he doesn't know, but has to find.

The ease of Sunday was upon Manhattan. How luxuriously, riotously swift the taxis ran! No trucks, no furniture vans to swipe against or avoid. The people trotted leisurely. There was a holiday mood. New Yorkers never get tired of seeking enjoyment, but now they were fresher than usual, for it was spring. Daffodils were being sold on the street and fair gasping roses. The sparkling dust added to all its other ingredients somehow the ashes of city-soiled flowers, the adulterated pollen that had brought forth so short a time before the small, thin, smart leaves.

I walked downtown toward East 30th Street, nearing the address of Van and Trip. The curtains in the big department store windows were drawn secretly over delicate wealth, the novelties and flimsy veils and stylized garments of the American woman at a time of boomtide years. All the annoying world of dollars and cents seemed to have been halted for my Sunday afternoon. But my feet still kept time on the pavements to the rhythm of the els. Yes, the wheels of vast American machinery at last for me were coming alive, they accompanied me downtown with their gay giants' noise, urging me faster and faster to deposit me at the feet of Miss Trip, with roars of mechanical cheer and don't-care laughter.

I felt I knew Trip already. I had only to offer a few side-glimpses of my personality, and probably she would recognize me at once as a kindred spirit. "As star meets star across the ethereal sea, so soul greets soul to all eternity." That would be enough, but so that she could not mistake me I began in my mind a summary of all my satisfactions and dissatisfactions with life up to date, my tastes in literature and poetry, how far I had come up to the present mentally and philosophically, something of my Oriental and Occidental adventures, etc.—all of which I planned to disclose at once on that afternoon.

The girls lived in one of those old, rather short houses below 34th

Street and off Lexington Avenue. Their names in actual print, the names of Van and Trip, made me feel I was walking in a dream. Would they be expecting me? This was the Sunday I was to come. I got in, by a faint, rather unfriendly click of the automatic opener, operated from above. And standing at the head of the stairs, peering down on me with faint reproof, was unmistakably Van. (Imagine Lysistrata as played by Blanche Yurka, a tall, broad, young Lysistrata—and you will have Van.) She was dressed—superficially at least—in a blue silk smock of a style usually reserved for small girls between four and fourteen. Underneath, one tell-tale leg of a pajama came tumbling down, a long striped pajama which looked very masculine. It was apparent they had been rolled up to answer the doorbell; one came down after the other, and Van had to bend down constantly to adjust them, after which she always towered back with flushed indignation. Aside from her size, she looked exceedingly ungrown-up. Her blond hair was bobbed and cut straight across like a medieval page's. Her skin, a nordic lily and rose of miraculously childlike texture, shone in the gloom from a tall height. Indeed, Van was a woman for a poster, a symbolic poster about America. She was Norwegian, from the Middle West, and of a Viking build.

The stage was all set, and I was ready to be a great actor. But Trip wasn't there. I could not believe it. I said I would wait, if Van didn't mind. Van hesitated, but I followed her into a large, darkened room made cool by the drawn shades. I still thought I must be expected. And Trip would come home soon. Against three of the walls were couches. One had the covers but newly drawn up. Except for that all was neat. Van sat down on the edge of a straight chair and waited, as if unhappily, holding her head. In fact she explained that she had an awful headache, and soon must begin studying for exams besides. But she knew who I was. That was something. (O, yes, Mr. Han.) Well, there was no help for it. Van said, firmly, she didn't know when Trip would be home. So I started to say it all to Van. (I thought she could report me to Trip, if I had to go off and wait a while, before coming again.) I told her of my student life in Boston, and gave, as I remember, some of my reasons for discarding medicine for poetry, asking, wasn't I right? Van looked at me so hard, I wondered if she went in for vivisection. Then I thought she would at least be interested in Laura, so I told her with serious manner how much Miss James had meant to me on Wednesday nights. It was very lonely in Philadelphia, I mentioned. I think I hinted that our wistful thoughts often sped toward New York, and Miss Van looked puzzled. "Laura lonely?" she exclaimed incredulously. "But she likes Philadelphia. Much better than New York."

"Oh, but she misses you both very much. She has told me. She so seldom gets any news of you. Especially from Miss Trip. It's very long since Miss Trip has written. She told me."

"No one ever expects Trip to write," said Van, with an obvious scepticism for the depths of Laura's longing about her friend. "She's too lazy and careless." As I looked pained at this, I felt, unfair characterization, Van bored me with round blue eyes queerly.

"Still, you see, I can't go back to Philadelphia without telling Miss Laura how Miss Trip is," I murmured politely. And Miss Van looked as if she were about to say, "Trip be damned!" She held her head again, shaking it from side to side on her long swanlike neck, like a person in some extremity. Instead she said, "Oh, Trip is fine, fine, Mr. Han. She's out somewhere with my roommate and a boy, having a grand time." And she hitched up her pajama leg viciously. "I wrote to Laura myself just the other evening telling all our little ways and doings. I guess she'll be passing through New York herself on her way home.... So, Mr. Han," added Van with a mirthless laugh, and with almost the haste of Miss Stein when she saw Mr Boshnack above on the balcony, "you'll have to take my word for it, Trip is all right! But I'm sorry she didn't stay herself this afternoon to receive you."

"Yes, I was to meet Miss Trip!" I cried in dismay. "That's what Miss Laura said."

"Well, well," Van rose brusquely. She pulled down the shade again, and turned back the cover of the bed. Her pajama leg came down and she made no attempt to repair it. "If you and Laura have made up your minds about that, why don't you come tomorrow when I'm not at home? While I'm at school, Trip's here by herself all day. And tomorrow you know I'll be taking perfectly beastly exams." Van stood by the door, with fallen pajama legs.

My relief and anticipation came flooding back. I felt warm gratitude toward Miss Van after all. Tomorrow was Monday. I was due at the store. I had that daily date of mine with Miss Stein. But I hesitated only a moment. I would cut it this time. I could not leave New York without what I came to find.

"Good-bye, Mr. Han." And Van's voice now held grace and penitence, with a good-humored friendliness creeping in. "Sorry—this frightful headache!"

3

Miss Van had told me succinctly that she would be out of the apartment by nine o'clock. But I waited until ten to be polite. I rang, and this time there was no click at all. I stood with sinking heart. (But it was only that Trip was one of those persons for whom clickers often didn't work. She had tried it impatiently, then had come down herself.) Another moment and we stood at the threshold of her house face to face. Without jolt, with suavest gliding motion, my dream took on its disguise of reality. I loved her. I loved Trip. I entered her house with confidence in God. And going before me, the smiling face, looking back over her shoulder with recognition, with merriment, seemed the mystic link to all the new life I had been seeking forever.

"Why, it's Mr. Han!" she had exclaimed, without waiting for me to introduce myself, "And here so early!"

The big room, the only room of the so-called apartment, occupied by three, had already lost the impress of Van's personality, a tidy, scrupulous neatness, and had taken on the impress of Trip's. There were the three beds as before, neatly made up, with their covers making them couches, but books lay around on the floor and a card-table was opened and spread with tumbling papers. Sunlight flooded the room, which appeared very comfortable.

It was an informal room. The manners of the girls were informal. Though Trip was rather silent and shy in her speech, she gave the impression of a person whose thoughts might become as involved and mixed up as her books and papers. So she had a certain helplessness, which was shot through sometimes by vigor. When she smiled, she looked rosy and pretty and natural. That rosy color over cheeks and short lips enhanced her feminine grace and seemed a half-shyness.... How gay, I thought, how innocent, hardly thinking she was a woman! In fact, she smiled continually when she looked at me, as if I were something amusing to think about.

Probably she was not thinking at all what I was thinking. Miranda, Rosalind, Imogene, all Western heroines, crowded to take their place behind the warm sweet face of my Western love, and the fanfare of all Western literature broke in my brain until she was like a mystic blossom set in the land of beauty forever.... But—to tell or not to tell?—I was realizing the great problem of the lover when he is struck. I decided reluctantly to conceal for the present. She would be frightened and shocked. Most practical of all, she might kick me out, so it would never do to reveal—for the present. Yet I kissed her a thousand times (I never did, I only imagined).... I gave her the Keatsian kiss that was never kissed, that's why it is immortal.

I came to with a start. Trip was offering me a cigarette from a silver cigarette box which stood on the gate-legged table, under the Indian print against the fourth wall. She seemed baffled that her attempts at conversation were all going astray. I stood up when she stood up. But she waved me down with light, peremptory hand. I watched her pretty slender figure bowing with cigarettes, and it seemed to have rainbow penumbras, in the jolly sunlit room. Oh, could a blind man have a greater shock in recovering his long lost sight?... She took one and reseated herself, crossing her legs. Now she resigned herself as with waiting. Her glance traveled once to the abandoned manuscript table.

"You are busy? I am taking up time?"

"Oh, no...."

And I feared desperately her attitude was a little like Miss Van's. I cast hurriedly about the room for the most immediate, the most practical thing to say in this emergency. My eye fell on the typewriter, on the scrambled piles of papers.

"I want you to help me," I said confidently, adopting the aggressive attitude of Mr. Lively in making a big sale. "I want to write a book. Would you help me to write a book?"

I had heard from Laura that Trip was engaged with writing a book as ghost for some one, which is partly what gave me this idea. But she looked much surprised. "You're interested in writing—in English?"

"Oh, yes," I said firmly. "A best seller. I don't know English well yet. But I have all the ideas."

That about the best seller made her get rosy and laugh, as if to herself, again. "I wouldn't be much help!"

"But I'm sure you would. How about letting me take some of your things back to Philadelphia to read?" I went on with authority. "Whatever it is you're doing."

But she shook her head decidedly, almost as if in alarm. She frowned. "No. I'm not any good."

"It looks as if you have written a lot," I said, regarding the piles of papers on the table. Trip frowned again, and gathering them up unceremoniously, half-thudded, half-piled them under the table. After that, as if feeling better, she leaned her arms on the table and played with a pencil. "Do you know the kind of mind that lives upon paper?" she said. "Every day, all day long, trying to get out of paper, out of words. And never doing it. You have to come out of paper before you can write. I take a thought and change the words fifty times. The poor thing is still-born! (without having much will-to-live in the first place).... I seem to be lost.... Oh well, some day, I'll find a real road, maybe.... What about you? What is your book, the best-selling one?"

"An autobiography!" I said promptly.

"Good. (Everything's that.) Tell me something about it, Mr. Han."

So I began to outline a book about my early life in Korea, spurred on by my need to interest her, fix her attention. It was something I'd thought on vaguely, of evenings in Philadelphia. Indeed, I'd read some biographies and travel books with that in mind. I had felt for a long time, I had much material to be shared with the West, in an ever-broadening, all-earth-embracing age, such as this we were in. And I was not going to write, like Kim, in classical Chinese; Asia, I knew, would be occupied for at least my lifetime with its throes of life or death. My moment seemed to have come now as I walked back and forth, swayed by the rhythms of prose and of public speaking. I told her of the land I was born in, its grassy, pine-covered mountains with great awesome stones, its sparkling clear air, which had never known factory smokes, the fields of tender green rice protected by devil scarecrows, the tiny houses with thatched roofs or roofs of bright green tile, decorously set within nature, nature worshipped with childlike awe just so for a thousand years. I told her of the people, those old-fashioned Korean scholars with tall hats, denying the earth was round and smoking their long pipes.

I touched the more personal note, she looked so gentle and persuasively smiling. "When I was born, it was a famine year," I paused, dramatically. "I never had a mother. She died. And I missed her so much."

However, Trip said, "*That* was probably a help. They don't seem to get on well with their mothers over here." And I was a little offended.

"But my father was no help," I insisted indignantly. "He beat me for running off to attend Western schools. And he tried to make me marry, at sixteen, some girl I had never seen and did not love."

Trip became interested. She marveled. She said she had known nothing about compulsory marriage for boys in the Orient at the age of fifteen and sixteen.

"My bride would have been some years older," I explained.

"Still, marriage might have been good for you too," she speculated, having got used to the idea. "A good way to learn, I should think. Better than prostitutes."

"That wouldn't be love," I suggested. "Now I know you must fall in love."

Just then the doorbell rang. Again Trip ignored the clicker. She ran down herself. She was gone quite a long time. She left the door open. I could hear murmurs below, and laughter. I walked restlessly around. I picked up a pair of tortoise-shell spectacles. I tried to look through them, but couldn't see anything. On the floor the papers were sprawled out. Some seemed to be verse. By putting my head on one side like a bird, I could read one, which seemed somewhat in keeping with words Trip had just said.

My beds are feathered with down,
Lily-white, lettuce-sweet,
With huge puffs of silk and satin and wool
Warm at neck and feet.

My tables are laden with cheer,
I am the most comforting cook!
Come, hang your coat with its world dust outside,
Come and look.

Look—Yet stand off, stand far off!
Oh, my tried traveller, beware!

All are but words, merely painted,
I give but painted word-fare.

The voices ceased downstairs. Trip was coming back up. She came in, her eyes still shining from the gay conversation downstairs I had not heard, and very wide and innocent, because she was near-sighted.

"Oh, yes. Now let's go on with the best-selling book."

"But you must take notes," I suggested.

"I wouldn't make you self-conscious?" She laughed outright.

"No. I am never self-conscious. Now here is the pencil. Where is the clean sheet?"

So I went on talking, and she taking notes now and then. That is how I spent the first morning with Trip. I was elated. I did not see how I could fail to make her remember me now. But good times must come to an end. At last Trip gathered up the few scrambled notes, and said, "Here they are. You write the first chapters now. Do begin. I should like to see it. Most interesting!"

"I want to leave the notes with you. You must write it."

But Trip was shaking her head very decidedly. "I don't want to write with anybody. I've stopped that. I want to try my own things." Then Trip ran to look at the clock. "Oh, I'm sorry," she said politely. "But it's time to get Van's lunch."

"It can't be time for lunch so soon?" I ejaculated.

"Not *so* soon. It's twelve o'clock. Van has only a few minutes to eat in. I must always have everything ready when she comes home."

I pleaded with Trip to come out to lunch with me. I had meant to ask her when I came in at ten o'clock, but so many things had distracted my mind. No, she said, she had to get Van's lunch. "But I wanted Miss Van too," I said sadly. "I must make full report to Miss Laura in Philadelphia." No, Van wouldn't have the time. She eats in an awful rush. Trip was already stirring briskly around. She shunted her papers under one of the beds, where already I saw there was a plethora of papers. Again she put my notes in my hands with that air, "Here is your hat." But I would have none of them. I determinedly returned them. So they went after the rest. Now she was spreading the card-table with oilcloth, paper napkins. Setting it for just two. "I'd ask you to stay," she apologized, "but really it is an awful rush, and isn't much. A mere snack. We always have just tea and toast and marmalade. Did you know that's very cheap?"

And I was wandering about the room restlessly like a disconsolate cat. Trip opened the cupboard doors of a little kitchenette. It was only a little stand with a sink and one burner. Below were some drawers. She was getting out sugar cubes now, slicing a lemon.

I examined the books in the bookcase. At first I couldn't see a thing by Browning or Shelley or Keats or Ruskin or Tennyson or Carlyle. There were poems by Emily Dickinson in a fat green volume, and a Kraft-Ebbing side by side. There were many medical books, big as great dictionaries. There was Dorothy Parker, inevitable at this time. There was *Arianne* by Claude Anet, and the *Birth of the Gods,* Merejkowsky, and *Albertine Disparue* in French, and something by E. E. Cummings. Poems of the Brontës from the public library. Lots of books by Hawthorne. *Elmer Gantry,* of course. A volume of Eugene O'Neill's earlier plays and several anthologies of modern verse. *The Waste Land,* which I had already encountered with Kim. And some Elinor Wylie. Finally at the far end, a small leather volume of Keats, very dusty on top, which I drew out, with the friendly feeling of meeting Trip in there. I opened it and found the signature of Miss Van across the flyleaf.

"Well, Van ought to be here in three minutes," said Trip inexorably into the kitchenette, her back turned.

"You will go out to dinner with me tonight?" I said desperately. "I wanted to show you some Chinese foods. So I can tell Miss Laura."

"All right," agreed Trip hastily. "Now you'd better go out and get yourself a nice lunch," she said with more coaxing smiles now. "Before Van comes in. She'll be in an awful hurry."

4

I had coffee around the corner, coffee and a doughnut—I didn't feel like eating—and composed myself for waiting until it would be a decent hour to call for the dinner invitation, and to enter the courts of heaven again. For I was in the mood of early Christian fathers receiving miracles. Which is of course the proper approach for the Christian romantic love.

I was about twenty-four years old, the age when many young men in Korea have five-year-old sons, in a country where sex maturity and procreation are considered as unavoidable as Western long pants. By the old-fashioned way, before the semi-Christianized, romantic Georges, a youth's first love meeting was carefully arranged by his parents, and it was no private matter, being initiated to the accompaniment of solemn family prayers for those time-traveling offspring which are seen as the main duty of organized life. Since a strict notion prevailed in the Orient that mistresses should be served second-hand rather than wives, all his subsequent meetings with the opposite sex might well be influenced by the equal bow exchanged with a veiled woman before society and her first right. Woman is approached realistically, and it may be gains in a certain amount of primitive physical respect, though this is not often granted by missionaries from the West. While love loses of course in the individual, romantic and spiritual aspect. One is not allowed to savor love, self-consciously, and individual growth itself by this is nipped. Degeneration of either society—Christian or Confucian—results in confusion, and it is probable that we are witnessing signs of both—in West as in East—during this strangely great age of disintegration and new combination.

But not for me, at such a moment, rationalistic reflection! Not for me, reason, to say I had been all along in the dawn of the Westernized Christianized ages, watching the livid borderline from which now the sun had just risen. True, by emotion I thought: for I thought, all my life I had felt stirrings and premonitions of this other light as much as a blind man might picture. Now it had come, for my love for Trip seemed sublimely natural, inevitable, born with me, carried from Asia, since the far moment when I set out to reach the West. Individuality, acute consciousness, consciousness of self and of other, which the love is, yes, these had been born in me like an unexposed roll of film, and with rapture they greeted the light. I hardly grasped yet that individuality is lonesome-minded. Indeed, my thoughts all turned *vice versa*. For me, here was sun with winter ended, and warmth and light and faith. I had asked for a sign from America and it had come. Having struggled rebelliously away from Nature, a child no longer cradled in her mystery and grand fatalistic control, I had been unconsciously miserable. Even while fascinated and committed mind and soul to the Western learning, I had been dismayed and alone. But now all nature took on an instant face, a face which was human, which could mirror my face and my thoughts, and the moon and the stars seen from Asia, Europe, America, Africa, Antarctica, anywhere I might turn, shone and twinkled to tell me, they had made in their enormous laboratory, Trip. Trip—as close to me as my own and as far away as the universe's utmost border, a point to which my whole being strove to attain. So I shaded my face in a dark corner of a drugstore in mid-afternoon and cried stealthily because I had been sent unkissed away.

At last I rose and with fast strides walked the streets. And perhaps people thought I was drunk or a crazy man. For I murmured to myself and from time to time wiped my eyes. The great variety of life eddied about me, and was my great Greek chorus, though it was composed of neither old men nor captive women nor sea nymphs nor classical maidens, but of all kinds of men on the globe. How grateful I was to New York, my magnet of worlds, my spiritual port, my rich harbor! How the stone pavements and dusty stalactite buildings surrounded with rugged grandeur the treasure of a still withdrawn room, that room where Van studied medicine, where Trip sat, charmed, amidst papers, helpless and as if alone!

I meant to take Trip to Chinatown for dinner, to give her some novelty. I invited Van, too. But Van had a date with her medical tomes, and she thrust us both out with relief. I felt both solemn and light-headed to be again with Trip. I started to get a taxi, for I remembered the words of George, "When with a girl, *always* take a taxi." But Trip wouldn't let me and said, "We patronize els." But when we got off at Mott Street, it was raining, so in a great bustle and hurry, I hailed a taxi after all. Since it was a new address I wanted to try, supposed to be more grand and suited to Americans, and I didn't know where it was myself, I gave the address to the taximan. And he drove just around the corner and stopped, it was only a few feet. I felt in my pocket to pay the man and I had no change. The smallest I had was a two-dollar bill. Idiotically, I pressed it into his hand and ran after Trip, to get her in from the rain.

We went upstairs to a large ornate Chinese restaurant, but nobody else was here now. A band off in one corner was playing jazz very mournfully. Trip sat down shyly and dubiously, as far from the music as she could get. But the whole place was lovely to me, lovely the murmuring rain outside, lovely the enforced intimacy of this Chinatown solitude. I noticed now, though, that the merriment, which had come in Van's apartment with Van before we left, had died out of Trip's face. A passive and somber expression had taken its place. She made little effort to talk. She seemed to be wondering quietly to herself, just what she was doing in here with an Oriental, Chungpa Han. Or she seemed to be bored. I asked her if she would dance. George said you had to dance. And we went around the small deserted circle of the dancing floor once or twice quite gravely to the dismal sounds.

Obviously the place was not suited for giving a young lady a good time in the vein of George. The quietness and melancholy of this place were more suited to spiritual revelations. So I told her about Boshnack Brothers, and Miss Stein, and how unhappy I was there. "I find that Americans can be very unhappy," I said.

"You have found that?" her chin lifted with interest. "I think that's so."

"Like Poe," I suggested.

"Oh, but that was romantic misery," said Trip. "There was some satisfaction in that. Yes, everybody seems rather unhappy and lost, in America, just now. You've felt that? But no, it isn't like Poe. It's more Chaplinesque."

"Chaplinesque?"

"Charlie Chaplin, you know. No dignity."

"Oh, yes! the fellow of laughs. Don't you like to laugh?"

"I resent being funny. I haven't much humor, I guess."

"Oh, but I'm sure you have. I like to laugh. More than to cry."

But my mind was suddenly on a paper I had written on Poe. It would be better to leave some costly jade behind, as if forgotten. Then she would have to communicate with me again. But I had no costly jade. I had only a paper on Poe.

"I want to send you a paper I wrote on Poe," I said.

"All right."

"And then I want to ask your advice?"

"My advice?" Trip laughed.

"Should I get out of Boshnack Brothers?"

"I shouldn't think you would be happy with them ever. A sensitive Oriental in America must surely find *that* hell. You were happier as a student, weren't you?"

"That, too, was a tiresome life. But I will get out of Boshnack's if you say so."

"Otherwise, when are you to write your best seller?" exclaimed Trip, dismissing the economics of my problem airily.

"When you are ready to help me."

But she immediately said she would rather write about America, and realism was the thing. And I forebore to mention that a tenuous life on paper was neither American nor realistic, for I sensed that consistency bothered Trip no more than economics.

Having prolonged our Chinese dishes, and tea, as long as possible, we went out. It had stopped raining.

We came to some posters not far from the restaurant, in brilliant colors, orange, yellow, black, cerise, and strong green. Trip stopped to look,

I to read the Chinese. I told her it was news.

"And is it colorful? I should expect it to be," said she.

"My, it's very exciting. Tong war."

"What! Going on here now?"

"But you needn't be frightened. There are more police around than usual, and there are always a lot." I suggested that we walk around some and see what was going on, though Trip wasn't so keen. So we walked those curved and intricate lanes, all with their flaming posters lit by dim street lights, for always at night Chinatown seems inky—it is no Broadway. I drew her with me into a small shop, and I bought some Chinese tea and some preserved fruits for her, the kind she had liked at our dinner. I wanted to buy her more things to sample, but she said hastily, no, we couldn't carry any more.

"Then I'll get some Chinese wine...."

"What is that like?"

"You will see. It is very strong, you know, like gin or whisky. I'll try here. Pardon me. Just walk along slowly by yourself. If you went down, they would not sell."

She seemed about to clutch my sleeve, then thought better of it. "Oh, we'd better go home!" But I was already moving off, in the direction of the cellar. "Just walk very slowly on. I'll be back in a minute." When I came out with the bottle inside my coat, she was having an angry conversation with a man. I saw something was the matter, and stepped quickly up. "Oh, Mr. Han!" she left me to do the talking. I spoke up very indignantly, though he had just drawn back his coat and shown his plain-service badge. He was apologizing now. He said to Trip he was a detective and had to protect American girls in Chinatown.

"Actually, he asked my age and my address and if my parents knew I was here!" exclaimed Trip, laughing incredulously, as we walked off together. "Marvellous! detectives! danger! Just what you always expect from Chinatown, and never get. I never saw a detective before in my life. But I wish you'd taken me into that dive with you, Mr. Han. The steps you went down were pitch-black, and *very* sinister." And I could tell she was merry and delighted with life once more, and the detective had done me a good turn, making Chinatown so interesting.

We took a taxi and got back to the apartment. Trip began to laugh as soon as we got in downstairs. "I hear Trip's giggle," I heard Van say gaily as she opened the door. And she welcomed her with open arms. There were two others in the room, another girl and a man. A babble of voices mixed together.

"Welcome sistah," said the tall pencil-slim girl with blue eyes and chestnut braids around her head, coronet style. She had a strong Southern accent. "Hey! What have you?" And Marietta, the third roommate, began grabbing things out of my arms, and examining them pertly, while Van, making a pretense of ferocity, choked Trip's laughter, and said, "Stop it—stop it—at once. Or tell what you're laughing at."

"Well, I've had a wonderful time," exclaimed Trip, throwing off her things and sinking down on one of the couches. "And Mr. Han is going to give us all a party now. Look! Chinese wine, whatever that may be!"

"Goody, goody!" cried Marietta, rubbing her hands together, and rolling her eyes. "Provisions, no end!" she winked. "And trust Trip for the wine. Good work, good work!"

"Libel, isn't it Trip?" said Van.

"Chinese tea. The very best!" exclaimed Trip, springing up to check them over. "Chinese ginger. Chinese fruits. I had them for dinner. All different kinds of mysterious things, and there is one thing—a little black ugly thing—when you break it between your teeth—you taste a marigold's smell—not at first, but slowly and gradually."

"Oh, Mr. Han, why didn't you take me along?—And what were you giggling about, please?" demanded Marietta imperiously.

"The girl always giggles!" said Van, with a mock-scowl. "It's the easiest thing in the world to make Trip giggle. Over nothing. Positively nothing. Isn't it nothing, devil?"

"No, it's something. Wait till you hear. While Mr. Han was bargaining for the wine, I got stopped on the street by a man."

"What, accosted!"

"What? For the wine!"

"No! For being in Chinatown with Mr. Han!" Trip leaned back

weakly against the cushions laughing. "But you see, a tong was going on...."

"What's a tong?" cried Marietta.

"I don't know. Something murderous. Mr. Han was explaining. A war in Chinatown. Policemen were all around. And on top of that, this plain-clothes man stopped me for loitering. Mr. Han had told me to walk slowly on, then slowly back again, while he was in that nefarious place where they sell Chinese gin.... That's when I got stopped for loitering. I became very respectable and haughty. And then the man displayed his badge. I was almost taken in. He should have got Mr. Han, who had the wine under his coat. But Mr. Han actually seemed to intimidate him. And he apologized very respectfully to *him*."

"Tut! tut!" Marietta held up a warning finger. "These loose ways! They'll come home to you in the end. Trip, you must look like a loose woman!"

"But suppose you had been along..."

"And she lost her naiyme again!" Van jumped up from the couch beside Trip, and with indescribable contortions of face and limb, she sang the song, the others joining in. Then Marietta ran for glasses. The tall gaunt ex-serviceman who was Marietta's cousin opened the bottle. Marietta handed drinks around. "Quaff, then."

Which Van did deeply—in milk. With a glass of milk in her hand, Van sang, "My name is Yon Yonson, I come from Wisconsin," taking deep draughts of milk, sighing huskily and wiping her mouth beerily with the side of her hand. (For she hated alcohol of all kinds.) She had a strong soprano voice, yet delicate and sweet, irresistibly lilting and droll. Released from the tension of hard study and grind, Van had become like some radiant natural phenomenon. The whole party rode the waves of her high animal spirits, and she seemed as exhilarated on her milk as any there. We melted into hysterics not only at her broad comedy, but at her delicate wit, turning this way and that like a bird in flight, suggesting deeper things in ridiculous foolery. Never had I seen a more bizarre American woman, or one more fitted to represent American woman's freedom (almost indeed to the point of caricature, including the tall skyscraper height that many of them reach). But no one could doubt the tender core of her womanliness, seeing her so unmasked and free like this, spontaneous as a little child. Her tenderness in particular guarded Trip, toward whom she always showed a special indulgence and protectiveness. She was not like Trip, resenting to be funny. (Van was more like me. At least I never objected very much to being funny. That didn't bother me.) I wished that George could see her. In Hollywood, I thought, she would have been a great success. For she was funnier than Charlotte Greenwood. And she hated what was too serious in thought. But she was very sensitive toward Trip and her desire for dignity.

The talk and the gaiety and laughter enchanted me. And Marietta and I drank most of the wine. I began to feel that Van was taking too much of the stage. Trip also must see me. I stood up before the old marble mantelpiece as on the lecture platform, a glass in hand—not of water but of wine—and Keats, Shelley, Browning, Tennyson, Ruskin, Carlyle, and Shakespeare rolled out in pages and sheets, all that had imprinted itself word for word on the retentive Oriental memory of one classically trained. The others now listened. They gave me the applause of clapped hands and laughter. I could not read the expression on Trip's face, which seemed to me trembling with the shake of water, water which held the nymph of youth, fountain of the eternal laughter. Finally she got out of sight. She was hiding behind Van's shoulder. Van sat at the head of the couch. Trip let her long bobbed hair fall down over her face, and I thought she held the handkerchief to her lips. I began to give them a Chinese poem in the old-fashioned singing, and I craned to catch Trip's eye. "Trip, you're choking! Hey! Something go the wrong way?" And Marietta clapped Trip on the back, meeting the hidden one's glance, her own face crimsoned with laughter.

Marietta's cousin got up to go. He showed Trip some book he had brought. I knew I had to go, too. That evening had passed into the realm of the lost evenings. Besides, I must catch my train back to Philadelphia, and greet Miss Stein with excuses on Tuesday morning. Still upon me the flush of the wine, and the joy of arriving in such a sweet world of eternal beauty and youth and delightful fellowship, I said good-bye to Van and Marietta. Van was kind but casual; still, past offenses seemed wiped out, old scores forgotten. Marietta was most free and cordial. I waited for Trip. Trip, her face still pink and shaken, eyes darkly moist, tossing back her dark hair with impatient gesture, gave me good-bye with a warmth somewhere in between that of Marietta's and Van's. But "Come again! Come again!" they all said. "It was a marvelous party."

The door of Paradise closed behind me. Marietta's cousin said a short good night and walked off. Still I lingered in the street below. Through the open windows, I heard Marietta's high staccato laughter, and Trip's in response as if she were shaken off her feet by mirth, held shaking and helpless, by an enormous God of laughter. I moved off, hardly knowing where, tears in my eyes, tears for the immortal kiss that had not been given or taken! Nor did I once think, in the innocence of my birth that day, ah, individualism! it is a lonesome world. Love, too, is lonesome.

By the middle of June, I had wound up my affairs in Philadelphia. And I severed all connection with Boshnack's forever. Afterwards, as a free but somewhat poor man, I went to New York to call on Trip again. True, I had not heard from her, though I had written.... It was just a polite letter, saying how much I enjoyed that day in New York with her. And soon after, too, I forwarded my paper on Poe. But I never received any answer. When I approached that apartment again with high mounting hope, already warmed by the thought of its informal welcome, I found it had become vacant, and neither Trip nor Van nor Marietta was anywhere to be reached. Their landlady could tell me nothing, except that they had rented there that past winter by the month. All three had vanished like the fox ladies in Chinese fairy tales, leaving no trace behind.

I wrote to Laura James. I asked her cautiously of Trip. Trip, she wrote back, had gone home. And she sent me Trip's address, which was South, amid Southern mountains. I wrote Trip again. Oh, with what care I had chosen my paper, remembering the counsels of George! With what care I had penned those pale meager words! And nothing came of that either. Trip seemed a dream, or if real, hidden now by all the obstacles of fate, time, space and the world. But I did not forget her. Nor what I had come to America to find. I set out now inspired to seek the romance of America. And spurning Boshnack's and the mean security it had offered me, I took the immemorial gypsy's trail. I became the man who must hunt and hunt for the spiritual home.

BOOK THREE

1

I COME TO a period in which I was literally a wandering student, a steady occupant of libraries, leading actually a hobo's life, but with the outward leisure of gentleman and scholar. I supported myself by small jobs of free-lancing or other efforts of the brain, and what I lived on is all but incredible. I met many people, but I made few ties. I may seem to have been derelict, but such was not the case, not so much as when I was working up to be a buyer for Boshnack's. I was waiting and watching constantly for some opening, that I might become a part of American intellectual life. When I got tired of one library, I packed my brief case and took up the hitchhiker's station along the road. All things I could not carry in that brief case, I left with George. To travel I found was very easy. And food in the South was cheap. The Library of Congress held me up for a long time, for I was much interested in its Oriental department. (Following Kim's advice, I was trying to specialize in Orientalia as from a Western viewpoint.) From Washington I went up to Johns Hopkins. These adventures I have now to tell found me in Baltimore.

On that day when I was to meet one of the strangest figures I had yet encountered in America, I had been to the Jewish Students' Home, where they served me with some kind of drink. It was strong. When I came out, I was so dizzy I could not work. I had been worrying over financial problems and the big opportunity that never turned up, so that under the influence of the drink I walked and walked, my mind eagerly searching the horizon for some future. In Baltimore I was made much of by this little group of Jewish students. They procured small lectures for me, and gave me many invitations. Their minds were keen and forceful and they savored my position in the West with true appreciation. But even with their help my funds were almost gone. I wondered when I would hear from my last free-lancing paper.

Having walked all afternoon, from one end of Baltimore to another, I found myself toward evening coming out of Druid Hill Park into the Negro section. It was a warm day in late October. At that very moment I was the witness to an unusual drama. An elegant light-colored gentleman was forcibly ejecting a large, coarse woman from a little tailoring shop. "You nigger, take your hands off me!" the woman screamed, clutching and kicking. Her dress seemed half unfastened. The immaculate gentleman threw out after her a woman's patent-leather belt, a purse and a hat. "Woman," he said impressively, "The Lord bids you—Git!" As the woman picked up her belongings, cursing and muttering, another man sidled out from the shop, a rough-looking oily-faced Jew in shirt sleeves. The Jew, behind the back of the Spanish-looking gentleman, was forming words with his mouth and making gestures as if for a future assignation, but the woman heartily cursed them both and made off. I lingered curiously, to hear the conversation of the two remaining actors.

"Brother Ginsburg, you done fallen into the quagmire. I caught you, Brother Ginsburg. What you guess the Lord's thinking now?"

"Well, Elder," whined the other doggedly, "I told you I couldn't hold out. You and the Saints is asking too much."

The dark gentleman, having wiped the sins of the world from his hands with a large, snowy, linen handkerchief, hand-hemstitched and mono-grammed, stopped now to apply the same handkerchief to his well-polished shoes. Over his shoulder he glanced at me standing and watching. From that moment he seemed to be very much aware of me, even while saying in a richly moving voice to the other, "That's what you and me is going to pray about, Brother Ginsburg. The Lord done told me to help my poor lost brethren, black or white or yellow—all peoples." Again he glanced my way. "So I ain't going to leave you to no devil, even though he might deserve to git you. But let us pray," he said abruptly. (Then he paused as if about to ask me to join them, but I made no move.) "There ain't no time like the present for repentance, Brother Ginsburg," he took up the same thread with passionate voice, "while sins of the world still burn as crimson and as hot as all hell-fire. Let us never be afraid to kneel down and put our troubles in the Lord's hands wherever we be, and rise up innocent and cleansed in Jesus' name, let us pray, Brother Ginsburg." He himself kneeled right down on the pavement in front of Ginsburg's tailoring shop, and his convert sheepishly followed suit just over the threshold. Since it was prayer, I took off my hat— a move which the Elder seemed to note with satisfaction. He made that prayer awfully short now, for he was in great haste to scramble to his feet again and take eager steps toward me. "Perhaps I could help out," he said courteously. "Are you a stranger to this city? Are you lost by any chance?" His dark rolling eyes moved eagerly over my face.

I thought I would play up to him, so I asked the way back to Johns Hopkins University, and admitted that I was a stranger to Baltimore. The Elder seemed in no hurry to answer my question. He said eagerly, "Just come over here and sit down, Brother—Brother" he groped for my name.

"Han," I supplied. "Chungpa Han."

"Ah, yes, Brother Han," he said it sonorously with satisfaction. "And then I'll explain your whereabouts to you." He ordered a chair brought out from Ginsburg's shop, wiped it with his great white linen handkerchief, and waved for me to sit down, in elaborate ceremony. He stood over me, his hand resting persuasively on the back of the chair, giving long involved directions in an emotional voice and always in the biggest words possible.

"Wait, Brother," I said. "I'm still confused in my way."

He took out a gold fountain pen and drew an elaborate diagram. By this time he had brought another chair, and he interspersed his directions with social questioning. In fact it was evident that I had made some great impression on this elegant light-colored gentleman quite out of proportion to my own importance. But he had never heard of Korea. He just wouldn't believe I hadn't come from China. (In fact, all the time I knew him, I could never make him understand about Korea. I remained Brother Han, from China, a "Chinee.") He seemed never to have heard of the big Eastern colleges either, nothing but Johns Hopkins. But he knew I was very learned, for my destination was Johns Hopkins that evening. When I rose to go, he said, "Well, well...er...Brother Han, are you in some hurry?"

"Only for some studying."

"First, won't you join me at dinner, Brother Han?"

He drew out his card and handed it to me. I read,

> Elder Bonheure
>
> Temple of The Saints
>
> Baltimore, Norfolk, and Atlantic Beach

"I would be delighted."

"Then step this way," said Elder Bonheure with a flourish. "My chauffeur is waiting."

Sure enough, around the corner from Ginsburg's shop, there was a big Cadillac car waiting, and in the driver's seat a very black and beaming Negro with a kind, honest, innocent face, dressed in the shiniest kind of chauffeur's uniform, with black leather puttees, cap, gloves, everything to match. He jumped out and bowed and bowed, first to the Elder and then me, and opened the door for us in the most aristocratic manner.

Bonheure motioned for me to go first. We sank back on the rich cushions and the car rolled grandly away. As we drove, Elder Bonheure asked me gently if I knew anything about God. Not much, I said modestly. Well, had I ever been converted, was I baptized a Christian? I hedged, at that, though of course I really had been baptized once in the Presbyterian Church. But I saw Bonheure did not really think I was a Christian. He would almost be disappointed if I was. I let him think that I was undecided. Still, I said, I thought the Christian faith very beautiful. I quoted the Sermon on the Mount, and St. Paul's words on Charity, and some other chapters that I knew by heart. Bonheure listened, enraptured. He wiped his face with his handkerchief. He sank back on the luxuriant cushions again, staring at me hard. Finally he jumped forward excitedly and gripped my arm. "Oh, Brother Han!" he cried with tears in his voice. "The Lord has planned it all! He was good to us this day. Blessed be the name of the Lord! He put me in your path, Brother Han, to show you the way home. This is our happy day, the day of the New Jerusalem!"

We drove up to a large three-story brick house of rather institutional appearance, still in the Negro section of Baltimore. Inside all was very neat and decent-looking. Everywhere were seen Negroes working. They all beamed and smiled at me and Elder Bonheure; they all bowed low. The chauffeur followed us inside. I noticed that as soon as we got in the house, Bonheure addressed him, too, as Brother, Brother Green. Then he introduced me to him for the first time. "Brother Han, meet Brother Green." All these working Negroes were the Elder's brothers and sisters, though they were humble while he was very fine.

On the ground floor, through an open door I saw a big, rough-looking dining room with long tables as in a charity house. But the Elder led me upstairs to his private apartment, which was more like a rich hotel suite. He threw open a large white-tiled bathroom and indicated with princely gesture one of the many snowy hand towels. When I came out, a tall, very dark-brown colored lady was standing there, whom the Elder introduced to me as "Sister Bonheure." She was plainly but neatly dressed in black taffeta and I remember especially her long skirt which fell below the ankles, and this at a time when the style for ladies, even grandmas, in America, was somewhere around the knees.

"Sister Bonheure," cried the Elder, clasping her round the shoulder ecstatically and looking at the ceiling, "I have just received a revelation from the Lord! The Lord has planned that I should meet this Chinee gentleman. I looked up from prayer, and I saw Brother Han standing there. Then it came to me what I should do. I went straight up and spoke to him, as the Lord breathed it into my ear. He harkened. And here he is, Sister Bonheure, he has not made up his mind yet to leave the world, but he followed to hear what more shall come to me from the Lord. I am sure the Lord has great blessings planned out for this Chinee. And all shall come about through me, the Lord's servant, Elder Bonheure. O praise God for His goodness, Sister Bonheure. Down on your knees and thank the Lord God!"

Both sank on their knees and Elder Bonheure plainly wished me to do likewise, so I sank, too. But Sister Bonheure was not quite so ardent and wholehearted in thanksgiving as Elder Bonheure. The Lord's plan seemed hidden from her, if not from Elder Bonheure. She regarded me hard and a little distrustfully. Afterwards, Elder Bonheure murmured in domestic confabulation with Sister Bonheure, "How about putting Brother Han in that little room off our own, Sister Bonheure?"

Sister Bonheure hesitated, but the Elder, without waiting for a reply, drew away and showed me a small room with bed and window and dresser and armchair, all very clean and comfortable-looking. "How about being our guest, Brother Han, while making up your mind? Step right in and make yourself to home. Later I hope you will join with us. We are all fellow workers for God here, and you are in the company of saints."

I protested that I couldn't think of accepting hospitality this way without doing some service in return. Was he in need of a secretary? If so, I might be his secretary for a while. (For I was very curious to learn what was going on here.) "The Lord will tell in time, Brother Han," answered Elder Bonheure mysteriously, "what it is you are to do. Now we must just be patient and not go against His will. He has some plan. He tell me it is best you stay now in the Saints' House. But we'll talk about this after dinner. Now whenever you're ready, Brother Han, we'll sit down to table."

I expected dinner to be served on those rough tables on the floor below with all the other saints, but no, there was a private dining room in the Elder's suite, with tablecloth and napkins and real silver, and no one had seats here but Elder Bonheure and Sister Bonheure and myself. But Brother Johnson, in white uniform, stood behind Elder Bonheure's chair to wait on him, and Sister Johnson, in white uniform, stood behind Sister Bonheure's, to serve her. What a dinner that was! My, but Sister Somebody downstairs could cook! There was real green turtle soup, and there was fried chicken, lots of it, great juicy drumsticks and many breasts, and pan-smothered sweet potatoes and many different kinds of fresh vegetables, and at the end a deep, fat blackberry pie straight from the oven.

After dinner, when we were all three feeling very plump and good-humored, Bonheure revealed a little more of the Lord's plan for me. He was telling Bonheure to take me with him when he went to Norfolk and Atlantic Beach in a couple of days. Sister Bonheure's face lighted up with comprehension, especially when Bonheure remarked, "Brother Han is a powerful speaker, Sister Bonheure."

And we did start off immediately for Atlantic Beach, before I got the chance to become better acquainted with the other brothers and sisters who ate downstairs and who seemed to hold a service of dancing and singing every night. Elder Bonheure did not ask me to join them, and besides I was very busy getting ready for the journey. But I remained curious about them, and wondered how they all came to be the servants of Elder Bonheure, while he, it appeared, took orders only from the Lord—the Lord's Servant.

After a tremendous breakfast in the private dining room (chicken again, with waffles, and honey-dew) Elder Bonheure and Sister Bonheure and I swept out like royalty, and all bowed before us, and Brother Green held open the door of the Cadillac car. And there to my surprise was Ginsburg, up in the space beside the driver's seat, with a clean shirt on, but no necktie and still looking very rough. He, too, it seemed, had some place in the Lord's plan. At least he was to accompany us to Atlantic Beach.

2

At Atlantic Beach was a house even bigger than the one in Baltimore—a five-story house, and it was occupied by a hundred of Bonheure's brothers and sisters who were all living communally and working for him like the ones in Baltimore. They lined up to greet Bonheure and to shake hands with me and with Ginsburg, after which they fell back to stare at us, with amazed rolling eyes, too stirred for speech. You could see it meant something special, our arrival down here. And Elder Bonheure, too, seemed much moved, and he called them his saints instead of his brothers. Saint White, and Saint Owen, and Saint Washington, he now addressed them, though on all ordinary occasions they were just Brother and Sister, or if Bonheure were talking to outsiders, "My Atlantic Beach cook, valet, or chauffeur."

My room was especially nice in the Atlantic Beach house, being large with a big double bed, and ruffled white curtains at the windows; the floor was so spotlessly clean it looked as if Sister White, who showed me in there, had cleaned it all round with her tongue. Later, I guessed she must do nothing all day but just wait around the corner, and as soon as I left for a moment, in she would jump, smoothing wrinkles, picking up every single hair or thread that had dropped, and plumping the big starched pillows until they were straight as boards.

I made myself at home and got out my copies of *The New Republic* and *The Nation,* and I placed *Elmer Gantry* on the table, to read in my spare time in my research upon Elder Bonheure. In fact, I was just beginning to like my room very much, when along in the afternoon, I found Ginsburg in it, too. Ginsburg had been washing up with my pitcher and bowl—he was still at it when I came in, and he had made an awful mess. I sat down on the big double bed and tried to talk to him, but there wasn't anything to talk about. He himself seemed in a dazed, humble, religious mood, after that excellent lunch in which he had joined Brother and Sister Bonheure and me in the Atlantic Beach private dining room, for he addressed me unctuously as Saint Han. But I couldn't help thinking he had come down for the ride, or just to get in on the ice cream and turkey. Certainly that man was very dumb. He couldn't read. He had nothing to say. And yet he could talk a few broken words, so it wasn't like having an animal in the room, which would have been better. Before words came to be, man got along with his fellow man without embarrassment, but as soon as language was invented, he became embarrassed when not talking.

By and by Bonheure came in and shook hands with us both. He acted as if he were surprised to see Ginsburg in my room, but I am sure Ginsburg had been led straight there by his orders. "Well, well," remarked Elder Bonheure, rubbing his hands in benevolent approval. "You two seem to be chums already. Do you think this is too crowded, Brother Han? Of course, there's room for Brother Ginsburg up on the next floor if you two brothers don't like each other. How about it, Brother Ginsburg?"

Brother Ginsburg said my room suited him. Elder Bonheure looked at me. I was sewed up. Nothing left to say. Oh, how it tortured me to nod "all right!" Oh, how I was tortured all that night with that dumb Ginsburg, who snored most horribly!

But meanwhile Elder Bonheure asked Brother Ginsburg if he would like to have a little conversation on spiritual matters. So they sat down on the side of the bed, and I listened.

The spiritual conversation was difficult, for they didn't have the vocabulary. Bonheure, of course, knew a few big words, but Ginsburg didn't know any. But their sex-phraseology was the most limited, at least when they wanted to be very delicate and nice as at a time like this, which was a pity, as this spiritual matter was all about sex. Though neither had even the word for that. So they had to use some expressions overtime, such as "sleeping with a woman" and "going to bed," and things like that, with intonation and quavering pause to convey the real meaning.

"Well, has the Lord done help you to overcome, Brother Ginsburg?" began Elder Bonheure cheerfully, "Has you done forgot that temptation I yanked you away from?"

Brother Ginsburg admitted he had received grace. He had been looking as timid as a rabbit ever since arriving in Atlantic Beach, but as Elder Bonheure went on, reminding him, some of his old irritation came back.

"Only I know sanctification can't last," he said doggedly. "Too much I got habit."

"*You* can't hold out, Brother, I know, not alone, but the Lord's going to be with you..."

"Take it this way, Elder, a man that's been having three meals a day all his life—he can't stop sudden, can he?"

"That's all right, Brother Ginsburg." (This was always Bonheure's first position in any argument. He always approved of you first, no matter what you said, and if possible he would always try to find a straw on your trousers to brush off. He sat a little nearer to Ginsburg and brushed off his trousers.) "That's all right. The Lord ain't going to let you hunger and thirst. It's the devil do that."

"It's sleeping with women, I mean," blurted Ginsburg. "I'm an old man, used to that thing. If I ain't never begun…"

"I know, I know, Brother Ginsburg, I understand. God plans everybody to have a woman. Ain't that good? He don't say you can't have no woman at all, never. What he say: Marry. Then everything's all right with God. It'll be all right with me too, Brother Ginsburg. Why don't you do what the Lord plan for you, marry and stay sanctified?"

"Well, Elder, I already got a wife."

"Then why don't you sleep with your wife, Brother Ginsburg? That's what all the saints does."

"You see, Elder, my wife don't live here. She's in the old country with all her kids. I ain't made enough cash to bring her already. How I going to do like your saints with all the Atlantic Ocean between, Elder?"

This was a poser, I could see, but Bonheure glided softly over it, saying, "Ah, we must pray about that, Brother Ginsburg."

But Ginsburg wouldn't be put off with anything superficial like that. He got irritated again.

"You talk like all people with money and a big house. Yes, prayer, prayer. What good it does me? You mean, if I pray, I get money and a big house? I bring my woman and kids over here, to stay? But I got only one room. Just my shop. A poor lonely old man…say, Elder, what harm does it do, if once in a while I get with that woman you drove out? I pay her a little money—everybody's made happy, see? You got all these big houses and a fine car. And a woman in with you every night.…"

"None but my own dear sister, Sister Bonheure," insisted the Elder firmly. "And money ain't much, Brother, under God's eyes. I'm a poor man. Them is not my goods, but the goods of the saints. Now when you're a good enough saint, Brother, all will come right for you. We bring your wife over, we baptize her, too—t'won't do for a saint to sleep with a Jew.…"

Ginsburg looked alarmed at the flow of Bonheure's mellow, juicy language making all things possible. He saw himself really a reformed man. "I ain't married to *her*," he exclaimed hastily, "though we got four kids. Four kids and her in one tailor shop, that's too much!"

"Oh, that's sin you ain't never told me about yet, Brother Ginsburg," said Bonheure reproachfully. "Now you got to make things right. You got to marry *her*. And after you marry, *stick*. That's it. Just one. Not like cows and horses and dogs; Brother Ginsburg, you're not a pig. The Lord says, just one."

Something about the "one" displeased Brother Ginsburg again, and he wormed and squirmed and complained, until the Elder said, sternly:

"This is all I got to say to *you*, Brother Ginsburg. When you think of the devil, you want devilish things. When you think of God, then you want heavenly things. You want to be one of these saints in this church, and eat with the saints, and sing with the saints, and pray with the saints—you don't want nothing to do with nobody but saints."

Well, Elder Bonheure worked on Ginsburg, until they both got up and danced around the room, shouting Glory, hallelujah.

After that the Elder turned to me a little awkwardly. "And now Brother Han, is there anything you would like to discuss about your sanctification?" he said with dignity. (He always treated me as one apart, the man whom he might like, someday, to make his partner; for he had already let many hints drop about this.) So he was rather surprised when I said, "Yes, Elder Bonheure. I've been reading and reading in this Bible Sister Bonheure gave me. And it bothers me a lot that I can't find out any arguments against smoking here. So I don't believe that is down in this Book."

"No, no, you're in error, Brother Han. I'll convince you."

"Still, I don't think we find the word 'smoking' here at all." (Smoking was one of the deadliest sins to the saints.) "And it certainly isn't in the Ten Commandments."

"True, of course," said Bonheure, after a pause, for his first sentence was always to approve you, "but there are many words in the Good Book that warns against this sin." Then he quoted to me several passages, among them the one about keeping the temple of the body pure. "You see, smoking's not clean, Brother Han. It's filthy and rotten."

"Then ashes are not really a clean form of dirt?" I inquired. "Do you think we could find a good argument there against smoking, Elder Bonheure? And yet people get cremated.... It worries me, Elder, not to be able to find that 'no smoking' verse in the Bible. Maybe, somebody might say, it's all right to smoke."

It pleased me to see Bonheure get irritated, for he lost his power when he got irritated. Very few people really irritated Elder Bonheure. But now he was irritated.

"Smoke, and you will go to hell," he said dogmatically.

"I, too, think smoking is a bad habit," I hastened to say. "Still, is it sin? But once I saw a man put a lighted cigarette down on a beautiful mahogany piano and scar the top. The furniture was ruined. And his mother wept. I might tell that man, to convince him, it is sinful to spoil furniture."

"Yes, yes, Brother Han. I ain't understood you, at first. I think we agree upon smoking."

Bonheure changed the subject. He wanted to get back to sanctification and Glory hallelujah. I saw that he was really no arguer. I might have helped Ginsburg out, too, citing verses I knew in the Bible about more than one woman. But Ginsburg was too dumb. Suppose I told him, when Bonheure went out, what to say? No, he could never remember it all.

3

I soon found out that God's plan was a revival in Atlantic Beach, with baptism of the converts in the river. Posters were already up all over town, advertising this revival. The posters read, "Jews and Chinamen to be sanctified!"

Then I thought I had been brought there under false pretenses. I went to Bonheure and spoke up. I refused to have anything to do with the baptizing. I had already been baptized once, and I wasn't going to do it again. Elder Bonheure listened thoughtfully and said, Well, did I object to speaking? No, I told him, I was a very good lecturer. I wouldn't mind speaking in his church. I would speak about the Bible and literature. So Bonheure said, "Well, well, Brother Han, yours is an exceptional case. And you know, we got to hang together, till we see what the Lord's going to do about us. The Lord told me to go and git you. He wasn't saying what for. As for the saints, you know we don't hold for no Presbyterian baptizing. Immersion or not at all with us. But your case is somewhat different. I think, having listened to you, Brother Han—you are very strong in the quoting of Scripture—I think

334

you have received immersion of the spirit, and your inner man has been rightly baptized. Something tells me, Brother Han, you is staying right by me in this revival, going to be my right-hand man."

Now while in Atlantic Beach I began to get more and more hints as to how this Saints business was run. To make those posters, Bonheure had his own private printing press. There was an office, too, in the Saint's House, with big typewriters and adding machines, where Negro girls worked all the time attending to "God's work." These girls were specially picked. Bonheure believed, with Carlyle, "There is a perennial nobleness, even sacredness in work, and blessed is he who has found his work." So he devoted a good deal of talent to picking the right person for the right job. He was really a genius at this, and all the saints seemed happy and industrious. "All work for one and one for all," said Elder Bonheure, and from what I saw, this was strictly true. And Bonheure was the one.

But my, what a marvellous and effective organization! That man really had the big business brain. Thanks to him, for the whole thing was his idea, the saints had a meat market of their own, a vegetable and fruit market, they had a business making ice cream and one making doughnuts. And the saints were not only self-subsistent. They engaged in commerce with the outside world and brought home the profits. Some of the women-saints could sew very well, and besides making clothes for the other brothers and sisters, they went out by the day; others went out as charwomen, washerwomen and cooks, and all the money they made they brought to "The Church." Yes, every cent earned by anybody went straight to the pocket of Bonheure, for the "work of God." He pretended this money was not his, but belonged to the common store. But why did he always dress so much better than they did, then? I knew a little about overcoats and his overcoat was the kind that sells in Wanamaker's for $200. His shirts were of the finest cloth, his socks of the best silk. His closets were full of clothes. Nothing fancy, of course. He always avoided the fancy or the bright as not being suited to one who had renounced the World. But everything elegant, expensive and grand. Why did he live with such luxury, he alone among the saints? I made my own investigation. In the common dining room, the saints had a good diet. Everything was well-cooked, clean and wholesome. But plain. And all the honey-dew melons and chicken and turkey and duck went to serve Elder and Sister Bonheure in private dining rooms.

The saints were supposed to live together communally, with clothes and food provided by the house. Every month each man and each woman received a pay envelope from the House, all neatly inscribed with his or her name. This was spending money. Each envelope contained exactly the same amount, only a few dollars. It was all a saint ever got, no matter what was originally earned. Even that, for the most part, found its way back to God's treasury (which was Bonheure's bank account). For the saints had no vices and no responsibilities and they threw it all on the collection plate again, as soon as they became intoxicated by the Gospel. All the saints worked hard, some inside, some outside. And Bonheure saw that there was a job for every man. And no new jobs were taken without consulting him. Sometimes he objected and vetoed, if he thought the new job might take a member too far out into the world, or could in any way slacken the old bonds. Of course, such a life was good for those unable to take care of themselves. Most of the saints were very lowly and ignorant and unquestionably better off working for Bonheure than before, cleaner and healthier and better-looking. But, as you can see, such a system was very bad for the abler ones. It killed all initiative and was just like slavery. So I could not help wondering how sincere Bonheure was. I tried to get his opinion on *Elmer Gantry,* by reading him certain passages and offering to let him borrow the book, but Bonheure was so ignorant he did not know what it was about, anyhow. "Well, what could you expect of any Baptist or Methodist minister?" was all that he said. Bonheure was of the "Holiness" persuasion.

Bonheure's church in Atlantic Beach had been originally a movie theatre; and once in a while it had been a sinful dance hall as well. He had bought it over with money earned by the saints and he was proud of having done this and so hatched it from the devil's hands. There it was, a permanent symbol of the saints' great fight that time with the devil. To spend an evening in Bonheure's church, I found, was as different from ordinary life as to spend it in heaven or hell. (Bonheure of course would say heaven and not pandemonium.) But Bonheure preached on *Black Sin,* and every time that God or Christ or Heaven was mentioned, the congregation would jump up

and cry Hallelujah. Every time Black Sin or Hell or the devil was mentioned, they would cry Hallelujah, too. So they had a great opportunity to cry
Hallelujah, for Bonheure liked to use the helliest, strongest Shakespearean,
and his topics, in spite of his limited sex vocabulary, were of the sort usually
prohibited by censorship and the Sumner committee. He made the most of
Ginsburg, whom he put up on the platform beside him and figuratively
stripped. He described how he had found this brother in a little dirty tailor
shop, with only a curtain between bedroom and business office, and behind
that curtain the *bed of Black Sin,* all soiled, shouted Elder Bonheure, and in
that bed, a woman of the streets. Elder Bonheure told how he hauled this
woman up and made her get dressed and told her to leave Ginsburg, for God
had him now. "Oh, oh, oh, Lord, what a difference!" and Bonheure pointed his long skinny finger at Ginsburg. "Brother Ginsburg is saved and
sanctified!"

"Thank God, brothers and sisters, thank God!" cried the Negroes.
"Hallelujah!"

"But think of the time he was on that soiled dirty bed naked with a
woman!" Bonheure shook his fingers and closed his eyes. "Yes, sir, Brothers
and Sisters, we all know what sin is. It's black, black. It's the way of flesh. It
is not God's way. What do God say unto you? If burning, get married.
Choose your own dear sister in Christ. All the fun we want, we can have,
brothers and sisters, when it's holy and sanctified!... Well, you know how
God come to me and say 'Save Brother Ginsburg. He's low, he's a black
sinner, he's a Jew, he crucified my son. But ain't nobody, Elder, too low to
be saved and sanctified.' That's what the Lord say to me. Welcome him,
brothers and sisters. Make him happy here among God's saints. No high, no
low, here among us. Brother Ginsburg done show now he wants to be a
saint before the Lord. Praise God, hallelujah!"

I looked and all the Negroes were crying about Ginsburg's conver-
sion. They cried so easily. All except Bonheure. He alone had the control.
Almost it left him sometimes. You thought the next moment he might
break, his quavering voice became choked in tears and hysteria, and his
whole body sink writhing in convulsions, as he swayed up there on the platform with shut eyes. (That was always the tensest moment, just before the

passing of the collection plate. When the collection plate went round, Bonheure recovered; his eyes were open then.)

Now all the Negroes were jumping. The women would start. "O bless our dear Brother Ginsburg," and they crowded around him, tears falling, to shake his hand, to hug him, then to turn and hug one another. The whole congregation joined in, jumping and shouting hoarsely, "I'se so happy. Lordy, I'se happy. Bless our Elder, our dear Elder Bonheure. Bless Sister Bonheure too!"

Rich waves of emotion and brotherly love buffeted you on all sides. It was a very moving atmosphere, and I found it hard not to cry too. I saw that the Negro is richer emotionally than other peoples. He could unite with his brothers harmoniously as if under one soul, but that soul was Elder Bonheure.

It was my turn to stand up and make a speech. I preached on racial prejudice, using Walt Whitman as text. And I told them to wake up, wake up and join the world of higher things. "Make something of yourselves. Be educated." My voice was fervent, too. I was deeply moved. Bonheure, sitting on the stage behind me, would pluck my coat every little while and whisper, "Brother Han, Brother Han, once in a while mention the name of God." That was easy, "My God, wake and come out of the slum! Leave off your ignorance and laziness, for Christ's sake! Don't depend on leaders. They can't help you. Nothing can, but your own will to make something of yourself!" With everybody round gaping to cry Hallelujah, it was the easiest place to swear in the world. Hell to it! Devil! Christ! Everything you couldn't say in polite missionary households, here for every swear-word the chorus came back, "Hallelujah! Praise God! Christ is here!" Even so, if Bonheure hadn't constantly prompted, "More about God, Brother Han," they might have been puzzled.

I stopped and for a moment there was a big silence. Then a Negro woman jumped up and cried, "A-ai-ai…. Praise God…. Judgment Day is comin'!…. Chinaman can speak, too! Chinaman can read!"

Bonheure bowed and shook hands with me, in tall impressive dignity. "Amen, Brother Han! Amen!" he turned to the congregation. "Now you hear what he say, Brothers and Sisters? Lift yourselves up. Listen to your pastor and learn. Watch your speech, Brothers and Sisters. I heard my sister say just now, 'Chinaman can speak.' Chinaman! That ain't the way. I ask you, Brother Han, is that the way to speak? No! You womans must speak good English from now on. One—Chinee…two—Chinese.…"

"Chinee—Chinee can speak!" they all cried, jumping up and down and embracing each other, and me as well.

"That was a good speech, Brother, you made," Bonheure took me aside confidentially. "But some words you don't speak right. You, too, Brother Han. It's genu-wine, you know, not genuine. You want to look out for that."

It was the longest church meeting I ever attended, for it lasted from half-past seven until twelve o'clock at night. They jumped more than if they had been to a dance. All solo performance, too—real blackbottom, hands clapping and voices shouting. Afterwards everybody was tired and happy. But that was the night I had to sleep with Brother Ginsburg. He kept up a steady snoring and groaning. To make him stop snoring, I would grab him by the shoulder and shake, "Brother, you're in nightmare. You're dreaming about Hell, Brother, too much." Because I couldn't say he was snoring. How glad I was to hear Brother Washington knock in the morning with summons to breakfast, hot cakes, melons, partridges, things like that…(eggs were always secondary with Bonheure). But afterwards I took Bonheure off and complained about Brother Ginsburg. Either Brother Ginsburg or I was leaving, I said. Bonheure smoothed me down and said Ginsburg had to go back to his business anyway after the baptizing. "But you, Brother Han, you must stay and help me out in the work of God." And then he said something vague about a Negro school he had in mind to found, out of the saints' money, and he wanted to place me at its head. Again I was impressed by Bonheure's big vision. I thought in that event I might play a real intellectual part in America. So I stayed.

4

Well, Brother Ginsburg had to have the baptizing, but I got out of that. I watched from the river bank. Bonheure had about twenty-five or thirty converts which he was to duck in the river. Tall and handsome, he waded out, a white silk surplice over his clothes, until he was over waist-deep. The converts were not so well protected. They wore white robes of a thin sleezy cheesecloth, and nothing on besides but the birthday suit. So I guess I was squared with poor Ginsburg, who was such an annoyance to me. How he sputtered and swore coming up, it was so cold in that water! And how ridiculous and vulgar he looked! Spectators were lined up ranks deep on the river bank, and I saw them laughing and laughing, for they had come for the show. It was a burlesque. I don't suppose Bonheure really meant it to be so sexy (though always he knew how to appeal to the crowd, white as well as black). But those nightgowns, as soon as they got wet, clung like filmy gauze and carved out every mold. Nudity would have been less noticeable. It looked as if the young girls had a thin veil, just to tantalize young men, and the young men also the same, to tantalize young girls. But the saints didn't see that, neither the old ones nor the new ones. They were exalted and serious. Tears came in their eyes, as they watched the long line of Negroes in white robes going down into the river, and coming up clean, with howls and hosannas, made more intense and vibrational by the cold water and wind. With the saints, the spirit was moving too much...the flesh wasn't weak enough to think how the flesh looks sometimes.

In Bonheure's Holiness Church, all the sanctification of the saints seemed founded on sex-morale. That was the perennial subject of his sermons; that was the point at which the Devil and the Flesh kept up perpetual opposition. The saints believed in the Devil as much as they believed in God, and they thought a man and woman saint, no matter how old or ugly, couldn't be together in private for an hour without the Devil proving too much. One day one poor young saint of seventeen or eighteen came to prayer meeting in a new blue dress that fell just below the knee. It was when all girls were wearing short dresses and showing much of the silk stocking leg—that which to George was the best part of a girl's looks. And, of course, here the Negro girl would have just as good a chance in the contest as the bathing beauties from Florida. To Bonheure this part was too much flesh. He pointed his finger at that poor girl, and he preached an extemporaneous sermon on the wickedness of short-dressing, how it is designed to arouse the devilish emotions of men and beckon them into the hell-fire of unlawful burning. That poor young thing was so overcome with shame, she repented herself so sincerely! She was one of the new converts Bonheure had just baptized, and now she felt she had fallen into sin again. Next night, her dress became as long as Sister Bonheure's and the saints rejoiced that she was won back to God. But she had ruined her dress to save her soul. She had to put on a flounce of a different color—perhaps she cut up another dress to patch it, perhaps ruined both. That was hard. No woman anywhere wants to look out of style. But Bonheure had no spirit of compromise.

Sex was the subject, too, of all the testimonials. In the first flush of revival the saints held testimonial over and over. The penitent, and everybody else, got a kick out of that. Nothing was too embarrassing to tell. Not even the women were shy, when they began to feel saved and sanctified.

"Two years ago, on Saturday night, the Devil came to me. And I wanted to run out with a man into the woods and under a bush. I didn't care about that man's soul! All I care about, that man's body, low-down dog in man's body. I went out with that man. I couldn't keep away from that man. Devil sent me to him all the time. Then my dear pastor come along. He pulled the Devil off of me. He said, 'Sister, you got to be saved and sanctified. You got to forget the flesh and come with me.' And I done went, Brothers and Sisters. Now I got a husband, brothers and sisters. There he is. Sitting right there beside Brother Washington. Now I don't want no low-down pig for a man. My husband, he's good enough for me!"

Brother Washington stood up. And when he spoke, I jumped, I was so surprised. He waited on Elder Bonheure in the Atlantic Beach private dining room, a little, meek, thin man, bow-legged, with a childish high thin voice. That voice didn't go with the words he was saying:

"Ten years ago, I was a wild man! I drank! I smoked! I fit with razor blades. I went out with women. Yes, sir, Brothers and Sisters, every night a wild woman lay by me. Not my wife neither. I never had no wife in those days, Sisters. A different one every night, and I left them all. Thank God, those days is over and done, I got a wife. (She's my dear sister over there.) Wild man ain't wild no more!"

He had all the emotional exuberance of the rest, but it wasn't thick-sounding, because of his trebling voice. Now when Brother Jones got up, he had a deep bass voice. He really sent a Mephistophelian thrill up the spine, when he counted off his sins, thrusting out his great broad chest: "Seven years ago, I was blacker than Hell. I went out with a virgin—my own cousin. I taught her to sin with me. That's what I done, low-down, dirty, black scoundrel! Now I let my cousin alone. My sister's good enough for me. I don't look at no woman's legs on the street. My eye's straight on the Lord. And I don't steal no more. When I go to that farm where the melons grow, I leaves them. Why, if I picked up a pocketbook with a hundred dollars in it, know what I'd do? Run to our good Elder here. He'll tell me what to do with all my money!" (And I thought, Brother Jones is right, there.) "Yes, sir, Brothers and Sisters, I sleeps with my own dear sister now, and I'se saved and sanctified."

Once every month the saints had a fast, to put the pinch on the flesh. A fast is all right, if you are used to it, a little, day by day. But not when you have been living on turkey and duck and turtle soup at Elder Bonheure's private table. Oh, how I suffered on those fast days! And how I hated them! Nobody was given anything to eat all day long, not even the guest in the house. I would debate with myself about running around the corner and buying a chicken sandwich at the drugstore, but I knew it wouldn't look right, and I couldn't bear to disappoint the saints. They must have felt it even more, for all were hearty eaters, and keeping up hard work besides. On fast day evenings, they met and jumped, too, higher than ever, all on the empty stomach. At twelve o'clock midnight, fast was broken. A big supper was served, with everything better than usual. Oh, how full they were then, and how good they felt and how happy!

Bonheure was certainly a man with ideas. Being a dictator, he had to keep his followers excited all the time. And besides the revival, he was training all the true saints to take part in an orchestra. He had hired a German music teacher whom he paid from the church funds. And he bought all kinds of instruments for them, cornets, drums, trombones, fiddles, banjos. I played the cymbals. I reminded Bonheure about my school. But he remained very vague as to that. Once he suggested that he and I might go to France sometime soon, and hold a revival there. That man had cosmopolitan ideas, all right! I kept wondering what was the truth about him. Was he interested in the glory and money-making, or was he interested in the welfare of the Negro race?

But one of the most eloquent sermons I ever heard him preach was on the subject of that new Pierce Arrow car he had set his heart upon. The revival was going very well. Every night that church, that had been a movie-house, was packed. Of course, Bonheure had all the saints' money anyhow, but most of that was tied up. He needed two or three hundred more, for that new Pierce Arrow car he had already picked out. It had to come from the audience and from new converts. I saw Bonheure, by his passionate and persuading words, make almost everybody there as interested as he in seeing Elder Bonheure of the Temple of Saints whirl down upon Atlantic Beach in that great shiny new car, like a chariot of fire. That car, before he got through, had personality, it had a soul, it almost grew wings, and you could see it had to belong to the Saints and to Elder Bonheure, as a symbol of sanctified glory. "United is heaven, divided is hell," he preached to those Virginia Negroes, who all their lives had watched and washed and driven only white people's cars for white people. "This way we rise up and climb the spiral way to the golden gates of new Jerusalem. Saint Brown, he digs the ditch, Saint Jones, he drives the truck. Saint Lee, he scrubs the floor, and Saint Green, he's the chauffeur to drive your pastor on errands of God's work, all round, saving and sanctifying for the glory of this colored man's Church of the Lord."

As soon as he got the money for the first payment, we rushed up to Baltimore to see a well-known Negro lawyer there, from whom Bonheure wanted to borrow enough to pay cash for the car. This lawyer was a Methodist...and Bonheure's doctrine was that all Methodists go to hell. But this lawyer was nice to Bonheure and only kidded him along a little.

"You know why I'm going to help you, Elder? So you'll help me when I go to heaven. I'm only a Methodist."

BOOK FOUR

1

A LARGE PORTION of America I now knew rather well. I had not seen New Orleans and Texas—or Colorado, California and the West. West and South I had not much explored. But a big slice of America from as far west as Chicago, running from Virginia as far north as Labrador—this was hitchhike and hunting ground for my two wandering years. I was not at all bored, and not very much despairing. It was the thought of Trip that comforted and contented me throughout this loneliness. Somewhere she existed. Sometime I meant to see her again. And the study I had undertaken, partly in libraries, partly in weaving a pattern of hitchhiking over the face of the land, appealed to my nature. In my way I was repeating the life of my grandfather, the geomancer, in another existence, a roving life of ever new contacts and scenes.

I was a very successful hitchhiker. I don't remember ever being refused a ride, with conversation thrown in, for I was an expert in spotting the man who would welcome a traveling companion and the man who would not. My racial oddity, inspiring curiosity, no doubt helped, securing me many a lift from a bored and lonely driver. Traveling salesmen especially were always glad to see me. And my! how many kinds of men sped over American highways! One day I would be picked up by a big fat swearing man, who would relate his experiences seducing women. Next, by the earnest iron-jawed kind, with a moving tale of how he got converted to Christianity. Many were strange specimens, with no more shape of soul nor purpose of life than amebas. Once in remotest Maine, I found myself with a stout black-haired young man with a flat oily nose and ingrained habits of swearing. However, he was very polite. At least he was to me. He immediately took a flask from the pocket of his car, took off the cup, carefully wiped it out with his handkerchief, and handed it to me saying, "You go first. That cup ain't been used yet."

I learned from him that his grandmother had been a Japanese and his grandfather a Jew. He had no Oriental features, except that his nose was not very high. He was very candid with me. He said he wasn't educated and he wasn't good for any damned thing but making money, but Goddam, he boasted, he certainly could make the money. His business was buying and selling antique furniture. He went usually through the northern part of New England getting an option on furniture in some old farmhouse, which he would buy and sell again without removing. Where he learned all this, heaven knows! But by this trick, he made lots of money.

Very polite in drinking, in smoking he was not so careful. He was not careful how he spit, especially when he began to talk about making money. But he took his handkerchief and smeared off the car window. He said he saw I was young. He had a piece of advice to give me. "Never get married."

"Why?"

"The best life is the free life. And a hotel's nice, ain't it? Why get settled so you can't move about? That would kill me. This way you can sleep late in the morning, go anywhere you want, talk to anybody you feel like, and there's a girl always waiting in the next town. So never get married. Oh, well, when you're forty-five or fifty—and your digestion ain't what it used to be. Yep, then's the time to be married. But not before. Not while you're young and life looks good."

We came to the first good-sized town and he said he would have to drop me here, because he knew a whole lot of beautiful girls waiting for him, and he was going to see them. He brought out $500 in bills.

"Made that wad all on one sale. Pays to know your business. Now I go spend it, see?"

Traveling salesmen—though cordial—had their disadvantages, if you wanted to get somewhere. Often you had to wait for them while they made a sale, and after that, like this man, they had to stop and spend some of the money before they could go on.

Once I was walking along somewhere in Ohio, with my little bag containing mostly books. That time I was picked up by a keen-faced man in a small, shabby roadster. "Well, what are you selling?" he asked, when we were comfortably settled together on the front seat. "This is a good chance to sell me something. Go ahead."

I told him I could only sell him myself, and that I was on my way East from Chicago. He asked me if I had been educated in the university there. I said no, in Boston. Then he got much excited. He said he had graduated twice from Harvard, and was ashamed of it. That damned committee who executed Sacco and Vanzetti! I thought he was going to throw me out of his car for having been to Massachusetts at all. But finally he subsided and became gloomy.

"This," he said, "is a rotten world. America is rotten. No good. Not a decent writer anywhere. Upton Sinclair used to be good, but he hasn't much blood now. There's some younger fellows coming along, but as yet they can't do much. What we need in America is more social-mindedness."

I became very much interested in this new sort of man and asked him what he was doing for a business.

He stopped his car, and pulled out a magazine on which was written in big letters the title, *Justice*. He was the editor of it, he said. He opened the magazine and pointed out to me editorial names. European editor, Frank Harris. American editor, Glenn Bates. Assistant editor, Mrs. Glenn Bates. "I'm Glenn Bates."

After that, he went on to kick New England a good bit.

"Devils! Hypocrites! Rotten souls!"

He began to examine me on what I had learned while in Boston. He asked me if I had read *The Brass Check*. I hadn't. *Oil?* But I hadn't read that one either. "You ought to have," said the American editor of *Justice*, frowning. "Look here, I'll send you a copy of those. What's your address?"

He seemed much struck with my wandering free-lancing life, and my study of Orientalia, as I told him about that. Then he went on to examine me on the subject of Frank Harris, the European editor of this magazine. And again Mr. Glenn Bates was horrified. "What! You never read anything by Frank Harris? The greatest biographer who ever lived?"

I liked Glenn Bates very much, he was so bristling and straight-forward. He seemed to like me, too, in spite of my not coming out well on his examination. He was very enthusiastic about his magazine and asked me how I liked the enterprise. I said I liked it fine, all except the title. That sounded to me too ethical and dogmatic.

"You mean you think it sounds too much like a missionary's product? But I have no use for Christianity. Neither has my wife. Neither has my daughter. Neither has this magazine."

After we had talked on a little farther, Glenn Bates suddenly looked at me as if an idea had struck him. "Look here. What references have you got? Whom do you know?"

I was puzzled.

"Well, we're in need of an Asiatic editor for this magazine. Who knows? You may be the man?"

I gave him some names in Boston and Cambridge, and in spite of his hostility for Boston, some names seemed much to his liking.

"Good. Then it's settled. I'm sure I'll receive a good letter about you."

So we talked some more on the project and my part in it, until again he held up a copy of *Justice*. "But this magazine doesn't sell. Can you believe that?"

And he explained that his real reason for being on the road was to canvass for subscribers in order to keep the magazine going. Besides being an editor, I must canvass, too, he said. "And I don't see how—until we get better established—you can get paid. But neither does Frank Harris get paid. And neither does Glenn Bates nor Mrs. Glenn Bates. But I will make this proposition: any money you get from subscriptions will be yours to pay for your editorial duties. And some day we hope to pay more than Mencken."

Yes, he was planning to compete with *The American Mercury,* he said. "The time of destroying is almost over. Don't you think things are pretty well destroyed—to all truth-seeking individuals? Boston—oh, Boston is practically dead and gone. America needs a new intellectual center."

I suggested that New York appeared to be that.

"Oh, yes, for the past decade or so, that is true. But New York is getting hard and Europeanized. And it always has been dollarized. New York is not strictly American. There should be a new intellectual center of America. Do you see any reason why some place in Ohio shouldn't be that?" suggested Glenn Bates.

"No."

"Youngstown, Ohio. Let's make it there. That's where I publish this magazine."

This was how I gained my first editorial job. My early lecturing was of an equally desultory character. Once I was in Pittsburgh all alone. I remembered I had a college acquaintance living in Pittsburgh, Harry Gordon, a friend of Edwin Parker. I looked him up and found him well established in a big office. He gave me most cordial welcome and insisted I should come home with him to meet his family. "Mother will be delighted!" he exclaimed.

I was somewhat surprised in Mrs. Gordon, for she turned out to be so much more intellectual than Harry. At least Harry never had any use for anything deeper than Bruce Barton. But Harry's mother was an ardent reader of Mencken and Broun, and a subscriber to several monthly book clubs. Naturally she did all the talking in that house on literary things. Harry appeared quite intimidated, while admiring her very much. She and I talked, and she said I must speak before a certain ladies' club called the Echo Club, of which she was the president. Bertrand Russell had been the speaker the week before. Here in this club after they had sent their husbands to work, ladies met to discuss all the latest best-selling books and new cultural ideas. So now I became the honorary guest. And all the ladies were enthusiastic and very friendly and liberal. They offered me cigarettes and gave me a special kind of spiced tea and chicken sandwiches. I was the only man there, for Harry seemed to feel uneasy at the mere notion of bearing me company. But my experience in preaching for Bonheure helped me a lot. I thought Harry was very funny to object to going so much. The ladies paid me twenty-five dollars for that lecture, the best pay I had yet received. And I thought, that was twenty dollars more than Emerson used to get when *he* lectured on the Orient! Business was improving.

Of all the places to choose a good riding companion, a frontier is the best. I had been up to Labrador, because some boys I had known in college, and met, told me it was the new Utopia. But it wasn't so much to my mind. I was again coming back, and heading toward New York to be there when the fall season opened, when all things speeded up and became sensationally thrilling. At Calais (not of France, but of Maine), custom officials examine baggage for a long time. That suited me, for I wanted plenty of time to pick out my car, intending to make a long jump, straight into Manhattan. I soon spotted it. A long, low, big, rich-looking car, open to the skies, except for its twinkling windshield. At the wheel was a tall, very good-looking, clean-faced man of forty-six or so with a healthy glowing tan and shining glasses. All the customs men were dodging in, to see if they could find whisky in this car, and the gentleman was saying blandly, "Well, well, you won't find what you're looking for on me, my man."

"Right, sir, pass on."

Then I, who was standing near, spoke up, and asked him if he were going in the direction of New York. He gave me a quick, shrewd look. "Japanese?" he asked in a kindly fashion.

"No, indeed, sir! I'm Korean."

"Get in, then. Koreans. Good God, I'll do all I can to help them."

I got in and we proceeded into the United States of America, talking on politics as we drove. My driver proved to be a strong Wilson man. Wilson, he spoke passionately, was America's greatest President. Washington, Lincoln—these according to him were just opportunists, but Woodrow Wilson...ah, there was the greatest brain the White House ever had! If principles of the Versailles Treaty had been carried out everywhere as Wilson first planned, Korea would be independent today! So he said.

After this promising opening we somehow got started on Shakespeare, and I found my driver knew all about Shakespeare and had read everything Shakespeare had written—but he had come to the conclusion that Shakespeare didn't write Shakespeare at all.

"Who did, then? Bacon, you think?"

"Bacon? The man who wrote his most important works in dead Latin, the man who had no faith in the future of the English? No, Shakespeare was more than Bacon. He said some Bacon, but Bacon never said any Shakespeare. 'Reading maketh a full man, conference a ready man, and writing an exact man,'…sounds like a college professor's lecture, doesn't it? That's Bacon for you. No, I'll tell you who wrote Shakespeare. Christopher Marlowe."

Then he quoted:

> If all the pens that ever poets held
> Had fed the feeling of their masters' thoughts,
> And every sweetness that inspired their hearts,
> Their minds, and muses on admired themes;
> If all the heavenly quintessence they still
> From their immortal flowers of poesy,
> Wherein, as a mirror, we perceive
> The highest reaches of a human wit;
> If these had made one poem's period,
> And all combined in beauty's worthiness,
> Yet should these hover in their restless head
> One thought, one grace, one wonder, at the least,
> Which into words no virtue can digest.

"There! Can you tell the difference between that and Shakespeare? And these two lived at exactly the same time."

Shakespeare at least must have been greatly influenced by Marlowe, I suggested.

"Influenced! Why, man, Shakespeare's plays are more Marlowe than Shakespeare! All the scope and daring of youth. What a young giant he was!"

Then my driver warned me that we had to pick up his lawyer. "My lawyer's a little odd," he told me. "An old bachelor, you know. (Not much Marlowe about him.) He's a little bit fussy about his beds and breakfasts, his coffee, etc., so we'll just let him decide everything. He won't be with us long, and afterwards you and I can do as we please."

Just as he said, this lawyer turned out to be a narrow, dried-up, fidgety little man, who was somewhat nonplussed to see me. He addressed my driver as "Senator Kirby," so that was the first time I knew I had been riding with a senator. Neither of them knew Boston very well, but I directed them to just the right hotel and of course I knew all the streets, and right turnings. The next night we were out in the country, and the lawyer had a better chance to finick. We examined farmhouses. But the lawyer found fault with every one. "This corner is awful," and the next place, "There ought to be another window in this room"; the barn was too near in another, and so on. Each time the lawyer was out examining the toilet arrangements, Senator Kirby would wink at me. "He's just a little odd, you see," he'd say.

But when the lawyer left us, we traveled very simply. Kirby was the most unpretentious of men. He showed himself as much at home in the most inconvenient farmhouse as in the most luxuriant hotel. And always he was very thoughtful about fitting my expense to the budget.

I have always remembered Senator Kirby as a sort of historic American. That is, he reminds me of *The American* written by Henry James. Not the American of the seething new age where all is changing, but the American along more classic lines. He was wealthy, and most of his life had been spent in making money. Some who make a lot of money are fat in the face somewhere as if they have put a few extra swindled rolls up there, but he had a beautiful, dignified face, very clean-cut, straight and definite. He was very fond of machinery, and at the slightest excuse would get into his khaki overalls and tinker around with that big car. I admired his accuracy in every move and gesture. (Always he stopped and let me get out to read the signs, never driving on and on like some motorists, for he said he detested backing, he detested a track that was wrong.) In his devotion to Wilson he had some of that missionary ideal of the classic American. Also about prohibition. He thought America ought to have prohibition, not from the individual's point of view but because of drink's social evil for poor people, whose families could not be protected. Kirby was not exactly puritan (he came from Chicago) but he was not exactly anti-puritan either. He said to me that he was much disgusted with ordinary American morality—he couldn't stand men who weren't serious fooling around with women; but on the other hand he was much disgusted, too, with American hypocrisy that said one thing in church and another in Elks meetings. He had not much use for churches, yet his morals seemed to be church morals...except that he would swear somewhat. I was reminded of Doctor Ko, who was a Korean Confucian to the marrow of his bones, though never speaking out, though actually divorced from that. In the same way Senator Kirby would remain Christian American to the end, no matter what church creeds he disbelieved. He was the product forever of American Jeffersonianism and American Puritanism blended, of American faith and American idealism, of all the Marlowesque stages of American industry. Kirby was on his way to California, where he had moved for the sake of his wife's health. But he himself was proud to call himself an Illinoisan, and obviously had much in him of the Midwest. When he spoke of Mrs. Kirby's health, his face was transparent in showing worry and clouds. She was in poor health. He mentioned her a great deal and it was always with great tenderness and pride. And I thought theirs must be a beautiful relation which had lasted through the span of twenty or more years.

I was with Senator Kirby for almost a week, for he had business in many places, and he liked me so much, he urged me to accompany him. We were very harmonious. I told him much about myself. He said, "Yes, young man, I can see you have come to America to stay, and I'm proud and glad. Now you must definitely make up your mind to *be* American. Don't say, 'I'm a Korean' when you're asked. Say 'I'm an American.'"

"But an Oriental has a hard time in America. He is not welcomed much."

"There shouldn't be any buts about it! Believe in America with all your heart. Even if it's sometimes hard, believe in her. I have seen many countries. But this is still the greatest country in the world for youth, for a full life, and ambitious enterprise. This land is like Christopher Marlowe's country when he was a boy. Young man, it's seldom I see any one with as much of that same spirit as I see in you. I tell you, sir, you belong here. You should be one of us."

"But legally I am denied."

Senator Kirby actually pooh-poohed this objection. "There are still ways and means of proving exceptions. And that unfair law perhaps will not always last. Next time I hold government office" (this was the time of the great reaction against Woodrow Wilson, and his party had been out for a long time), "write me and I will help you."

2

I was in New York once more. I now had a regular job, one I had more or less created for myself. I interviewed the editor of a certain critical monthly, and taking my free-lancing work on other papers, I told him I wanted to sum up Oriental news regularly for his review. He accepted the proposal. I was assured by that of about fifty dollars a month.

That fall, I was sitting in on a short-story course at Columbia presided over by a very well-known figure in American life, letters, economics and business, a man of enormous energy, still young, with a wide range of knowledge and experience. He was a new type of American professor to me, so new that it was hard to think of him as "professor" at all. To a solid scholastic foundation, he added a lucid sense of reality in human relations. He was a born popularizer, and practical manager of every piece of information he gathered; and in his great pigeonholing mind, he had the greatest assemblage of facts I have ever seen. Every fact he made do some work for him. Yes, his startling regimentation of scholastic facts arrayed on the march, to arrest and catch the mind of the ordinary American, is one of the most spectacular things I have seen in this modern civilization. He was engaged at this time as an American editor of the *Encyclopædia Britannica,* 14th edition. He and that work gripped my mind. I had a long talk with him, and the upshot was that, with the swift definite decision and action characteristic of him, he made me an editorial worker on his staff.

I felt that I had come back to New York for good, after a series of spiral flights. I had aimed. I had dropped. I had captured my little opening. It was significant more as an entering wedge in the professionally intellectual world, than as anything else. But my satisfaction was supreme. It was enough to make New York loom up powerfully again as the dream-come-true dazzling city. And as I walked New York streets, it did not seem possible that Trip could not be here, she who had been mystically interwoven into my whole dream of America. I was desperately eager to find her somewhere. I wrote to Laura James. I urged her to visit New York, to try for something on the art staff of the *Encyclopædia Britannica,* for many young artists I knew were being employed there. And I asked with emphasis for Trip's address. Laura wrote that she was at work in Boston, and could not come to New York. And she made no mention of Trip or Trip's whereabouts. Well, no business can ever be done by a letter, that was my sad thought. I must go to Boston and interview Laura, in person. This conspiracy of time and of silence could not forever keep up. I was a disciple now of my editor-superior's action.

One cold night in early winter I was in Chinatown, my mind still habitually abnormal with thrilling possibilities, bright-hued hopes, my mind still in New York fever, thoughts conscious of an electric pulse, thoughts a harbor rim of dark sea where lights sparkled questioning an unknown space. I was in my favorite downstairs eating place, the one that had first received me when I had only five cents. And there I found somebody else. I could not believe my eyes. The last I had heard, he had been in Europe on a newspaper, but of course you never can tell where Oriental exiles will be turning up next. Certainly I had always associated this exile with New York. (Boston for Helen, but for Kim New York.) For it was Kim. It was surely Kim. But I was terribly shocked. At first I noted the physical man so changed, his shabbiness, soiled shirt, frayed clothes, broken shoes—and Kim in personal appearance had always been rather elegant, rather nice. But far worse was the spiritual transformation, for I seemed to be looking at the empty shell of a Korean, one not so old in years, but broken in mood and in heart.

My dear friend showed himself not especially glad to see me and yet not sorry. The spark in his eyes flickered once more, but the old Kim did not come back. We sat there together. And he didn't say much. He had been eating a cheap meal, eating with a routine air and without much pleasure. When I ordered something good by way of a celebration, he didn't eat much of that. Yet Koreans always like to eat. They like good things at a Chinese restaurant. At first he listlessly parried my eager questions, my surprise and delight at having found him once more after so long a time. I thought to myself, he looks so fatigued and lusterless, as if having just come from some long imprisonment—or maybe just out on bail. Indifferent he seemed to contradiction or argument, whether you called a cow a horse, or named black white. Had he merely grown more secluded in his monastic world, more disciplined in social intercourse and less dogmatic? But where was that exalted far-seeing eye of pessimism, where those ironical quips as well as the childlike glee—were these all gone? More or less in a stolid disposition he seemed, as if a prisoner already proved guilty, content to wait for the execution hour.

I went with Kim to his lodging. As if some word of explanation was necessary, he told me of the failing of his family. His father had been a fabulously wealthy man, with the annual income from many bags of rice. His father had died. Possibly half-brothers had mishandled the estate. But in these times of stress, not like the old days, there was nothing unusual in that ruin. The biggest Korean fortune now will often fail, leaving the heirs stranded penniless abroad, on student passports. I know of many many cases just like Kim's. At any rate, Kim lived no more on Eastern bags of rice.

Since he would not say much, I began to tell him of my new work, how I had followed his advice all these years and now was ready for his help again. I could give him much to do in my department. (One of my duties in the Encyclopædia was the picking of men for various Oriental articles.) He was the very man I had been looking for. But Kim listened without much interest. He appeared to feel that his ideas would never command attention nor his personality cause any sensation. And he rebelled no longer. He was perfectly willing to be a caged animal looking out on the world through the steel bars of his own isolation. But what had he done, I wondered, with his soul? Where had he buried that ironic laughter and all those sarcastic remarks? No more an undertaker to bury an idea, no more a philosopher to play with anything—no praise, no blame, no cry, no sigh.

He was in a cheap room near Bleecker and 8th streets. It was up over a stable. At least it smelled so. However, it had a mysterious gateway to indicate that there was a mysterious man inside and around the corner. And the inside was better than the outside where Italian children played amidst horses and trucks. You crossed a small soiled courtyard of flagstones; a narrow stairway then led straight to his room. He had inside a fireplace with a coal skuttle, a few odd chairs and a stool, a rickety small couch for sleeping and a good-sized old and scarred table for eating and writing. On the table was half a loaf of bread sticking out of waxed paper. The room was not so small; it had a gas stove in the bathroom and two windows. But there was not much light.

What was his financial state? I kept insisting to know. He laughed, as he confessed he had sold everything he once owned. Furniture, clothes, ring, watch. He had kept his books to the last, but they, too, were all gone now. He had made them over to a second-hand dealer recently for $125.

"That wasn't much!" I cried, horrified, remembering all his rare Oriental books.

But he showed me a roll of bills that he still had, as if to put my mind at rest. While I was there, a kitten crept into the room, wandering up from the courtyard, and Kim wanted to turn all my attention to watching that kitten, its funny lithe movements, its leaps, its springs and its antics in chasing its tail.

I asked about Mr. Brown. He had not seen Brown since he saw me. I asked about Helen Hancock.

"Helen?" For a moment he looked as if he did not know whom I meant. "Oh, yes. Helen."

He considered the name. He told me, so far as he knew, just what had happened...and without emotion. He had not heard from Helen since leaving America. His days in Europe at first had been spent wandering about, thinking of her and waiting. He certainly expected some message, some word to the waiting lover of rendezvous, some word of good-bye, if the Helen he knew had been changed. No word ever came. Well, he hardly knew what he had done since we met....

"But you were writing good things. I read them in various Korean papers. I always looked for your name."

Yes, he agreed, perhaps. He only knew he had lost interest. At last something stirred in his brain. He had to get back to New York. He was in Italy at the time. He had gone out to the English graveyard. And somehow he could not bear it—the death of the dead that lay there. "Even to die in America," said Kim slowly, "seemed to have more of a future than to live like a ghost with them." He had had much trouble getting in.

"And then? Why didn't you go straight to Helen?"

"I began to think that there wasn't any such girl," Kim smiled wistfully—he was blinking and watching that kitten, and in the dim light of that little cheap lampshade, he really looked a man of shadow—"that with Helen, I had been like that kitten chasing its tail."

("No! Oh, no!" something in me cried violently.) And I said, "I do not believe they let her get your letters." And Kim said, that might be. But the story did have a sequel. For Kim was not so removed from it all then as now. Unknown to the Browns, he had haunted their street, he had intercepted their maid. He had taken her out to dinner and questioned her minutely, making her promise never to tell this to Arthur Brown. He had asked her of Helen. Well, queer as it may seem, she had overheard something. And how much she made up and how much she heard, one can't say. Even as Kim told it to me, it seemed blurred and hazy, and one felt that for him the fate of Helen was wrapped in an unending mystery. But according to this maid, Helen had stayed alone with her father and aunt, not seeing anybody, and being sent off from time to time to various sanatoriums for rest cures. She had been interviewed by many psychiatrists. It was over that, Brown blew up, and loudly gave his views which had been overheard by the maid. He hated Helen's branch of the family anyhow, and while they accused him, he accused them, and according to him, the psychiatrists had finished what Helen's upbringing began.

All of this was, as I say, a blur to poor Kim. The thing he got from the maid was, Helen was dead. She had died in a rest home outside of Boston. But all along Kim seemed to be talking of someone he only casually heard of and never knew well. He couldn't tell how she died. Kim seemed impassive more or less, but I remembered his friend Hsu Tsimou's words, that Kim had no road now but Helen or communism. He had come to America again, not to Russia. And there was no Helen.

Then I tried to preach to Kim, to come out of his lethargy, to work in the actual world, since surely work now was to him a physical necessity. I could not rouse Kim.

"But man, you know you must work for self-preservation."

"I have no instinct for self-preservation," Kim argued listlessly. "Animals use all sorts of shields and shells, strong teeth and legs and claws, to protect themselves. Plants, even plants, know how to develop poisonous secretions and sharp thorns. The cuttlefish blackens the water so it can remain unseen in isolation. But I have none of this art. Or I have lost it.... Rats, while appeasing their own hunger, eat up the bodies of plague-dead rats, and so contract deadly disease. That is like me. Get away from me. I advise you. I don't want to give that disease, as the rats give it to other animals.... Really, the sight of the dead body, that moves no more, gives me no panic. I have seen too much. And what is one more corpse over so many dead worlds?"

I left him, heartsick, intending to come back soon. But a kind of horror was upon me, too. Almost I did dread the effect of Kim upon myself. I seemed to hear in my ears Kim's unsaid soliloquy: "Was only I insane? No, all the West is. Insane since the time of that first Helen whose ghost destroyed one world and built another. Without Helen, Ulysses would never have been shipwrecked again and again in the black treacherous sea. Always he tried to reach the receding horizon. The Israelites were more wise, half-Asiatics, playing upon the Red Sea, sailing cautiously along some near-by coast. And look, they inherit the earth. Not like the Greeks, the unruly Greeks who fashioned Helen and fostered Jesus Christ. And all of this means that we have to stick close to this miserable earth. We must not imagine ourselves to be immortal. Man may fill the earth with grand ideals and may draw deep breaths of lofty philosophies. But wait and see—there is no way out. Reality, there is none. Man's drunken imagination hunts in the haunted garret. Terrors, fears, heartbreak, these only wait. Let him follow the

Israelite. Let him stay close to the earth that fed him, let him never look up, let him toil and sorrow close to the dust that will suffocate on the last day his breath. Suffocated, dead, buried and no more...what then remains of high thoughts?"

Yes, I ran from Kim. A silent life, a motionless life, an unpraised life, an unblamed life, and now a wholly undistinguished life at the end—a life that had lived in the ego and in the inner dream, that did not know if it was in inner dream or in outer reality, a life that had never accepted its real worldliness, did not know if it came once to be transplanted or was hopelessly in exile, did not even know if it felt real grief that its Helen of the new age of time had been lost, or if it had only contracted some disease from the Western dead men. I ran from Kim....

3

I went to Boston after my meeting with Kim. And I found Laura, and I made my inquiries concerning Trip. Laura was plainly reticent now, and a little horrified at such importunity. That was mortifying, but I kept on. Trip was still living with Van and Marietta. Where were they? And Laura gave me a worried laugh. Why, I could find their phone number under Marietta's name in the phone book. (Plainly she did not want to be implicated this time in my calling.) But she gave me Marietta's last name. Such a small thing as that had been at the root of my trouble in finding Trip. Many times I had looked under Van's name and under Trip's in the New York phone book— yes, for three years—but I had never tried Marietta's.

I returned to New York with the definite, accurate way—as swift as thought—of addressing a dream and a vision...something grown fertilely in mystic splendor enclosed in a soul's inner life. A number and telephone wires. How fantastic, how feasible! (How perhaps impossible!)...but what would my Browning say from his comfortable spiritual chair before Fichte was quite discredited, Don Quixote went sparring again, or science invaded forever the West and the East?

There are flashes struck from midnights,
　　There are fire-flames noondays kindle
Whereby piled-up honors perish,
　　Whereby swollen ambitions dwindle,
While just this or that poor impulse
　　Which for once had play unstifled,
Seems the sole work of a lifetime
　　That away the rest have trifled.

Anyhow I reached for that telephone book with all my heart and faith behind that gesture.

I was so frantic to hear Trip's voice soon, to feel that she really existed, that I called very early. It was hardly decent. She was not even up. But I had to be saved quickly from going quite empty like Kim. It was real emergency. And in a way, she was at the mercy of an early telephone caller—she would be there and she could not refuse to answer, for she would not know who was calling, I thought grimly. Well, she could not think any worse of me than she had when she had not written. Better to keep on with the madness. A calmness and deliberateness fell upon me. I might have been making a business call. Now I was repeating aloud over and over, across the wire to reality, the very name that had lived in my innermost chambers for so long. I had to repeat it, Van or Marietta answered the phone, I do not know which. I think, one after the other. And this much I made out indistinctly—in a minute they were going to make Trip get up and come to the phone. They thought it was something important, a wire perhaps from home. I had phoned at half-past seven—the time I got in from Boston.

Then the third voice came. "Yes, yes, I am she. But I don't understand—who is calling?"

"Oh, don't you remember me?" I cried in despair. "I'm Chungpa Han. Mr. *Han*."

"Mr. Han!" the voice turned staccato, as if with relief. And it held now astonished laughter. "Why, where *have* you come from? Of course I remember you. And you are still in this country? Are you still with Boshnack's? But that was in Philadelphia, was it not?"

"No, no, I am not with Boshnack's any longer," I went on joyously. "I am with the *Encyclopædia Britannica*. And I just got your address. I have seen Miss Laura."

"Britannica? That sounds good! You'll inspire us with awe. You certainly must have *arrived*."

"O, may I come to see you?" And I clutched at the promise and I seized on the definite date. Then I put down my head on the desk and cried a little before any one else came around, for I was in the *Britannica* office where I came straight from the train, and nobody else had arrived yet except the janitor....

I had found Trip. Oh, I was safe! I was not to be the prisoner condemned without a hearing. I had a reprieve. This time, I swore, I would be, oh, so clever, Trip should never escape me again like that. But wasn't it an ironic fact, she had been in New York all this time, just around the corner from the apartment where I had first gone to call? Not only had I been there many times to examine her old house in vain, but I was in the habit of visiting frequently, all that autumn, at the home of one of the *Britannica* editors who lived two or three streets up on Lexington Avenue. We should have met at least once, or passed on the street. Now since for so long all ordinary rules of chance had been against me, luck couldn't go the bad way again....

I was in New York now—on the scene, business always is done *on the scene*. I would make her translate Oriental poems, I would get her interested in that. Or I would pose as "material." I would get her mind working with me. And that was a good book, she must see we had to write. Was she still sitting charmed like that in the midst of those papery papers? Oh, let me be her servant forever and put myself in paper's place! I hadn't much paper in me, but I had all the stuff. Boshnack and Lively both said I had personality. I knew, like Bonheure, I had a big executive brain. And like George, all the love sincerity. Love sincerity...paper sincerity...which shall life take? Both in one man are very hard to find.

4

Just at this time I forgot about Kim. I forgot about Kim for almost a week. One day somebody at the Korean Institute showed me casually a paper several days old, a New York paper in English. One small paragraph reported the suicide of a friendless "Japanese" on Bleecker Street. The Korean who saved it and showed it to me did so, saying, "I believe that fellow isn't a Japanese, but a Korean. The name is surely Korean. Do you know anything about this poor fellow here?" I read. And it was Kim. I went at once to Bleecker Street and hunted up the landlady of that apartment. True to the traditions of landladies, she was very vague. She could tell me little of Kim. He had left slightly over a hundred dollars in bills and had been buried on that. The death had been reported to the police. But I couldn't find out even where Kim's grave was.

O Kim, why did you do it, I thought! Yours was not the spirit of Pehyi-and-Shutsi, who starved on roots of grass, rather than come out and accept a high post under an alien dynasty. You had no reason like Chu-yuan, who drowned himself to convince his king, who would not listen to counsel. You were no patriot like the Japanese Samurai. And it could not have been done in the mood of the high Korean official Minyung Whan, who had lost his fatherland to those same Japanese. Neither had you conspired like Achitophel with Absalom against King David. And you had none of the ambition of Zambri, who usurped the throne of Israel and burned himself with the king's house rather than give it up. You did not have the gloomy conscience of Saul, nor of Judas Iscariot. Nor were you forced like Socrates to drink hemlock. Yet was it done for the mind's sake, at the end of a blind alley, because death was the logical conclusion?

Yes, you always argued death was natural, inevitable. But then this natural death is a long, sloping, gradual sinking down. Why should you die while still blooming, still at the age of the full-leafed tree? No tree of that sort dies a natural death. Such trees are cut down unnaturally, by an outside force. Then was Kim, too, destroyed by the world's outside forces? I believe that he was.

Perhaps, like the Eastern landscapes he loved in painting, he had too much that was diffused, mysterious and dynamic, and not enough that was anthropomorphic, static, and composed. One moment the dark clouds drift swiftly, a summer storm showers vehemently down. Clouds disband again quickly from mountain summits and over faraway valleys. Memory of unearthly bliss seems upon all nature. As if uncovering revelation, great masses of clouds roll back revealing long pure slopes rising from deep ravines where the sunlight is bright once more after darksome hours. Evening follows with its blending succession of different colors, gradually all being absorbed and melted away by the night shadow, as the marblelike twilight slowly changes to thick somber vapor. What different moods over the same landscape—the moods of storm, of blissful recollection, of impenetrable gloom! From cruel to smiling, from dignified to playful—the uncertainty and unevenness of nature was like the temperament of Kim. He seemed always at the mercy of his moods, never controlling them with a steel-lined purpose. The secret ways of nature, the mystery of Kim. You could never tell what was going to happen from either. You had to take Kim as you found him. Never seek, you never get. Neither sceptic nor believer, neither optimist nor pessimist, neither a yea-man nor a nay-man, he was one in one moment and another in another moment. He would be wise, then foolish, an old sage once, and next a helpless child. Now most egoistic, now most humble. At all times willful and unsatisfied. What are you to do with a man like that?

But it seemed unfair to pass any judgment on him. He was what he was. The romantic Korean exile, my brother, who had died. Like Byron

> ...From my youth
> My spirit walked not with the souls of men,
> Nor looked upon the earth with human eyes.
> The thirst of their existence was not mine,
> My love, my griefs, my passions and my powers
> Made me a stranger....

He was a child of revolution, whose soul passed from one continent to another never to find peace, denying earth as home...a strange, gifted creature born with the instinct for noble human things. He was wasted. All his work had been burned in that Bleecker Street fireplace, nothing was left. But the greatest loss to me, Kim's friend, was himself, his brain which bore in its fine involutions our ancient characters deeply and simply incised, familiar to me. And over their classic economy, their primitive chaste elegance, was scrawled the West's handwriting, in incoherent labyrinth, and seamy Hamlet design. To me—to me almost alone—a priceless and awful parchment was in him destroyed. Could it not have been deciphered, conveyed to the world?

My first instinct had been to go to Trip, to make her mourn with me over Kim's death and waste in a strange land. And then I did not dare. For I thought I would speak out all my thoughts, and I feared she would shut me out. No, I must write to Hsu Tsimou, his friend. Vision dimmed, eyes blurred as tears fell on my paper. And though I did not know it, I was writing to another dead man. The joyous Chinese lyricist had been killed in an airplane crash, but on his native soil, expressing his firm belief in the future of Western science transported to China.

All sinks to death in the end. It is the "coming to pieces" as the baby of four can explain, "to make more lives." All lives rise from nature, express it a moment, then come to destruction in the undying world—the scientist with his laboratory invention, the explorer with his passion for the undiscovered land, the mother with her devotion of love, the lover with heaped agony, all doomed and destined to be ashes under the volcanic destruction of death, as Pompeii under Vesuvius. It is all a matter of how soon. Life the eternal butterfly flutters into its natural web. Yes, the philosopher, too, dreaming he may be that butterfly, moves on to his death, and only the undying universe remains, the bird of two wings. Then the universe to which man is attached, like some mean parasite, it alone proves living of positive worth, it alone stands to verify faith?... but over Kim's death I still puzzled and mourned. How could he let the universe pass on and beyond him without cleaving full strength? If our values are not deposited in living, then are they in dying? We give up the gem of life to obtain the pearl of death, Chinese philosophy says. But if we find no enthusiasm for life, how can we for death? And life was no gem for Kim. I only knew that dying must have been a source of comfort, the first peaceful dream and undisturbed sleep for a long time that the King of Terror could present to him. Somewhere he must be in American earth, stones for a pillow under the head, a grass-woven blanket on top, all his hopes, fears, ambitions, ironies, love, lying buried there, too.

Easter season would come—Manhattan Easter—with its bright sunshine and gay flowers. How brisk and debonnaire those people, not unlike Helen and Kim, dressed in the spirit of spring and walking on Fifth Avenue! Those little children, how beautifully they would be dressed, running hand in hand through the parks and the streets! New hats would show all around, new shoes, everything new, to symbolize the new season—the new life of an Easter morning as gay as the Easter flower. From that time on, the Park would gather more people as it gathered more leaves. Here Trip and I would walk, under little city fruit blossoms and willow streamers. We would walk carefree and hungry, toward China Garden, the Peking restaurant uptown which served fried shrimps that Trip liked (flaky cocoons, their little red tails curling, crisply). With the expanding spring, the flower of our relationship was to bloom fuller and fuller, containing seed of all our future days.... Yes, everywhere gloomy weary hearts of winter would be softened. But not Kim's. The heart that was frozen in the winter's cold snow, in death, too, it must lie frozen. Rain would drip on the green roof, but for Kim still ash and dust-powder. Forever frozen heart, forever cold body that could never embrace love's naked arms! It obsessed me that the exile in life must remain the exile in death. Nothing here would visit his grave with wholeheartedness. The gray moon would touch it but half, the snow would leave half to the black shimmer of branches. The August sun might blaze with an outer wholeheartedness, but the heart that had never felt its humanity but by half would keep the oblique touch of winter even under a softened and fertile earth.

I looked everywhere and seemed to have passed unharmed through a vast destruction. And Kim with greater talents had been lost. Because of Helen he died in America. He chose Greenwich Village as a grave, he, the man without a village. But he died a Korean exile to the end. America was not for Kim. He would never have been convinced by *Life Begins at Forty*...nor would he have nodded his head to syncopated tunes, "I-can't-give-you anything...but...love, Baby!" And Helen, too, died like the cutting down of a tree; she was a bough off the puritan tree of America. I had come to America, I had lived just while trees were falling. I watched the ax descend. Helen, who looked eagerly for love with a racial nostalgia, with a Boston uncompromising soul, she, too, was gone. Yes, for a long time everybody over the world had been steadily at work destroying. Down, down with the ancestor's house. For they pointed out how it was not built on a firm foundation, and how the rain leaked, the storm shook. "In my father's house are many mansions"…still not a blueprint could be found.

In the East it was the same with a difference. It was much worse. Chaos, however, there was on both hemispheres. Kim and I came when the Village spirit was upon America. It was the time when everybody wanted the artist's and rebel's life. Marriage was a failure. Exile was the only refuge. Men and women everywhere tried free love, companionateness, everybody wished hard to live the life that did not smell of baby diapers, corned beef and cabbage. In Asia, Christianity, church-going and monogamy had just commenced to be heroism—drinking, polygamy, wild life, and free verse-making to be labeled by some reckless young radicals vice. While in the West, vice versa. But on the whole, Christianity, Confucianism, both seemed to have come to much the same pass. Both seemed dying, like Helen and Kim, cut down and apart.

Everything ends…even the merciless virtue of destruction, even the proud individualist's rebellion and anarchy…sooner perhaps in the West than in the East. I saw my meeting with Mr. Glenn Bates was a sort of American milestone. It seemed to be right, what he said, how the great work of destruction was being finished off. That magazine *Justice* after about three issues never came out any more. I don't know why. And after that I never heard from Mr. Glenn Bates. I regret the failure of that magazine. Suppose it had kept on. Maybe by now it might have got the circulation of *The Nation* or *The New Republic*. Back numbers of *Justice* are now selling at a very high price. Frank Harris has died. Everything he ever wrote becomes an item. I have noticed in *Publishers' Weekly* that one copy is wanted for the price of ten dollars. So I hope those copies left over each month and stacked up in the closet have at last come into dealers' hands…. What I mean to say is, *Justice,* too, was a sign of the times, for it tried to be socially conscious. In the early twenties, the more sensitive American writers were touching no political issues. Politics—like all shades of domesticity and like church-going—was a form of the older generation's vice. I had seen all this changing. Now it began to seem Village life was somehow over. A few years of wild living, and everybody gets sick, gets lonesome.

Some commit suicide. Some fly forever away. But those who are left get tired, and begin to want something the opposite. Nostalgia creeps in for the man in the comfortable rocking chair with the child on the lap and the woman near-by knitting.... And the artist's skylight studio begins to say "For Rent." Anarchy, good or bad, has gone into retreat. Now a few advanced Americans were just beginning to come out for Communism and Catholicism, taking their cue from abroad. Soon politics, economics, some social philosophy was to be the whole thing. What a change from the mood of lonely Bohemia! Ten years from this time, intellectuals, too, will range themselves with keen interest behind Roosevelt or Landon.

Even George Jum had changed. I received this letter: "You will want to ask me about Hollywood. Only minor parts there. I was disgusted. So I have come to Hawaii, where lazy monkeys can pick up the nuts without working. It is a hot country, and that means there is more love. I am going to get married and settle down. I am engaged to a Korean girl, one American-born, with a good stenographic training, and very pretty to see. (Of course I think she is beautiful!) So here in Hawaii I will spend all my hours in eating, loving and sleeping. Is love the be-all and the end-all, am I still romanticist? I never go back on my words. But what is the difference? Man has to love, and it costs the same amount of energy either way.... P. S. For the rest, I have not failed. I have only not succeeded."

5

My exile seems as if ended. But I have never gone back. The opportunity has not come. My father's family is all dead or scattered. My own beyond-time, time traveling ties have been made on American soil. There are, besides, political difficulties besetting the Korean who returns to the native shores. Perhaps spiritually, it would be difficult to return wholeheartedly, and

I would be there as an exile from America. The soul has become molded to the Western pattern, the whole man has become softened somewhat by the luxuries of Western living. I could hardly hope now to run barefoot over ice and snow, as in my village the boys were proud to say they could, on feet as flexible and padded as the puppies' armored shoe of skin. When I finally go back, it will only be for a visit.

Once here in America, I had a dream…a dream that I had climbed to the top of a lofty tree. And looking over a leafy ocean of verdure, I saw stretching across wide water a hairlike bridge, like those suspension bridges we often used in Korea. Creeping across this bridge and beckoning with eyes of glee were Yunkoo and Chak-doo-shay—the little boys I played with as a child. Then I saw at the other end of the bridge, so long and precarious, a paradise of wild and flowery magic, with mountains and waterfalls and little gushing streams on which as in an old Chinese landscape could be discerned the scholars with their brush-pens or tranquil fishing-rods. I waved and shouted to Yunkoo and Chak-doo-shay, and I struggled to reach the bridge, which seemed somehow attached to my tree. Panting with the effort of climbing, I looked down and gasped with fear at being so far above ground. But Yunkoo and Chak-doo-shay were daring me to follow, standing up now and running back and forth like men on a tightrope across the little trembling bridge. I had almost reached it. Yunkoo held out his hand and pointed back to what was now a never-never land. But all in a moment, things began tumbling out of my pockets, money and keys, contracts and business letters. Especially the key to my car, my American car. I clutched, but I saw it falling.

Now, always before in my dreams when I entered that village, it was with Trip, in a car.… I must not lose the car key. "The car key, the car key!" I cried to myself in my dream, forgetting Yunkoo and Chak-doo-shay. "It fell in the bushes at the foot of the tree. I must find it."

I half climbed, half slid down the tree and began grubbing in the leaves and sticks, and ever present in my mind was the urgency of finding the car key, of recovering all of the money.

And now, as is the inconsequential way of dreams, I was running down the steps into a dark and cryptlike cellar, still looking for my money and my keys. The cellar seemed to be under the pavements of a vast city. Other men were in that cellar with me—some frightened-looking Negroes, I remember. Then looking back, I saw, through an iron grating into the upper air, men with clubs and knives. The cellar was being attacked. The Negroes were about to be mobbed. I shut the door and bolted it, and called to my frightened fellows to help me hold the door.

"Fire, bring fire," called the red-faced men outside.

And through the grating I saw the flaring torches being brought. And applied. Being shoved, crackling, through the gratings.

I awoke like the phoenix out of a burst of flames.

I have remembered this dream, because, according to Oriental interpretation, it is a dream of good omen. To be killed in a dream means success, and in particular death by fire augurs good fortune. This is supposed to be so, because death symbolizes in Buddhistic philosophy growth and rebirth and a happier reincarnation.

NOTES

In preparing the text of *East Goes West* for this edition, we attempted to match Follett's 1965 reprint, which both corrected a number of typographical errors from the original Scribner's edition and introduced some of its own. While we corrected obvious errors and imposed some standardization (such as the consistent capitalization of "Westernized" and "Machine Age"), it was a priority to retain Younghill Kang's unique and often idiosyncratic style. We also retained markers of Kang's times, such as frequently hyphenated compound words and archaic spellings.

Dedication   In the Scribner's edition, the dedication read:

DEDICATED

TO

FRANCES KEELY

who has saved my life from the fate of exile
and collaborated in the making of this book

p. 10   Younghill Kang spells the name of his protagonist inconsistently, alternating between "Chung-pa" and "Chungpa." We chose the spelling that appeared more often, "Chungpa."

p. 65   "Fusan" is the romanization of the Japanese name of Pusan. Since Kang was writing at the time of the Japanese occupation of Korea, we retained the Japanese name.

p. 217   Inexplicably, the quotation in the Follett reprint, which we republished here, is completely different from that in the first edition. In the Scribner's version, Kim's hero is not Li Po but the Sung painter and poet, Su Tung-p'o, and the poem is given only in translation:

The flower's center rises from a black halo
And all the beauty of Spring flows from the brush.
Let its shape take form out of mist,
Let it spread in a manner wholly natural.
A bending lotus tells of the wind's force,
A rotting apricot indicates the rain.

THE UNMAKING OF AN ORIENTAL YANKEE

BY SUNYOUNG LEE

"I AM A POET." Spoken by a writer of prose, this simple statement, made by Younghill Kang in a 1946 lecture, seems less a description of occupation than an assertion—a deceptively concise distillation of the passions and convictions behind his life and work (110).[1] The first Korean American novelist and a pioneering voice in Asian American literature, Kang was already edging past his prime when he made it. He had successfully published two autobiographical novels and a children's book, earning him gushing praise from the likes of Rebecca West ("After Mr. Kang, most books seem a bit flat...What a man! What a writer!") and H. G. Wells ("Here is a really great writer.") (138). He had drunk gin and talked shop with literary giants of the age, counting among his closest friends fellow New York University freshman English teacher Thomas Wolfe. And at a time when, on the opposite coast in California, anti-miscegenation laws banning Asian/white marriages were still in place, he had even met and married Frances Keely, the pampered daughter of a Virginia industrialist turned professor. (In an essay written shortly before Kang passed away, his daughter Lucy Lynn would write of her parents' relationship: "He regarded her as the princess with the many mattresses on top of the pea, and he was the foreign prince. In Don Quixote fashion, nothing was impossible." (119))

But if Kang sampled some rare triumphs for a young Asian immigrant, he also suffered the inevitable humiliations of America's entrenched racism: Kang slipped into the U.S. just before Congress passed a 1924 law effectively banning Asian immigration, and he was ineligible for citizenship because of his race.[2] Like most Koreans at this time, he was a man without a country. Asked to explain his nationality on his 1931 application for a Guggenheim Foundation fellowship, Kang would write: "In practice an American and permanently located here, but debarred by the United States Government from naturalisation as an Oriental. I am not a citizen elsewhere, since the Korean Government was dissolved [by Japan] in 1910" (65).

A poet, Kang went on to explain in his lecture, is someone essentially solitary, someone who feels human sorrow. Kang had elaborated on a similar theme in his first novel, *The Grass Roof*, published in 1931: "[I]t seems to be that the poet alone has no home nor national boundary, but is like a man in a ship. His nearest kin is the muse up in the clouds, and his patriotism goes to the ethereal kingdom" muses Chungpa Han, the book's young protagonist and Younghill Kang's fictional alter ego (3:376). This realm of the poet, pregnant with the possibility of cultural mediation, is essentially one of expectation: and indeed, as Han considers it, he is himself on a ship, suspended between the faltering traditions of his native Korea and the seductive promise of American modernity. Now, more than ten years after penning those words (and more than twenty years after he himself had emigrated), Kang was back in the land of his birth—not as a returning hero, but as an American military attaché, gathering information for the U.S. Army while it presided over the simultaneous liberation and division of Korea.[3] To the end of his life, Kang remained a man stranded—as much by historical circumstances as by early success and his own singular ambitions—in a state of profound exile.

When *East Goes West: The Making of an Oriental Yankee* was published in

1937, the success and modest acclaim generated by *The Grass Roof* had already begun to crest. Largely on the merit of that first book, Kang had become the first Asian ever to be awarded a Guggenheim Foundation fellowship—an opportunity he used to travel with his young family to Europe and write. "He was young and successful and plucking the plums from the Western world into which he had entered," remembers Lucy Lynn Kang (119). Kang's most accomplished work, *East Goes West* is a unique and vividly realized account of the heady cultural mix taking place on the margins of early twentieth-century America's growing prosperity. In its portrait of a young man's fracturing idealism, it is also an extraordinary, if coded, critique of American materialism.

Chungpa Han, first introduced in *The Grass Roof*, is the precocious and much doted-upon eldest son of an eldest son who ventures forth from the rural seclusion of his hometown to look for his place in the world. *The Grass Roof* describes Han's early childhood in northern Korea, and follows his exploits in Seoul and Japan. *East Goes West* picks up Han's story where *The Grass Roof* leaves off. Having witnessed the destruction of his childhood's bucolic tranquility by Japan's brutal colonialism, and unable to envision a productive role for himself in Korea, Han decides to head West. He explains:

> Korea, a small, provincial, old-fashioned Confucian nation...was called to get off the earth. Death summoned. I could have renounced the scholar's dream forever (plainly scholarship had dreamed us away into ruin) and written my vengeance against Japan in martyr's blood.... Or I could take away my slip cut from the roots, and try to engraft my scholar inherited kingdom upon the world's thought.... (2:8–9)

Han arrives in New York at the tender age of eighteen with little more than four dollars and a suitcase full of Shakespeare to his name. There, and in his subsequent travels throughout the United States and into Canada, he encounters prep school girls and Village bohemians, entrepreneuring salesmen and radical leftists, fire-and-brimstone preaching evangelists and stalwart Yankee farmers. He also meets, befriends, and is befriended by a rich diversity of fellow immigrants—Siamese, Italian, Filipino, Chinese, and Japanese among others—most of whom, like him, are forced to work a variety of menial jobs to make ends meet. Han's closest and most constant companions, however, are to be found amongst his fellow Koreans. Most prominent among them are the eager-to-assimilate but ever self-possessed George Jum, with his nattily pressed pants, his elaborate theories on love, and his infatuation with a white Harlem nightclub dancer; and To Won Kim, the exquisitely educated artist and scholar whose self-imposed exile in the West ends in tragedy.

With its keen eye for details, *East Goes West* is at once a picaresque adventure, an exploration of immigrant urban life in the 1920s, and a bitingly satirical critique of the hypocrisy and pretension behind America's gleaming industrialized facade. Yet from the time of its publication until now, it has been persistently misread as little more than a charmingly informative memoir. A contemporary review, published in *The New Yorker*, reports that *East Goes West* "describes with much humor and charm the author's difficulties in adapting himself to American life, and his successful search for the formula that was to make him an 'Oriental Yankee'" (91). In a *New York Times* review, this assumption of the book's essential non-fiction becomes explicit: "[Kang's] story attracts and holds the attention as if it were a novel.... But of course, *East Goes West* is not a novel. It is the candid record of 'the making of an Oriental Yankee' as its subtitle states; and its author has been so successfully Americanized as to become Assistant Professor of Comparative Literature in New York University and a member of the staff of the Department of Far Eastern Art at the Metropolitan Museum" (100). In other words, Kang's own life becomes proof of Han's successful assimilation.

This fraying of boundaries between fact and creation is most starkly revealed in those reviews where events from Kang's biography are carelessly leaked into the supposed contents of the book. For example, the *Springfield Sunday Union & Republican* blithely reports that "[*East Goes West*] concludes with [Kang's] winning of an American wife and achieving the first rung of an intellectual career"—although it remains unclear whether or not the book's hero, Chungpa Han, ever does win over Trip, his elusive idealization of American womanhood (100).[4] Certainly, as Kang himself readily admitted, portions of the book were derived from his own experiences; it is, after all, an autobiographical novel.[5] But to assume that this exchange runs in both directions—i.e. that Kang's life could be read back into the book—is a slip that implies more than just sloppy journalism: it indicates a presumption of artlessness in Kang's work.[6]

The potential damage of such a claim can be seen in the lengths writers such as Thomas Wolfe, Kang's close friend and contemporary, went to address it. Bothered by criticisms that his work was little more than a recapitulation of his life, Wolfe included a note "to the reader" at the beginning of *Look Homeward Angel* that stated: "Fiction is not fact, but fiction is fact selected and understood, fiction is fact arranged and charged with purpose."[7] For Kang, an Asian immigrant, such allowance for creative license was hardly considered. The craft of *East Goes West* was diminished instead into the uninspired and impossibly bland "story of a human being among other human beings in an amazing diversity of human experience" (100). Kang the writer is replaced by Chungpa Han the character, and in the process, Kang becomes an early victim of the still-prevalent belief that the only contribution any writer of color could possibly have to make is the story of his or her own life.

Kang's reviewers were joined in their assessment of his work by his editor Maxwell Perkins, the powerful Scribner's institution who also edited Wolfe, Hemingway, Fitzgerald, and a host of other illustrious American authors. Introduced to Kang through Wolfe, Perkins' starkly different attitudes towards both is revealing. In an introduction to Scribner's reprint of *Look Homeward Angel,* he writes of Wolfe: "Many of [his reviewers] asserted that Wolfe could only write about himself, that he could not see the world or anything objectively, with detachment—that he was always autobiographical.... But all that he wrote of was transformed by his imagination."[8] This transformative power of the imagination is not in evidence in Perkins' reading of Kang's work. His attitude towards *East Goes West* is much more matter-of-fact. *The Grass Roof* had been quite successful, with steady sales, translation rights sold for several languages, and even a tentative offer for a movie option; and Perkins undoubtedly expected *East Goes West* to be a book along the same lines⁹—the relatively straightforward, marketable tale of a young man's eventual acceptance into Western culture.¹⁰ Explaining his suggested cuts to the manuscript in a letter to Kang, Perkins wrote: "The principle I went on was that in the first place this was the story of a man, and in the second, of an Easterner in the West." In an effort to emphasize this aspect, Perkins urged Kang to include more information about Trip "and to show definitely that you married her, because the fact that you did, makes one of the principal points of the book, in that the Easterner became a Westerner through this experience" (147: 8 Feb. 1937).¹¹

Such an approach to *East Goes West* seriously underestimates Young-hill Kang. Certainly someone like Kang—who had mastered both Asian and Western traditions of poetry and philosophy, and who demanded in an assignment that his students "select for elaborate commentary a literary masterpiece which is chiefly notable for the ethical, social, or religious truth it presents" (64)—would have loftier ambitions for his second major work than merely recording his life. Nevertheless, most readers, including Perkins, continued to see in *East Goes West* what they expected from it: the candid account of a hardworking immigrant who, through his unwavering belief in the American dream, comes to attain it.

That Kang's ambitions for this second book were much more complex than what his editor or his reviewers comprehended becomes evident in the fellowship application he submitted to the Guggenheim Foundation in October 1931. The book he hoped to write, tentatively called "Death of an Exile," was to be a companion volume to *The Grass Roof,* though one "more mature in style and technique." And unlike *The Grass Roof,* which "treated of the Orient," it was to

> treat of Orientals in America, being the reflection through the hero's eyes of this mechanical age, of American civilization, and of the literary and cultural epoques he experiences here over a period of ten years; also a history of his spiritual evolutions and revolutions while love-sick, bread-sick, butter-sick, education-sick, he is lost and obliterated in the stone-and-steel jungles of New York City... (65)

Kang staked out his literary territory very clearly: the book was to be both a novel of ideas and the portrait of an era. The issues he proposed to address might not have been strikingly innovative in and of themselves, but they were to be explored from the unique perspective of an Asian living in the U.S. with access to the literary, philosophical, and social conceits of two traditions. Through his travels, the "hero" was to experience "the various religions of mankind, Buddhism, Taoism, Confucianism, Christianity," as well as "the various philosophies, pragmatism, naturalism, humanism, neo-realism, etc." Racism was also to play a formative role in the proposed book: "The theme of race prejudice recurs, in the lives of minor characters and in the life of the protagonist, and the whole alternates between the mood of satire and the mood of a stirring prose poem." (65)

The title Kang originally proposed for the book further attests to his conceptual sophistication. For Kang, "Death of an Exile" could be read in two ways. First, as a reference to the tragic character of To Wan Kim, "a beautiful and romantic spirit in exile," who dies by himself in Greenwich Village "after many bitter experiences" and "being thwarted in love and ambition." The deeper meaning of the title, however, is to be found in the philosophical underpinnings of the book, not its plot. "Death of an Exile" also alludes to "the idea of a rebirth in the soul of the hero, which had also been in exile. At the end of the novel, the romantic soul in him is dead, and the soul that remains and feels itself at home in the world is the soul that is facing life in the real sense, pragmatically."[12] The hero, having worked his way through quandries both metaphysical and material, "finally identifies himself as a poet with a belief in the significance and hence immortality of the soul." (65)

This notion of the irreducible soul, purged of abstractions and living in itself, is a theoretical quote of, among other things, the literary source with which Kang closes out his proposal. He writes: "*Grass Roof* may be said to have been written in the mood of the Everlasting Nay of Carlyle; *Death of an Exile* may be compared to the mood of the Everlasting Yea" (65). The concepts he refers to are taken from Thomas Carlyle's *Sartor Resartus* [The Tailor Retailored], a book whose eclectic combination of autobiography, novel, and essay might have been an inspiration for *East Goes West*. The

Everlasting Nay refers to the loss of faith that accompanies the difficult passage from certainty to uncertainty: "Such transitions are ever full of pain: thus the Eagle when he moults is sickly; and, to attain his new beak, must harshly dash-off the old one upon rocks."[13] This description of crisis resembles the radical break with the past that Chungpa Han recounts at the beginning of East Goes West: "It was my destiny to see the disjointing of a world …I saw myself placed on a shivering pinnacle overlooking a wasteland that had no warmth…. And I felt I was looking on death, the death of an ancient planet…In loathing of death, I hurtled forward, out into space, out toward a foreign body…" (2:5). Carlyle's conclusion that "'It is from this hour that I incline to date my Spiritual Newbirth, or Baphometic Fire-baptism [a transformation by a flash of spiritual illumination], perhaps I directly thereupon began to be a Man'" becomes a fitting assessment of Han's situation at the end of The Grass Roof and the beginning of East Goes West.[14]

The Everlasting Yea elaborates on the idea of release from incertitude through the assertion of individual freedom. It hinges on the notion of self-understanding—that you create your own circumstances and knowledge. "'Fool!'" Carlyle writes, "'The Ideal is in thyself, the impediment too is in thyself; thy Condition is but the stuff [out of which] thou art to shape that same Ideal…'"[15] In other words, wherever you go, there you are. Or, stop looking for answers outside of yourself. Early on in East Goes West, Han considers the aim of his journey to the U.S.: "This world, which had sucked me in by its onward, forward magnetism, must have that in it, too, to feed and anchor man in the old durability…. It was here…here in America for me to find…but where?" (2:5). A passage in Carlyle's Everlasting Yea answers this question:

> "May we not say…that the hour of Spiritual Enfranchisement is even this: When your Ideal World, wherein the whole man has been dimly struggling and inexpressibly languishing to work, becomes revealed, and thrown open; and you discover, with amazement enough…that your 'America is here or nowhere'?"[16]

The "rebirth" of Kang's hero—or rather, the death of the state of exile—

comes from the realization that the spiritual home he had come to America to find would by necessity be a place of his own making, not an impossible ideal.

Illuminating though it may be, Kang's Guggenheim application lists only intentions. When Kang submitted it in the fall of 1931, he was still eager to join the intellectual ferment around him and confident of his ability to do so. It seems appropriate that the tone of his proposal resembles the self-assurance expressed by Han at the end of *The Grass Roof*: "And there are many more dreams within me, greater and greater, also going to come true soon through my own act" (3:376). But, after all, defining oneself is only half the struggle. How society defines you is not, for most, a matter of choice—even more so when you are an Asian immigrant living in the America of the twenties and thirties. It is hardly surprising that the portrait of an extremely complex man—driven by equal parts ego, intelligence, and idealism—that emerges from Kang's characterization of himself as a poet contrasts sharply with the good-natured, somewhat naive "Oriental Yankee" that his reviewers and critics saw in him.

In the intervening half-decade between the Guggenheim proposal and the actual publication of his second novel, Kang's aspirations for the limitless agency of the individual matured and darkened. The *New York Times* book reviewer who wrote that Kang "is no cynic. He never picks up a big stick. He merely tells us what happened, good and bad, the sad and the merry, and always alive," could not have been more mistaken (100). Kang was in fact quite skeptical about the rosy promise of assimilation and success advertised by the American dream. However, such a reading only becomes possible when *East Goes West* is looked at as a novel and not as autobiography. Splitting the figure of Chungpa Han from the presumed identity of Younghill Kang proves to be a liberating act: it restores Kang's creative muscle, and a more radical and more subversive critique of American modernization is revealed.

From the beginning, the process of Americanization for Han is both a process of marginalization and an initiation into the rigors of materialism. Starting off at the main office of the Y.M.C.A., Han hopes that a letter of introduction from a missionary will secure him an entrée into the bustling

world of opportunity and work embodied by the Y.M.C.A. office itself—
"high up in a skyscraper, [it] seemed one of the busiest places to judge by the
typewriters all about...clickety-clacking at enormous speed" (2:16). He is
disabused of this notion "with businesslike finality" by the organization's
president, who refers him to the Harlem Y.M.C.A. (2:16). There, in turn, he
is told that the only available position must "not be given to a Negro or an
Oriental...precisely because [this] branch was up in Harlem" (2:19). Having
unwittingly spent almost all his remaining money on a haircut and shave,
Han ends up in a flophouse, an experience he describes as being comparable
only to the extreme deprivation of a Japanese prison cell. The flophouse is
even worse in some respects: unlike the Korean revolutionists, who had
been placed in jail "for a single integrated feeling, a hard bright core of fire
against oppression," the homeless bums of New York with whom Han
spends the night are "like pithess stalks, and the force that swept them here,
the city's leavings, was for the most part...a personal disintegration" (2:22).

Han might still be charmed enough by the possibilities of American
individualism—"where individual disintegration was possible, as well as
individual integration, where all need not perish with the social organism"—
to brush off the flophouse misery, but as this first day draws to a close, he is
jobless and without clear prospects for the future (2:22). The situation
becomes desperate: "I had known the famines of poor rice years in Korea.
Now, in utter solitude with a chilling heart, I feared pavement famine, with
plenty all around but in the end not even grass to chew" (2:30). Around him
swirls a world of commerce and exchange, but it is mechanical and unsus-
taining. Alone in his unheated room, Han tries to eke out some spiritual
nourishment by reading Shakespeare, but finds himself unable to concentrate—"Even in the midst of Hamlet's subtlest soliloquies, I could think of
nothing but food" (2:30).

Significantly, Han is aided in and saved from this hand-to-mouth
existence by fellow outcasts—first a bum, then a Chinese restaurant manager,
and finally his friend George Jum. On the margins of New York's unre-
lenting efficiency, other models for social interaction exist. During another
hungry period of his life, Han notes:

[I]f I wandered through the streets of Chinatown about nine o'clock at night—the dinner hour for Chinese waiters and restaurant men—some waiter was almost sure to see me and call out, "Come on…Dinner time!" Always they cooked enough to be elastic either way—five more or five less made no difference—and if I joined them, they just brought out another bowl and chopsticks. Such was the Chinese custom. They had a psychology which would seem strange to American businessmen. A spiritual treat for a material, a material for a spiritual—they saw no difference. (2:79–80)

Such generosity is hardly characteristic of Han's encounters as he seeks to join the mainstream of American life. As he continues in his adventures, Han comes to realize that as a person of color, his difficulties always begin when he steps outside the narrow boundaries of acceptable, unthreatening behavior. So, for example, his stint as a houseboy with one American family ends when the father, Mr. Lively, encounters George Jum and his white girlfriend and begins to suspect that Han might be romantically interested in his teenaged daughter. "'My dear boy, see here,'" Mr. Lively admonishes. "'I love you just as much as if you were my own boy. But you are getting wrong ideas. I don't want to see you marry an American girl. Neither would I want to see Elsie marrying an Oriental. And all decent people are like that. It is not as the Lord intended.'" Han's surprise is complete: "I was very solemn and silent and unable to open my mouth to say anything." (2:150)

For the non-white populations of this time, making one's way in the U.S. becomes a matter of negotiating around racist—and often ludicrous—misassumptions. Anti-miscegenation laws still held force in California, and for an Asian man to even be seen with a white woman often meant trouble. Stereotypes dictated the very conditions of your life in other ways as well: in one Chinese restaurant, eight of Han's nine fellow waiters have college degrees—three of those also have Ph.D.'s from Columbia University. Han's friend George Jum, formerly an ambassador to Washington from Korea, makes his money as a cook (2:81).[17] Wagstaff, another friend who works as an elevator man while getting a law degree, asks, "'What room is there in America for an educated Negro? There is not much else but the "yessuh" job. And either way, I shall hardly be assured of a decent living way'"

(2:273). Han asserts that "Through Wagstaff I was having my first introduction to a crystallized caste system, comparable only to India, here in the greatest democratic country of the world," but in fact he has been learning this lesson since he first set foot in the United States (2:273).

If Han seems naive initially, he is also a quick study. Leaving the scene of his first New York encounter, he notes:

> [S]oon I became convinced that everyone in New York felt the same way as this dry-voiced, kidding man I had first met...the need of sustaining a role, a sort of gaminlike sophistication, harder and more polished than a diamond in the prosperous classes, but equally present in the low, a hard shell over the soul of New-World children, essential for the pebbles rattling through subway tunnels and their sun-hid city streets. (2:16)

Cultivating a persona, Han realizes, is a necessary survival tactic, especially in a society where you are almost entirely subjected to distorted expectations. At one point, Han complains to his more cynical and experienced friend, To Wan Kim, about Boston. Kim replies,

> "You will get along somehow.... Boston has treated you well on the whole.... professors in Boston have great sympathy for any adopted Oriental child. As long as you are willing to be docile and obedient."
>
> "That's just it!" I agreed indignantly, and Kim smiled. "I hate being nicey-nice."
>
> "Well, I'm afraid we cannot do much against Boston," said Kim. "Morals and manners are greater strongholds than fortifications..." (2:255)

Through his experiences, Han comes to understand this lesson quite well. The disjunction between the circumstances that Han finds himself relegated to and the lofty hopes he fosters for his adopted land is not bitter irony, it is an inevitable by-product of America's racist culture. For an interloper like Han, the trick is to figure out how to negotiate those expectations without capitulating to them.

Perhaps the most revealing instance of the pragmatic survivalism Han develops can be found in the series of dinner parties given by Miss Churchill, an elderly Quaker woman who "used to entertain in a quiet way all kinds of people, particularly young people and many of them from foreign lands, such as India, Japan, or China." At first, Han is one of many guests, often accompanied by "the Hindu student Senzar, or the Japanese Miyamori." What follows is in essence a detailed explanation of how Han alone of the three foreign students manages to secure his place at such gatherings. (2:296)

Miyamori, on the one hand, makes the mistake of admiring American civilization too uncritically. According to Han, "[Miyamori] frankly envied me as a more or less permanent exile, and advised me never to go home, since all was primitive and barbaric hell back there. Tall buildings, subways, autos, universal sanitation, great department stores...these seemed like Utopia to Miyamori." For this fault, and for the fault of writing bad poetry to all his American friends, signed "Very respectably," he is invited by Miss Churchill less and less. (2:296)

Senzar's excision from the group comes about in a much more dramatic fashion. An "Indo-Oxford product...in America studying engineering," Senzar seems "handsome, poetic and sad" as long as he keeps his mouth shut. (Such a characterization gives an apt depiction of Orientalism—the illusion of exoticism and mystery can only be maintained through silence.) Conflict arises one evening when he seizes upon Han, the only other non-white in the room, and begins berating Han's American schooling, "unconsciously parodying the English-felt superiority of the English university man." The complexities of a colonized mentality are clearly articulated in Senzar's simultaneous identification with Oxford's superiority and his rage at the second-class status it relegates him to. "'You think you're educated,'" mocks Senzar to Kang, "'You don't know how to talk English!'" The other guests, who had been "listening attentively to this, with sly glances of amusement and surprise," are less entertained when the scope of Senzar's tirade widens to include them—"'Then, Americans are not sound,' Senzar kept on, and the Americans and English began to get very uncomfortable." Another Oxford man protests, and Senzar becomes even more enraged, excoriating the colonial system and exclaiming, "'Soon we will drive you English out.'" (2:296–99)

Attempting to save the situation, Han jumps back into the fray, countering Senzar's rant with the claim that "You Hindus are better off under the English than we are under the Japanese." The conversation goes on and on, but Han finally manages to engage Senzar's attention once again: "I deflected his words and his wrath toward me. Not without enjoyment, too, I sought to stem that lava which Miss Churchill felt to be such a social catastrophe." Afterwards, Han is "almost decorated for merit by the exhausted Westerners." He comments matter-of-factly: "Senzar, for want of tact, was never invited by Miss Churchill again. I became a regular guest now, for dinner and the evening, every Wednesday." (2:299)

The irony of all this is that the statements made by both Miyamori and Senzar are remarkably similar to ones made throughout the book by Han. For example, both Senzar and Han are critical of colonization. Han is diplomatic about his situation—"For me there was always special favor, special kindliness, special protection...the white-man's-burden attitude toward the dark colonies. Ralph's kindness...Leslie's brutal cruelty...I weighed them in my mind, and it seemed to me better to miss the kindness and not to have the cruelty" (2:118)—while Senzar bristles with indignation at his: "So you think you know the English? No! This cold-blooded, thieving, wooden, two-faced race? Oh no!" (2:298). Moreover, Han's frustration with the disjointed, assembly-line instruction that passes for Western pedagogy parallels Senzar's assertion that there is "Nothing to get from their education anyway. Only mechanical things" (2:298). And both are aware of their own exiled status in the West. When Han describes Senzar's attitude towards his native country—"Of course, he was a fanatic patriot, but his words were so much in the clouds, you could not make out whether he intended to go back to India or not"—he could be discussing his own conflicting sense of self-interest and love of country (2:297). Similarly, Miyamori's reluctance to go back to the "primitive and barbaric hell" of "home" (2:296) is echoed in Han's realization that he has become "softened somewhat by the luxuries of Western living" (2:368).

In contrast to both Senzar and Miyamori, however, Han has learned to master the fragile balance of accomodation. If he is unwilling to remain silent and inscrutable on the fringes of conversation, at least he knows how to function within the strict rules of polite company. He is not, like Miyamori, overly eager to Westernize, thus making him uninteresting to a Western audience. He is also not, like Senzar, so flamboyant in his criticisms of Western culture that he is deemed uncivilized. Han's deflection of Senzar's attention away from the others, using Korea's colonization as bait, is a classic middle-man maneuver; it might be disturbingly opportunistic, but it is also extremely astute, earning him the gratitude of his hostess even as it grates on our modern-day multicultural sensibilities. Because of this performance, Han is invited back again and again—an opportunity that gives him access to free food and the social connections that eventually lead him to his beloved Trip.

In its dramatization of the racial politicking happening in the parlor rooms of American society, this episode is both more complex and more informative than it might appear to be at first: the dissonance between Chungpa Han's persistent idealism and his clear-eyed observations of the hypocrisy around him is not mere inconsistency, it is a carefully constructed conceit, with Younghill Kang as its master architect and principal beneficiary.[18] At the time Kang was writing *East Goes West,* America was going through a profoundly xenophobic stage, and to be an Asian in such a society —even one who operated in the oftentimes more progressive world of academics and intellectuals—required a certain decorum and polish, and an acute sense of survival. Kang the writer, like Han the character, needed to tread the middle ground between the extremes of honest expression and diplomatic restraint. Like Han, he could not afford to alienate his audience. And like Han, he was vying for a place at the table.

For Kang, however, a place at the table meant access to American citizenship—that sense of home—that was denied to him by law. Like all Asian immigrants, Kang was prevented from becoming naturalized because of his race. "I know I am an American," he would write, "[in] all but the citizenship papers denied me by the present interpretation of the law of 1870, under which a Korean is not racially eligible for citizenship" (33:63). Nevertheless, his previous successes had made him cocky about his ability to surmount these difficulties. Taking up the challenge voiced at the beginning of *East Goes West*—"Out of action rises the dream, rises the poetry. Dream without motion is the only wasteland that can sustain nothing," (2:6)—he set about trying to accomplish what even Thomas Mann had been unable to do—get a law passed through Congress that would make him a U.S. citizen. The bills that eventually came before Congress (H.R. 7127 in the House and S. 2802 in the Senate) were not introduced until the fall of 1939, but Kang had grasped the importance of pro-American boosterism long before. As Kim points out to Han, "'In this country, in this age, art becomes the instinct for self-preservation'" (2:165). Later in his life, Kang would conclude even more explicitly, "Artists are propogandists. They propogandize themselves" (110).

Kang was ultimately able to scratch out a place for himself as a writer within the crippling limitations of the role assigned to him because he managed to subvert them. Just as Han uses his own history (i.e. Korea's colonization by Japan) to get into the good graces of the assembled company, Kang played off the assumption that his book is autobiography to prove to his audience—the American public—that he was citizenship-worthy. He manipulated the misperception that he and Han are the same person. Han's clever positioning of himself between the extremes of Senzar and Miyamori thus becomes both a lesson in survival skills—a description of how to stay afloat in the frigid waters of social acceptability—and a demonstration of Kang's own balancing technique in *East Goes West*. Thus, the book's harshest critiques of America's bigotry and ignorance are placed in the mouths and actions of other characters, while Han narrates from a seemingly inoffensive fly-on-the-wall perspective. (As Han discovers in his very first job, "It was interesting in a sense, being treated just like a dog or cat. One could see everything, and go unnoticed…" (2:62).) Through Kang's shrewd construction of Han as an amiable fellow who understands the rules of the game and who knows how to make himself useful (which in this case means making oneself palatable—not too strong and not too weak—very much like an acceptable dinner guest), he was able to negotiate between his ambitions for the book, his insights about American society, and his own political self-interest.[19]

The recommendations that Kang's citizenship bid received from university presidents, best-selling writers, philosophers, politicians, and publishers represent the initial success and the ultimate limitations of such a strategy.

Maxwell Perkins writes: "I have known Younghill Kang both professionally as an editor, and personally, for some ten years now, and I believe him to be thoroughly qualified—in his understanding of American principles and in his love for this country—to be a citizen of whom Americans can be proud" (112). Kang is thus singled out as a talented intellectual who, through his demonstrated commitment to "American principles" can be trusted with the honor of citizenship. A comment by the popular author Louis Adamic expresses a similar sentiment: "Younghill Kang is, emotionally and intellectually, identified with America; his interests in America, in fact, are greater—in many respects—than those of all too many native Americans" (112). By out-Americanizing the Americans, Kang is deemed worthy of becoming one.

Both these endorsements, like the citizenship bid itself, presuppose a utopian vision of reasonableness, a belief that for the exceptionally gifted, exceptions can be made—that the racist structures that had conspired to shut Kang and countless other immigrants out could, under the right conditions, be flexible.[20] They are an appeal to the seductive if elusive humanism on which Kang's hopes for success in the U.S. were built. In an article requesting support for the bills, Kang would write: "Democracy is the only possible medium in which men may struggle individually toward poise and dignity and self-respect.... [I]f we behave ourselves and move with high thoughts, each man attains kinship with a king" (33:62). But neither Kang's illustrious connections nor his personal and literary achievements nor his "high thoughts" ultimately proved sufficient to remove him from the ranks of those barred from citizenship because of their race. The congressional bills that had been introduced as part of his citizenship bid were never passed.

It is a testament to Kang's perspicacity that his book already contains within it a critique of the racist culture that would burst his idealism. Kang might have been enticed by the possibilities offered by an idealization of individualism, but he is not stupid. Unlike Han, he is not surprised to find that a "crystallized caste system" exists in America. *East Goes West* might open with the hopeful optimism of Carlyle's Everlasting Yea, but it closes on a much more ambivalent note.

In the last pages of the book, Han describes a recurring dream: he is trying to reach his childhood friends who are playing on a rope bridge that leads to a "paradise of wild and flowery magic." As he descends to meet them, things begin to fall out of his pockets—"money and keys, contracts and business letters. Especially the key to my car, my American car" (2:368). He chases after them, suddenly finding himself in a cellar. He notices that he is not alone:

> Other men were in that cellar with me—some frightened-looking Negroes, I remember. Then looking back, I saw...men with clubs and knives. The cellar was being attacked. The Negroes were about to be mobbed. I shut the door and bolted it, and called to my frightened fellows to help me hold the door.
>
> "Fire, bring fire," called the red-faced men outside.
>
> And through the grating I saw the flaring torches being brought. And applied. Being shoved, crackling, through the gratings. I awoke like the phoenix out of a burst of flames. (2:369)

In pursuit of that ultimate icon of the American dream—his car keys—Han is cornered by the ugly reality of his position in society. The fire-baptism that he experiences here is not the birth into a newfound sense of freedom that Carlyle envisioned as the Everlasting Yea. It is the realization that to be non-white in a fundamentally racist society is to be trapped by others' fear of you. It is a birth into an expectation of violence. In the end, Han has more in common with the "frightened-looking Negroes" than with the "red-faced men" gathering outside—he too is trapped.

Kang's belief that he could escape the metaphorical fate he depicted in *East Goes West* was based on an arrogance that was both his strength and his greatest weakness. In an essay called "Younghill Kang's Unwritten Third Act," James Wade writes:

> Somewhere in [Kang's] middle years those vaulting aspirations were realized to be impossible, an experience that happens to all of us, except the most unassuming. Kang, in his pride and sense of superiority (and he *was* superior in a great many ways), apparently wilted under the realization. If he could not be the greatest, he would not settle for second-best: for him it was genius or nothing. Rather than compromise those ambitions cherished from child-

hood, he fell silent and saw his career ebb away into relative obscurity. For such a man, the late-learned lesson must have been a bitter one. (108:59)

Blaming Kang's lack of productivity on ego alone is not entirely accurate, however. This "relative obscurity" was triggered as much by profound disillusionment with the political situation as by the onslaught of middle age. "It has been hard for me to retake my place in American life after World War II," Kang would write, "partly because of my restless anxiety about the world situation, particularly the recent Korean events" (66). In the aftermath of these upheavals, Kang found that he could not maintain the level of poise required to balance between the twin poles of his intellectual ambitions and his pragmatic, social needs.

The mental and material cost of all this for Kang was great. As Lucy Lynn Kang poignantly writes, her father "was not equipped to survive in a system of capitalism and free enterprise, once the bubble of success broke" (119).[21] Moreover, by assuming that he could transcend the restraints on his fellow Asian immigrants, he had become complicit in the diminution of his own work. Kang's youthful idealization of the opportunities awaiting him in the United States must have seemed like that first haircut Chungpa Han receives upon arriving in New York—sitting back in the barber's chair, he is seduced by the luxuries of the moment. He doesn't yet realize how much this momentary indulgence will cost him (2:17–18). By 1954, Kang would write:

> I was of the Western generation that had matured believing in Northrup's *Meeting of East and West*. I foresaw great cross-fertilization of science and art. I thought of myself...as a cultural go-between, never as a member of any political party. In more ways than one I was seeing the death of all I had hoped for. Such a job is hardly possible now and I seem to have no job, a small enough tragedy in the greater one holding us all." (66)

As he crisscrossed the country in an old Buick, supporting himself through lectures and occasional teaching jobs, Kang would become alienated from even a sense of his own literary accomplishments.

If, in the end, *East Goes West* is flawed, it is still remarkable in its aspirations and achievements. The passion for literature that sustained Kang in his youth stands out against the ruins of his life, forcing a closer look at the lessons of this first generation of Korean immigrants. "To me literature is the most important of all the arts," Kang would say in 1941. "Good literature cannot be destroyed. A hundred years from now people who read American history to learn about the Roosevelt Administration will not have the whole truth. They will find more truth in Dreiser or Sinclair Lewis, for literature alone can give the emotional side of human beings" (134). Certainly, Kang's depictions of urban centers like New York through the eyes of Chungpa Han makes for a richly entertaining and informative account of the cosmopolitan subculture of immigrants in the twenties and thirties. Kang's portraits of the small urban Korean community on the East Coast, driven by nationalism while scrambling to sustain a livelihood on the margins of the mainstream, is probably the only literary account of its kind from that time.

The significance of *East Goes West* extends far beyond mere historical documentation, however: it is a unique portrait of one man's journey through idealism, in all its complexity and contradictions, its difficulties and unique pleasures. Kang is not, and perhaps never imagined himself to be, a visionary writer. In many ways, he is still very much a product of his times. But he is also a man of undeniable insight. So, for example, while his portraits of African Americans relies largely on popular stereotypes—invoking in one instance the "flamboyant lazy magic of disintegration" of "Negro jazz" (2:18–19) and in another, the "Negro humor which found some funny side in lack of dignity, in losing face" (2:75)—his assessment of their situation in relation to his was remarkably astute. The image of imminent lynching at the end of the book is just as potent a premonition of the urban riots of today as it is a reference to the racial unrest of the time. It is as a record of one man's response to the world around him—of his questing intelligence—that Kang's work transcends the shuttered expectations of his own time.

Out of print for much of the past fifty years and all but un-anthologized, the impact of Kang's books on American and Asian American literature has been largely limited to the influence he had on people such as Carlos Bulosan, the pioneering Filipino American writer. Bulosan, who published his own account of immigrant life, *America Is in the Heart*, in 1946, credits Kang as an inspiration: "I returned to the writers of my time for strength. And I found Younghill Kang, a Korean who had immigrated to the United States as a boy and worked his way up until he had become a professor at an American university.... But it was his indomitable courage that rekindled in me a fire of hope. Why could I not succeed as Younghill Kang had?" (143:265).

Kang's failures are as much a part of his legacy as his successes, however. Kang saw himself as unique, apart from the rest—the Korean who could become an American through force of will, the Asian immigrant who could sustain a career as a successful writer—but his life is, in its hopes and disappointments, actually the life of many first-generation immigrants who come to this country and find themselves disillusioned and alone. The lessons he learned are worth remembering: The "Oriental Yankee" of *East Goes West*'s subtitle might read as an antiquated version of today's term "Asian American," but "The Making of an Oriental Yankee" is in fact that process of deconstruction—of simplistic nationalism, of naive faith in America's gleaming promise, of a stable, color-blind identity—that is implicit in the construction of a new sense of home.

Proof of Kang's singular abilities—his perceptive eye, his acrobatic talent for mediation—ultimately comes not from his inclusion on a guest list, but from the writing and publication of *East Goes West* itself. In his book, if not in his life, Kang emerges as the singular writer and poet that it was his greatest ambition to become. The story is there, for anyone to read.

This essay—and this reprint—would never have been possible without the contributions of Juliana Koo, whose editorial insight, thoughtfulness, and commitment is always an inspiration. Thanks also to Lawrence Chua, for his ever-incisive comments and suggestions.

1 The citations refer to the following bibliography, which assigns each source a number. The source number is followed by a page number when appropriate. References to *The Grass Roof* are taken from Follett's 1959 reprint. References to *East Goes West* are from this edition. Materials not in the bibliography are listed in these notes.

2 As a result of the 1790 Naturalization Act, only "free whites" were able to become citizens of the United States. This and subsequent laws and interpretations by courts excluded Asian immigrants from voting and owning property as well.

3 "I'm still in Korea..." Kang wrote his editor at Scribner's, Maxwell Perkins, on January 1, 1947. "I don't enjoy myself very much. Thirty million frustrated, confused, and humiliated Koreans are trying to become a nation. The only excuse for the continued presence of Americans in Korea is to help prepare the Korean people for their promised independence. The steps in accomplishing this mission are clear: we are getting nowhere." (147)

4 The clearest allusion to a future for Chungpa and Trip occurs in the still very ambiguous lines: "With the expanding spring, the flower of our relationship was to bloom fuller and fuller, containing seed of all our future days..." (2:366)

5 To find clues to Kang's life in his books, it is useful to study those portions that he explicitly claimed as autobiography—for example, in sketches such as "Oriental Yankee," published in *Common Ground* in 1941.

6 A particularly snide review that ran in the *Times Literary Supplement* explicitly states: "[Kang's] autobiography is of great length, and yet it is told in an artless way that makes it rather fascinating." (98)

7 Thomas Wolfe, *Look Homeward Angel,* introd. by Maxwell Perkins (1922; New York: Scribner's–Simon & Schuster, 1995) xv.

8 Wolfe xii–xiii.

9 Perkins' view of *The Grass Roof* can be seen in a draft of the recommendation letter he wrote for Kang's 1931 Guggenheim Foundation fellowship application. "[*The Grass Roof*] makes the Western reader feel at one with the Oriental characters." The

next line is visible through Perkins' pencilled cross-out: "Generally they seem to be hopelessly alien and incomprehensible." (147)

10 Of the *New York Times* book review describing *East Goes West* as "not a novel," Perkins writes: "The first really adequate review we have had." (147: 14 Oct. 1937)

11 Much has been made of Perkin's suggestions that Kang cut descriptions of "the frivolous Easterners" in early drafts of *East Goes West*. Taken in the context of the correspondence as a whole, it becomes clear that Perkins' comments have more to do with his assessment of Kang in terms of commerce rather than art—and thus with keeping the manuscript within an acceptable, or publishable, length—than with attempts to censor Kang. Perkins might not have been sufficiently visionary to ascertain the potential value of Kang's portraits of Koreans for future generations, but on the basis of his brief notes to Kang, it is difficult to assert that he manipulated the original text without Kang's approval. (147)

12 The eventual title and subtitle of the book, *East Goes West: The Making of an Oriental Yankee,* were the result of a collaborative brainstorm by Thomas Wolfe and Maxwell Perkins (and presumably Kang). Perkins originally suggested "The Americanization of Younghill Kang" and "Rebirth in America" (the former giving further indication of how Perkins hoped to package Kang's book) while Wolfe's first offerings were "Yankee out of Korea" and "Oriental Yankee." (147: 5 Apr. 1937)

13 Thomas Carlyle, from *Sartor Resartus, The Norton Anthology of English Literature,* 5th ed. (New York: Norton, 1986) 964–65.

14 Carlyle 970.

15 Carlyle 984–85.

16 Carlyle 984.

17 Ever pragmatic despite his extremely romantic views on love, Jum notes that: "'The wages of a good cook are $50 a week with board, room and laundry. Better than a bank clerk or a college instructor, you will find. And it's much better money than when I was an Ambassador for the Korean Government in Washington, D.C.'" (2:35)

18 In its dead-pan portrayal of the attitudes goading such opportunism along, the Senzar episode also gives a sadly accurate commentary on the condition of some multicultural interactions—two colored folk duking it out over the same tiny scrap of privilege while an appreciative audience looks on.

19 A passage in *East Goes West* describing the battle of the wills between a professor

of Greek and Vidol, a Siamese classmate of Han's, is a useful indication of the rationale behind such literary dissimulation. Whenever Vidol is called on by the professor, he refuses to admit that he hasn't done his homework, saying instead that he can't remember the answer: "[B]efore such alien falsehood, the professor lost all control; he would grow white and shake with fury. It was an obsession with him to break down Vidol, to force him to confess he was not telling the truth." Han interprets Vidol's stubbornness to another friend:

> "Of course the East does not put the same emphasis upon the words of fact as the West," I tried to explain. "A gentleman says what is respectable and decent to say. No doubt Vidol really means 'I ought to have read.'"

Han portrays this attitude as an East/West dichotomy, but as used by Kang, it can be read as a kind of strategy—an indication of what to expect from Han himself. (2:178–79)

A later discussion of race with Wagstaff further justifies such a tactic: "'They say that Negroes always lie. Why shouldn't they?'" Wagstaff asks.

> "They must lie to exist. They see around them a world of lies, a cruel unfriendly world from birth, where they are gyped because of color. There is only one philosophy that can come from that. It will not be 'honesty is the best policy' or any lie like that. Learn the language of gyp, learn to gyp too. Confess honestly that right isn't might, but might is right, always since the world began."

Likewise, Kang realizes that he could never hope to pass in society by remaining completely honest. His use of Han as a mask becomes less a matter of deception than an instinct for self-preservation. (2:274)

20 This promise is articulated by Senator Kirby, one of Han's road companions. He says: "'Now you must definitely make up your mind to *be* American. Don't say, 'I'm a Korean' when you're asked. Say 'I'm an American.'" When Han observes "'But an Oriental has a hard time in America. He is not welcomed much.... legally I am denied,'" Kirby comes back with: "'There shouldn't be any buts about it! Believe in America with all your heart. Even if it's sometimes hard, believe in her.'" (2:353–54)

21 In a April 20, 1986 letter to the *New York Times*, Lucy Lynn Kang would hint at political difficulties as well: "My Korean-born father, Younghill Kang, a writer…, sought American citizenship and political freedom; he, too, could only live as part of a free society.… During the McCarthy era, when people were blacklisted for expressing such sentiments, my father, along with countless others, suffered adversities." (118)

THIS CHRONOLOGY has been assembled from writings that Kang himself explicitly claimed as autobiography (articles, letters, applications) and secondary biographical sources. The dates are as accurate as possible, given Kang's sometimes vague account of the number of years he spent in a particular place or his age at the time of a particular event. Several irresolvable inconsistencies that exist in Kang's own chronology of his life have been noted. Among the facts of Kang's life that remain unclear: when exactly he died and when his youngest son, Robert, was born.

1903   The son of a farmer, Younghill Kang is born on May 10th in Song-Dune-Chi ("Village of Pine Trees"), Hamkyung Province—"a sheltered, beautiful valley some 300 miles north of Seoul." (38:110)[1]

            Kang proves his intellectual promise by becoming fluent in Korean and Chinese classics.

1910   On August 29, Korea is formally declared annexed by decree of the Japanese government.

Shortly thereafter, Kang witnesses the beating of his grandmother by Japanese police. She eventually dies from injuries sustained in this attack. His uncle is imprisoned on false conspiracy charges; while in jail, he is tortured and permanently crippled.

1914   Against the wishes of his father, Kang leaves the countryside and travels to Seoul in search of further education. He makes the 300 mile journey over 16 days on foot with the equivalent of 3 dollars.

1915   Kang leaves Seoul for Japan. "I knew the Japanese language and tried to study the Western science. I found the Japs did not allow it to be taught in Korea. I wanted to go to America, but had no money or means to get there. First, I saw, I must go to Japan, among my enemies, to learn the Western science. I bought the clothes of a Japanese boy and stowed away on a boat for Japan." (38:110)

1916–18   Attends Youngsaing [probably a high school], graduating in 1918.

1918   Works as a math instructor in Kobe, Japan.

1918–19   Returns to his hometown and then to Seoul. In 1919, Kang takes part in the March 1st Independence March, a nonviolent mass protest of Japanese occupation that was calculated to put "the Korean people on the record before a world court as claiming their right to their own independence" (34:13). He is, as a result, beaten and imprisoned by Japanese police.[2] He would later report that according to Japan's own records, they imprisoned 50,000 Koreans and killed 7000. (34:30)

Kang publishes essays and poems in Korean, and an article by him is printed in a Korean newspaper.

1920   Kang assists Mrs. H. H. Underwood in the translation of work by John Bunyan. He also translates poems by Browning, Keats, and Shakespeare into Chinese and Korean.

Attempts to escape to the West through Siberia, but is caught by Japanese agents, beaten, and given another prison term.

1921   Through the help of a missionary, who smuggles him out of Korea as a servant, Kang immigrates to the United States.[3]

Kang goes to Canada to attend Dalhousie, a Nova Scotian missionary college, on a scholarship.

1922   Attends Harvard University in Cambridge, Massachusetts.

1923–25   Pursues studies at a Boston university and graduates with a Bachelor of Science.[4]

1924–27   Continues writing in Korean and Japanese. Of this time, he later writes: "When I went to college in America, I meant to study in some definite field of science, as being most valuable to myself and most serviceable to society. I found myself very unhappy and I did not feel at home in the laboratory. The only subject that gave me relief and delight was literature and poetry, read and re-read and unconsciously memorized in the solitary room. Writing was forced upon me, since I could not find my peace anywhere else." (127:744)

1925–27   Resumes studies at Harvard, graduating with a Masters in English Education.

1926   Works for the Chinese Commission at the Sesqui-Centennial

International Exposition in Philadelphia.

1928   Begins to write primarily in English.

     Kang spends the summer with the family of his fiancée, Frances Keely, a graduate of Wellesley College and a poet. They are married on the lawn of her grandmother's family home in West Virginia.

     Hired to work on the 14th edition of the *Encyclopædia Britannica,* Kang acquires and edits pieces on Asian art and literature in addition to writing over 100 signed and unsigned articles. Kang later credits this work as helping him to acculturate to the West.

1928–29 Begins writing what would become his first autobiographical novel, *The Grass Roof.*

     During this time, Kang also works as a contributing editor to the *Korean Student Bulletin,* a monthly periodical of Korean and Korean American news, and writes articles for the *Review of Reviews.*

1929   Begins work as a lecturer in the Comparative Literature Department of New York University. In September, Kang meets fellow freshman English teacher, Thomas Wolfe. Kang would later say of Wolfe that "He was one of my best friends in America, although my association with him was only about ten years.... There were about 75 teachers of English in the Department...and it was hard to know them well.... But Tom Wolfe often invited me to come to his apartment near the University, and we talked about many things including Shakespeare, Milton, and modern authors." (67: 31 Aug. 1957)

     Translations of Oriental Poetry is published by Prentice-Hall in New York. Kang also publishes an article in the New York-based *Korean Nationalist Weekly* entitled "Why I am Studying Literature."

1929–30	Publishes articles in the *Saturday Review of Literature, New York Herald Tribune,* and *Kidok-Shinmun* (in Korean). He also continues to contribute essays, poems, and book reviews to the *Korean Student Bulletin.*
1930	His daughter, Lucy Lynn, is born.

Kang's first autobiographical novel, *The Grass Roof,* is contracted by Scribner's: "[Wolfe] was very much interested in my work and asked me to read it. I gave him the first four chapters, which he took to Maxwell Perkins of Charles Scribner's Sons. Perkins was [Wolfe's] editor for *Look Homeward Angel,* which came out that fall. From that time on we often had lunch at...the same place where he always came in for lunch with Hemingway, Scott Fitzgerald (whenever they were in the city) and many other writers. My first book was accepted by Perkins with $500 advance" (67: 31 Aug. 1957). With the publication of this book, Kang becomes "the first Korean novelist ever to be introduced to the English speaking world" (124:3).

1931	*The Grass Roof* is published. The book is favorably reviewed in a number of prominent journals and papers, and praised by Pearl S. Buck and H. G. Wells among others. In a review that ran in the *New York Post,* Thomas Wolfe would write: "Kang is a born writer, everywhere he is free and vigorous: he has an original and poetic mind, and he loves life." (138)

Gaining wider recognition as a scholar of Asian culture, Kang continues to lecture and publish book reviews, articles, and autobiographical portraits in a number of newspapers and magazines including the *New York Times, New Republic, Nation, Asia Magazine,* and *New York Evening Post.*

1931	Applies unsuccessfully for a Guggenheim Foundation fellowship, proposing to write a sequel to *The Grass Roof* to be called "Death of an Exile."

1932	In October, Kang resubmits his application to the Guggenheim Foundation.

1933   *The Happy Grove,* a children's book based on the first part of *The Grass Roof,* is published by Scribner's.

         Das Grasdach, a German translation of *The Grass Roof,* is published by Hesse & Becker in Leipzig.

         A Hollywood agent inquires about motion picture rights to *The Grass Roof,* citing MGM's production of Pearl S. Buck's *The Good Earth* as proof of the "considerable interest being shown at present in Chinese stories" (147 [letter from Adeline M. Alvord, authors' and producers' representative, to Scribner's]: 6 Sept. 1933).

         In the spring of this year, Kang receives notice that his Guggenheim application was accepted. He becomes the first Asian to ever receive a Guggenheim Foundation fellowship. He is given a stipend of $1800 to be used towards writing a novel abroad. In September, Kang sets up residence in Rome with his wife and baby daughter.

1934   Kang requests and is granted a six-month renewal of his Guggenheim fellowship, stating that he plans to finish his book by February of 1935. Leaving Rome, he eventually settles with his family in Munich. He later writes: "In Germany I was more popular than the high-nosed American in the Hitler thirties, because I could be mistaken for a Japanese, the only race descended from the gods outside of the Aryans." (66:2)

1935   Returns to the United States.

         The Grass Roof is translated into French as *Au Pays du Matin Calme* by Librairie Plon in Paris.

1937   *East Goes West: The Making of an Oriental Yankee* is published by Scribner's.

Au Pays du Matin Calme wins Le Prix Halperine Kaminsky, France's annual award for best book in translation.

In November, an interview with Kang and dramatic readings of several passages from *East Goes West* are aired on WHN in New York City.

His son Christopher is born.

Kang is promoted to the position of Assistant Professor at New York University's Washington Square College.

1939   Begins working part time as an assistant curator in the Department of Far Eastern Art at the Metropolitan Museum of Art while continuing to teach at New York University.

World War II begins.

On July 10th, Representative Kent E. Keller of Illinois and the Committee on Citizenship for Younghill Kang, headed by the novelist John Chamberlain, introduce a bill to the House (H.R. 7127) that seeks to naturalize Kang. Congressman Keller argues that "[The exclusion law] was [passed] for the purpose of preventing the competition with American labor and not with American scholarship. Therefore, it is out of keeping with the American spirit to have this law operate against a man who has through his own genius written some fine books and become a teacher of English in a great University. There was no such thought that anything like that would ever happen and therefore the law has no moral force and should not be applied in the case of Younghill Kang.... If we grant citizenship to Younghill Kang, it will liberate and finally completely free a mind unusual in its grasp of America and American ideals." (112)

The bill includes statements of support by a number of prominent literary and cultural figures: among them, Malcolm Cowley, Pearl S. Buck, Lewis Mumford, Nicholas Murray Butler, William Lyon Phelps, Maxwell Perkins, and Charles Scribner. Perkins is instrumental in rounding up signatures and support letters for Kang, though one senator confides that such a bill would never pass, citing a similar citizenship bid by Thomas Mann that had ended in defeat. A second bill is introduced by Senator Matthew M. Neely of West Virginia to the Senate (S. 2801). Editorials are written to various newspapers asking readers to call their congressmen to support the bills.

1940   In a newspaper interview concerning the bills for his citizenship, Kang comments, "'Whether my bills now pending in Congress concerning my status are approved or not...this is my country. I married an American, have two children born here. All my roots are here, and I must do everything in my power for America.... My one desire is to serve this, my country, when the time comes'" (125). Both bills are eventually rejected.

1941   After the bombing of Pearl Harbor in December, Kang is called by the U.S. War Department. He gives up his professorship at New York University, as well as his curatorial work at the Metropolitan Museum of Art, and works for the U.S. Army and other government agencies, "doing whatever I could for the war effort." (66)

     During the war, Kang would publish several anti-Japanese propaganda articles, including "The Japanese Mind Is Sick," "An Appeal from Tyranny to God," and "When the Japs March In."

1942   Kang works as Director of the Army's Japanese Language School for 10 weeks over the summer, as well as Orientation Lecturer for the Public Relations Division of the U.S. Army.

1943   Works as Principal Economic Analyst for the Korea and Manchuria Section of the Board of Economic Warfare in Washington, D.C.

| 1944 | Works as a language consultant to the Education Division of the U.S. Army in New York City. Also compiles and edits the *Japanese Phrase Book* for the army language unit.

The Grass Roof continues to sell steadily, though it goes out of stock for several years because of wartime paper shortages.

East Goes West goes out of print. |
|---|---|
| 1945 | World War II ends. Korea is promised independence but is divided at the 38th parallel. As the Soviets had already done in North Korea, the United States erects a military government south of the 38th parallel. Kang would later write: "The 38th parallel is…Korea's dead line. Korea's life and blood circulation was stopped on that line and could not flow from either direction…." (66:2) |
| 1946 | A contract is renewed for the reprint of a Czech edition of *The Grass Roof,* originally published before the war. |
| 1946-47 | Travels to Korea as Chief of Publications for the American Military Government's (USAGMIK) Office of Public Information. "I was always safe from the terrorists and the Japanese-trained Korean police, as others were not, because of my immunity with A.O. cards. On the other hand all types of Koreans with different political shades would tell me things they felt too ashamed or embarassed [sic] to tell my American colleagues…. With these advantages I was naturally able to gather a good deal of information on Korea, on the way things were going, making out my report like amny [sic] other to generals" (66).

While in Korea, Kang lectures at Kyongsong University. His experiences in Korea provide him with material for the provocative essay, "How It Feels to Be a Korean…in Korea," published in *U.N. World* (May 1948). "If the reactionary politicians do not ruin South Korea, inflation almost surely will," |

he writes. "Certainly if an honest secret election could be held in South Korea today...the victor would have the difficult task of reviving a people and an economy that have been all but starved by being fed on money, all but deathly poisoned with graft, corruption and terror" (28:21).

In a May 3, 1947 letter to Perkins, Kang writes: "General Hodges has made *The Grass Roof* required reading for every G.I. in Korea." (147: 3 May 1947)

1947–48   Works as a political analyst and advisor to the XXIV Corps Office of Civil Information.

    Serves as President of Tongyang Waeguko College.

    With his wife, Kang finishes a translation of Han Yong-woon's *Meditations of the Lover,* the first Korean book of poetry to be translated as a whole into English.

1948   Returns to the United States. He teaches summer sessions at New York University without tenure until 1953, and continues his lecture tours.

    Meditations of the Lover is rejected by Scribner's.

1950–53   The Korean War takes place. In its aftermath, the country remains divided at the 38th parallel. Kang's restless anxiety in the face of these events makes it difficult for him to reacculturate to American life. He will write later of his conflicting feelings: "It is natural for me to love America and to fight for her, it is natural for me to love Korea. Why then this conflict? It is strange for man to have more conflict when...he has sought two sides of the story. How well I see, had I known only one side of the story, the American side, I would feel differently! I know why the U.N. or Mr. Truman has done what has been done. But I also know we have spent millions and lives and created enemies in Korea.... What is it they fight? communism? democracy? both are alien enough ideologies. In the hands of a few leaders these rally-cries are about like longitude and latitude to Alice, grand words to use in Wonderland, but to the average Korean what do they mean? The typical Korean is a hunted uneducated farmer. One thing makes him go mad, that 38th parallel, separating parent from child, husband from wife.... Whichever the force won this war from without shall lose it politically. The operation was a success, but the patient died— it's that kind of success." (66)

1950   Yale University asks Kang to survey the East Asiatic collection in the Sterling Memorial Library and to recommend additions to the book collection.

1950–51   Serves as a visiting professor at the Asia Institute in New York.

1952   Lectures as an English professor at Long Island University at Oyster Bay, New York.

1953   Receives the Louis S. Weiss Memorial Prize in Adult Education from the New School. A notice announcing the award writes of Kang: "He has brought about in his own mind and heart a fusion of forces which in the world at large are still fighting one another. A patriot without provincialism, a lover of freedom without prejudice or pretense, he has made his personal life a model of achievement under adversity and described it movingly for all of us to share. As a poet, a writer and teacher remaining whole and wise in a divided world, he has proved himself a great adult educator." (111)

1954   Kang's translation of *Anatahan* by Michiro Maruyama is published by Hermitage House. Josef von Sternberg's film based on the novel also premieres.

            Unable to support his family with royalties he receives from Scribner's or by selling other publications, Kang applies for another fellowship with the Guggenheim Foundation, proposing to write a book on the cultural history of Korea and northeastern Asia tentatively titled "Dragon Awakened." He explains at the end of the application that "It is rather discouraging to have on hand the work of years, much unpublished" (66). Kang's application is rejected.

Kang continues to support himself through lectures. *The Heath Anthology of American Literature* notes: "Always a visiting lecturer, [Kang] was never offered a stable teaching position. Instead, he traveled from speaking engagement to speaking engagement in an old Buick, spellbinding Rotary Club audiences with his recitations of Hamlet's soliloquy and his lectures on Korea" (139:1747).

1959   *The Grass Roof* is reprinted by Follett Publishing with an introduction based on Rebecca West's review of the book in the *London Daily Telegraph*.

1965   Kang teaches courses on philosophy and Latin American studies at Western College for Women in Oxford, Ohio.

1966   *East Goes West* is reprinted by Follett Publishing.

1970   Kang is awarded an honorary doctorate in literature from Koryo University, where he is a guest with his wife and daughter at the 37th P.E.N. Congress.

Kang donates his extensive collection of more than 4000 books to Koryo University.

Kang's translation of *Meditations of the Lover* by Han Yongwoon is published at last by Yonsei University Press.

1972   Kang dies in the middle of December at his home in Satellite Beach, Florida.[5]

1 In an obituary that ran in the *Korea Times,* Jong-gil Kim writes: "The official year of his birth is the seventh year of Kwangmu, that is 1903, though a friend of his suggests that he was actually born in 1898 or thereabouts. It matters little anyway, as that is often the case with Koreans of his generation." (122)

2 Kang gives conflicting reports of how long he was imprisoned. In an article entitled "Prelude to Korean Independence," he writes that "after several days, the Japanese released us, mere children, from a cell without washroom or toilet" (34:30). In "When the Japs Marched In," he writes: "I...got off relatively lightly.... I was beaten and tortured into unconsciousness, revived, beaten again, revived—for four successive days, and then given three months in prison on a diet of beans" (38:111).

3 A remembrance of Kang in the *Long Island Forum* reports that Kang "eventually sailed from Yokohama to San Francisco, arriving with only four dollars in his pocket." (115:84)

4 It is unclear from existing documents whether Kang attended Boston College or Boston University.

5 Kang's *New York Times* obituary states that Kang died the Monday prior to December 14, 1972, while other published reports state that he passed away on December 15.

BIBLIOGRAPHY

WORKS BY YOUNGHILL KANG

Books

1. *Anatahan.* By Michiro Maruyama. Trans. Younghill Kang. New York: Hermitage, 1954.

2. *East Goes West: The Making of An Oriental Yankee.* New York: Scribner's, 1937. Chicago: Follett, 1965. Afterword Sunyoung Lee. Kaya, 1997. Excerpt rpt. in *Asian-American Heritage: An Anthology of Prose and Poetry.* Ed. David Hsin-Fu Wand. New York: Washington Square, 1974. 217–50.

3. *The Grass Roof.* New York: Scribner's, 1931. Introd. Rebecca West. Chicago: Follett, 1959. Excerpt rpt. in *Korean Student Bulletin* June 1932; "The Marriage of the Prodigal Son" in *The Golden Book Magazine* July 1934: 44–49; "Doomsday" in *A World of Great Stories,* eds. H. Haydn and J. Cournow, New York: Crown, 1947: 789–96.

4. *The Happy Grove.* Illus. Leroy Baldridge. New York: Scribner's, 1933.

5. *Meditations of the Lover.* By Han Yongwoon. Trans. Younghill Kang and Frances Keely. Seoul: Yonsei UP, 1970.

6. *Translations of Oriental Poetry.* New York: Prentice-Hall, 1929.

Articles

Translations

7. "I Do Not Know." By Han Yongwoon. Trans. Younghill Kang and Frances Keely. *University of Kansas City Review* Summer 1951: 270.

8. "I the Ferry Boat, You, the Faring." By Han Yongwoon. Trans. Younghill Kang and Frances Keely. *University of Kansas City Review* Winter 1950: 90. Rpt. in *Yalu: Korea's Liberal Journal* 1 Jan. 1961.

Reviews

9. "An Appeal from Tyranny to God." *The World Outlook* March

1941: 18–21.

10. "Changing Japan." Rev. of *Economic Aspects of the History of Civilization of Japan,* by Yosoburo Takekoshi; *Japan's Economic Position,* by John E. Orchard; *Realism in Romantic Japan,* by Miriam Beard. *Nation* 19 Aug. 1931: 190.

11. "China and Korea in Revolt." Rev. of *Korea of the Japanese,* by H. B. Drake; *The Inner History of the Chinese Revolution,* by T'ang Leang-li; *The Spirit of the Chinese Revolution,* by A. N. Holcombe. *New Republic* 7 Jan. 1931: 224–25.

12. "China Is Different." Rev. of *The Good Earth,* by Pearl S. Buck. *New Republic* 1 July 1931: 185.

13. "China's Thinkers." Rev. of *History of Chinese Political Thought,* by Liang Chi-Chao. *New York Herald Tribune Books* 2 Nov. 1930: 10.

14. "Chinese Saga." Rev. of *The Buddhist's Pilgrim Progress,* by Helen M. Hayes. *New York Herald Tribune Books* 15 Mar. 1931, sec. 11: 23.

15. "Confucius as a Humanist." Rev. of *Confucius and Confucianism,* by Richard Wilhelm, trans. by George and Annina Danton. *New York Evening Post* 15 Aug. 1931: 9.

16. "In Chinese Drama, Music's the Thing, Not the Play." Rev. of *The Chinese Drama,* by L. C. Arlington. *New York Times Book Review* 30 Aug. 1931: 10.

17. "Korea as the Battleground of Foreign Interests." Rev. of *Undiplomatic Memories,* by W. F. Sands. *Korean Student Bulletin* Mar. 1931: 3.

18. Rev. of *Korea of the Japanese,* by H. B. Drake. *Korean Student Bulletin* Dec. 1931: 3.

19. "Novels of World War II: Younghill Kang Looks at American Literature." *America* Feb.–Sept. 1948. [Monthly, by American Office of Civil Information in Korean, Japanese, and German in Korea, Japan, and Austria.]

20. "Oriental Life." Rev. of *The Pillow Book of Sei Shonagon,* trans. Arthur Wales; *Dream of the Red Chamber,* by Tsao Hsueh-Chin

and Kao Ngoh, trans. Chi-Chen Wang. *The Saturday Review of Literature* 20 Apr. 1929: 900.

21. "Young China Writes." Rev. of *The Tragedy of Ah Qui,* trans. from the Chinese by J. B. Kyn Yn Yu and from the French by E. H. F. Mills. *New York Herald Tribune Books* 22 Mar. 1931: 10. [This review was published under the name Frances Kang, but Younghill Kang included it under the title "Chinese Writers" in his Guggenheim application.]

Commentary

22. "The Amateur Spirit and Korean Letters." *New York Times Book Review* 26 July 1931: 8, 19. Rpt. in *Korean Student Bulletin* Dec. 1931: 5–6.

23. "China Turns to the Short Story." *New York Times Book Review* 20 Aug. 1933: 2.

24. "Christ on the Japanese Stage." *Review of Reviews* Aug. 1929: 100.

25. "Chuntokyo, Korea's New Religion." *Review of Reviews* Feb. 1929: 94–96. Rpt. in *Korea Student Bulletin* May 1929: 1+.

26. "Famine." *Review of Reviews* Mar. 1929: 90.

27. "The Flight of the Dragon-Cloud." With Frances Keely. *Dalhousie Review* Winter 1954: 239–45. [Includes the poems "Embroidery Secret" and "I am the Ferry Boat, You are the Faring."] Rpt. of "Embroidery Secret" in *Yalu: Korea's Liberal Journal* 1 Jan. 1961.

28. "How It Feels to be a Korean...in Korea." *U.N. World* May 1948: 18–21.

29. "Japanese Literature." *The World Through Literature.* Ed. Charlton Laird. New York: Appleton-Century Crofts, 1951. 75–96.

30. "The Japanese Mind is Sick." *Tomorrow* May 1945: 39–41.

31. "Japan's Secret Plans." *Picture Scoop* Dec. 1942: 27–30.

32. "Oriental Section." *A World of Great Stories.* Eds. H. Haydn and J. Cournow. New York: Crown, 1947: 737–46.

33. "Oriental Yankee." *Common Ground* Winter 1941: 59–63.

34. "Prelude to Korean Independence." *Travel* Sept. 1946: 9–13, 30.

35. *Thesaurus of Book Digests.* Comps. and eds. H. Haydn and E. Fuller. New York: Crown, 1949. [79 articles on Asian literature scattered throughout 831 pages.]

36. "The Tiger Lost His Tail by a Man, But Was Killed by a Woman: A Korean Folktale." *Korean Student Bulletin* Oct./ Nov. 1935: 2–4.

37. "Western Hat." *Asia Magazine* Jan.–Apr. 1931: 6–13+, 84–91+, 156–63+, 239–45+.

38. "When the Japs March In." *The American Magazine* Aug. 1942: 42–43, 110–11.

39. "Why I am Studying Literature." [In Korean.] *Korean Nationalist Weekly* 1929. [New York.]

Articles in Encyclopedias

40. "Bed (Modern Metal Bedstead and Eastern Beds)." *Encyclopædia Britannica.* Vol. 3. 14th ed.

41. "Changing China." *Commonwealth Encyclopædia.* [1932 ed.?]

42. "Chinese Literature." *Commonwealth Encyclopædia.* [1932 ed.?]

43. "Chinese Literature." *National Encyclopedia.* 1954–1955 ed.

44. "Dance (Dance of Japan)." *Encyclopædia Britannica.* Vol. 7. 14th ed.

45. "Dress (Far Eastern Dress)." *Encyclopædia Britannica.* Vol. 7. 14th ed.

46. "Japanese Literature." *Commonwealth Encyclopædia.* [1932 ed.?]

47. "Japanese Literature." *National Encyclopedia.* 1954–1955 ed.

48. "Korea." *Americana Annual.* 1949 ed. 366–68.

49. "Korea." *Collier's Yearbook 1953.*

50. "Korea." *Collier's Yearbook 1954.*

51. "Korea." *Commonwealth Encyclopædia.* [1932 ed.?]

52. "Korea." *Encylopedia Americana.* 1949 ed. 1952 ed.

53. "Korea." *National Encyclopedia.* 1954–1955 ed.

54. "Korean Literature." *Commonwealth Encyclopædia*. [1932 ed.?]

55. "Korean Literature." *National Encyclopedia*. 1954–1955 ed.

56. "Li Po or Li Tai Po." *Encyclopædia Britannica*. Vol. 14. 14th ed.

57. "Societies of Art." *Encyclopædia Britannica*. Vol. 20. 14th ed.

58. "Tibet." *National Encyclopedia*. 1954–1955 ed.

59. "Tonghak or Chuntokyo." *Encyclopædia Britannica*. Vol. 22. 14th ed.

60. "Tu Fu." *Encyclopædia Britannica*. Vol. 22. 14th ed.

Unpublished works

61. "An Seunghwa." Ms. character sketch [probably for *East Goes West*]. Younghill Kang file. Huntington Historical Society. Huntington, New York.

62. "Murder in the Palace." Unpublished play/opera libretto. [Listed in a few biographical sources but never fully described.]

63. Manuscript fragment of *East Goes West* draft [dialogue between Helen Hancock and To Won Kim]. Younghill Kang file. Huntington Historical Society. Huntington, New York.

Letters and Miscellaneous

64. "Assignment V." Younghill Kang file. Huntington Historical Society. Huntington, New York.

65. Guggenheim Fellowship application, 29 Oct. 1931. Guggenheim Foundation, New York.

66. Guggenheim Fellowship application, 6 July 1954. Guggenheim Foundation, New York.

67. Letters to K. W. Lee. 1957–1967. K. W. Lee papers.

68. Manuscript. Autobiographical statement. K. W. Lee papers.

69. "Philosophy 204: Final Exam." May 1965. K. W. Lee papers.

Reviews

Of The Grass Roof

70. "Aus dem Leben eines Koreanischen Freiheitskämpfers" [From the Life of a Korean Freedom Fighter]. Collection of reviews in German. Leipzig: Paul List.

71. Ayscough, Florence. "The Life Story of a Korean." *New York Herald Tribune* 15 Mar. 1931, sec. 11 (books): 7.

72. *The Boston Transcript* 25 Apr. 1931.

73. *Cincinnati Times Star.*

74. Carter, John. *New York Times.*

75. Choy, Martha. "The Old and New Korea in a Novel." *Korean Student Bulletin* Mar. 1931: 3–4.

76. *Detroit News.*

77. Gannett, Lewis. *New York Herald Tribune.* 17 Mar. 1931.

78. "The Grass Roof." *Thesaurus of Book Digests.* Ed. Haydn, Hiram and Fuller, Edmund. New York: Bonanza, 1968.

79. Hansen, Harry. *World-Telegram.*

80. Hosie, Lady. "A Voice from Korea." *The Saturday Review of Literature* 4 Apr. 1931: 707.

81. *Manchester Guardian.*

82. *New Republic.* 1 Apr. 1931.

83. *Providence [Rhode Island] Journal.*

84. "A Scholar of Korea." *Times Literary Supplement* 16 Apr. 1931: 297.

85. Walton, Eda Lou. "A Charming Autobiography." *Nation* 25 Mar. 1931: 332–33.

86. Whang, Harry. "Eminent Critics Discover a Masterpiece." *Korean Student Bulletin.* 1–2. [Younghill Kang file. Huntington Historical Society. Huntington, New York.]

87. Wolfe, Thomas. "A Poetic Odyssey of the Korea That Was Crushed." *New York Evening Post.*

Of The Happy Grove

    88.   Chamberlain, John. "Books of the Time." *New York Times* 11 Sept. 1933: C15.

    89.   Eaton, Anne T. "The New Books for Children." *New York Times Book Review* 31 Dec. 1933: 11.

    90.   Lewis, Elizabeth Foreman. "Tales of the Sea and Far Overseas: *The Happy Grove*." *New York Times*. 12 Nov. 1933, sec. VII: 14.

Of East Goes West

    91.   "Briefly Noted: General." *New Yorker* 18 Sep. 1937: 98.

    92.   Cha, Ellen. "A Book Review." *Korean Student Bulletin* Feb./Mar. 1938: 5–6.

    93.   Geismar, Maxwell. "Gentle Arapesh." *Nation* 30 Oct. 1937: 482.

    94.   "A Korean-Born Lad Ventures Into the West." *The Boston Transcript* 18 Sept. 1937, books sec.: 3.

    95.   "Life in America Viewed by Korean." *Springfield Sunday Union & Republican* 26 Sept. 1937: 7E.

    96.   *New Republic* 8 Dec. 1937: 153–54.

    97.   Thompson, Ralph. "Books of the Times." *New York Times* 18 Sept. 1937: L++17.

    98.   *Times Literary Supplement* 30 Oct. 1937: 805.

    99.   Weil, Elsie. "Of Orientals Shipwrecked in America." *New York Herald Tribune* 3 Oct. 1937.

    100.   Woods, Katherine. "Making of an Oriental Yankee." *New York Times Book Review* 17 Oct. 1937: 11.

Of Meditations of the Lover

    101.   Kim, Jong-gil. "Han's Poems in English." *Korea Times* 14 Mar. 1971.

Critical essays

    102.   Kim, Elaine H. *Asian American Literature: An Introduction to the Writings and Their Social Context*. Philadelphia: Temple UP, 1982. 32–44.

103. ———. "Kang's America Fraught With Failure." *Koreatown Weekly* 19 Nov. 1979: 3, 13.

104. ———. "searching for a door to america: younghill kang." *Asian American Review* 1976: 102–16. Rpt. in *Korea Journal* July 1977: 38–47.

105. Ku, Robert Ji-Song. "Ethnography, Protest, and the Korean American Self: The Primitivism of Younghill Kang's *The Grass Roof*." M.A. Thesis. UCLA. 1996.

106. Takaki, Ronald T. *Strangers from a Different Shore: A History of Asian Americans*. New York: Penguin, 1989. 184–86, 351.

107. Suttilagsana, Supattra. "Recurrent Themes in Asian American Autobiographical Literature." Diss. Bowling Green State U. 1986.

108. Wade, James. "Younghill Kang's Unwritten Third Act." *Korea Journal* Apr. 1973: 57–61.

Biographical material

109. "The Case of Dr. Younghill Kang." *New York Post* 21 Sept. 1939.

110. Chee, Chang Boh. Personal interview. By Sunyoung Lee and Chisun Lee. 16 Aug. 1996.

111. "Commencement, '53: The Louis S. Weiss Prize in Adult Education for 1953 to Younghill Kang." *New School Bulletin* 2 June 1953.

112. Committee on Citizenship for Younghill Kang. "Citizenship for Younghill Kang." 13 Feb. 1940.

113. Enslow, Catherine Bliss. "Younghill Kang's Citizenship Bid Goes to Congress." *Advertiser* 6 Feb. 1940.

114. "Ford, Bought in 1930 for $800, Ran Up 400,000 Miles for Keeley." *Long-Islander* 1966. [Younghill Kang file. Huntington Historical Society. Huntington, New York.]

115. Gibbs, Alonzo. "Thinking of Mr. Kang." *Long Island Forum* 1 Aug. 1989: 83–84.

116. Han, Jae-Nam. "In Search of an Earthly Utopia: Younghill Kang." *We/Woori* Summer 1996: 50–51.

117. "Introducing Younghill Kang." *U.N. World* May 1948: 5.

118. Kang, Lynn. Letter. *New York Times* 20 Apr. 1986, sec. 6: 94.

119.   ———. "Thoughts of The Times." *Korea Times* 16 July 1972: 3.

120.   "Kang, Younghill 1903–1972." *Contemporary Authors*. 37–40: 285.

121.   Kim, Jong-gil. "Kang Showed Korean Culture to World." *Korea Times* 17 Dec. 1972: 3.

122.   ———. Personal interview. By Sunyoung Lee. 2 Feb. 1997.

123.   "Korean Novelist May Get American Citizenship." *Korean Student Bulletin* 1940.

124.   "Korean Novelist Returns From Abroad." *Korean Student Bulletin* Oct./Nov. 1935: 3.

125.   "Korean Seeks Army Training." *New York Sun* 25 June 1940.

126.   Kunitz, Stan, ed. *Twentieth Century Authors: Supplement.* New York: Wilson, 1955. 509.

127.   Kunitz, Stan, and Howard Haycraft, eds. *Twentieth Century Authors: A Biographical Dictionary of Modern Literature.* New York: Wilson, 1945. 744.

128.   Lee, K. W. "Kang and Wolfe: East-West Friendship." *Koreatown Weekly* 7 Jan. 1980: 1+.

129.   ———. "Friendship Between Wolfe and Korean Scholar Told." *Kingsport [Tennessee] Times*. 6 Oct. 1957.

130.   ———. "Souls of Korea." *Yalu: Korea's Liberal Journal* Jan. 1961.

131.   ———. "Tribute to So Few." *Yalu: Korea's Liberal Journal* Jan. 1961: 6.

132.   ———. "Younghill Kang: Wolfe's Books Autobiographical." *Koreatown Weekly* 14 Jan. 1980: 2, 6.

133.   "Mr. Younghill Kang is with the Metropolitan Museum of Art in New York City." *Korean Student Bulletin*.

134.   "An Oriental Yankee Talks of Love, Life, Literature, and Interracial Marriage." *New York Post* 2 Oct. 1937: 9.

135.   "Our Own Hall of Fame: Five New Stars in the Firmament of Korean Scholarship." *Korean Student Bulletin* Apr./May 1934: 7.

136.   Reissig, Rev. Herman F. "In Behalf of a Chinese Scholar." Letter. *St. Louis Post-Dispatch* 19 Sept. 1939. Rpt. in *Madison [Wisconsin] Progressive* 14 Oct. 1939.

137.   "Seven Guggenheim Fellows." *Boston Evening Transcript* 1 Apr. 1933

books sec.: 1.

138. "Younghill Kang." Promotional flyer for lecture services. [Younghill Kang file. Guggenheim Foundation, New York.]

139. "Younghill Kang 1903–1972." *Heath Anthology of American Literature.* Vol. 2. Lexington: Heath. 1747.

140. "Younghill Kang to Give Talk at Western C." *Oxford [Ohio] Press* 15 Oct. 1964.

141. "Younghill Kang in WCW Chair." *Hamilton [Ohio] Journal-News* 28 Jan. 1965.

142. "Younghill Kang, Writer, 69, Dies." *New York Times* 14 Dec. 1972.

Other published material

143. Bulosan, Carlos. *America Is in the Heart.* 1946. Seattle: U Washington P, 1973. 265.

144. Lee, K. W. "Revolt Will Topple Red China's Regime If Needed, Speaker Says." *The Charleston Gazette* 18 Apr. 1959.

145. "Our Culture Likened to China's in 800 B.C.; Dr. Kang Sees Economic State Only Difference." *New York Times* 11 Oct. 1931, sec. 2: 1.

146. Young, A. A., and T. J. Teague. "Mrs. Buck and the Chinese." Two letters concerning Kang's review of Pearl S. Buck's *The Good Earth.* [1 July 1931:185.] *New Republic* 6 Jan. 1932: 219.

Unpublished material in collections

147. Scribner's archives. Letters to and concerning Younghill Kang by Maxwell Perkins and others, 1930–1962. Also contains letters from Younghill Kang and inventory records for *East Goes West* and *The Grass Roof.* Princeton University. Princeton, New Jersey.

148. Guggenheim Foundation files. Letters from and concerning Younghill Kang's Guggenheim Foundation fellowship, 1932–1955. Also includes applications, clippings, lecture notices, correspondence, and other materials pertaining to Kang and his work. New York.

149. Huntington Historical Society files. Archived materials about Younghill Kang. Includes photographs, original manuscripts, and articles about Kang and his work. Huntington, New York.

ACKNOWLEDGMENTS

WE THANK THE FOLLOWING people for their help in putting together this edition of *East Goes West*: K. W. Lee, Chang Boh Chee, and Jong-gil Kim for generously sharing their memories of Younghill Kang; Sam E. Solberg and Hasig Bahng for their invaluable research suggestions; Jiwon Lee, Chisun Lee, and Caroline Lee for helping to research and write the bibliography and chronology; Robert Kuwada and Darryl Turner for their editorial acumen; Elaine Kim for her support and encouragement; Sharon Gallagher; Ira Silverberg; Myles McDonnell; Robert Ku; Chinh Q. Vo; Steven G. Doi; Mitzi Caputo of the Huntington Historical Society; G. Thomas Tanselle of the Guggenheim Foundation; and the estate of Younghill Kang. This project would never have been possible without the steadfast commitment and vision of Soo Kyung Kim. We would also like to acknowledge Walter Lew and Brian Stefans for their involvement in the early stages of this project. Finally, we remember the late Lucy Lynn Kang Sammis for her dedication to her father's work and legacy.